Traitor

in the Realm

A Next World Over Story

Linda,
Enjoy the adventure!
Patricia J. Boyle

PATRICIA J. BOYLE

A Russian Hill Press Book
United States • United Kingdom • Australia

Russian Hill Press

The publisher bears no responsibility for the quality of information provided through author or third party websites and does not have any control over, nor assumes any responsibility for, information contained in these sites.

Cover art, interior artwork, and maps by Susan Marchand
Cover design by Jordan Bernal with Dragon Wing Publishing

ISBN: 978-1-7351763-8-3 (hardcover)
ISBN: 978-1-7351763-4-5 (softcover)
ISBN: 978-1-7351763-5-2 (eBook)
Library of Congress Control Number: 2020921437

In memory of my mother, who nurtured my passion for reading, and my father, who gave me a love of words.

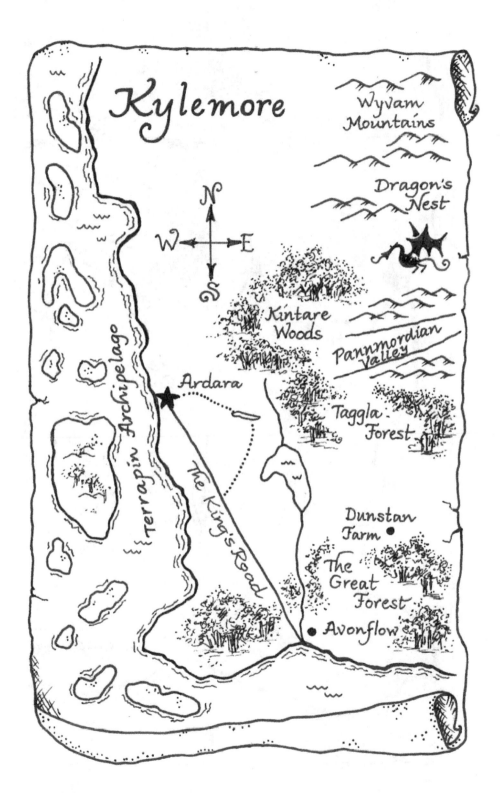

Kintare
Woods

Pannmordian
Valley

Canibri

Ardara

Lowri River

Taggla
Forest

Phelip's
Pond

Maulden Trail

Lake
Carlow

Daire

Dunstan
Farm

The King's Road

River Catriona

Gateway to Earth

The
Great
Forest

Avonflow

CONTENTS

1 THE FINDING_____ 3

2 INTRODUCTIONS _____ 11

3 COMPLICATIONS _____ 17

4 QUESTIONS, ANSWERS, AND MORE _____ 27

5 DISAGREEMENTS _____ 37

6 SECRETS PRESENT AND PAST_____ 47

7 ILLNESS STRIKES _____ 57

8 HIDDEN TALENT _____ 67

9 A MATTER OF TRUST_____ 77

10 CAPTURE_____ 87

11 NORTH FROM AVONFLOW_____ 95

12 BREAKING NEWS_____ 105

13 IMPORTED DANGER_____ 113

14 TRAVEL TROUBLES _____ 119

15 AFTERMATH_____ 129

16 PRISONER_____ 139

17 JOURNEY'S END _____ 147

18 AUDIENCE WITH THE KING _____ 153

19 EXPLANATIONS_____ 163

20 CASTLE DAYS _____ 169

21 CALL FOR AID _____ 179

22 OF FLOWER AND FLAME _____ 187

23 BY TRAIL TO THE VALLEY _____ 195

24 PLAYING WITH MATCHES_____ 205

25 UNEXPECTED ENCOUNTER _____ 213

26 PANNMORDIAN VALLEY _____221

27 TURMOIL_____231

28 SHOW AND TELL _____241

29 CHOSEN _____247

30 A VIOLENT DISTURBANCE_____255

31 LOFTY RESCUE _____261

32 ENTANGLEMENTS_____267

33 JOINING FORCES _____277

34 ONE STEP BEHIND _____283

35 FLIGHT_____293

36 CONFRONTATION _____301

37 CHOICES_____311

38 CONSEQUENCES_____319

∞

Characters_____331

Creatures _____333

Places _____334

Acknowledgments _____337

About the Author_____339

Traitor in the Realm

I was careless once
and got lost.
It took a long time
to find my way home.
~Kallan MacKinnon, tenth-grade essay

1

THE FINDING

*L*ooking back, I cannot say whether it was the fox, or Ethel, or simple procrastination that changed our lives forever. That summer I learned the hardest tests in life don't come from a teacher.

Picture a dark-haired teenage girl running through the woods, ponytail swinging from side to side. I trotted along a shadowy path right after sunrise, ignoring my empty stomach while keeping Ethel in view. The hen ran an erratic course, staying well out of reach. I had to catch her before she got near the waterfall. The noise would terrify her. Besides, I'm shaky when it comes to heights, and the trail there is twenty feet above the stream. Even though I was near home, the gloomy woods disoriented me. I'd dashed out of the house without my cell phone, which made me feel even more lost and alone.

"Come on, Ethel," I cooed.

Ethel was our best egg layer and our favorite. My foster brother, Matthew, and I expected her to win an award in the county fair the following week. We had plans for the prize money; soccer gear for him, art supplies for me.

3

"Ethel, stop. I have yummy food." I ran with my arm outstretched, a mound of chicken feed bouncing in my palm. I kept my eye on the hen instead of the trail.

Bad idea.

I tripped on a root and sprawled on the forest floor. The chicken feed flew in the air, then rained down like hail. I swore and sat up. A small fantailed bird swooped down from a maple tree. It pecked at Ethel's back while she zigzagged down the trail. When it raised its beak for another jab, sunlight glinted off a row of pointy teeth. I gasped and covered my mouth with my hand. At the taste of dirt, I spat and wiped my mouth on my sleeve.

Toothed birds died out millions of years ago. I'd learned that at the age of six from my paleontologist father. Matthew and I were nearly sixteen now. I wished my dad was still around. He'd love the bird's disturbingly prehistoric appearance. I figured it must be a mutant like the snake with the clawed foot I saw online.

The strange bird chased Ethel out of sight. As her squawking faded away, I became aware of another sound— the pounding of water on rocks.

The waterfall. Crap. I slammed my fist on the ground and cursed the fox that riled up our Rhode Island Reds that August morning. There were always chores to do at our summer cabin in the Adirondacks. A couple of days before, Matthew, Grandpa, and I removed the old chicken coop roof. The next day we were busy and didn't get to replace it. We thought it wouldn't matter, but this morning the fox scattered the chickens all over the property.

I got to my feet. Matthew strode down the path toward me. He held our youngest chicken, Tess, under one arm and Chanticleer, our rooster, under the other. As I brushed dirt and leaves off my clothes, I remembered the hard words Matthew and I had shouted at each other the week before. Since the argument, we hadn't had a conversation unless Grandpa was with us. To be honest, he's Matthew's grandfather and, for the last year, my foster father. I've known him most of my life though, so I call him Grandpa too.

I rewound the elastic on my ponytail and waited for Matthew to speak.

"Hey, Kallan. Who're you after?" His voice was soft.

I matched his quiet tone. "Ethel."

"She's the last one to catch. Grandpa and I rounded up the rest." Hands full with Tess and Chanticleer, he nodded at my arm. "You're hurt."

Dark beads of blood oozed from my forearm. I wiped the blood off with my tee shirt. I cleared my throat. "We should have fixed that coop yesterday."

He was silent for a while. "I wish we had," he finally said. "We were all busy until dark, though."

"I didn't have to paint so long. The art show's not for a few weeks. And you kicked the soccer ball around for hours after helping the vet at the ranch."

"Can't make varsity without practice." His mouth widened in a yawn. We usually slept in on summer vacation.

I stifled a yawn of my own and reached out to smooth Tess' feathers. "You'll make it."

Matthew smiled at my vote of confidence. "Thanks."

"Anyway, it wasn't only us. Grandpa worked on his book late into the night." He taught medieval history at a university and was writing a book about games in the Middle Ages.

"That's all in the past," Matthew said. "Let's find Ethel."

I pushed past a branch that blocked the trail, and we entered a noisy, misty space. The hill was steep on the right of the narrow path, the sky hidden by leafy trees. The stream lay below us to the left. On the far side of the stream stood a tall cliff of ivy-covered rock. Ahead of us, hazy spray from the waterfall filled the air and glistening droplets spattered the ivy leaves.

We had explored every inch of the woodland on

5

Grandpa's property over the years. When we were little, we pretended it was a magical world and searched for fairies in the bushes and leprechauns under ferns. Ethel was nowhere in sight. I knew magical beings hadn't taken her.

"Ethel must've gone behind the falls." I bit back my fear of slipping off the trail and smashing into the rocky stream bed. "I'll get her."

"I'll come with you."

"No way. The noise will spook the chickens."

Where the trail went behind the waterfall, a rock ledge jutted out, forming a narrow roof. The fantailed bird flew out and nipped at my hair. Busy with the chickens, Matthew didn't notice. I batted it away and said, "Oh, come on."

Matthew clucked to Tess and Chanticleer as we continued on the path, stepping around the muddy patches. I glanced to my left where the ground sloped down to the churning stream. My knees wobbled. I swung my head away and focused on Matthew's slim back.

The space behind the waterfall shone with greenish light. The chickens cackled and Matthew tightened his hold on them. We hurried as much as we dared to get past the curtain of water. A few steps beyond the falls, the path ended at the rock wall on the far side of the stream.

Matthew shook his thick chestnut hair out of his eyes, flinging water everywhere. "Where's Ethel?"

Before I could answer, the prehistoric bird flew out of the tangle of vines that covered the cliff and landed on a scraggly bush near us.

Matthew's jaw dropped. "What is that? Are those teeth?"

"Yep. Where could it have come from?" As if in answer, the bird flew back into the mass of leaves.

Matthew nodded at the cliff. "D'you think it has a nest in there?"

I pulled aside a handful of vines. What had always been

a solid rock wall now had an opening six feet high clear through it. I blinked. Nothing changed. The space was three feet long and wide enough for a person to walk through. Keeping a tight grip on the vines, I leaned forward to get a better look and flinched when a tingling sensation flowed down my spine like a trickle of electricity.

The air shimmered; its fuzzy edges fluttered against the rock as if in a light breeze. On the far side of the opening hung another tangle of vines. Through gaps in the leaves, I saw Ethel strut like a princess across a meadow. Unlike our dim early morning woods, midday light bathed the meadow. A creature flew across the patch of sky in my view. It had a thick body and reminded me of a dragon illustration in my old fairy tale book. A sensation of squirmy caterpillars filled my stomach, making me grateful we'd missed breakfast.

"Do you see a nest?" Matthew asked.

"Nope. No nest."

He squinted at me. "What's wrong? You're pale."

I bit my lip. "The cliff. I can see through it."

"What d'you mean?"

"There's a . . . I don't know what to call it. An archway. A tunnel. I can see daylight on the other side."

"Pipit, that's not possible." I grinned at his pet name for me. *Maybe he's forgiven me after all.*

I pulled the vines farther to the side. "See for yourself."

Matthew stepped in front of the space and let out a low whistle. He squared his shoulders. "Ethel's out there. I'm going after her."

"Wait. That tunnel. It's not natural. Where does it lead to?"

"I don't know. Maybe it's the back of one of the camps down the road."

"Can't be. The cliff is the side of a hill. There shouldn't be any daylight."

His shoulder rose in a shrug. "We'll figure it out after I get Ethel back."

"Don't go. That place gives me the creeps."

He considered me. "It probably gives Ethel the creeps too."

I stamped my foot. "Forget about animals for once!"

The color drained from his cheeks. He seemed as shocked as if I'd slapped him. I let the vines fall into place. "Sorry. I feel bad about losing her too." I took a deep breath. "It's crazy to go through there. We don't know what's on the other side."

"Looks like a meadow."

His mouth was set in that stubborn way that meant he wouldn't change his mind. I gave it one more go anyway. "Something's not right. Please stay here."

Ignoring me, he said, "I'll be back in a few minutes." He thrust the chickens toward me. As I took them, Chanticleer struggled and jabbed my scraped arm with his beak. I yelped and lost my grip. Chanticleer and Tess dropped to the ground with a noisy flapping of wings and raced through the gap in the rock. Matthew took off after them.

He was my best friend; I couldn't let him face the unknown alone. My pulse beat in my ears, drowning out other sounds. I thought I heard Grandpa calling from across the stream. Peering through the haze of droplets though, I couldn't see anyone. I stepped into the cool air of the rough archway. The same buzzy, electric sensation zinged through my body as before, and the hairs rose on the nape of my neck. When I reached the end of the short tunnel, I took a step back to make sure it worked both ways and we wouldn't get trapped on the other side. Reassured, I hurried after Matthew.

After a few steps, I turned around to get my bearings so we could find the tunnel again after we caught the chickens. I saw a rockface similar to the one in our woods. Vines covered this one too, although the leaves were pale green and heart-shaped, not dark and lobed, like ivy. My fingers trembled as I tore off handfuls of foliage to mark the spot.

Matthew had stopped his chase to watch me. A hand

on his hip, a smirk on his face, he pointed to the top of the cliff. "The archway is below that oak. Easy to find, since it's the only tree up there."

I stuck my tongue out at him. We laughed, like old times. I caught up to him and we went in search of the chickens.

The sun shone hot on our heads and the air smelled of cherries. The scent came from an orchard that filled the back end of the meadow. Holes large enough to trap a foot littered the uneven ground. Tall birds with long necks and small heads grazed in a fenced enclosure. They resembled moas. My dad said moas had been extinct for hundreds of years. Could these be emus? Whatever they were, their tough beaks and clawed feet could have pitted up the earth.

To our right sat a two-story house, several outbuildings, animal pens, and a stone barn. As much as I wanted to believe it was a farm in upstate New York, I couldn't. Two dark shapes passed overhead. With their long narrow heads and short bodies, I would have called them pterodactyls if they weren't extinct too. My toe caught the edge of a hole and I stumbled. When I raised my head again, the creatures were distant smudges in the sky.

We'd picked our way halfway across the grassy meadow when Matthew stopped short and I almost collided with him. Behind us, Grandpa called out our names. I waved him over. The three of us could round the chickens up faster.

I nudged Matthew. "Grandpa's here. Where do you think we are?"

"No idea."

"Did we go through some kind of time warp? Are we in the past?"

"Don't think so."

"Why not?"

"That's why." Matthew's voice was strained, and he stared straight ahead.

Two people dressed in pine green tunics and fawn trousers approached us. They appeared to be about our age and could have passed for students from our high school, dressed for a play about the Middle Ages. Except for one difference.

Furry, catlike tails hung a foot below the hems of their tunics.

My heart thumped in my chest, pounding out a rhythm: "not real, not real, not real." I wanted to run back home, but my legs had forgotten how to move.

The tailed pair stopped a few yards away. The girl had a short stick she held straight out toward Matthew. Her expression was serious. Still, I thought she might be joking around. The boy eased a gleaming dagger out of a sheath and pointed the tip straight at me.

Not a joke. We were in trouble.

From time to time unexplained
events occur. The appearance of
tailless outsiders is one example.
~Handbook of the Eyes and Ears of the King

2

INTRODUCTIONS

I raised my arms straight in the air with my eye on the tailed teens. My mouth was dry, my palms sweaty. The girl's stick was blunt and not much longer than a ruler. No danger there. The boy's dagger on the other hand could be a problem.

Stick Girl wore her black hair in a thick braid woven with bright yellow flowers. She stood a few inches taller than me and had a firm, muscular build. I glanced around, searching for possible weapons. I didn't see any rakes, shovels, axes, or other tools lying around the tidy farmyard that might be used to fend off the strange pair should they decide to attack.

I heard swishing sounds in the grass as Grandpa caught up to us. He slipped between Matthew and me and was a step in front of us when Dagger Boy spoke. "Halt there, aged one."

Grandpa halted and flung his arms out to the sides to shield Matthew and me from the tailed pair. Matthew held his hands in the air, same as I did.

One positive, the stranger spoke English. He was kind of cute too, tall, with curly black hair, and the same muscular, athletic build as the girl. Even if we could get the dagger away from him, we were at a physical disadvantage if this came down to a fight. Matthew's a lightweight compared to Dagger Boy, and Grandpa's had a bad heart for years.

"Excuse us," Grandpa said. "We stumbled onto your land by accident. If you lower your weapons, we'll collect our chickens and go home."

Grandpa's a master at putting people at ease. Although his mind must have been working overtime, his face was smooth, and his arms hung loosely by his sides.

What if they don't let us go? Escape plans swarmed through my mind like bees around a hive. I felt a feather light pressure in my head, a shiver sweeping through my brain. In an instant, it went away. Imagination mixed with fear does strange things to a person.

The boy said to the girl, "Their intentions aren't evil. Mind you, they could still be dangerous."

We only wanted to get the chickens and clear out. Not an evil desire. The boy thought we might be dangerous, though. I stiffened my spine and held my head high.

Stick Girl nodded at her companion. Her dark eyes were nearly black, and it was hard to read her emotions. "We have questions," she said. "Your chickens must wait. They'd best stay out of the moa pen." I wasn't happy about recognizing the bird species. I still had no idea where we were or if we could convince this pair to let us go home.

"We'll answer questions after we catch our chickens," Matthew said. "There are three of them." He kept his hands above his head and took a step toward the nearest bird.

In a flash, the girl flicked her stick at him and uttered words I couldn't understand. The air in front of Matthew wavered, like heat over a highway in summer. Bright blue sparks crackled six inches in front of his face when he was in midstep. Thrown off balance, his foot came down in a hole. We heard a loud snapping sound as Matthew crashed to the ground with a yelp, landing on his left side with his foot twisted beneath him. Gripping his ankle with both hands, he rocked back and forth and moaned.

When Grandpa started to go to him, the girl shouted, "Stay put!" We stood still, as in a game of statues. Matthew struggled to his feet, keeping his left leg bent and most of his weight on his uninjured right foot.

"What'd you do?" I asked Stick Girl. Matthew would never make it back to our cabin in this condition. She pointed the stick at me and remained silent. Anger overcame my fear. I crossed my arms. "What kind of weapon is that?"

Dagger Boy's brows drew together. "A wand. What else would it be?"

I opened my mouth to reply. No answer occurred to me, so I closed it again.

"Come. We'll talk indoors." The girl waved her wand toward the rambling two-story farmhouse, indicating we should go ahead of them. Even Grandpa didn't argue. Matthew hobbled at my side; one arm draped across my shoulders while I kept an arm around his waist. Grandpa stayed between the strangers and us.

We hadn't gone far before the toothed bird flew toward us from his perch on the fence that enclosed the moa flock. I stopped in my tracks and shielded my head with my free arm. However, the soft whirr of its wings passed over me. The bird landed lightly on Matthew's far shoulder as though it belonged with him. I relaxed a little. If anyone knew how to relate to animals, it was Matthew.

"Aeron, come to me, fellow," Dagger Boy said to the bird, holding out an arm for him to perch on. Aeron remained where he was. The end of the boy's tail twitched from side to side. After waiting half a minute, Dagger Boy dropped his arm.

When we reached the house, Wand Girl ordered us to hand over our weapons. I was surprised she hadn't thought of that earlier. Then again, they appeared to be ordinary kids, not soldiers trained to disarm the enemy as soon as possible. Grandpa, Matthew, and I were dressed in jeans, tee shirts, and sandals. We turned out our empty pockets.

"Only lint," I said with a small smile. Wand Girl didn't react to my attempt at humor.

"Check them for knives," she said to the boy. "Do any of you have magical skill?" she asked, keeping her wand pointed at us.

"Magic isn't real," I said. "There must be a scientific explanation for what you did back there."

"The skill's real, though it's rare," Dagger Boy said.

If he was telling the truth, I may have seen an actual dragon flying around when I peered through the gateway in the cliff. The hairs on my arms rose at the memory.

Dagger Boy said no more as he patted Matthew's pant legs, doing as thorough an inspection as any airport security worker.

While the boy checked Grandpa, and Matthew was safely propped against the house, I took a step backwards. I intended to edge out of wand range before turning around to sprint home for help.

The girl noticed me. She aimed her wand over my head and shouted, "*Solidiom.*"

I felt, rather than heard, a *boom*. When I took my next backward step, my heel hit something hard. I whirled around. Nothing blocked my way. I stretched out my hands. They met an invisible wall of air, smooth as a pane of glass. I hit it with my fist and got only sore knuckles for my effort. The girl grabbed my arm and pulled me over to the others. She patted me down herself while the boy kept us trapped between the house and the air wall with his dagger.

When they were sure we were weapon free, the boy opened a door and we shuffled into the kitchen. Grandpa and I supported Matthew between us. We took seats around a long wooden table as directed. The girl pointed her wand through the doorway at the air wall and said, *"Reversion,"* then shut the door tight. Aeron flew to the top of a dish cabinet and settled in.

A dog bounded into the room in a blur of brown, tan, and white. It had the same big ears and goofy grin as one of my foster family's Welsh corgi. This one was shaggier and had longer legs. It sniffed each of us in turn and licked Matthew's face when he bent down to pet the creature.

A sharp command came from Wand Girl. "Howell, get away, boy."

Howell gave Matthew's hand a lick and lay down by his chair, resting his head on Matthew's uninjured foot. The girl glared at the pair of them. Howell glanced up at her and stayed put. Both Aeron and Howell had defied their masters to side with us, or at least with Matthew. Small victories that filled me with a warm glow of satisfaction.

While I considered ways to escape, I rubbed the silver ring I wore on my right hand. It was a gift from my mother, passed down from her father and countless Irish ancestors before him. The knot design on top was shaped like an infinity symbol. Swirls of red, blue, green, and gold flowed across the surface in patterns that changed with the light. Although my mom passed away when I was in middle school, rubbing the ring brought back memories of her and helped me think.

Grandpa clasped his hands together on the table, as if he were leading a faculty meeting at the university. "We got off to a bad start. Let me introduce myself. I am David Webbe, and these are my grandchildren, Matthew Webbe and Kallan MacKinnon. I'll take them home now. Before we go, may we know your names?"

The boy sheathed his dagger and leaned against the door. "You must stay a while longer. I am Cadoc Dunstan, and this is my twin sister, Carys. How did you find your way onto our land? What is your purpose in Kylemore?"

"What's Kylemore, the name of your farm?" I couldn't

help blurting out. I was as confused as Cadoc was.

His brows scrunched together as they had when I asked about the wand. "The *Kingdom* of Kylemore. The greatest of Betherion's kingdoms. You ask the most peculiar questions, lass." He turned to Grandpa. "What kingdom are you from, aged one?"

"We're from a world called Earth, not Betherion. Our 'kingdom,' I guess you'd say, is New York." He sighed. "We entered a gap in a cliffside on our land and somehow walked out of the cliff onto your farm."

"There are no gaps in our cliff. It's as solid as the rock of Orrkane." Cadoc pushed himself upright and fingered the hilt of his dagger.

"Are you calling my grandfather a liar?" Matthew curled his hands into fists. "Your bird, Aeron, came into our world and chased one of our chickens through the opening."

"He attacked Ethel too," I said, twisting my ring around my finger as I spoke. "If you let us catch her, we can prove it."

Cadoc scratched his head. "Who is Ethel?"

"The chicken Aeron chased, of course," I said. "Now who's asking peculiar questions?"

We heard voices in the farmyard. Carys turned toward the door, and a slow smile brightened her face. "They're back."

Her announcement did nothing to soothe my nerves.

*It can be difficult
to distinguish between the
innocent and guilty, yet it is
of primary importance to do so.
~Handbook of the Eyes and Ears of the King*

3

COMPLICATIONS

Three adults entered the kitchen. A thin careworn woman with a long scar over one eyebrow walked with a limp, favoring her left leg. She and a brawny man with wavy brown hair appeared to be middle-aged. The third person, a lean man with a silver ponytail, was probably as old as Grandpa. Each had a long, furry catlike tail.

It hit me that the twins had purposely held us captive until the adults returned. No matter. Grandpa would make the adults understand we meant no harm, and then we'd be on our way home. We'd have to splint Matthew's ankle and take it slowly. We could leave the chickens behind as a gift. Afterward, we'd each block up our end of the tunnel and forget this whole bizarre adventure.

Cadoc cleared his throat. "Da. Ma. Poppa. We found these intruders in the field."

"They claim to be from a place called Earth," Carys said. "They're humans, not Pannmordians. They have no weapons, no magic, no tails. The enemy might have sent them here to—"

"We're not enemies," I said. "All we did was follow Aeron and our chickens here." I stopped myself from asking

17

what Pannmordians were. This didn't seem the best time.

"My granddaughter's right," Grandpa said. "We only want to collect our chickens and return home."

The older, ponytailed stranger spoke up. "Chickens? Are you daft? Chickens died out a hundred years ago."

"They may have died out here," Grandpa said. "Where we live, they're common birds."

Cadoc moved close to the ponytailed man and spoke quietly to him. I caught a few words: "Eyes and Ears" and "force the truth."

I heard "baron" and "see the king" in the man's reply.

Cadoc rose up on his toes. "Take me with you."

"No." The word came out a gruff bark. The man shook his head, then spoke in an ordinary voice. "I'm sorry, lad. You're still a youngling. Besides, your da needs you here."

Cadoc crossed his arms, a stony expression on his face. He glanced at me and I shrugged. Like at home, kids here didn't always get what they wanted. Cadoc's arms relaxed a little, and he studied the flagstone floor.

The older man spoke to Grandpa. "I am Beli Whelan." He gestured toward the middle-aged couple. "My daughter and her husband, Marilea and Rolant Dunstan, the parents of these outspoken younglings." He smiled at the twins. Turning serious again, he said, "Soon, Baron Colum Humphrey will arrive. He's passing through on his way from a mission in the kingdom east of here. As the king's representatives, Lord Humphrey and I need to ask you some questions. We'll need to take you to King Darren for questioning as well." Carys and Cadoc exchanged wide-eyed glances, and a chill passed through me.

Grandpa asked, "Is that necessary? Can't we settle matters here?"

"Nay. King Darren has commanded that we take anyone from outside the kingdom to him in the royal city of Ardara. Your names?"

Grandpa made the introductions, then rubbed his hand

across the bristly stubble on his chin. "How far is it to this royal city of yours?"

"Around two weeks travel, if the weather holds," Rolant said.

I sucked in my breath. It would take a month to go to the royal city and back. So much for a quick return home. A lot could happen in a month.

Grandpa ran a hand through his snowy white hair. "We don't have that much time. In three weeks, classes begin at the university where I teach, and my grandchildren must return to school." We'd be juniors in the fall. It would be hard to catch up after a late start.

"I'm afraid Rolant's right," silver haired Beli said. "At least ten days there and ten back. Four weeks for the round trip, plus whatever time the king wants to question you."

"There are five days in a week?" Matthew asked.

Beli chuckled. "Aye, lad. Five days."

Grandpa said, "We might make it. As Kallan says, we're not enemies." He shifted in his seat. "This morning we stepped through a brand-new opening in a cliff on my land and found ourselves here. It sounds impossible, I know, but it's true. Betherion appears similar to Earth, yet I've seen creatures here that are long gone from our world, and you say chickens no longer exist in yours. Nothing I've seen today makes any sense."

It didn't make sense to me either. I pinched myself to see if this was all a dream. The tailed people were still there.

Grandpa narrowed his eyes at Beli. "How long has the gateway in the cliff been open? Will it close again? Can we afford the time to satisfy King Darren's curiosity?"

It hadn't occurred to me the gateway might close up. *It isn't a dream after all. It's a nightmare.* I pinched myself again with the same result as before.

Beli fingered the cleft in his chin. "Can we afford not to satisfy it? There have been attacks on our kingdom in recent months. Someone is waging war on Kylemore. We must be certain you're not part of that." He stared out the window, lost in thought. After a few moments, he turned back to Grandpa. "As for the gateway, we likely have as many questions as you do."

Rolant addressed his father-in-law. "Beli, if you and Lord Humphrey are satisfied after you question them, I request that the younglings stay here while you take David to Ardara."

"No," Matthew and I said at the same time. Matthew added, "We won't leave Grandpa." He half rose from his seat, then winced and sat down quickly. The others didn't notice his pain. I caught Matthew's eye, but he gave his head a tiny shake. He wouldn't bring attention to his injury unless he had to.

Beli said, "That's not possible."

"Be reasonable," Rolant said. The hairs on his bushy tail stood on end. "Beli, if they're cleared, let the aged one speak for all of them with the king. I won't risk the younglings being mistaken for the enemy."

Beli's face took on a pained expression. "That wouldn't happen in Kylemore."

I had no idea what they were talking about. It sounded like Rolant wanted to keep Matthew and me safe. However, if we were separated from Grandpa, it would be a lot harder to escape. "If Grandpa goes, so do we," I said.

Rolant moved close to me and held my gaze. I saw concern in his eyes. "Lass, you don't know what you're saying. King Darren is a fair man. However, some of the royal guards and the king's counselors can be . . . harsh."

Carys tucked her wand inside her tunic. She sat at the table and spoke in a soothing tone. "Da's right. They're a rough bunch. The dungeons are cold and dark, and their whips are—" She clamped her mouth shut at a sharp expression from her grandfather.

"They'll be under my protection," Beli said. "There's no need for them to stay here."

Rolant gripped the back of an empty ladder-back chair, his fingers wrapped tight around the top bar. He appeared to be fighting to control his temper. "Beli, consider this. If we split them up, David will be more cooperative on the journey and complete in his answers to the king. He'll do nothing to bring harm to his grandchildren."

When Beli didn't answer, Rolant tried another approach. "Think of the twins. Would you want them to be guarded by the likes of Iron Beard?"

Beli grimaced. "Your words bear weight. If I'm satisfied, the younglings will stay here." He looked out the window to the yard between the house and meadow where a group of uniformed men sat on horseback. "The baron has arrived. I must talk with him." Beli went outside while Rolant kept watch over us.

If we couldn't convince the kids or their family to let us go, how would we ever convince a baron? If Betherion was anything like Earth, once government officials got involved, it could take a long time for them to see reason. It had taken Grandpa years to convince New York State to allow him to be my foster father.

My stomach rumbled. Marilea's eyes crinkled. "Carys, come near," she said. "We'll set out the meal. Cadoc, have the farmhands help you gather the chickens. I want to see these ancient creatures."

Grandpa rested his chin on his hand, deep in thought, and Matthew squirmed in his seat and adjusted his bad foot. Marilea and Carys sliced bread at a long wooden counter and rinsed cherries with water from a hand pump that emptied into a deep sink. Their silky tails hung still while they worked. Without thinking, I took the elastic band off my ponytail and put my hair in a tight braid. After a while, I couldn't bear to sit any longer. "What's there to do?" I asked as I pushed my chair out. "'The more hands, the quicker the work,' my mother always said."

Rolant took a step toward me. "We appreciate the offer,

lass. Kindly stay where you are." I scooted my chair back in. For the next quarter of an hour, I studied the kitchen and imagined what it would be like to have a tail.

By the time Marilea and Carys set the last dish of food on the table, Cadoc and Beli had returned, bringing with them a tall, elegantly dressed man. The baron, Lord Humphrey. His clothes were indigo trimmed with yellow braid and his overtunic was dotted with silver buttons. His formal outfit reminded me of a military uniform. Lord Humphrey was clearly a man of authority. It didn't matter that a thin layer of dirt covered everything from his bald head to his black riding boots. He must have ridden a long distance to get that grimy.

My insides contracted with fear at the sight of the man. I was afraid because of his imposing size. More than that, the power he represented filled me with fear. Mom and I lived with the sadness of losing my dad, but we lived a free life. After she died, Family Services placed me in foster homes with people more interested in the money I brought in than my happiness. Some parents were strict, others simply indifferent. One was cruel. I learned to fear the Family Services staff. They had the power to choose where I lived, and my foster parents decided where I could go and what activities I could do.

Spring of freshman year, I told a teacher about the weekly beatings my latest foster father gave me for minor infractions of his rigid rules. After that, Grandpa was given permission to be my foster father in spite of his age. I was happy again. There'd even been talk of adoption, something I'd dreamed about for a long time. Under the baron's suspicious glare, I reverted back to the scared kid I'd been for three years. Slumping in my seat, I made myself as small as possible.

Lord Humphrey's response to meeting us was worse than I expected. He stationed a guard in the doorway and issued an order to the three remaining guards. "Until we know who they are and what they're about, chain them to the table."

"Chains?" I squeaked. Grandpa objected to our treatment. The baron held firm. The guards produced manacles connected by thick iron chains and locked the heavy metal around our ankles and the table legs. Howell growled when the guard put the leg iron around Matthew's uninjured ankle. Rolant grabbed the dog and pushed him outside. Aeron flew out the open door, barely escaping before Rolant shut it with a bang.

Marilea's mouth twisted in distaste as she studied our leg irons. "My lord, are you sure we need to—" She broke off at the questioning look the baron gave her. "I suppose we do," she finished and took her seat, followed by the twins and Rolant.

The guards stationed themselves at the corners of the room, and Beli and the baron sat with the rest of us. The heavy oak table was long enough to hold more than a dozen people. It was much bigger than their family needed. In addition to the cold food, Marilea served a fragrant stew out of a pot hanging from a hook in a brick fireplace. It had been a long time since our last meal, and my mouth watered at the scent of herbs mingled with the tangy aroma of cooked meat, carrots, and potatoes.

Carys filled glazed mugs with cherry juice. Before she handed them out, Lord Humphrey took a small vial out of a leather bag at his waist. He rolled it back and forth in his palm with the tip of a forefinger.

"We can do this two ways," he said. "Beli and I can question each of you, trusting our judgment about your answers. After that, we'll decide whether to take one or all of you to Ardara shackled as prisoners." He held the vial up in front of the window. Sunlight passed through the translucent green liquid.

"Or," he said, "We can put a few drops of this in your drink and have a pleasant conversation over the evening

23

meal. That would be quicker, and I'd have complete faith in your answers. David, if I am satisfied, you alone would accompany us. You would travel as a trusted representative of a foreign land rather than a captive. The younglings would stay here, free to move about instead of being chained together for weeks." Carys bit her lip. Cadoc stared at the tabletop.

Grandpa squinted at the small container. "What's in the vial?"

"Truth serum. Quite effective and difficult to obtain. Drink a small quantity and you'll not be able to tell a falsehood for hours."

"What are the side effects?"

The baron waved the concern away. "I've seen nothing extreme. Nausea, or perhaps a slight headache. Some become sleepy."

"I'm willing," Matthew said. He was more trusting than I. "Freedom sounds better than being locked up." He looked the baron in the eye. "No matter what, I'm going with Grandpa to the royal city."

"Freedom's a maybe, not a promise. Your answers will determine my decision. And you'll not accompany us to Ardara if I say otherwise."

Matthew's chin jutted. He and Lord Humphrey glared at each other, locked in a mute struggle. *Stubborn as boulders, the pair of them. What will the baron do if Matthew pushes him too hard?* Despite my fear of the man, I spoke up. "I'm hungry. Let's do it."

Grandpa put up a hand. "We'll drink it on the condition that one of the Dunstans takes it as well. With all due respect, I have only your word, my lord, that the liquid isn't poisonous."

Cadoc gave me a quick wink, then said, "I'll drink it. If I'm to be an Eye of the King, I want to learn about the potion firsthand." He wasn't permitted to travel with Beli, but he was determined not to be left out. I had a feeling he would become an Eye of the King someday, whatever they were.

Rolant gave his permission, and the baron removed the stopper from the vial. He tipped five drops into each of four cups of juice. Cadoc took a large gulp. Matthew did the same. Grandpa and I sipped ours slowly. I couldn't detect the truth serum; the cherry juice overpowered any flavor the potion had. When I'd drunk it all, I held out my bowl for a ladle of stew.

4

QUESTIONS, ANSWERS, AND MORE

The meal went on for a long time. As we talked, a headache formed behind my eyes, then crept across my skull. The only plus was that the baron sat far away from me at the end of the long table. Cadoc didn't eat much. I guessed he had a stomachache. Grandpa appeared to have no side effects from the truth serum. Matthew was pale and answered questions directed at him in short, clipped sentences.

Beli and Lord Humphrey took turns interrogating us, sometimes asking the same question in different ways. Where were we from? What did Grandpa do for a living? What did we know of Kylemore's history and politics? They were quite interested in our chickens since they'd only seen drawings, not live ones.

"David, your grandchildren have different surnames," Beli said. "Tell us how the three of you are related."

"Matthew's father was my son. I've raised Matthew since his parents died in a boating accident when Matthew was a baby. Kallan's relationship is more complicated . . ." He stopped, searching for words.

"I'll tell them," I said. "Matthew and I have been best friends since preschool—since we were three years old. My father died in a work accident when I was eight. My mother, she got sick . . . she's been gone four years now." I drank some juice to swallow the lump in my throat. I didn't talk about my parents often. The memories made me hollow with loneliness.

Cadoc leaned toward me. "I'm sorry about your parents." His voice was thick with emotion. Since he'd drunk the truth serum, he must have meant it. Carys looked glum. *Have they lost a loved one? What else would explain their sadness over the deaths of two people they never knew?*

Matthew picked up my story. "The government passed Kallan from family to family. A year ago, they let her come live with us."

The baron asked no more questions about the topic. The bare facts told him all he needed to know. We had no family to miss us. Family Services would hunt for me when I didn't show up for school, but even if they searched Grandpa's land, I didn't think they'd discover Betherion. We wouldn't have found the tunnel without Aeron. We'd left our cell phones at home. It didn't matter; they would be useless here. My head throbbed with the realization that we were on our own.

"You say someone's waging war against Kylemore," Grandpa said. "What's going on?"

Lord Humphrey shook his head. "You've no need to concern yourself with our troubles. My guards will keep you safe on the journey, and the less you know, the shorter your interview will be with the king."

Rolant flung his napkin on the table. "Blessed Ancestors! My lord, if he's to travel through our kingdom, he has a right to know what he may encounter."

The baron's face reddened. The guards edged closer to the table, gripping the hilts of their swords.

I cringed, ready for the guards to seize Rolant, the only person intent on keeping us safe. He realized he'd gone too far. He returned his napkin to his lap and cleared his throat. "I beg forgiveness, my lord. Yet I must ask, after all this talk, do you not trust them?"

The baron studied Rolant for a long time. No one spoke. My leg itched where the manacle rubbed. I didn't dare scratch it. Finally, the baron said, "I believe them. That's not the same as trusting. Go ahead, give them some facts. No more than a few, mind."

Rolant nodded. "I'm not divulging royal secrets. You'll hear the same talk in the common room of every inn on the way to Ardara. The problems began several months ago. Raids on villages in the north. Swarms of insects infesting fields in the southern part of the kingdom. Burned fields right in our area. Many fish have died in Lake Carlow—the largest lake in the kingdom. A lot of folks' drinking water comes from the lake."

He twirled a cherry stem between his fingers. "We haven't had rain in four months. Folk hunting in the Great Forest for deer, cainos, and agrios, have found animals starved to death or dying of thirst. Some of it might be natural. Then again, maybe magic's involved."

Matthew frowned. "Excuse me. I know deer, but what are cainos and agrios?"

"They're furry critters," Beli said. "Cainos are small, about as long as your forearm. They browse in the underbrush while the larger agrios scramble along tree branches to eat the leaves. That's caino in your stew. It's moist, tender meat, don't you think?" He helped himself to more of the fragrant mixture.

As much as Matthew liked animals, he wasn't a vegetarian. He explained his reasoning when I asked him a few years ago. "We're omnivores. Consider our teeth— canines for tearing and molars for grinding—makes sense to eat meat and veggies both." Even so, he preferred to stick to familiar foods. He carefully set his spoonful of meat in his bowl and then chewed on a thick slice of bread.

Grandpa asked Lord Humphrey, "Who's behind the attacks?"

"I'll not pass on any suspicions King Darren may have. Rest assured he is looking into all possibilities. That's why I must take you to see him." He took a sip of juice before continuing. "For true, I have no reason to believe you're involved in our war. Still, anything out of the ordinary must be investigated. When we travel, I'll post guards at the gateway between our worlds to make certain no one passes through in either direction. Now, I want to see it for myself."

Beli stood and patted his stomach. "Excellent meal, Marilea. As good as your mother's. Perhaps better."

"Enough flattery," Marilea said. "Let us see this hole in the cliff."

The baron stepped in front of her. "I'll leave the younglings here in your care." His tone didn't invite argument.

Marilea gave a small bow of her head. "As you say, my lord."

The guards removed our shackles. When the heavy iron left my ankle, I rubbed out the soreness and wiggled my foot, celebrating the freedom to move it as I wished. Lord Humphrey still frightened me. However, aside from the tense scene with Rolant, he had remained calm, never yelling or threatening us during the questioning. Since he hadn't changed his mind about taking Grandpa to Ardara, our fate now rested with the king.

The baron went outside with Grandpa, Beli, and Rolant, leaving one guard behind. Cadoc left to check on the chicken coop the farmhands were building. One of the farmhands, a man named Rafe, had interrupted our meal to let us know they'd managed to capture all three of our birds and none had been harmed. Marilea told Matthew and me to go into the next room while she and Carys cleaned up the kitchen.

"We'll stay here, if it's all right with you," Matthew said.

"It'll be easier to work with fewer people around. Off you go." We stood, then Matthew swayed and gripped the edge of the table. Marilea put down the pile of plates she held. "Whatever's wrong?"

"Carys startled me this morning with some magic and I twisted my ankle. Or broke it. I can't tell."

"He's taken truth serum, so it must have happened," Marilea said, studying her daughter.

Carys crossed her arms. "I only crackled the air in front of him. They were traipsing through the field and I didn't trust them."

"Lass, what you did is understandable. Keeping the fact hidden was a poor decision. If you're to be a healer, you must remember the primary rule. Always relieve pain as soon as you are able."

"Aye, Ma. I'll remember," Carys said in a meek voice. She caught me watching her and scowled.

"Mind that you do." Marilea carried the stack of plates to the sink.

Carys and I helped Matthew hobble into the large room off the kitchen. We eased him onto a padded wooden bench covered in dark leather. His ankle was swollen to twice its normal size. Carys knelt and removed his sandal, then gently explored the area around the purple joint with her fingers. "It's broken, at that," she said. "I'll stabilize it with a little magic."

"You're using magic to heal? Is that safe?" My words came out in a rusty croak.

"Aye, it's safe. Though my skill's not fully developed. We'll have to wait for Nuala—our local healer—to fully mend the break. She's off for a week, collecting herbs in the Great Forest."

"Okaay . . . what can you do if you're still a student?" Matthew asked.

"The best answer is to show you. Mind you, healing magic has side effects." Matthew narrowed his eyes, and she hastily added, "Not to worry. I expect they'll be minor."

"That's what the baron said about the truth serum, and I have a wicked headache on top of the ankle pain," Matthew said.

Carys looked offended. "I promise I will make you feel better than you do now."

"All right," he grumped. "Let's get it over with."

Carys placed her fingers on either side of Matthew's foot. She took long, slow breaths while stroking his ankle from his foot toward his calf, then in the other direction. After a minute or two, she wrapped her hands around his ankle and pressed lightly for a while. She muttered a chant in a voice too low to make out any words.

I was mesmerized. This was real magic. She'd used it as a weapon before and now used it just as easily for healing. Matthew bit his lip. Every once in a while, he uttered a low moan. I wondered about Carys' knowledge of magic. Would she damage his bones more than the accident?

When her chant ended, she asked Matthew how he was.

He flexed his ankle. "Amazing. Much better. Hardly any pain."

"That was my intent." Carys looked satisfied with herself—satisfied, but not cocky.

"I've still got the headache, though."

"We might as well finish the job," she said and touched her fingertips to his temples. "Be still."

He closed his eyes. Soon, his breathing slowed, and he lowered his hunched shoulders. A couple of minutes later, Carys released him. He rubbed his forehead gently. "My headache's gone. How'd you do that?" After a pause, he added, "Uh, thank you."

I reached out to help her up and nearly let go when she grasped my hands. Her fingers were icy cold, and she was shivering. "What's wrong?" I asked.

"That's one of the parts of healing I haven't mastered.

As my magic pours from me into another person, I lose heat. Magic always saps energy from the one who uses it." She tucked her hands under her arms to warm them. "Nuala says when I'm fully trained, I'll be able to keep my body heat normal."

I'd thought to ask her to magic away my headache. I changed my mind; it would only make her condition worse.

"What about side effects?" Matthew asked. "I don't, *hic,* feel anything. Wait a minute. *Hic,* could hiccups be the, *hic,* side effect?"

Carys laughed. "They could. The effects vary from person to person. They should be gone in a few hours, though sometimes aftereffects last for days or weeks."

Now I knew for certain I didn't want magical help for my headache.

Carys wagged her finger at Matthew. "Don't walk on that foot. Remember, the bones aren't mended. I've merely lined up the joint and eased the swelling."

That reminded me of Marilea's limp. "I don't mean to be rude, but can't you or Nuala heal your mom's leg?"

She lowered her gaze. "It happened long ago. There wasn't a healer around at the time, and it's too late now."

"I'm sorry." I studied the room while we waited for Grandpa and the others to return. Decorative hangings softened the rough plaster walls. Some were bright weavings and others were made of furs that blended white with shades of brown and gray. One was trimmed with long feathers. Thick candles sat in sconces along the walls. A fireplace took up most of one wall, as did the fireplace in the kitchen that was used for cooking.

No electric lights or refrigerator, no microwave oven or telephone. It finally sank in, and my own hands grew icy. The Dunstans' life was far more primitive than ours at Grandpa's summer cabin, and we had no idea how long we'd be trapped here.

I wandered around the room. My toe bumped

something, and I took a quick step back. A winged reptile, about a foot long, napped in front of the fireplace. It was dull green with a pointed face. Half of its length came from a skinny tail. A frill ran along the back of its head. Disturbed by my foot, it spread its wings, showing patterns in red, yellow, and brown. It yawned and stretched, then curled up again, closing its eyes for another sleep.

Matthew pointed. "What, *hic*, is that?"

"Solo, our insect hunter. She keeps down the bugs in the house and outbuildings. In the evening, she glides along the cliff to feed." Carys stroked Solo's back. The little creature grunted in return.

I squatted down and ran a finger along the creature's rough, scaly skin. "She's a Coelurosauravus. At least that's the name our scientists use. They're extinct on Earth."

"Extinct?" Carys asked.

"They all died out like the chickens here."

"How do you know what she is?"

"I recognize her from one of my dad's books. He was a paleontology professor at the same university where Grandpa teaches."

Carys wrinkled her nose. "I know about professors. What's paleontology?"

"It means he studied fossils . . . um, remains of creatures and plants long dead." I smiled at the memory of my burly dad telling me stories while I sat on his lap, his beard brushing my cheek. "My mom gave me his sketchbooks and reference books about ancient life. Sometimes I put the prehistoric creatures in my own drawings."

Carys pulled on her braid, studying me. "You can draw? There's no teacher in these parts, and it's a skill I've always wanted to learn. Will you give me lessons?"

"Sure. We'll be here for a while." Pushing that thought away, I went back to exploring the room. A few paintings made on squares of wood perched on the mantel. There was one of Cadoc when he was small, and two of Carys at different ages. "These are good."

Carys hesitated before saying, "We had those painted in Ardara. Artists flock to the festivals there."

At the other end of the mantel, I noticed a small, framed charcoal sketch of the farm drawn on parchment. I tapped the frame. "Was this done in Ardara too?"

"Nay. It was a gift from a wandering artist who took ill near our farm. Ma treated him, and he gave her the drawing in payment."

"Why'd he draw two moons? Or is one the sun?"

She frowned. "Moons. He drew two because there are two." She looked from Matthew to me. "Blisters! You truly aren't from Kylemore, or anywhere else on Betherion." She shook her head, then pointed to the drawing. "Metiri is the larger moon, and Kuklos the smaller. Metiri is brighter and white. Kuklos is reddish. He couldn't show the colors with the charcoal, of course."

"Of course not." My chest tightened again. There must be countless ways Betherion differed from Earth. I rubbed my silver ring, thinking of weapons, wild creatures, magic, and Grandpa's weak heart. School didn't seem so important anymore. The question was, could we survive long enough to get home?

Many differences can be bridged
with a positive attitude and
simple kindness. It should be
noted, these methods are
not always effective.
~Royal Guidebook of Diplomacy

5

DISAGREEMENTS

Nausea from the truth serum woke me in the night.
Marilea had put us up in guest rooms on the second
floor of the farmhouse. The place had far more bedrooms
than one family could use. With the extra rooms and large
kitchen table, I wondered if the building had another use
besides serving as the family's home.

A guard stood watch outside my room. I hated to
disturb him but had no choice. I opened my door wide, then
told him I'd barf all over his shiny boots if he didn't take me
outside to the privy. When I returned to bed, I slept hard
until midafternoon and was groggy and irritable when I
woke. I'd missed breakfast two days in a row. This time I'd
also missed lunch.

I found Matthew downstairs where we'd left him,
resting on the bench in the sitting room. His leg was
propped up on a folded blanket and his hair was brushed.
A large book lay open on his lap. It had thick pages and a
leather cover, like all the other books I'd seen when I
explored the room the evening before. Matthew greeted me

with a smile that quickly faded. "Pipit, you look awful. Ask Carys to use her magic on you. She's good."

I quirked an eyebrow at him. "I'll keep it in mind. Where's Grandpa?"

"Gone. He left with Beli and Lord Humphrey hours ago. He went to your room to say goodbye but couldn't wake you."

"Crap. I never heard him. D'you think he'll be all right? There's no telling what he'll face out there."

Matthew closed the book and traced the cover's embossed leafy pattern with his forefinger. "He'll be careful. I tried again this morning to make them take me. No luck." His face brightened. "There is good news. I told Carys about Grandpa's heart. She made Beli promise to take care of him."

"She's doing a lot of good deeds for us. Or at least for you. I wonder why."

"She's a nice person?"

Carys came in then, carrying a tray of food which she set on a low table in front of the bench. "That looks delicious," Matthew said, rubbing his hands together. She gave him a small curtsey. I blushed with embarrassment. *Is he attracted to her?* He picked up a biscuit and slathered it with honey.

Carys handed him an embroidered napkin, then acknowledged me. "Greetings, Kallan. I didn't know you were awake. I'll fetch tea for you." She left the room, her tail held high, the end curved in an arc.

I cleared my throat. "I see you're not hiccupping anymore."

Matthew answered in between bites. "Gone this morning. The swelling in my ankle's down too. I told you she's good."

He is attracted to her. "Matthew, I say this as your friend and sister. Please don't get emotionally attached to that girl. We don't even know if they're fully human. Besides, we'll be here such a short time. I . . . I don't want you to get hurt again."

I closed my eyes, waiting for the eruption. A heartbeat of silence, then a curse, followed by an outburst in low, angry tones. "Don't be an idiot. I'm not getting 'attached.' If you're so concerned, remember that if you hadn't interfered with Sarah and me, we'd still be together."

"She cheated on you! I thought you'd want to know."

"Maybe it was just the one time. She might have realized she'd made a mistake and let him go. She might have told me herself, and we'd be able to work things out. Now we'll never know."

"I was trying to protect you."

"Don't bother. I'm a big boy. I'll take care of myself."

Carys chose that moment to return with my tea. "Everything all right?" she asked, handing me the steaming mug.

"Yes. I mean, aye. It's all good," I said, grabbing two biscuits before stalking out of the room.

I ate sitting cross-legged on the ground next to the chickens' new coop. The scent of fresh wood chips sprinkled around the pen didn't entirely cover up the ammonia smell from the chicken's droppings. I didn't care; the sight of Tess, Chanticleer, and Ethel scratching the ground for bugs was a comforting reminder of home.

It may have been smarter to keep my mouth shut, but Matthew was in such pain after he and Sarah broke up, I had to say something. We'd been best friends nearly our whole lives. Lately, for reasons neither of us understood, we sometimes got on each other's nerves. Carys, whom he'd known for a day, made him happy. I scowled at the irony and bit into my second biscuit.

Matthew didn't speak to me for the rest of the day, and I avoided Carys. Except for two guards Lord Humphrey left behind to keep watch at the gateway to Earth, we were alone with the Dunstan family and their farmhands.

Despite the fact home was only a field away, escape was out of the question until Grandpa returned. I spent the afternoon helping Cadoc with chores and badgering him with questions about Kylemore.

∞

The next morning, the Dunstans took me with them to the village of Daire where the family sold produce and baked goods at the market faire. We took two wagons, the twins and I in one, Marilea and Rolant in the other. The wagons were filled with baskets of juicy cherries; small, hard peaches; and huge white mushrooms; as well as loaves of bread and potpies stuffed with caino stew. Howell trotted alongside the wagons when he tired of riding.

Matthew stayed behind since he still couldn't put weight on his bad ankle. Marilea had refused my request to keep him company, instructing the farmhands to take care of his needs. In spite of the guards and Grandpa's absence, I thought Marilea worried that we'd try to escape. Before we left for Daire, I apologized to Matthew for reporting Sarah's cheating to him, and he grunted his acceptance. Not complete forgiveness, but a start. I also decided to be friendlier to Carys. If I had to leave the safety of the farm, I needed all the friends I could get.

When we loaded the wagons, Marilea told me they would donate some of the food to the village's poorest families. It was difficult for those families to get enough food in a normal year; the drought and farm attacks only made things worse. She said if they didn't have expenses of their own and farmhands to support, they'd give even more food away rather than sell it. Marilea and Rolant reminded me of my own parents and their generosity and care for others. I gave myself the same advice I'd given Matthew: don't get too attached. We'd be home in a few weeks and would never see the Dunstans again.

The early morning sun warmed my back. After a couple of hours, our wagon topped a small rise. Below us, houses were lined up along lanes surrounding the village green. A few large ones were made of stone. Most were small wooden structures surrounded by grassy lawns withered tan by the drought. Some streets were lined with rows of closely spaced buildings—shops I guessed. In the distance off to our left, a castle stood on a hill. "Who lives there?"

"Lord Humphrey," Cadoc said. "He's our liege lord. If the attacks spread, Da will fight under the baron's command. If it continues past my birthday, I'll join Da. Carys and I will be sixteen and fully grown then."

Carys grimaced. "Blessed Ancestors! May it never come to that."

Fields and farm buildings filled the land between the baron's grounds and the village. More farms lay to the west. Leafy woods separated Daire from the western farmland. As we drew closer, I noticed wooden market stalls on the village green. Bright triangular pieces of cloth hung from cords strung along the top of the stalls. The pennants flapped in the breeze, and hungry dogs nosed around for handouts. The air was filled with the sounds of goods being unpacked and children's high-pitched voices. I pointed to the waving sea of color. "The pennants make it festive."

"Each farmer and merchant have their own set of colors," Carys said. "Ours are green and yellow for our farm, Meganeara. Green, because we're on the edge of the Great Forest. Yellow's for the rising sun since we see it first in the kingdom, living on the eastern edge of Kylemore."

My tee shirt, jeans, and sandals were stowed under my bed at the farm. I wore old clothes Carys had outgrown. In tan trousers, dark green tunic, and leather boots, I could blend in at a Renaissance faire. We'd gone to one in southern New York the previous summer. There, people dressed in medieval outfits for fun. Here, they were ordinary clothes. Most grown women in Kylemore wore dresses, but

Carys said plenty of youngling girls wore trousers, same as the boys. That suited me just fine.

Cadoc guided our horses to an empty slot in a row of wagons. In a short time, we organized everything in the Dunstan's stall. Marilea handed Carys a small leather bag full of clinking coins. "Buy the items we talked over. Take Kallan and Cadoc with you. Howell can go too. Stay together and mind you keep to our story that Kallan's your cousin."

"Aye, Ma, we'll take care." With that, the twins drew me into the crowd.

Cadoc explained that Daire held a small weekly market on the village green. Once each month people gathered for the much larger market faire. It was a special occasion that mixed sales of necessities like food and cloth with trinkets such as jewelry and toys. Musicians, dancers, jugglers, and other performers provided entertainment. Knots of adults gossiped all over the green, and children played around them, imitating knights with wooden swords, tossing balls, and rolling barrel hoops with sticks.

As we wandered from stall to stall, I examined stacks of bright cloth and shelves of clay pottery and other wares while Carys made her purchases and Cadoc stored them in a cloth sack. I stopped in front of one stall that displayed mounds of colorful ribbons, rows of wooden tops, and stacks of bracelets braided from thin cording. The rotund merchant's greasy hair hung in front of his face as he bent over a bowl of black objects. When he straightened, he held up a smooth heart-shaped stone.

"Put this under your pillow at night, lass. The love of your life will return the sentiment. They've been touched by a magic spell woven by a sorceress I know well. Her spells never fail."

He held out the stone on the tips of his fingers. I shook my head and then glanced up. An assortment of feathers hung from the same cord as his green and black pennants. Soft teal ones brightened the row of long brown plumes with black bars and ashy grays with white spots. The merchant followed my gaze. "Those are from rare birds of the north, from the Kingdom of Kelby. First-rate adornments for your shiny locks."

"No, thanks." A woven basket held a mound of long, curving, ivory teeth. I pulled one out. "What are these?"

"Dragon fangs, as anyone can see. Bring you luck, those. Went through terrible danger to collect 'em. Got this gash on me arm nabbing the biggest one." He held up his right forearm, exposing an angry red streak. It appeared to be a recent but healing wound. "Lucky to get away with me life." The wound was straight and smooth-edged. I thought it more likely a cut from a knife fight than a tear from an animal attack.

"No thank you. We're happy for your escape," Cadoc said. I tossed the tooth in the basket and Cadoc steered me away from the merchant. The greasy man continued to call after us and exclaim about his rare objects.

"He's an annoying wretch of a man," Carys said as we walked away from the faire down an empty lane. "Waste of coin, buying his rubbish."

"Was that really a dragon tooth?" I asked, remembering the heavy-bodied shape I'd seen in flight when we came through the gateway in the cliff.

Cadoc snorted. "Of course not."

"Oh." I hadn't expected it to be real but was disappointed all the same.

He said, "That peddler's a fraud selling overpriced wares. For real dragon fangs, go to the Equinox Festival in the royal city. The autumn one's in the ninth cycle of Metiri. The other's in the third cycle for spring. The festivals last two weeks. Folks come from all over the kingdom."

A flare of excitement gave way to a sense of loss. The day before, Cadoc had explained how they measured time by the cycles of the white moon Metiri. Each of the ten cycles lasted thirty-five days. We were in the middle of the sixth cycle. I shook off my disappointment. "We'll be gone long before the autumnal equinox. When Grandpa tells King Darren what happened to us, he'll have to let us go."

"Then we must show you as much of Kylemore as we can before you leave. Let's begin. There are only twenty-five hours in a day." He turned his warm brown eyes on me and smiled, making my stomach flutter.

My emotions were a mess. I was attracted to Cadoc and wanted to get to know him better. At the same time, I missed my friends and our life back home. Fun things like movies and the county fair where we'd planned to show off Ethel, and everyday stuff like my soft bed, computer, cell phone, electricity, and running water. I wanted life to be the way it was before the chicken disaster. Before Matthew got moody. I wanted life to be simple again, but deep down I feared it would become more complicated the older we got.

With all my worrying, I lagged behind the twins. Someone tugged on the strap of my leather satchel—a beautiful gift from Marilea. I whirled around and yelped at the sight of a tall, thin boy holding a dagger.

He stepped closer to me and held the braided leather tight. "Give it here, you tailless freak, or I'll cut you."

"No way." I tugged on the satchel strap and brought my knee up, striking him in his most sensitive area.

The boy doubled over, groaning. Cadoc grabbed a branch lying in the lane. He rushed in and whacked my attacker on his back. The boy collapsed. Howell circled the action, growling low in his throat. When the fiend pushed himself up, Cadoc punched him in the jaw. Defeated, the thief collapsed again, breathing hard. "You'll pay for this, Dunstan," he snarled.

Cadoc pried the boy's dagger out of his hand and tucked it in his own boot. "Let's go." We raced with Carys to the nearby woods. Howell gave a last sharp bark at my attacker, then bounded after us. When we reached a thick part of the forest, we dropped to the ground, panting for breath. There was no sign of our foe.

"You've made an enemy now," Cadoc said.

"Maybe he'll think twice before trying to rob someone else. I hope he didn't follow us." Shading my eyes with my hand, I scanned the woods in the direction we'd come from. There was no one in sight.

"Don't fret. Fergus is a puking coward, not a true cutpurse."

"You know him?"

"He's a schoolmate of ours," Carys said. "His father's a cloth merchant. Wealthy, though he won't give Fergus much coin. What Fergus wants, he takes." She glanced at her brother before continuing. "He's hated Cadoc for years. Fergus has no magical skill, and what burns him more is that Cadoc's form of magic is rare."

"What is your magic, Cadoc?"

"My sister exaggerates. It's a minor talent I have."

Carys sat up straight. "It's to do with spirits and—"

"And that's enough about that," Cadoc said, cutting her off.

"Forget I asked." I was curious, but he clearly didn't want to be pushed. Lying down on the soft ground, I gazed up at the pattern of sunlight on leaves. It was cool in the shade, and the air was thick with the scent of white blossoms that dotted the nearby bushes. Bees swooped from flower to flower, their droning shutting out the sounds of the faire. Howell slept, whimpered, then quieted down again.

We'd been silent for a while when Cadoc raised his head, listening. I could hear nothing. He motioned for us to stay still and pointed toward a rough path that wound through the woods. His voice was a husky whisper. "Beware. The forest is unsettled. Something evil approaches."

6

SECRETS PRESENT AND PAST

The twins and I heard voices raised in argument. Lying flat, peering through the lower branches of the dense bushes, we watched three men traipse through the woods and stop about twenty feet away. Two sat down on a fallen tree trunk and took swigs from a bottle they passed back and forth. One of them was a thin, curly-haired man.

"It's a lot of coin," he said, "but it ain't worth it if we get caught."

"Who's gonna catch us, Seisyll, tell me that?" asked the burly and bearded man who paced in front of the other two. "We set the fires or put the creepy crawlies in the fields in the black of night. We strike with no pattern. They can't spare enough men to guard everywhere, every night. None of 'em can afford a mage to protect the fields." He spat tobacco juice in the weeds at his feet and then resumed chewing his wad.

"Don't matter who catches us, Morcant," chimed in the third companion from the log. He was a stocky man with a tattered vest missing the top two buttons. "*If* we're caught, we'll be hanged for sure. Our leader may be a royal like you think, though I don't reckon the king would take that as an excuse."

47

"Durst talks sense," put in thin Seisyll, a gap showing where a front tooth was missing. "A lot of folk are gonna starve if we keep this up. It don't feel right."

Morcant stroked his beard, gazing steadily at the two seated men. "Right or not, we're in it up to our necks. If we keep quiet and don't act suspicious, no one'll be the wiser. What d'you think they'll do to us if we quit now? That one 'at hired us made it clear, once we started, we're in it 'til the end." He took out a knife and used it to clean his fingernails.

"We can't quit, and it's wicked to keep on," Seisyll said. "Blessed Ancestors have mercy on us all." He put a stopper in the bottle and stowed it in a leather satchel.

Morcant pointed the knife at him. "Keep your thoughts to yourself. I won't suffer any back talk."

Howell stirred in his sleep. His front legs pumped, running in his dream. The movement scraped dry leaves against each other.

Hand still on the satchel flap, Seisyll raised his head and stared at the bushes that hid us. "What was that?"

"What was what?" Morcant asked, his voice rough with irritation.

My stomach tightened and I held my breath. Howell whimpered, then grew still. Seisyll stood and scanned the woods. "I heard a crackling noise. May be there's spies listening in."

A bee buzzed near my face. I held my arms tight against my body, forcing myself not to swat it away. It swooped close to my cheek, then swerved to land on a flower. I blew out a silent breath of relief.

"What are you goin' on about?" Morcant snorted in disgust and put his knife away. "No one's followed us. It's a lizard or some such, skittering around in the duff. Don't hunt for trouble where there ain't none." He took off his brown felt hat and slapped it, releasing puffs of fine dirt.

"Let's get a move on," Durst urged, tugging on the hem of his vest.

48

"Let's do," Morcant said, putting his hat back on. "Time's a wastin' and this heat's gettin' to me. It'll be cooler by the sea in Avonflow."

They headed south in a bedraggled line. My mouth was dry as I watched them go.

"Did you hear that?" Carys said once the men disappeared from view. "Now we know who's ruining the crops."

Cadoc rubbed his chin. "I wonder who hired them. They said their orders came from someone important, maybe even royal."

"Shouldn't we report this?" I asked. "Don't you have a police force or village guards, or . . . anyone who can tell the king about them?"

Cadoc looked at me, his brown eyes thoughtful. "Police? Don't know what they are. We need to think this through before we tell anyone. A traitor that destroys fields doesn't care who they hurt. Besides, we don't know what authorities we can trust."

"Aye," Carys said. "If we tell the wrong person, we could be in danger ourselves. We need to know more."

"What about your parents? Can't they tell this group . . . what's it called . . . the Eyes and Ears?"

Cadoc shook his head. "Ma and Da wouldn't put much weight on our words. I swear, sometimes they still see us as thumb-sucking tots."

"Da knows we're nearly grown," Carys said. "Only he's worried about who'll work the farm if you join the Eyes. He wants you to be in charge someday."

"Farming's not for me. He'll have to hire more help. What about you? Will Ma let you go to university? Even with Nuala in your corner?"

I coughed. "Um, we're getting off track. Can we tell Matthew? We can trust him. We have to find a way to stop these guys before they destroy your fields."

"Aye, we can tell Matthew," Cadoc said. "Kallan, can

you make a sketch of those men?"

"Sure." I'd made a sketchbook from sheets of handmade paper Marilea had given me. I tugged it and some charcoal out of my satchel. In a few minutes I produced drawings that captured the men's features reasonably well.

Cadoc nodded his approval. "Keep 'em hidden. We'd best get back to help Ma and Da."

I was afraid Fergus might pop up again, so I paid attention to our surroundings on the way back. My heart went out to a thin woman with a pinched face at a cheese stall. She offered to trade wildflowers for a hunk of cheese. Two wide-eyed boys peeked out from behind her skirts. Their bony limbs and sunken cheeks showed the effects of the food shortage from the drought. The cheese man shooed the family away. The mother turned and walked slowly toward another stall.

I begged a coin from Carys and rushed over to the woman. Pressing the money into her hand, I pointed to a small bouquet. It must have been too much money for the little bunch of flowers because she tried to give me all of her bouquets. Carys waved her hand at me in a 'go on, it's all right' gesture, so I folded the mother's fingers over the coin. "Only the one bunch. Buy food for your family."

"Thank you, m'lady."

I hurried away with the twins, breathing in the scent of lilies of the valley and some fragrant purple blooms I didn't recognize. When we returned to Rolant and Marilea, I helped out where I could, handing out fruits and vegetables to the customers that clustered around the stall.

After a long afternoon, we headed back to the farm. The heat had eased off a little. I saw clouds to the west, but they were too thin to bring any rain. About halfway to the farm, Carys spotted Nuala bent over a clump of plants with fuzzy leaves growing in the ditch by the road. The slightly built healer looked ancient. Her skin was a weathered brown and her silver hair hung in a long braid down her back. She wore an ankle-length, cobalt blue dress belted at the waist.

Carys called to her. "Healer Nuala, you've returned early."

"Aye, a wasted trip. This blasted drought has delayed the flowers I need. How was the faire?"

"Business was good," Carys said. "Food's getting harder for folk to come by. We're lucky. With two springs on our farm, our crops have done well."

"Aye, your family and I have water, and our lands are at the kingdom's border. We'll be safe for a while." She climbed out of the ditch, noticing me as she came toward the wagon. I shrank back from the piercing glare of her pale blue eyes. "Who's the lass?"

"A visitor from the east," Cadoc said. "Healer Nuala, I'm pleased to present Kallan MacKinnon. She and her brother Matthew are staying with us for a while."

"In fact," Carys said, "We need your help. Matthew's ankle is broken beyond my talent to mend. Can we offer you a meal and moa eggs in exchange for a healing?"

Nuala's gaze was still on me, but she spoke to Carys. "Aye, lass, I'll come. And I'll find out what you've not a mind to tell me at present." She hitched up her dress and climbed into the wagon, settling in next to Howell.

As soon as we arrived at the farm, Nuala went to Matthew where he rested on the leather bench. Carys made the introductions.

Nuala said, "Let's get you on your feet again, lad."

"I know you're supposed to heal as soon as possible. However, I'd rather eat dinner first if I'm in for hiccups again."

She chuckled. "As you wish."

During the meal, Rolant and Marilea filled Nuala in on how Matthew and I came to be with them. *Is it wise to tell more people about us? Can we trust her to keep quiet?* The healer asked us about the kinds of medicine we used at home and what sorts of plants grew there. Then she peppered us with questions on all kinds of topics, including the constellations in our skies, the animals that roamed our woods, and the relative numbers of humans, dwarves, and elves on Earth. That last one was easy. She was skilled at extracting information; there was no pattern to her inquiries and no pause between one answer and the next question. No time to think up lies, even if I'd wanted to.

I didn't understand her quick acceptance of us and the facts we told of another world. While we ate a dessert of raspberry tart, I asked her about it. "Healer Nuala, you don't sound surprised by what we've told you. Have you met others from different worlds?"

"Nay, lass, I've not met outsiders before. The ease with which you answered my questions, and the details you provided, convinced me of your honesty. When we met, Cadoc claimed you came from the east. Why would that be?"

Cadoc answered for me. "The gateway to their world is in the cliff on the eastern edge of our land."

Nuala narrowed her eyes at him, then turned back to me. "To answer your question, my gran told me stories when I was a wee tot. Some told of folk crossing over from other worlds in ancient times. She wouldn't say if the stories were fancy or fact. You and Matthew prove them true."

I looked at the Dunstans. Marilea's lips were pressed tight together. Rolant turned his spoon over and over in his hand. The twins' eyes were wide with interest. I couldn't keep the shock out of my voice. "You mean this has happened before? People know about it? Rolant, Marilea, you knew about it?"

Rolant laid the spoon next to his bowl. "It's been said that now and then boundaries between worlds grow weak. Cracks open. Not for long, mind you, and they don't open again once they've closed." A flash of panic jolted me. How much time did we have before the doorway disappeared?

He took a drink of water before continuing. "Not many know the stories. The royal spies, the Eyes and Ears of the King, know of a handful of times it may have occurred. The last passage, if it happened, was hundreds of years ago."

So, the Eyes and Ears are spies. Beli is one, but how does Rolant know their secrets?

Marilea answered my unspoken question. "I suppose there's no harm in telling you. Years ago, Rolant and I served in the Eyes, so we've seen the records. The gateway you came through matches ones described in the accounts, though there's no proof, lass, remember that. The reports read as myth, not fact. And who believes a myth come to life on their own homestead?"

I glanced at Matthew and he shrugged. "If it happened hundreds of years ago, I don't see how it helps us now." He ran his fingers through his hair. When he spoke again, it was more to himself than the rest of us. "The two worlds are connected in some way . . . maybe parallel universes. A physicist might know. Betherion's the next world over from Earth. We share a lot of species. Gateways could have opened more often in the distant past. The species would have started out the same in both worlds. Evolution took a different path in each place. That makes sense." He nodded, then noticed the others staring at him.

He cleared his throat. "Nuala, could you take a look at my ankle?"

The Dunstans and I cleared away the dishes, then we all gathered in the sitting room. Aeron flew to Matthew's shoulder and folded his wings. Since he'd led us into Kylemore, the little bird had grown quite attached to my foster brother. Nuala knelt beside the bench where Matthew sat. "Carys has a sensitive touch," she said. "Still and all, her main talent lies with plants and ointments, not bone and sinew."

Carys had smeared a pale green cream with a minty odor on Matthew's foot and ankle. Nuala rubbed some of it between her fingers. "Good choice using your own concoction, lass. Keeps the pain down better than any mixture I've made." Frowning in concentration, the healer turned Matthew's foot from side to side, probing and pressing. He squirmed and bit his lower lip. Aeron flew out the open window.

Nuala nodded at Carys. "Excellent work. You've lined up the bones well. I can heal it straight and strong."

Carys blushed at the praise. "Thank you, mistress."

"Now for the knitting of the bones. We'll put you right soon enough, lad. This will tingle, mind." The healer grasped Matthew's ankle once more and spoke in a curly-sounding language, her voice rising and falling in a musical way. Her eyes were closed, the muscles of her arms taut. Matthew balled his hands into fists and stared at the charcoal drawing of the farm and two moons.

When Nuala released him after a few minutes, beads of perspiration stood out on her wrinkled forehead. Marilea handed her a cup of water and she took a long swallow. "It takes something out of me now, the healing. I recall one battle when I was newly trained. Mended a hundred folk—men, elves, Pannmordians even. Full of vigor, I was. That was a long time ago. A long time." Her pale blue eyes had a faraway look of remembrance.

"Thank you," Matthew whispered. He stood and shifted his stance until he bore weight equally on both legs.

Nuala returned her attention to him. "Do you hurt, lad?"

"It itches a little. No pain." He cleared his throat. "Sorry, I can only whisper."

"It may be a week or more 'ere your voice returns to full force. I know not why healing one part of the body affects another. The best mages in the land have studied magic for more than an age, yet many mysteries remain."

"My voice will come back, right?"

"Aye. Rest it as much as you are able. The more the

strain, the longer the weakness. Carys brews a fine soothing tea."

"We're so glad you came," I said, reminding myself of my mother thanking neighbors who visited during her illness. I made a small curtsey before I could stop myself. When I straightened, I let go of my tunic and clasped my hands together. My cheeks grew hot.

Nuala inclined her head and stared at my ring. I heard her say under her breath, "Curious." She looked me straight in the eye. My breathing quickened and I turned the top of my ring around, hiding the knot design in my fist.

She said, "I share my gifts with pleasure for the benefit of the kingdom. As should we all." She rose and headed for the door.

Outside, Rolant had hitched up one of the horses to a cart. He helped Nuala onto the seat beside him. Then they were off with a cloud of dust billowing in their wake.

I rested my head against the cool glass of the window. Stars dotted the sky in unfamiliar patterns, making me long for home. *Is there any way to stop the men we overheard in the woods? Is the traitor that hired them really someone in the royal family?* Nuala's interest in my ring unsettled me. It had been in my mother's family for hundreds of years. Why would it attract the attention of anyone in this world?

Some illnesses cannot be cured
but must rather be endured.
Provide what comfort you can.
With time and proper care,
the patient may recover.
~Elementary Guide for Healers

7
ILLNESS STRIKES

𝒯he morning after Nuala healed Matthew's ankle, Marilea and I collected eggs from Tess and Ethel. These were the first ones they laid since we followed the chickens into Kylemore. Even though the morning was warm, Marilea wore a woolen cloak over her tunic. Her hand shook when she placed an egg into the small basket I held. She pulled her cloak tighter.

"You're shivering. What's wrong?" I placed a brown egg in the basket next to her tan one. Carys had told me that neither of her parents, nor her grandfather Beli, had magical talent, so Marilea's shivers couldn't be caused by using magic.

"I'm chilled. An old illness comes to haunt me now and again." She turned toward the house. "I shall take to my bed. The eggs must stay cool. Carys can show you where to store them."

As soon as we entered the house, Marilea headed upstairs while I went to find Carys. When I told her about her mother, she ran up to her parents' bedroom. I followed, but Carys shut the door in my face. I waited for her in the kitchen with the basket of eggs. A few minutes later, she shouted down the stairs, "Fetch my da."

I found Matthew, and we each searched a different part of the farm. He discovered Rolant in the barn and gave him the message. Rolant sprinted to the house while Matthew and I waited outdoors for news. Before long, Cadoc came by with a load of firewood he'd chopped. We told him about Marilea while we helped stack the wood.

He wiped an arm across his sweaty forehead. "I feared something bad would happen today."

"Why's that?" I asked.

"At breakfast, the air around her was dark . . . shadowy. Didn't know what it meant, though."

"She said she gets this way sometimes. Is it bad?"

"It can be. She's real sick for a few days, then it eases off. It happened two or three times when I was small. Da says she was taken with it more often before Carys and I were born." He cleared his throat. "It's serious. And after losing Annie . . . well, Da would be broken if he lost Ma."

Matthew stopped adding logs to the woodpile. "Who's Annie?"

Cadoc scrubbed the toe of his boot in a patch of dirt, not answering right away. When he finally spoke, his voice was shaky. "Our little sister—her full name was Annilea. She died about four years back. Only six years old. She and I got sick—not the same as Ma's illness. Terrible coughing. Couldn't suck in enough air. Weak as a newborn pup. In the end, I pulled through. Annie, she was too little." He blinked away tears.

Now I understood the two paintings of girls on the fireplace mantel. They weren't both of Carys; one must be little Annie. A lump formed in my throat. I reached out and squeezed Cadoc's hand.

Matthew crossed his arms and studied the ground. "Sorry, man. That's rough."

"Aye, it is." Cadoc swiped at the tears with the back of his hand.

Rolant came around the corner of the house but was too distracted to notice Cadoc's distress. "Son. I've a shipment of cherry tree seedlings coming into Avonflow in a few days. I need you four younglings to pick them up from the warehouse. I'm staying with your ma."

I wondered what Lord Humphrey would say if we left the farm without Rolant or Marilea to supervise us. I didn't want to risk the baron's anger. When I opened my mouth to protest, Rolant held up a hand to silence me. "You must go," he said. "I'll have my hands full with my wife."

"Cannot Carys stay with you?" Cadoc asked. "She's a good healer."

"I'll not risk any of you getting sick. I've been through this with Ma before. If she . . . if she gets worse . . ." He stared into the distance, talking to himself now. "No. She'll get well, as she did before." He ran a hand through his wavy brown hair. His tail twitched back and forth in agitation a few times, then his face cleared. "Kallan, you and Carys fetch Nuala while the boys gather supplies."

Next, he spoke to Cadoc. "I need those seedlings. Leaf curl's taking over half the orchard. Do what hunting you can and teach this pair some skills." He nodded at Matthew and me. "They must learn to defend themselves. With all the attacks on farms near Daire, there's no knowing what you might come across in the Great Forest."

He turned toward the house, sending his last words over his shoulder. "You best leave for Avonflow in the morning."

∞

Carys led me to a small stone structure built over one of their springs for keeping food cool. After storing the eggs in the springhouse, we set off for Nuala's place. We found her preparing ointments in her snug little cabin. Bunches of herbs hung from the rafters. Wooden shelves full of clay jars and woven baskets piled high with dried herbs lined one wall of the main room that served as kitchen and sitting room. I was careful to keep the top of my ring turned toward my palm. Nuala didn't make any comment when she glanced at my hands. Instead, she asked about Marilea.

The four of us had decided to inform the healer about the criminals we'd seen at the market faire. The twins trusted her completely, and she thought well of Carys, so she would probably help us. While Nuala packed her clothes and medical supplies, Carys told her what we'd overheard in the woods. When she was upset, Carys tugged on the end of her ebony tail. She did so now, saying, "Nuala, is there any way to get word to the king? He should know that the traitor could be someone in the royal family."

"Think, lass. The criminals mentioned no names. Didn't hint if the leader's a man or woman. Not much to go by, is it?" Carys sighed. Nuala added, "Don't worry yourself. I'll get a message to a friend who works in the castle. She'll see it reaches King Darren." She patted Carys' shoulder. "The king will be on his guard. Mind that you four are on yours. There's the Great Forest to travel through, and Avonflow's a busy seaport with plenty of villains hanging about."

Nuala returned to the farm with us. While she tended to Marilea, Carys and I packed our bags. I wasn't anxious to leave the safety of the farm for unfamiliar woods infested with wild beasts and traitorous criminals, but I had no choice.

∞

We left the next morning after breakfast. Kylemore horses were small and sturdy. Cadoc had chosen Willow, a shaggy brown mare with white stockings, for me. Colby, Matthew's black gelding, was a hand taller than my mount, although still pony-sized. We'd been riding since we were eight years old, although we hadn't been on a horse all summer.

Our first day on the trail to Avonflow passed quickly. The ground was level, the trees sparse. I gave shaggy Willow lots of attention, and by the time we made camp that evening, we'd begun to develop a bond. The next morning, my legs ached so much that each step was an ordeal. I was hungry and tired from a restless night on the hard ground. Cadoc ignored my complaints, insisting Matthew and I needed a hunting lesson before breakfast.

"Isn't Carys coming?" I asked.

"She's tending to the horses."

"Shouldn't we help her and hunt later?"

"Some animals are active right after dawn. We hunt when the time is right. Follow me and step lightly."

We walked single file with me in the middle. After Cadoc sent dirty looks my way three times for snapping twigs, I stepped directly in his faint footprints as often as I could. My muscles screamed in protest as I placed each foot down with care.

After we'd walked for twenty minutes or so, we stopped in an area that resembled an outdoor cathedral. Sunlight streamed between branches lush with emerald leaves swaying in a soft breeze. I tilted my head back to find the treetops. Seventy feet high? Eighty? A hundred? Their trunks looked too slender to hold up their massive crowns. Mushrooms, the color of cream, sprouted in the shade, and wildflowers grew in the sunny open area, brightening the carpet of decaying leaves. I stared in wonder, forgetting my sore legs.

"What kind of trees are they?" Matthew said, his voice still whispery soft from Nuala's healing magic.

"Rough elm," Cadoc answered, his voice as quiet as Matthew's. "Look. Straight ahead." I peered beyond his outstretched arm. A small, slender-bodied green dinosaur with muscular thighs and short front limbs stood on its hind legs watching a lizard sunning itself on a rock. The dinosaur was about as tall as my chest and so well camouflaged that I wouldn't have seen it if Cadoc hadn't pointed it out. The graceful creature turned its head in our direction, and then it bounded away before Cadoc could let loose his arrow. The lizard fled into a bank of giant ferns.

"Rule one, step silently," Cadoc said. "Rule two, never stand upwind of your prey. They'll catch your scent and your meal is gone. A breeze that shifts direction like we have today is no help to the hunter." He shrugged. "No matter. Those dinosaurs, hollow tails they're called, have tough meat. At least we can pick mushrooms. They won't run away."

Cadoc squatted by a cluster of the creamy white fungi that grew in the shade and cut one off with his knife. "Rule three, never eat mushrooms, or any other plant, unless you know it's safe. It's better to be hungry than dead. These are queen's buttons—safe and delicious." He pointed out features to identify them and tell them apart from poisonous imposters. By the time we were done collecting, my stomach ached with hunger.

I was pleased that I only snapped one twig on the way back to camp.

When we returned, I expected to eat right away, but Carys had a new lesson in mind. We paired off, Matthew with Cadoc and Carys with me, to learn how to defend ourselves with daggers. We used wooden trainers, not the real thing.

Between my hunger pangs and sore legs, I couldn't focus. Carys barked out one correction after another. "Tight grip! Hold it straight, not over your head. Step back with care. No! Not that way, you'll . . . trip over the tree root."

She offered me a hand. I waved her away, rolled onto all fours, and eased myself up. "Enough!" I threw my wooden dagger on the ground. "I want breakfast."

Carys jerked back like she'd been struck, while Cadoc appeared to hide a grin behind his blade. Matthew, who knew well how grumpy hunger made me, quickly put his trainer away and dug a packet of biscuits and a bag of dried cherries out of a saddlebag. We ate in silence, which was fine by me.

Afterward, we followed a brook for a couple of hours. The trees were closer together in this part of the Great Forest, evergreens mixed in with rough elm, ash, and oak trees. Between the running water and decaying leaves, the air was moist and smelled musty.

We took a break in the early afternoon and watered the horses at the brook. Cadoc taught Matthew how to use a sling, a common weapon in Kylemore. A rectangular leather cradle connected to cords at either end held the stone to be flung. Cadoc demonstrated a few different ways to wind up before sending his missile straight to whatever target he chose. He moved so fast, and his motions were so complicated, I had no hope of copying him. I decided to stick to my dagger.

Carys and I left the boys to their training while we foraged for healing plants along the bank, then dangled our feet in the cool water while we ate our lunch. When we returned to the boys, we sorted our collection into cloth bags. Matthew sat on the ground next to me, wincing as he rubbed his wrist and shook it out.

"How's it going with the sling?"

"Not so well. It's totally different from the slingshots we made back home."

I grinned at the memory of our homemade rubber band contraptions. "I remember flinging stones at apple trees around the cabin. You always hit more fruit than I could."

He bumped fists with me. It was good to see him relax. Still, our peace was a fragile thing; there was no telling how long it would last.

"Cadoc makes it look easy. The sling takes a lot of coordination. You have to swing it fast enough in the right direction and release it at precisely the right moment to hit the target." He rubbed his wrist again. "If we stay here for a few months, I can get the hang of it."

I stiffened but kept my voice casual. "That's not going to happen. You'll have to practice back home." Unlike me, Matthew seemed more comfortable in Kylemore as time passed. He enjoyed exploring new places, aside from the unfamiliar foods. In foster care, I'd learned to keep my guard up and be suspicious of the unknown. A headache bloomed, and I massaged my temples.

"Pipit, what's wrong?"

"The subjects we studied in school are worthless in this world. The twins can use all sorts of weapons and magic besides. Drawing's my talent. Big whoop. As far as survival in a place like this, drawing isn't any more valuable than your soccer skills. I'm so . . . useless."

Rubbing my ring, I sighed. "There's another thing. I hate to admit it, 'cause it's silly. When I was small and my mother told me stories about elves and other magical creatures, I wasn't jealous of their talent because I knew the stories weren't real. Now that we're in a world that actually has magic. . . I don't want to be left out."

Matthew said, "Then again, you and I never really fit in, even at home. Maybe 'cause we're orphans. Or because we'd rather roam around the woods instead of playing video games. Doesn't matter why. But sometimes . . . sometimes this place feels more 'right' to me than home does. Even if I can't do magic."

My heart pounded in my chest and my ears rang. I spoke slowly, willing him to take in every word. "Don't. Say. That. We belong on Earth. We have no idea how to survive here. Think of this as a vacation, nothing more."

We dropped our conversation when Cadoc came and sat near Matthew. "You do well with the sling," he said. "By the Living Spirit, you'll bring down game before we finish this trip."

"Don't swear," Carys said automatically as she joined us.

"Beg pardon," Cadoc said, his reply as mechanical as her scolding. He rummaged around in a satchel, pulled out two small loaves of dark bread and tossed one to Matthew. "Are you two hungry?" he asked us girls.

"We ate while you lobbed your rocks," Carys said. "We're off again. She pointed toward the stream with her collecting bag. "My feverfew supplies are low."

I trailed her, letting the soothing sound of the burbling water replace the memory of Matthew's words. We followed the stream, going farther than we had earlier. On the streambank, the bright feverfew flowers shone in the midday sun. The attraction of the big, yellow centers with halos of pure white petals was canceled out by an unpleasant, bitter smell.

"Ma should be well by the time we get home. In case the sickness lingers, she'll need more of these," Carys said, breaking off a plant low on the stem. Before long, we'd filled the collecting bag and started back to camp. All of a sudden, Carys stopped in midstep. "Shh, listen."

Something rustled in the woods. We crept through the underbrush. Twigs snagged my tunic and I scraped my knees on tree roots hidden under leaf litter. In a few minutes we discovered what made the noise. "Would you look at that?" Carys whispered. "I cannot believe our good fortune."

The full meaning of a discovery may
not be uncovered for a long while.
~Handbook of the Eyes and Ears of the King

8

HIDDEN TALENT

I pointed to the animals that had caught Carys'
attention. "I think I know what they are, but why are
we fortunate to find them?" At the sound of my voice, the
taller creature swiveled to stare at the shrub that hid us.
Carys put a finger to her lips and we watched the feathered
couple in silence.

"Come," she whispered after a few minutes. "I'll tell you
my idea on the way."

Back at camp, she announced our discovery to the
boys. "We found a troodon nest."

"Small dinosaurs?" Matthew asked.

Carys nodded. "Aye. Small but fierce fighters. We had
their eggs in Ardara once. The tastiest you'll ever eat."

I said, "We would've collected eggs now, except the
parents were too close."

"They hunt at dusk," Carys said. "We can raid the nest
then. They haven't started to brood yet, praise the Living
Spirit. There'd be no point in collecting anything if they had.
Who wants to eat eggs full of feathers?"

Matthew laughed. "How do you know they haven't
started to brood?" His voice was only a little husky now.

Carys shifted to her teaching mode, speaking slowly

and holding our attention. "The female lays pairs of eggs over a couple of weeks for a total of sixteen to twenty-four. The father won't sit on the eggs until they're all laid, so they'll hatch at the same time. They have five or six in the clutch so far. We can gather a few today and more on our way back home."

"They look dangerous," I said. "Do you think we can do it without getting hurt?"

"If we're careful," Carys said. "We must be alert. One parent may stay near the nest."

"We have a lot of experience with moas," Cadoc said. "These creatures shouldn't trouble us much."

Carys scowled. "Troodons are powerful. Our moas know us, they aren't as big, and they don't have that sharp claw on their foot."

"It'll be easier to get close if we distract them," Matthew said. "Cadoc, if you hurl stones into the bushes with your sling, that might give one of us time to nab the eggs."

"Worth a try."

"Sounds possible," I said. "Still, can we agree to quit if it feels unsafe?"

Matthew knew I avoided danger whenever I could, especially after my dad's fatal work accident. He said, "Sure, Pipit. The eggs aren't the only food in the forest."

Carys nodded slowly. I wondered if she was having second thoughts. Cadoc scoffed at my suggestion.

"We'll take care enough." His voice softened. "There is some risk. If you'd rather, you can wait here for us."

I was touched by his concern and angered by his suggestion that I was afraid. "I'm no coward. I'll come."

"As you wish. Remember, my da gave us orders to teach you to fend for yourselves. This is good training."

"That's settled, then," Carys said.

We relaxed for the remainder of the hot afternoon. Aeron entertained us with aerial acrobatics when a female of his species flew into our camp. She was not impressed and turned her attention to cleaning her feathers. Aeron flew to Carys, who found grubs for him under a flat rock. Matthew made a list of plants and animals in Kylemore while I drew the Dunstan's farm from memory. I was getting accustomed to quills and homemade ink. While the twins and I were at the market faire in Daire, Matthew had made a set of chicken feather quills. They were a small reminder of home that I preferred to the Dunstans' moa quills.

When the light faded, Carys and I took the boys to the dinosaur nest. It was on the ground, bowl shaped, and formed out of sand. Eggs stood on end, partly buried in the sand with their tops poking out. We hid quietly in the brush nearby and waited. The troodons were sturdy dinosaurs that stood on two legs with short arms in front. They were about three feet tall and six feet long, including their tails. They must have weighed close to a hundred pounds. Downy feathers covered their bodies, and muscles bulged under the soft covering.

One of the pair was in the bushes a distance away. The other stood near the nest. I could see the pointed tip of a retractable claw on its foot. I winced at the thought of it slicing through my flesh. Cadoc readied his sling, then winked at me and mouthed, "Watch this."

I rolled my eyes. *Why do boys have to show off?*

The nearest one had its back to us. It appeared to be watching a fat lizard perched on a tree trunk. Cadoc took one step forward, and *snap*. The sound of the cracking twig echoed in my ears. Rule One, I thought, *step silently.*

The troodon pirouetted and trotted toward our hiding place.

"Run!" Carys shouted.

I raced after her and the boys. My sore legs screamed with every step. The troodon was on my trail and closing in. *The claw. Must escape the claw.* I kept to the denser vegetation to slow it down. My breath came in ragged gasps.

It was nearly upon me. I caught a flash of movement to

my right. Cadoc dashed onto the path and crossed to the woods on the other side. The dinosaur charged after him. I stumbled and nearly fell into a thorny bush.

Cadoc screamed in pain.

Carys whipped out her wand. *"Solidiom!"* The trooden smacked into her air wall. Matthew came and held me upright as my knees gave way. We watched the creature stagger around and bump into trees as I recovered my strength. Cadoc emerged from the woods, blood streaming down his face. The four of us sprinted away, leaving the invisible air wall in place.

Back at camp, Cadoc sank onto a log by the fire pit. The color had drained from his face. He was sliced open from the middle of his forehead to his temple. A flap of skin fell over his eyebrow. Rose-red blood flowed freely from the gash.

"Lie down," Carys ordered. "Kallan, fetch cloth strips from my medicine bag."

Matthew and I took a first aid course each summer. Grandpa insisted on it since his cabin was pretty isolated, and it would take time for help to arrive in an emergency. I recalled my training while I fetched Carys' bag.

I handed her a clean strip of cloth. "Put pressure on the wound. It'll stop the bleeding quicker."

"I know what to do," she snapped. She laid the fabric in place and pressed. It took three cloths before the bleeding stopped. Then she cleaned the gash while Cadoc swore through gritted teeth. Next, she placed her hands on either side of his head. She closed her eyes and chanted a spell in the same flowery language Nuala had used. When she finished, she sat back on her heels and examined her handiwork.

I looked at Cadoc. "Better? Whoa, that's one bushy brow." The gash was gone, but thick black tufts sprouted in all directions from his eyebrow. I covered my mouth, trying not to laugh.

Cadoc explored the thatch of hair with his fingertips. "Dung balls!"

"At least you can still talk," Matthew said.

Carys shivered and moved toward the fire. She leaned against a log by the fire and gazed into the distance.

"You all right?" I asked.

"Aye. Using magic always does this. It's peculiar. I feel powerful and connected to everything."

"What will happen to your air wall? Will animals run into it forever?"

"Nay. If you don't reverse the spell, it lasts an hour or two, depending on the barrier's size. It warms slowly and turns back to ordinary air."

Matthew said, "Carys, why do you use a wand for air walls and starting fires, but your hands for healing?"

"The wand helps throw magic at a distance. For healing, I need to direct my magic into the injured spot and use precisely the right amount of energy, or it'll cause damage. With a wand, I might use too much or miss the injury." She tilted her head. "Matthew, you're the fastest runner of us all. Want to try again with the eggs? I can take the dinosaurs' attention away from the nest."

"Do you think they've settled down?" he asked.

"Probably. They have short memories."

"Someone could get hurt a lot worse than Cadoc this time," I said. "Are you sure it's a good idea?"

"Come along," Carys said. "It'd be safer with you watching for danger."

I agreed and went with them, leaving Cadoc behind to nurse his bruised ego and care for the horses. The sky was indigo; we didn't have much time before the troodons settled down for the night. Carys climbed a tree, securing herself by wrapping her tail around a slender branch. Using her sling, she sent a hail of stones to a cluster of bushes on the far side of the nest. We were lucky. Both dinosaurs rushed to investigate. Matthew ran in and gathered four of the leathery eggs. Carys kept up the barrage of stones until he was back in hiding.

Darkness had fallen by the time we ate, but the meal of scrambled eggs and mushrooms seasoned with rosemary tasted better than anything I'd eaten in days.

∞

We broke camp early the next morning. Matthew's voice was nearly back to normal. Cadoc's eyebrow was still bushy, giving him a wild, unbalanced appearance. When he grumbled, Carys assured him the extra hair would fall out in a few days.

We rode at a good pace. As we drew closer to the seaport of Avonflow, the air took on a salty tang. Around noon, we stopped for a meal. Using their slings, Carys killed an agrio and Cadoc and Matthew each took a caino browsing in the brush. The twins cleaned the carcasses and cut the meat into strips. We cooked it in salted water with wild onions we'd gathered at the midmorning break. I put my pieces on a slice of bread for an open-faced sandwich and grinned when Cadoc copied me.

He cleaned his hunting knife and tucked it in its sheath. "Kallan, do you have those drawings of the men we saw near the market faire? I want to remind myself of their appearance. They must have reached Avonflow by now. If we locate them and learn anything useful, Da will have to tell the Eyes and Ears."

I retrieved my sketchbook and turned to the drawings of the men. The burly bearded man, Morcant, and Durst, the one with the tattered vest, were on one page while Seisyll, the thin, curly-haired man, was on the facing page.

Carys peered over my shoulder. "When did you add the backgrounds?" she asked. "Why'd you draw buildings when we saw them in the woods?"

I frowned, puzzled. "I only drew the men. I've never seen

buildings like those." The details grew more distinct. I was hot and cold at the same time and broke out in a sweat. I wiped my sleeve across my forehead. "Something's wrong. My skin is ten times more sensitive than normal, and the light hurts my eyes." I handed the sketchbook to Carys.

She sucked in her breath. "The backgrounds are fading! Take the book back." She shoved it into my hands. The backgrounds became clear and sharp again. Carys' voice was full of wonder. "Kallan, this is magic!"

I stared at the book. "What? No way."

She dismissed my objection. "Though you may not be able to do magic on Earth, you can here. I think your drawings show us where the men are." She studied the picture. "Cadoc, you've been to Avonflow with Da. Do you recognize those buildings?" Her brother looked at the drawing.

Matthew hopped up from his resting place on a flat rock. "What do you mean, Kallan can do magic?"

"It must be magic," Cadoc said. "I've never seen the like before, yet there's no other way to explain how the drawing changed." Matthew came over to see the picture for himself.

"No. No. It can't be that," I said, not wanting to utter the word "magic." As jealous as I'd been of the twin's magical abilities, I didn't want any part of it now. It made me sick, and I had no idea how it worked or how to control it.

"Those buildings are warehouses near the pier," Cadoc said. "That's where we'll pick up the cherry seedlings."

"What's going on here?" Matthew asked. "Can you explain it?"

Carys drew a deep breath. "All magic needs something to work with, a . . . a bit of tinder to set it ablaze, so to speak. Kallan's magic is kindled, you might say, by the drawings. I think her art can show us what's happening in another place." She nudged me. "Kallan, let's see your sketch of our farm."

I flipped to the page. "It's the same as when I drew it."

Carys tugged the tip of her tail. "Do you have an image of someone or someplace that's really important to you? Grandpa, for instance?"

"Yes, of course." I'd drawn Grandpa sitting in front of our Adirondack cabin. Now the page showed him in the common room of a rustic inn. Lord Humphrey and the twins' grandfather, Beli, sat on either side of him. As far as we could tell, they were having a friendly conversation. My stomach lurched and I flung the sketchbook away. "I think I'm gonna be sick."

Carys picked up the book and brushed off the cover. "Lie down. You'll feel better." She smiled. "This is rare magic you have."

I put my hands over my ears. "Stop calling it *magic*." With a groan, I lay down on the bare ground. Cadoc rolled a woolen blanket under my head for a pillow, then covered me with a second one. Matthew paced in a circle.

I shivered uncontrollably. With eyes closed, I breathed deeply the way one of my teachers had taught us to do before a test. Eight, nine, ten, and done. My stomach calmed down and the shivering stopped. I opened my eyes and forced myself to pay attention to the others' conversation.

"Sis," Cadoc said, "what do you know about this? I've never met anyone with Kallan's ability."

"There are all kinds of magic," she said. "I think Kallan is what Nuala calls a Far Seer. Some people can use an object to channel magic and see what's happening to another person. It can be something personal, like strands of hair or a fingernail, or something the person uses often, say a tunic or mug."

Carys perched on a broad, low branch of an oak tree. Below it, the end of her tail hung motionless. "Using an object for viewing is an unusual talent in itself. What Kallan can do is even rarer. If her need is strong enough, she doesn't need an object. She can discover what's happening

74

to anyone or any place she sketches."

Matthew stopped pacing. "Why didn't it work with the farm drawing?"

The tip of Carys' tail swept out an arc. "Mmm . . . well, she doesn't have a deep connection to that place, does she? Or, perhaps we have no great need to know what's happening there."

"Kallan couldn't do magic before today," Matthew said.

"Magic varies from person to person. In some folks, the ability shows up when they're tots, in others, not until they're almost fully grown. Both our grandmothers had strong talent. Our parents can't do magic at all." She grew thoughtful. "Cadoc and I showed the talent early. Also, getting it from both sides of our family, our abilities are stronger than most."

Matthew said, "Is magical ability rare?"

"There are many kinds of magical talent, yet most folks can't do any magic. Only one in a hundred or so. Sometimes it runs in families, like ours. Anyone who has the ability can learn to do common magic; that is, light fires, heal cuts, make air barriers, and such. Some have special skills."

Matthew cocked his head. "For example?"

"Cadoc can sense people's intentions and the emotions that linger in a place. Mind you, it's an undeveloped ability. He refuses training." She tugged on her braid. "My magic's strongest with plants. Nuala's teaching me how to use it, though one day I hope to study at university."

"If Ma will let you off her apron strings," Cadoc said. "Since Annie died, Ma's held onto Carys with a tight grip. It's understandable she doesn't want harm to come to her only remaining lass, yet it's annoying. True, sis?"

"Suffocating, sometimes."

Cadoc rubbed the back of his neck. "We'd best keep Kallan's talent secret for now. We don't want the wrong people to learn of it. Magic this strong could be useful to the king."

Someone coughed in the shrubbery nearby, and then a dark-haired man strolled into our camp. "What magic could be useful to the king?"

There may come a time
when your life depends on
knowing whom you can trust.
~Royal Guidebook of Diplomacy

9

A MATTER OF TRUST

At the stranger's question, Cadoc sprang to his feet, dagger in hand, and stepped in front of the rest of us. I peeked from beneath my tan blanket, trying to imitate a carpet of dead leaves.

Three older men emerged from the underbrush. Swords drawn, they flanked the younger man. He appeared to be a few years older than the four of us. Jet black hair fell to his shoulders in waves and framed his tanned face. His body was lean and muscular. Feet planted, arms crossed, he radiated power.

Cadoc pointed his dagger toward the man's chest. "Name yourself."

The older men's tan tunics and trousers were cut from finely woven cloth. A thin band of crimson topped by gold braid ran along the edges of their tunics and down their trouser legs. The twins had told us much about the kingdom over the past few days. If I remembered correctly, crimson and gold were Kylemore's royal colors. Cadoc swallowed hard. He must have recognized the royal colors too.

Aeron flew at the strangers, beak snapping. Carys commanded him to land and clapped a hand over him when he lit on her outstretched arm.

The young man raised his hand in a calming gesture. His clothes were trimmed in the royal colors too. The fur on his tail was black mixed with sable. The men blended in so well with the trees, we hadn't seen any of them until the youngest made his presence known.

"Be at peace," he said. "I am Prince Brenden." He nodded at his companions. "These are my overeager bodyguards. "Put your weapons away, men. You as well, youngling."

If Morcant, Durst, and Seisyll were right, Prince Brenden could be the traitor behind the attacks. How much of our conversation did he overhear?

The guards sheathed their swords only after Cadoc slid his dagger in its own scabbard. "Your Highness," he said, bowing low. "I beg forgiveness. I am Cadoc Dunstan of farm Meganeara. This is my sister Carys, and our friends Matthew Webbe and Kallan MacKinnon." He indicated each of us in turn. I ran my fingers through my hair in a fruitless attempt to make myself presentable.

Matthew copied Cadoc's bow and Carys curtsied, clenching the edges of her tunic to hide a mended tear. I remained seated on the ground, still too unsteady to rise.

Prince Brenden acknowledged the signs of respect, then knelt next to me. He put a hand on my clammy forehead. "Is the lass ill? What makes her chilled in this heat? I have some magical skill, perhaps I can help." He stood and noticed Cadoc's bushy eyebrow. "Lad, your hair. Is it always so . . . twiggy?"

Cadoc opened his mouth, but no sound came out. Blushing, he licked his fingers and swiped at the ragged tufts. Carys spoke in a quiet voice, looking directly at the prince. "Your Highness, I assure you Kallan will be fully recovered in a short while. She has recently used magic for the first time. My twin is suffering the side effects of my healing a rather nasty troodon wound."

The prince opened his arms in a gesture of apology. "I am sorry to hear of your injury, lad." His gaze passed over each of us. "Now, I wonder. Would Kallan's newfound skill be the magical tool that might be of use to my brother, King Darren?"

After a slight hesitation, Carys said, "Aye, it would."

"Tell me about it." Prince Brenden sat on the ground and indicated the rest of us should do the same. He made it a request, not an order. I had no doubt of his power and authority, in spite of his kind and gentle tone. He didn't behave the way I expected a prince to act. *Is it his personality? Or a trick to make us lower our guard?* I folded my blankets and sat between Matthew and Carys.

Carys explained how we'd discovered my talent as a Far Seer. The prince nodded from time to time. When she was done, Cadoc told him about the three men we'd overheard talking near Daire. Despite Prince Brenden's kindness, we had no way of knowing if we could trust him. I shot a warning look Cadoc's way, but he continued talking.

Neither of the twins revealed where Matthew and I had come from. If Prince Brenden wondered at our lack of tails, he kept his questions to himself. After all, accidents happen, and I supposed it wasn't unheard of to meet people with stubs of tails or none at all.

When the twins were done explaining, Prince Brenden said, "You've given me useful information. We've been investigating the destruction of the fields with fire and insects. The insects aren't local to Kylemore. They must be imported."

One of the guards handed him a flask, and he paused to take a drink. The days were still hot with no relief from even a small rain shower. Following his lead, the rest of us took long cooling swallows from our own flasks. The other guards brought their horses over from where they'd picketed them. Understanding that we had accepted the intruders, Aeron flew to a branch high above us where he perched, as if on alert for new dangers.

When we had settled again, Prince Brenden continued. "Reports have come in from agents in the western seaports. However, we've had no luck in finding the source of the insects. Avonflow is our next stop. What sends you there?"

"We're taking delivery of cherry seedlings," Cadoc said. "The drought's given our trees cankers and they're beset by insects. Our da knows a nurseryman on the Terrapin Archipelago who grows cherry trees that do well in dry times. His agent's due in Avonflow this week."

Prince Brenden turned to me. "I could use your help in tracking down the villains you younglings discovered. Are you well enough to show me your sketches?"

I glanced at the twins. Carys nodded her permission, and Cadoc said, "It's all right." I still didn't know if we could trust Prince Brenden, but I retrieved my sketchbook.

The drawing showed the criminals in front of the warehouse. They were talking with a stranger. The open building door revealed wooden crates and plump sacks piled high on the floor. As before, the magic only worked if I held the sketchbook. This time, I was pleased as well as anxious when I viewed the drawing. *I, Kallan MacKinnon, have magical talent. The skill will probably leave me when we return home, but for now, magic is part of me, and there's no point denying it.*

The warehouse stranger was heavyset and bearded. I saw nothing remarkable about his appearance to help identify him. Then he walked toward us, displaying a distinctive gait, tilting to one side as he lifted a leg that appeared to be shorter than his other one. I held the drawing at arm's length. "The people in the drawing move!"

"That's fortunate," Cadoc said, accepting it as natural. "We know something now that makes the fourth man stand out."

As he turned to go, Warehouse Man appeared to look straight at me. I shook off a spasm of fear and asked the prince, "Can he see us, or is this a one-way drawing?"

"Don't worry yourself, lass. Far Seeing only works the one way."

I felt ill again, so I put the sketchbook away. Considering that Carys was only cold, not nauseous, when she used magic, I hoped this was a temporary effect I'd overcome with time. The twins and Matthew packed our supplies while I sat out of the way, wrapped in a blanket. We would continue our journey in the company of the prince and his guards.

Prince Brenden said, "My brother, Prince Aiden, is also in the Great Forest searching for the villains. His party is to the west of us, not far away." I hoped his brother was as nice as Brenden, and we could trust him. The prince turned to one of his guards, a muscular man with thick, wavy hair. "Alec, give Prince Aiden our news and tell him I wish him to meet us by the docks in Avonflow tomorrow morning."

"Aye, Your Highness." Alec mounted his horse and headed west.

A cool sea breeze wended its way through the forest as we rode, bringing some relief from the heat. We neared Avonflow at dusk and prepared to camp one more night in the woods. Carys showed me how to light the cooking fire using magic. "Send the energy through your fingertips with your mind, then push it through the wand."

It took four or five attempts. Finally, the kindling caught. Flames leaped high in the air. A pine branch ignited overhead. Crackle! Pop! Scalding sap droplets rained down. Carys dipped her wand in the water bucket. "*Climbanin.*" A waterspout formed. She directed it to the flaming branch. The water sizzled and extinguished the fire, leaving behind a charred mess. I let out my breath.

"Try again," she commanded.

"No."

"You must face what frightens you."

"Easy words, hard to do."

"If you cannot control your magic, it will escape at the worst times. When you're frightened, angry, tired. You could injure others. Kill them. Is that your desire?"

"Of course not!"

She spoke softly. "Then you must learn to handle it."

"Cadoc isn't trained. Why must I be?"

"He knows enough. Nuala taught him the basics. Do not fear, I will teach you. Ready?"

"I suppose."

I held my wand arm with my other hand to keep it from shaking and uttered the spell. Yellow tongues of flame lit the kindling. They reached five feet in the air before settling down to a reasonable height. In spite of my earlier mistake, I was excited. What happened with the drawings was out of my control. With a wand, I could use magic to do what I intended. This might be fun after all.

Alec returned in time for the evening meal. "Your Highness, Prince Aiden's agreed to meet us in Avonflow on the morrow."

After we ate, I found myself alone with Cadoc when we gathered more firewood. I confronted him. "What were you thinking, telling Prince Brenden about the criminals? He could be the traitor."

"Do you remember when you entered Kylemore? Did you notice something brush your mind when we stood in the field?" I recalled the feathery touch that I had put down to my imagination and fear. I nodded mutely.

"That was me. I was sensing your intentions."

"You were inside my head?" Instinctively, I took a step back as if it could protect my innermost thoughts from detection. "How'd you do that? What gave you the right?" I stared at him, anger boiling inside me.

He licked his lips. "The kingdom's under attack, remember? I had to find out if you were a danger. Be at ease. I only did it the once. Besides, I can't read thoughts, only moods and intentions. Even so, the skill is useful in detecting trickery and evil."

I was still angry. "Never do that to me again."

He put a hand over his heart. "On my honor, I promise I won't ever use the mind brush on you again."

"Okay, then." I cooled down a little. "I guess it made sense to do it when you met us. We were trespassing on your land. I'd probably do the same to protect my family if I had the ability."

"For true, you would. You're clever as a dragon, not a brainless woodenhead." He gazed at me with such pride that I realized he meant it as a high compliment. My anger melted away like an ice cube in the summer sun.

"What does your power have to do with Prince Brenden?"

"While we were talking with him, I used my ability on him and his guards. I sensed nothing bad in any of them. I believe the prince is as honorable as he appears."

"What if you'd sensed evil in him?"

"If I didn't trust him, I would have told bald-faced lies, so you'd get the hint and lie too. When Carys and I were small, we made up private signals. I'd use one to warn her to defend us with magic."

"Wouldn't Prince Brenden feel the mind brush and wonder what it was?"

"Aye, he'd feel it. I'm counting on him knowing what it was."

"Why?"

"Da wants me to take over the farm. I want to join The Eyes and Ears of the King—that's their full name. If the prince decides my talent's useful to the kingdom, I'll get my chance." His jaw stuck out in a determined way, but I saw pain in his eyes.

I felt a stab of sympathy for him. During my years in foster care, I rarely could do what I liked. I babysat or cleaned, did whatever my foster parents demanded. Only when Grandpa took me in could I choose how to spend my free time and plan my future. Cadoc gazed down at me. I put a hand on his cheek. "I'm sorry your da doesn't understand what you want, but you have to live the life that's right for you."

He smiled sadly. "He does understand. He and Ma, Poppa and Ma's mother, Nan, were all in The Eyes and Ears. Nan died in service to the kingdom, and Ma has a limp for life. Da doesn't want anyone else hurt. We understand each other perfectly. We simply disagree."

I understood Rolant's concern. "Why do you avoid using magic? Why have you refused training?"

He didn't answer right away. I wasn't sure he would answer at all, then he sighed and said, "All right, I'll tell you. When I was young, I was excited to learn magic. Clearly, I had the talent, same as Carys did. However, I was headstrong and attempted things on my own that I shouldn't have. One day, a storm headed our way. The day was windy and cold. I tried to light a fire behind our barn to warm up—a small one, mind. It got out of control. I set the barn ablaze and burned myself badly."

His eyes grew bright with unshed tears, and he swallowed hard before continuing. "We lost three horses. The whole barn would have burned down if the rainstorm hadn't arrived in time to save some of it. Nuala used her magic on me, except Ma made her leave one patch of skin to heal naturally as a reminder of how dangerous magic can be." He lifted his tunic and showed me the spiderweb-patterned scar on his stomach, an area about the size of my palm.

"I'm so sorry." I touched the scar lightly, then pulled his tunic down.

He took an acorn out of a pocket and held it between his thumb and forefinger. "Ma gave me this after Nuala went home. Ma knew that patch of skin would be painful while it healed. She said the acorn had given her courage during a difficult time in her life, and it could help me be brave too.

Since the fire, I've avoided magic, used it only when I had to. Now I feel different. This talent I have might be the only way for me to leave the farm and become an Eye and Ear of the King. I want to serve the kingdom as my parents and grandparents did. Like Poppa still does."

He pocketed the acorn and drew me close. I laid my head on his chest and breathed in the clean, fresh smell of pine boughs and the spicy clove scent that belonged to Cadoc alone. We stood in silence, holding onto each other for a long while.

When we brought the branches that we'd collected back to camp, Prince Brenden asked to speak privately with Cadoc. My friend tugged on his bushy eyebrow and followed the prince. Soon he'd know how valuable the prince considered his talent.

I took my time to prepare for bed and was still awake when Cadoc returned. Judging by the swagger in his walk, the prince agreed his talent was useful.

In the morning, we checked my sketches again. I noticed the drawings were fainter than they'd been the day before. Prince Brenden, who was studying magic at the royal university to qualify as a mage, explained that magic leaked out of the pictures with each use. Eventually, they'd become too faint to use. The four men in the drawing were entering an inn. A carved wooden sign hanging in front read "Mariner's Rest." Fearing the men would soon leave with sacks of insects to do more damage, Prince Brenden decided we wouldn't wait for Prince Aiden. "We'll arrest them on our own."

We left the horses at a stable in town and then continued on foot, passing by the docks on our way to the inn. Puffy clouds littered a sparkling blue sky that brightened the surface of the sea. Conroy, a cheerful, apple-cheeked guard, pointed out the ships, describing the different types, but I was too distracted to pay attention.

Cadoc asked me what was wrong. I pointed to a line of

pterodactyls that flew parallel to the coast. "They give me the creeps."

"They're not dangerous." He narrowed his eyes and watched them for a minute. "Odd. I can normally sense animals' intentions. These tell me nothing. They're blank." He brushed a strand of hair off my face and gave me a reassuring smile. "We're not likely to see them often, so I wouldn't worry."

Kain, a serious, slender man who was Prince Brenden's third guard, called to us. "Time to go."

"Coming," I said, focusing on the sensation of Cadoc's touch on my face instead of the dark creatures overhead. I grabbed his hand. "Let's catch some villains."

When employing magic to remove
a threat, use the lightest force
possible and protect the
innocent from harm.
~Master Ailfrid
The Art and Discipline of Magic

10

CAPTURE

*W*e followed a maze of cobblestoned streets until we arrived at the Mariner's Rest. The inn was a long, whitewashed building. A row of windows on the second floor marked the guest rooms. As we prepared to enter, I touched Prince Brenden's sleeve and pointed to a window above the doorway.

"What is it?" he asked.

"A couple of the criminals were standing at that window. Morcant—he's the leader—and the man from the warehouse too." Warehouse Man had locked eyes with me for a second. I didn't have Cadoc's talent, but I knew the man's intentions were evil.

By the time the prince looked at the window, it was empty. When we went inside, he gave us instructions. "I want you four well out of this. Sit there and order breakfast." He waved a hand at a table in the corner of the large room and tossed some coins to Cadoc. "Alec, Conroy, Kain, upstairs. Keep the damage to a minimum. I'll keep watch at the foot of the stairs."

The guards left, and the prince took up his position. He was dressed in Cadoc's spare clothing. His guards had covered their royal colors in plain, lightweight cloaks. Alec explained that disguised as commoners, no one should connect them to the palace this far from the royal city.

I was ready for a meal indoors. I gave Cadoc my order: tea, sausages, and porridge with fruit, then headed out back for the privy. Passing the prince, I nodded toward the door to the back yard. "Be quick," he said and leaned against the wall to wait for the guards to bring down the criminals.

A stout wooden fence covered in climbing plants completely enclosed the yard behind the inn. Morning glories gave the area color and honeysuckle kept down the privy odors. I averted my gaze from a man whizzing against the fence and walked straight to the wooden shack at the back of the yard.

The privy was similar to others I'd seen in Kylemore. A bench of polished wood ran the length of the small building. A hole was cut in the center of the bench and a basket in the corner held a stack of torn sheets of paper. A trench under the building which emptied into a covered pit caught the waste. As the prince requested, I was quick.

I washed my hands at the pump and watched the water flow through a clay pipe into the trench. My thoughts drifted to all the conveniences we took for granted back home, like flushing toilets. I dried my hands on my tunic and followed the slate path through the yard. I was working out how to explain modern toilets to Carys so they could build an indoor bathroom at the farm when someone yanked me from behind.

I yelped. A man twisted my right arm behind my back and wrapped his other arm around me, pinning my left arm to my side. I caught the glint of a knife in his hand, then its tip pressed on my tunic, above my navel. He put his mouth next to my ear and the smell of ale filled my nostrils.

"Not a peep, lassie. What brings you to yon inn with the pretender prince?"

I twisted my head to look at him and realized he was Warehouse Man. He must have gone outside by a back staircase after I saw him in the window.

He sneered. "Didn't think I'd recognize him, did you? All subjects of the Rightful Heir can spot the royal pretenders. Question is, how much is the life of a tailless brat worth to the mock prince?" A good question. I wasn't sure I wanted to learn the answer. I hoped my talent as a Far Seer put some value on my life.

Holding me in front of himself like a shield, he marched toward the inn. There was no one in the yard to rescue me. The man who'd been peeing on the fence was gone. My heart sank with the realization that Peeing Man and Warehouse Man were the same person. Seeing him from behind, I hadn't recognized him. It was a lucky break for him that I had to use the privy.

My captor kicked open the back door of the inn. Prince Brenden's head jerked up at the noise. We made our way to where he stood. Kain and the other guards clattered down the stairs with Morcant, Durst, and Seisyll in chains. Warehouse Man kept a tight hold on me. There was no space for Carys to create an air wall between us, no way for anyone to attack him without going through me.

Warehouse Man glanced at the three captives in the grip of the guards. He poked the knife through my tunic until it pricked my skin and spoke to Prince Brenden. "Prince Dragon Dung. See what I found."

Prince Brenden took a step toward us, then noticed the knife and came to an abrupt stop.

Warehouse Man's chin bobbed up and down against the back of my head as he nodded in approval. "I propose an exchange. This tailless youngling for my three mates. Once we board a ship of my choosing, you can have her back. Refuse, and the lass dies."

It was no idle threat. The knife tip pierced my skin. I whimpered. A trickle of blood made its way down my stomach. My hand lay against the brute's abdomen. I didn't dare scratch him. He might push the knife in deeper. Everyone in the common room stood still, expressions of horror etched on their faces.

Prince Brenden studied my captor. I silently begged him, *stay still, don't do anything heroic.* With the brute's knife already poking me, I'd probably be dead before he could draw his wand.

The prince began to speak, but Warehouse Man wasn't finished. "Don't try to stop us. The Rightful Heir has loyal subjects scattered from one end of Kylemore to the other."

The prince drew himself up to his full height of six feet. His cheeks were flushed. "My brother Darren is the rightful king. He'll have your head, and the heads of all traitors."

"He has no authority over me," Warehouse Man said, his voice dripping with scorn. "Listen, pup. You want the lass to live or not? Do we have a deal?" He yanked on my arm. I squeaked like a trapped mouse.

During their conversation, Carys' words about magic came back to me: *All with the ability can do common magic . . . use the right amount of energy to heal, or it'll cause damage . . . Send the energy through your fingertips.* My fear was replaced by anger, then anger by an icy calm.

Magical energy swelled inside me. I forced it down my arm. It pulsed inside my forearm, surging toward my hand. Hot streams of it poured from my fingers through my captor's tunic, burning his skin. He howled and loosened his hold on me. I pressed my fingertips into his soft belly. He squirmed with pain and his knife fell to the floor.

Prince Brenden pointed his polished oak wand at us and shouted, "Step away, Kallan!" I released the magic, took a step forward, and dropped to my knees. A ball of violet light burst out of the prince's wand and flew over my head. Warehouse Man collapsed with a thud.

Matthew and the twins quickly hauled me over to a bench next to a broad table. Carys swept aside dirty bowls and mugs, and I rested my head on my arms. My captor lay on the floor, unmoving. The prince knelt and checked for signs of life. He shook his head. "Dead."

Carys cleaned and bandaged the cut in my abdomen. It wasn't deep enough for magical healing. The innkeeper stood beside Prince Brenden, hands shaking and face pale. "Pardon, Your Highness. I knew nothing of these men's plans. Traders, they said they were, meetin' a ship. Collectin' island spices and whatnot."

Prince Brenden answered, "Innkeeper, I do not hold you responsible." He pressed some coins into the man's palm. "This is for his burial. Give the extra to his kin." He handed over more coins. "For your trouble. We'll remove these three"—he pointed to the men still held by the guards— "and return shortly for our meal."

Most of the customers had fled, leaving only a few to gawk at the dead man. The innkeeper spoke with them and arranged for Warehouse Man's body to be taken away. I didn't care where they took him, so long as I never had to see him again.

Prince Brenden told Morcant, Durst, and Seisyll they'd have a chance to explain themselves to the royal examiner in Ardara. The prisoners were chained securely to a bench outdoors, facing the morning sun. The guards took turns overseeing the surly trio, while we ate a subdued breakfast. I couldn't eat more than a couple of bites. I'd never seen a person die by violence before. The prince saved my life by killing him, but I wished there'd been another way to end the standoff.

While we ate, I wrapped sausages in a napkin for the prisoners. Hunger doesn't encourage cooperation, and I'd had enough rough stuff for one day.

After breakfast, we walked toward the prisoners' bench where Conroy kept guard. I remembered the men's conversation in the woods and pictured Morcant pointing his knife at Seisyll. Even chained, they might be dangerous up close. My steps slowed as I thought about what to say to them. All the while, several scruffy stray dogs pranced around me, yipping and jumping at the napkin, which I held high above my head.

Alec, a few steps behind me called out, "Kallan, that's some company you're attracting. Need help?"

I turned toward him, my face a hot blush. "That'd be great."

Handing over the greasy napkin and its contents, I asked him to divide the food between the prisoners. His lips pressed together as though crushing a smile. He agreed to my request, and the dogs abandoned me to follow him. When I heard the men's grunts of gratitude and noisy finger-licking, a glow of satisfaction filled me.

Prince Brenden joined the guards to question Morcant and his pals. The twins, Matthew, and I waited for the prince under a shady maple tree in a corner of the inn's enclosed front yard. We sat in a tight group, ignoring the interrogation.

"I've never seen a killing before, even in self-defense," Carys said. "Sometimes you have no choice though, like when Ma and Pa were in the Eyes and Ears."

"What happened?" Matthew asked.

"It was more than twenty years ago. Before Ma and Da were married. It's how Ma got her limp," Carys answered. "There was an uprising on the Terrapin Archipelago—on the biggest island, the one with the royal city. Their queen asked our king for help. She needed to find out who the leaders were so she could squash the rebellion. The Eyes and Ears are the best spies of any kingdom around."

Cadoc took up the story. "King Darren's father, Raghnall, was king then. He sent Ma and Da to meet with the queen and find out what she could tell them. They docked their boat near a small fishing village where they were to meet the queen in secret."

Carys said, "Ma won't talk about what happened. Da

will only say that a couple of royal guards tried to kill him, and that Ma put herself between the attackers and him. She saved his life. He and Ma killed one of the guards and seriously wounded the other one. During the fight, Ma broke her leg and got a deep cut on her head. She nearly lost an eye."

"Why ever would royal guards attack them?" I asked.

"The queen had guards posted all over the kingdom to search for rebels," Cadoc said. "The story from the wounded guard was that they mistook Ma and Da for the enemy. I don't believe it. Those two must have been part of the rebellion themselves and got word of the secret meeting. The queen and King Raghnall didn't want to blow it up into a big incident, so they kept the whole mission quiet."

Carys said, "There was no magical healer near the village. Ma's leg and the gash on her head had to heal naturally. She was left with the limp and the scar. It wasn't all bad, though. During the weeks they spent in the fishing village while she recovered, she and Da fell in love. They married as soon as they returned to Kylemore."

Cadoc took out his acorn and rolled it around his palm with a finger. He said, "Ma knew that mission would be a risky one. Before they left, she collected two acorns from an oak on the castle grounds in Ardara. Oaks are strong trees and one of the symbols on Kylemore's royal crest. She took the acorns for courage, one for her and one for Da. When they married and moved to the farm, she planted one on top of the cliff on our land. This is the other one."

It was comforting to know that the oak marking the gateway to Earth was a symbol of love as well as courage. Kain separated himself from the group with the prisoners and walked toward us. Cadoc pocketed the acorn and rose.

"Kain's taking us to the warehouse to pick up the cherry seedlings," Carys said. "Come along? It'd take your mind off what happened in there." She jerked her head in the direction of the inn.

I wanted time to think. I shook my head. "Thanks. I'll be all right here."

"Matthew?"

"I'll stay with Kallan." He leaned against the maple's trunk.

"See you in a while." She rose and walked down the cobblestoned street with Kain and Cadoc.

I breathed in the salty air.

"Pipit, you okay?"

"Not really. I know Prince Brenden killed that man to save me, and I don't want to think what would've happened if that creep had gotten me on a ship. But with one flash of a wand,"—I snapped my fingers—"a life over. No questions, no trial . . . dead."

Matthew tried to speak. I put up a hand and kept talking. "Listen. Even I hurt him enough to make him let me go. I didn't really care how much damage I did." I plucked a fallen maple leaf from the ground and twirled its stem between my thumb and forefinger, staring at the spinning tips. "I always thought of myself as a peaceful person, but not anymore. The other day I fought Fergus. Today, this. I hate to think I have that much violence inside me. Makes me want to get away from my own body."

"Kallan, people are made of peaceful and violent parts put together. It's who we are. Most of the time the peaceful side wins out. Sometimes anger's useful . . . to fight evil or injustice or save a life. Man, that sounds like something Grandpa would say." He grinned. "You're the only person I know who's been rescued by a prince. No one back home will believe us."

He picked a black-dotted golden caterpillar off his sleeve, gave its long hairs a gentle stroke, and set it on the grass. Peering past me to where Prince Brenden and the others were talking, he sucked in his breath. "Prince Aiden's arrived."

It is a wise person who knows when
to stand up to an enemy and
when to refrain from argument.
~Royal Guidebook of Diplomacy

11

NORTH FROM AVONFLOW

A rusty-haired bear of a man strode through the gate that separated the inn's front yard from the street. His sleek red tail announced his self-confidence, rising straight and tall from the tail-slit in his tunic. Hands on hips, he gazed down at Prince Brenden, who took his time raising his head to meet the eyes of the larger man. Prince Brenden appeared unruffled, but his sable tail drooped.

Three guards followed Prince Aiden into the yard. If they hadn't worn Kylemore's royal colors, I would have thought they belonged on the bench with Morcant and the others. Thickly bearded, their eyes were hard, their expressions surly. They looked as rough as Prince Aiden, while Prince Brenden's guards matched his civilized manner. I hugged my knees, watching from the shade of the maple tree. Matthew sat still as a boulder next to me.

A deep voice carried over to us. "What have we here, little brother?"

Prince Brenden stood up straight. "Traitors. These pawns of the enemy claim they don't know who their leader is."

"It's the truth!" Morcant shrieked. "I swear by the Blessed Ancestors, Your Highness."

Prince Aiden faced Morcant, who leaned back as far as his chains would allow. "You'll speak when questioned and not before."

Chin touching his chest, Morcant mumbled a few words, then fell silent.

The red-haired prince continued, "You may not know who's in charge of the attacks, yet I'll soon learn what you do know."

Prince Brenden stepped between his older brother and the chained men. "I've already questioned them, Aiden. Strangers contact them when they pass through villages. They aren't given names. They merely follow orders. There are layers between them and the leader."

Prince Aiden patted Prince Brenden's shoulder. "Good capture. I'll take charge now. These three will be no match for my men. The king can decide their fate when we get to Ardara."

I hated the way Prince Aiden treated his younger brother. *Why does he want to take over? Does his bossiness come from being older, or is there more to it?* Quick as a darting dragonfly, an answer came to me. *If Prince Aiden is the enemy leader, he'll want to keep his troops close to himself and away from Prince Brenden.* I studied Prince Aiden from his rusty red hair to his worn leather boots. I couldn't decide if he was a loyal royal or a scheming traitor.

Prince Brenden's tail twitched. "They were no match for my men, either. I'll see to it the king hears the facts of their apprehension upon my return." He turned on his heel and gestured for Matthew and me to follow. We jumped up and hurried through the gate, close behind Conroy and Alec.

The prince's pace didn't let up until we met Kain and the twins at the stable. Cadoc moistened the root balls of the cherry saplings they'd collected from the warehouse. Then he wrapped them in burlap and placed them in his saddlebag, letting the leafy branches stick out. They were slender young things. It would take years before they would produce cherries. We mounted our horses under the watchful eyes of two pterodactyls perched on the stable roof. Eerie and primitive, they gave me goosebumps. When we turned the horses north to head out of the city, they rose in the sky on leathery wings and flapped their way westward.

This time, we took the King's Road through the Great Forest rather than the remote trail we'd followed on our way from the Dunstan's farm to the seaport. Cadoc said the wide, hard-packed dirt road led all the way to Ardara. Thinking about the royal city made me wonder about Grandpa. He must be on his way back from his meeting with King Darren by now. He would probably reach the farm a day or two after us. It wouldn't be long before we'd take Chanticleer and the hens back home. I was ready to leave prehistoric creatures, criminals, and royal traitors behind. But I had to admit, I would miss the magic.

∞

The following morning, we lingered around the cooking fire after breakfast. The prince didn't want to attract attention, so we passed through the villages quickly and camped deep in the woods. Well hidden from the road, we hadn't heard many travelers. At a lull in the conversation, Cadoc put his fingers to his lips for silence. The sound of rattling branches came from over the lip of the hollow where we'd made our camp. With a soft whirr of his wings, Aeron flew off to investigate while the guards drew their swords and padded in the same direction.

Half a minute later we heard Aeron screech. We all dashed up the angled side of the hollow. Carys stumbled to a stop after running down the other side. She dropped to the ground next to the little bird, who lay still on a scattering of decaying leaves. Two boys stood frozen in place several yards away, staring at Prince Brenden's guards. One of them was Fergus, my enemy from the market faire.

The other boy was younger. They looked so much alike they had to be brothers.

I stared at the hunting sling dangling from Fergus' fingers, and the anger I'd buried from our last encounter resurfaced. "What have you done?" I shouted.

At my words, the younger boy turned and fled. Fergus chased after him, and Cadoc and the guards followed. Prince Brenden and I stood by while Matthew knelt next to Carys, who sat in shocked silence. Matthew gently took Aeron from her and laid two fingers on the bird's breast. He let out a breath of relief. "His heart's beating."

Cradling Aeron in the crook of his arm, Matthew ran his fingers over the little body. One wing could move back and forth normally. The other one had an unnatural bend along one side. Matthew probed the bones with a fingertip. "I can splint this. I've done it before."

Carys rested a hand on Matthew's arm. "It'll take ages to heal that way."

Matthew bent over the little body as though protecting Aeron from Carys. "Natural healing's best for him—there's no telling what side effects your magic might have. He could end up with horns or feathers sprouting in all directions so he couldn't fly."

Carys pressed her lips together. "All right. We'll do it your way."

Matthew gave a quick nod. "Kallan, can you get me a flat twig? Carys, I need one of those strips of cloth from your medicine bag."

I cut a small branch off a maple tree with my belt knife, then peeled the bark and trimmed some of the moist wood from one side to make a flat surface. Carys gave Matthew a piece of cloth. Matthew splinted Aeron's wing and handed him back to her.

"Thank you," she said. "Do you really heal everything on Earth without magic?"

"Earth, what's Earth?" asked Prince Brenden.

Carys licked her lips and stood up. In a stumbling way, she explained who we were and how we'd found our way into Kylemore. She finished by saying, "Matthew's grandpa—his name is David Webbe—went to Ardara with our poppa—Beli Whelan—and Lord Humphrey."

"A gateway to another world? How do you come by such secret knowledge?" The prince rounded on me. "Are Carys' words true?"

I didn't have the courage to speak. Matthew stood, ran a hand through his hair, and spoke in his most soothing voice. "It's true, Your Highness. Just as the old tales say."

This time his words didn't have the intended calming effect. The prince considered each of us in turn, his dark eyes stony cold. "Why didn't you tell me earlier? If I find you're withholding any other critical information, you'll all be in the royal dungeons until we've conquered the enemy, however long that takes. Am I clear?"

Carys' eyes glistened, and her lower lip trembled.

Matthew took a step forward. "Your Highness, Carys has told you everything important about us. We didn't say anything before because we're trying to go home without getting involved here any more than we have to."

I nodded. "We've told the Dunstans and Lord Humphrey about Earth, and the king must know about us by now. We didn't think anyone else needed to know." I took a deep breath.

I decided to trust Prince Brenden completely. Cadoc sensed he was noble and safe, and if he were the traitor behind the attacks on Kylemore, he probably would have killed us already. "There's only one other thing we should probably tell you. When we overheard Morcant and the others talking at the market faire in Daire, they wanted to stop working for the enemy. But they're too scared to quit. They said their orders came from someone in power, maybe someone royal."

Comprehension dawned on the prince's face. "I see. You

thought I might be their leader. The royal traitor. Understandable, however false." He rubbed his chin. "We've had suspicions about . . ." He broke off, apparently saying more than he meant to. "They didn't mention a name?"

I shook my head.

"We'll leave it at that. It's disturbing news, although it shortens the list of suspects." He started to walk back to camp.

Carys' boot drew a crescent in the loose soil. She cleared her throat. "Prince Brenden? There's one last incident you might want to know about."

He wheeled around. "*Another* matter?" He crossed his arms. I saw a vein throb in his temple. "Out with it."

She spoke in a rush. "A white roc flew in circles around our farm a couple of weeks ago. It landed in an oak at the top of the cliff that borders our meadow. All afternoon it perched in the tree. In the evening it flew away to the west."

"What's a roc?" I asked, not sure I wanted to hear the answer. If it was anything like the mythological rocs on Earth, I never wanted to see one.

"A giant bird, the largest there is," Carys said. "It's fierce and can carry away any creature it wants to. Except a fully-grown dragon."

I gulped. Her description exactly matched the giant bird of prey in Earth myths.

Aeron lay quietly in her arms. She stroked his feathers. "Kallan and Matthew showed up the next day. The gateway to Earth is right under the tree where the roc perched."

Matthew stared at Carys. She continued. "Poppa says he's never seen a white roc. He says rocs live by the sea. They don't fly inland. Since it's so rare, I thought you should know. That's all there is, Your Highness. For true."

Prince Brenden nodded. "Rocs nest on the islands of the Terrapin Archipelago. I've never seen a white one either."

Carys said, "The Terrapin Archipelago? Isn't that where your aunt, the Sorceress Mairsil, fled years ago?" She closed her mouth and turned bright red. "I'm sorry, Your Highness, I shouldn't have mentioned her."

Prince Brenden's mouth twisted in a grimace. "It's all right. The entire kingdom heard the news at the time. She moved to the islands to pout when my father, Raghnall, was named ruler instead of her. What you don't know is that several years ago we received a report of her death."

Carys' fingers touched her lips. "Nay, I didn't know that. I'm sorry for your loss, Your Highness."

He gave a wry smile and said, "I've come to a decision. I will take the four of you to Ardara with me. There is too much going on that I don't understand, and you may be able to help the king untangle the meaning."

Even if Lord Humphrey didn't approve, the prince outranked him. *With luck, Grandpa will be at the castle when we arrive, or our paths will cross on the way. If we aren't lucky . . .*

My thoughts were interrupted by the guards' return. They pushed Fergus and the younger boy in front of them. Cadoc strode ahead of the pack, his tail puffed up in anger. He stomped over to Prince Brenden. "They were spying on us, Your Highness. Fergus would've told the whole village we're your prisoners. I know what he's like. He's big on spreading lies, this one." He glared at Fergus. If it weren't for the guards, I think he would have punched him.

"Bow, and address Prince Brenden," said Kain, giving Fergus a push in the prince's direction. The boy obeyed, scowling the whole time.

Conroy nudged Fergus' brother. He bowed clumsily and stammered, "Your Highness."

"We had a talk," Alec said. "The lads picked up a shipment of linen in Avonflow for their da. He's a cloth merchant in Daire. Fergus admits he injured the bird. He claims it was in self-defense."

"Aye. That monster dove at our heads." Fergus struggled to free himself as Kain held his arms behind his back. He slipped one arm out of the guard's grip, but Kain grabbed his tail and he settled down.

Cadoc said, "Your Highness, they may be on an errand for their da. Still, Fergus is a known troublemaker. Carys and I have lived near his village all our lives. Last week he tried to steal Kallan's satchel. Now he's attacked my sister's bird. Aeron protects Carys and our whole family."

Prince Brenden studied the brothers. "Needless violence is an offense that requires a consequence. Your father is a cloth merchant?"

Fergus nodded, his face pale under a sprinkling of freckles.

"Then it is fitting that you purchase high-quality wool and have a cloak made for each of the lasses."

Fergus' eyes blazed. "My father will make me work extra hours for weeks to pay for them."

"All the better," said Prince Brenden. "Alec, write an order describing the fine. I want this lad to work off the cost of the cloth and the seamstress' labor."

He turned back to Fergus. "Do you have good wool available in your shop, and a seamstress nearby?"

"Aye, Your Highness," Fergus said in a flat voice.

"Good. I will visit your father's business in about a week. If your da tells me you've given him trouble, you'll work as a servant for me. Or, I might decide to hold you in prison for a while. Clear enough?"

Fergus nodded, his cheeks pink under the freckles, his hands bunched into fists.

The prince signed the instructions Alec had written out. Conroy lit a small fire. Alec held a little pewter dish of wax over the flames with long-handled tongs. When it softened, he put a dollop of wax on the folded note. Prince Brenden pressed his signet ring into the wax and handed the paper to Fergus. Then he turned his back on the boys, dismissing them.

Kain and Conroy tailed them for a distance along the

King's Road to make certain they headed toward Daire. We broke camp and set off when the guards returned, taking the same route as the brothers.

Before we left, Carys lined a narrow, woven basket with soft cloth for Aeron. She nestled it in a wide loop of linen that she draped over her tunic. The basket swayed gently with the motion of her horse, and the normally fierce little bird tucked his head under his good wing and slept.

I felt exposed on the wide road and scanned the sky every few minutes for pterodactyls and rocs. I peered into the woods for a glimpse of Fergus and his brother, in case they'd doubled back to spy on us again. After we'd traveled several miles without incident, I relaxed. I'd seen nothing to stop us from going home as soon as Grandpa returned. *We'll start junior year in another week or so. Soccer for Matthew, painting lessons for me. Soon, life will be back to normal.*

Disturbing news may reach your ears.
Do not let emotions guide your steps.
Reason through the best course of action.
~Handbook of the Eyes and Ears of the King

12

BREAKING NEWS

We didn't learn about the rebel attack until we reached the Dunstan's farm. Riding in ignorance, the three-day journey from Avonflow with Prince Brenden and the guards was as ordinary as a trail ride at home. There were no signs of dinosaurs or queen's buttons. I missed the troodon eggs and tasty mushrooms, but I didn't see any pterodactyls after we left the coast, so it all evened out.

Carys, usually as calm as her sleek chocolate mare Epona, became more distracted and moodier the closer she got to home. One day she lost her temper with Cadoc when he spilled a mug of tea at breakfast and growled at Matthew when he was slow to mount up after the midday meal. I thought I knew what bothered her and nudged my shaggy mare Willow next to Epona.

"Want me to do a viewing of your mom when we stop tonight?"

Carys' back stiffened and her tail curled tight against her thigh. "Nay." The word came out hard and cold, like a slap.

My cheeks grew hot. "Okay. Thought I'd offer."

Her posture relaxed a little. "Beg pardon for my

rudeness. Consider Ma's condition. What if she's sicker? Or . . . gone with the ancestors? I'd have to live with that knowledge for the rest of the journey with nothing I could do about it."

I winced. "I understand. I didn't mean to upset you." I dropped back in line behind Epona.

The night before, after everyone else fell asleep, I'd tried to do a viewing of Grandpa. There wasn't enough light to see the drawing, though. I could make out a lumpy shape under some covers, probably indoors. Maybe he was still at the castle, or they might have stopped at an inn on the way back. When I thought about what Carys said, I agreed with her. I'd rather wait for bad news than know about it and be helpless. I decided not to do another viewing of Grandpa. Just in case.

When we arrived at the Dunstan's farm a couple of days later, it was past suppertime and already dark. Candlelight filled the kitchen windows, showing us a handful of men seated around the table. The only one I recognized was Rolant.

By the time we'd gotten the cherry seedlings to the farmhands and taken care of our horses, the men had moved into the sitting room off the kitchen. Carys raced upstairs to her parents' bedroom. Cadoc, Matthew, and I stayed in the kitchen and rummaged around for food. Prince Brenden motioned to Alec, who told Matthew and me to go upstairs.

The guard grabbed a candle from the kitchen table and followed us up, so we didn't hear any of the visitors' conversation. When we reached the hallway at the top, Alec said, "I'll bring you dinner. Stay here." He handed me the candle and headed back down the stairs, preventing any argument.

I pulled Matthew into my room and shut the door behind us, then set the candle on a small table. I didn't want to get the bed covers dirty from my traveling clothes, so I sat on the floor while he perched on a wooden chair.

I didn't even try to hide my annoyance. "Who d'you think those people are, and why can't we meet them?"

"Dunno."

"Aren't you curious?"

"Yeah, but obviously no one will tell us anything, so why waste energy fuming?"

I glared at him.

He spoke in that quiet tone of voice he uses to soothe riled animals. "Pipit, you'll wear yourself out. Wait until we see Cadoc. Maybe he'll tell us something."

I sighed. "You're right. It doesn't matter anyway. Those visitors have nothing to do with us."

Someone knocked at the door. When I opened it, Alec handed me a tray of food.

"Thank you. How's Marilea?"

"Still weak and in bed. Rolant says she's past the danger point, and it's only a matter of time until she's fully recovered."

"That's great."

"Aye. You two stay upstairs 'til morning. Sleep well."

After a full day of riding, I was beat. When we finished eating, I grew pleasantly drowsy. Since we weren't allowed downstairs, Matthew set the tray on the floor in the hall and went to his own room. I washed my hands and face in the glazed bowl on the washstand, brushed the dirt out of my hair, then changed into my borrowed nightgown. I blew out the candle and fell asleep as soon as my head hit the pillow.

∞

It couldn't have been more than a few hours later when a light tapping at the door woke me. The room was pitch black, and I was groggy with sleep. I groped my way to the door and opened it a crack, letting in a whiff of the clove scent I detected whenever Cadoc was close. Instinctively, I

ran a hand through my tousled hair even though it was too
dark for him to see me.

"Come in," I said and pulled the door open wider.

Cadoc took a step inside, then closed the door. He laid
a hand on my shoulder, warming my skin through the
fabric of my nightgown. He spoke, but distracted by his
touch, I missed the meaning of his words. "What'd you
say?"

He drew me closer and whispered in my ear, his breath
tickling my neck. "We need to talk. Stay here while I get
Matthew." He released me and slipped out the door.

I opened the curtains, and Kuklos' soft red light poured
into the room. I touched my shoulder and remembered the
weight and warmth of Cadoc's hand.

A minute later, the boys arrived. Cadoc said, "The
guards are patrolling. They'll be back upstairs before long."
We sat on the floor, then Cadoc spoke in an urgent tone.
"The men you saw here tonight. They're Eyes and Ears." All
thoughts of romance fled my mind.

"Why are they here?" Matthew asked.

"This is one of their way stations. A safe house—part of
a secret network that spans the kingdom. Agents stay here
sometimes, hold meetings. That's what this place was built
for a hundred years ago. Folk outside of the Eyes don't
know that, though. They think of Meganeara as an ordinary
farm."

"I knew there had to be more to it," I said.

Matthew nudged Cadoc's knee. "You learned
something." It was a statement, not a question.

"Aye. I'm not allowed in their meetings, since I'm not
one of them. I listened in as best I could while pretending
to do chores. Rebels attacked Lord Humphrey's party."

Grandpa. "What happened?" I asked.

"The baron took the Maulden trail to Ardara. Not sure
why. It's not the quickest route. Maybe he wanted to hide
your grandfather. Maybe he wanted to pry information from

folk in small villages. The spies didn't give a lot of details. Beli's all right, though your grandpa was wounded."

My stomach did a flip-flop.

"How bad is he?" Matthew asked.

Cadoc cocked his head to listen for the guards. After a moment he said, "Don't know. Someone said the rebels were defeated, and then the baron went on to Ardara."

Matthew's jaw tightened. "I'll hold the baron responsible if Grandpa doesn't survive this."

"Listen," Cadoc said. "The best healers in the kingdom are in the royal city. They'll take care of him. Matthew, we need to go to our rooms. The guards will be back any minute."

The boys padded away, and I stared out the window at a tree lit by pale moonlight. *How bad are Grandpa's injuries? We should have insisted the baron take us with him. How will we ever get home?* I drew the curtains tight again, plunging the room into darkness. My sleep was troubled by nightmares of men fighting on horseback, giant rocs flying low over the farm and carrying moas off to the Great Forest, and a wizened healer shaking her head at Matthew and me, mouthing words I couldn't hear.

I woke in a tangle of covers with weak morning light seeping in around the edges of the curtains. I dressed quickly, then headed downstairs. In the hallway, I collided with Prince Brenden and stumbled backward.

"Sorry, Your Highness."

"Steady there. I'm saying my goodbyes to Mrs. Dunstan. Afterward, I'd like a word with you and Matthew. Wait for me downstairs."

"Yeah, I mean, aye." I knocked on Matthew's door and told him to pack up. I stuffed clean clothes from the supply Carys had lent me into a bag. I had no doubt the prince would be ready to leave for Ardara right after breakfast. Matthew and the twins were already eating by the time I got to the kitchen. There was no sign of last night's visitors. I slipped into a chair and was spooning honey on my porridge when the prince joined us.

"When do we leave for the royal city, Your Highness?" I asked.

He poured a mug of tea and took a sip before answering. "I've decided you and Matthew will remain at the farm. I'll take only the twins."

"What? No!" Matthew said, at the same time I asked, "Why?"

Prince Brenden set down his mug. "It's a long journey in a world that's unfamiliar to you. There are dangers you're not prepared to face." I didn't believe for a second that was the reason. He didn't want us to find out about Grandpa.

"Our world's a pretty dangerous place too," Matthew said. "Didn't you say Kallan's talent might help the king?" He kept pushing his hair out of his eyes, a sure sign he was agitated.

"Aye, I did. However, I must weigh the cost of your safety against the value of her talent."

We needed to reach Grandpa. I didn't give Matthew a chance to reply. "Thanks for thinking about our safety. Would you like me to do a viewing of Prince Aiden before you go?"

The prince's eyes widened. I don't think he expected me to give up so easily. Matthew's mouth twisted in disgust. He didn't expect me to give up so easily either. Prince Brenden said, "I'm grateful for your understanding. I appreciate the opportunity to see how my brother fares."

Carys eyed me suspiciously. I retrieved my sketchbook, ink pot, and quill, then opened the book to a clean page.

I remembered Prince Aiden's features and what his guards looked like well enough. Once I'd sketched them, I pulled my chair next to Prince Brenden's and held the drawing flat on the table. Before long, the background began filling in, and I grew nauseous and cold. Prince Aiden stood in a forested area, talking to two of his guards. Prince

Brenden's grip tightened on his mug. "He's taking a strange route. I thought he'd stick to the King's Road."

"Why is that?" I asked.

"The King's Road is the shortest route to Ardara," Cadoc said.

"Aye, that's right," Prince Brenden said. There was motion in the drawing. Prince Aiden waved his arms around and glared at the guards. One backed away from him. The other shook his head, frowning at the prince.

Cadoc said, "Can Prince Aiden be trusted?" Although he'd said it quietly to Carys, we all heard him. Both Prince Brenden and Cadoc flushed pink with embarrassment. It seemed Prince Brenden didn't trust his brother any more than we did.

"That's enough of the viewing," Prince Brenden said. He stood and paced the kitchen. I let go of the paper and took deep breaths to fight the nausea.

"You say your world is a dangerous place?" he asked Matthew.

"Yes, Your Highness. We have wars on Earth too, and sometimes people assault others or rob them. There are also animal attacks. As you know, we ended up in Kylemore because a wild animal tried to kill our chickens."

The prince continued pacing. "Perhaps I underestimated you. You'll be fully grown in a couple of months." He glanced at the drawing. "If you're willing, you may come with us." We assured him we were willing and made quick work of cleaning up the breakfast dishes.

One cannot anticipate
all the enemy's tactics.
~Handbook of the Eyes and Ears of the King

13

IMPORTED DANGER

arys left Aeron in the care of one of the farmhands, and before the sun was halfway to its peak, we set out for Ardara with Prince Brenden and his guards. The day was hot and dry with cottony puffs of cumulus clouds dotting the sky.

We stopped in Daire to collect the cloaks that Prince Brenden had ordered from Fergus. His father's shop was well lit with large windows on the front and back walls of the main room. A doorway opened off to the right. I guessed it led to the living quarters. One wall of the main room was lined with cubbyholes filled with neatly folded piles of cloth in colors as bright and varied as my tubes of paint back home.

A compact man with muscular arms and brown hair streaked with gray cut a length of linen at a large table in the center of the room. Fergus stood at a table in the corner, folding a jumble of cloth into neat stacks. He looked up when we entered. "Da, Prince Brenden's here."

The man bowed to the prince. "Your Highness, Norman Brady at your service. Welcome to my humble shop. Your order is ready." He went over to Fergus and dragged him by his ear to stand in front of the prince. He gave Fergus' head

113

a shake. When he released the ear, I saw a red mark where he'd held it. "You'll apologize for your villainous behavior."

In spite of the mean things Fergus had done, I was sorry to see him treated so roughly, especially in front of the prince. Fergus bowed and stammered an apology to Prince Brenden and then to Carys and me, his freckles stark against his pale face.

We accepted his apologies and thanked him and his father for the cloaks. Norman Brady handed them to the prince with another bow. The edges were embroidered with hunter green vines, setting off the mulberry color of the wool. The cloth was smooth and the stitching even; the vines flowed along the cloth in graceful curves. They were beautiful and heavy enough for winter weather. Fergus cast one last glance at me, then busied himself with his piles of cloth.

"He resents us more than ever," Cadoc remarked as we walked back to the horses.

∞

An hour after our midday meal, we met a man walking along the road. Even on such a hot day, he wore a long, colorful cape; stripes of yellow and blue alternated on a tan background. A scuffed leather instrument case hung across his back. His hair was thick and curly, the sandy color matched in a full beard and thick tail. Warm tawny eyes smiled out of his bushy head as he straightened from a low bow holding a floppy, broad-brimmed hat in a slender hand.

"Good day, fine folk. Master Dolph Molyngton at your service. I am a minstrel wandering the fair kingdom of Kylemore and offering songs, stories, and news in exchange for a coin, a bit of food, or a drink. I see some of your party wear the royal colors of Kylemore. You must be Prince Brenden, sir. Much has been said of your goodness and comely features, Your Highness." After this peculiar speech, he bowed deeply again, then gazed up at the prince.

The guards were on alert, their hands on the hilts of their swords. Prince Brenden chuckled and spoke in a kind voice. "Good day to you. May I see your minstrel medallion?"

The strange man fished a disc out of a tunic pocket and handed it to the prince. It was made of metal and resembled a large coin with an imprint of a flute in the center.

Prince Brenden inspected it before giving it back. "Thank you. That will do, Master Molyngton."

"Please call me Dolph, Your Highness, everyone does."

"As you say. Good day, Dolph. We're on our way to the royal castle in Ardara. Would you be good enough to accompany us? We can provide meals and conversation in exchange for your songs, stories, and news of the kingdom."

"It would gladden my heart to travel with a prince of the realm." I wondered if Dolph was always so formal, or if he was showing off for royalty.

"I'll ask you to ride our spare horse, as we have not the time for walking," the prince said.

Dolph stared at the horse placidly nibbling grass at the edge of the road. The minstrel's Adam's apple bobbed up and down with rapid swallows. "Must I ride, Your Highness?" he asked, trying to look at the prince and the horse at the same time.

"I'm afraid you must, Master Dolph."

"So be it." Dolph sighed and awkwardly mounted the little horse we'd brought to carry extra supplies. He gripped the reins tightly, and we set off again.

The sun had nearly set by the time we found a level camping site off the main road. The minstrel entertained us after the evening meal with folk songs and stories of ancient heroes. Stars filled the sky when Dolph announced he had one more story before the final song of the evening. "This is a true tale, and not from history either. It's been happening for months in the northernmost mountains of our kingdom."

Prince Brenden stiffened and gave the minstrel his full attention. Dolph's eyes were wide, the whites showing bright in the firelight "There is a little cove near a thick forest that runs almost to the edge of the rocky shore. Boats glide into the cove some nights and pull up to a pebbled beach. They unload a few passengers and slip back out to sea, not waiting to learn if the travelers get settled and all. I wager that's due to the passengers being wild creatures. Not humans, Pannmordians, wood elves, or any other intelligent folk."

Sipping ale from a tankard, he scanned our faces to gauge our reactions. "I heard it myself in an inn on the edge of one of the northern outposts. The beasts are fearsome, over three feet long, with spotted hair, and two long pointed teeth."

He leaned forward. "A villager spied one attacking a caino browsing on the ground. It dropped from a tree onto the poor creature and stabbed it 'til it was dead. What the man remembered most were the sharp teeth. They were tucked into pouches in the creature's cheeks. When it attacked, it jabbed with 'em like a set of knives." Dolph's fingers stabbed at his palm over and over.

He paused, fingers suspended over his palm. "The beasts are imported murderers. I ask myself, what are they, who's bringing 'em to that cove—and why?"

Does this have any connection to the person that Morcant, Durst, and Seisyll work for? Is Prince Aiden involved?

After letting his words sink in, Dolph strummed his lute and said, "A soothing tune to shake off the memory of those wild creatures. Put 'em out of your heads, they're far north and no threat to us here."

Prince Brenden let Dolph finish his quiet song, then sent the rest of us to our bedrolls. Trailing behind the others, I watched the prince approach Dolph as he stowed his lute in its battered case. The prince spoke so quietly, I could barely make out his words. "Let us walk. I would hear more about these strange happenings." Alec appeared at my side and led me to the others, cutting off Dolph's mumbled reply.

For all its power, there are
some conditions that
magic cannot heal.
~Master Ailfrid
The Art and Discipline of Magic

14

TRAVEL TROUBLES

Five days into our journey, I joined Matthew and the twins for breakfast in the common room of the Crooked Chimney. We'd slept in inns on this leg of the journey, but this would be the last time we'd sleep indoors until we reached Ardara. After this, we would take the Maulden Trail and camp in the woods. Loaves of coarse, brown bread were set out on each table, filling the air with their tantalizing aroma. My order of porridge arrived, topped with slices of small, pale peaches. Ignoring the pitcher of milk, I reluctantly poured a stream of cider over the contents of the bowl and sighed. "I wish you had cows here. I'm not crazy about goat's milk."

Realizing I sounded whiny, I quickly apologized. "Sorry. Don't mean to be rude."

"What's a cow?" Cadoc asked.

"A fat horse that gives milk as sweet as a baby's breath," said Matthew. "They have soft brown eyes, and they're about as brainy as that bowl of porridge."

Carys snorted. "They wouldn't last long around here."

"Yeah," I said, seeing a chance to make up for my rudeness. "Lots of Earth creatures would have trouble surviving here. Grandpa, Matthew, and I wouldn't have

119

lasted a day without your help."

Cadoc frowned. "You mean getting chained to the table by the baron, being forced to answer questions after drinking truth serum, and letting David be taken away? That help?" He took a savage bite out of his bread.

I gaped at him. "Those things weren't your fault."

Matthew nodded. "Dude, don't beat yourself up."

Cadoc grunted and ate a handful of blackberries. He was normally self-assured. His apparent guilt about the way things turned out after he and Carys detained us on their farm surprised me. It was a relief to see he sometimes doubted himself.

We packed our bags after breakfast and headed north again with Prince Brenden, his guards, and Dolph. After leaving the village, we rode through rolling hills covered with brush, then entered a forest of oak, birch, maple, and pine trees. For the first time since we'd arrived in this world, I saw thick, gray clouds hovering in the distance. The air was hot and sticky. Shiny green bottle flies pestered us all afternoon. I was jealous of the others who could flick their tails at them as well as swat them away with their hands.

Carys and I rode side by side in the middle of the group, discussing differences between Earth and Betherion. We spoke quietly, not wanting Dolph, who rode ahead of us, to overhear. Carys said, "Your world sounds peculiar, with one moon. We use Metiri, the large white one, to measure months. Kuklos, with its dim red light, is the moon for romance. When a lad wants to show he cares for a lass, he waits until Kuklos is full, then he—"

She broke off at a shout of "Halt!" from Dolph. The minstrel reined his horse in as a thin brown snake with long ochre stripes slithered across the dusty road. Dolph held out a hand to keep us back. "Beware the winding beastie. We don't want the horses spooked."

I tried to remember what the snake reminded me of. I let my mind go blank, and it came to me. "That's a garter snake. They're harmless. Even better, they hang out near water. Maybe it'll lead us to a stream."

Kain heard my comments. "The youngling speaks truth. Stay here while I talk with the prince."

He rode up to Prince Brenden, who was in the lead. At the prince's direction, we all searched the woods for a source of water. Before long, Conroy discovered a narrow stream trickling through banks of mossy shale. We knelt and scooped up water with our hands, pouring it down parched throats and splashing it over sweaty faces before filling our leather flasks. We flopped onto the shady ground and ate dried meat and bread while the horses drank their fill.

Prince Brenden allowed us a long rest. Later, he sat near me, making small talk. After he'd complimented me on my knowledge about the snake, he paused, as though not sure he wanted to say what was on his mind. When he spoke again, he kept his gaze on the ground. "I know using magic wears you out. However, I need a viewing of my brother Aiden. It's important."

He was considerate for a prince. "Sure, no problem." I also wanted to know what that bully was up to. I opened my sketchbook to the image of Prince Aiden and stared at it, wondering how close he was to the castle. No background appeared. Nothing happened at all.

"What's wrong? Why isn't it working?" I asked Carys.

"You're thinking, not feeling. Magic's not a mathematics problem. You can't make it happen by reasoning or force of will. Simply let go—like you told me you do when you paint."

Shutting out my thoughts, I sank into emotion. An intense dislike of Prince Aiden filled me. I couldn't tell if it was due to his condescending attitude toward Prince Brenden, or if there was something sinister in his intentions. The picture stayed the same. Finally, I gave up puzzling it out and sat with my emotions.

Dim shapes became visible, then grew clearer. Prince

Aiden sat in front of a massive oak tree in the center of an open grassy space. He held his head in his hands. I could make out a pond behind the tree. When Prince Brenden saw it, he cursed and smacked his palm with a fist. As curious as I was about his reaction, I didn't dare break the spell by asking questions. Finally, he said, "That's enough. Thank you."

I wrapped myself in my new woolen cloak until the magic's chill and nausea wore off. I'd have to ask Nuala or some other healer how to stay warm after doing magic. The recovery period was annoying.

While I warmed myself, I overheard Prince Brenden talk with his guards. "Aiden's at Phelip's Pond. He's still days away from Ardara. He should've taken the fastest route. The prisoners will have valuable information for the king."

Cadoc came over and recruited me to collect wood sorrel leaves for a salad for the evening meal. Prince Aiden slipped out of my thoughts as Cadoc and I walked side by side, scouring the woods for the plant's heart-shaped leaves and delicate yellow flowers. We didn't talk much, but every time he glanced at me or his hand brushed mine, a lightness filled me. I wouldn't have been surprised to find myself floating above the ground.

There were no villages near this part of the trail. Prince Brenden decided to set a night watch in case there were any rebels or common criminals in the area. The twins, Matthew, and I asked to be part of the rotation. The prince agreed, as long as we were paired up with him or a guard. I'd noticed that Dolph, who was always ready with a song or a story, shied away from difficult work. Because of our insistence, the minstrel was shamed into taking a shift as well.

Three-quarters of an hour into my watch, I heard a sound in the bushes. I froze as my mind ran through the possibilities of what might be hidden in the shrubbery. I whistled a signal to Kain, who was on guard with me. Or rather, I tried to whistle. All I managed was a loud whoosh of air. It must have been loud enough, because Kain crept over to where I hid with my arms wrapped around my trembling knees.

"It's over there," I whispered, pointing to the clump of bushes. Clouds hid the full moon of Metiri and Kuklos, which was in a gibbous phase. We couldn't see anything in the blackness. Then the cloud drifted away from Kuklos, and in the eerie red light we saw a small, shrew-like creature perched near the top of the bush.

Kain was a serious man. He didn't chat with us as much as Alec, and he didn't laugh as often as Conroy, so I was surprised to see the flash of his white teeth as he smiled in the darkness. "It's only an eomaia, lass." He chuckled, and with that friendly, ordinary sound, I stopped shaking. "They're fine, furry creatures. They eat insects. Completely harmless. Why, Princess Skyla even keeps one for a pet. Doubtless you'll meet the princess when we reach the royal city."

Grateful he couldn't see my reddened ears, I mumbled my thanks and settled in for the rest of our watch.

∞

The next day, the weather changed dramatically. In the middle of the morning, Cadoc rode up to me and said, "There's a breeze kicking up. See the leaves?" The leaves on the birch trees lining the road shivered, showing silver undersides as they rubbed against each other.

"Look there," I said, pointing. The road curved and a view opened up to the west. Dark clouds lined the horizon. "Rain's on the way."

Dolph trilled an old song he called, "Rains of the Year."
Rains in the autumn bring leaves to the ground,
Rains in the winter chill me to the bone,
Rains in the springtime start green things a growing,

But it's the soft rains of summer that welcome me home.

"His voice is sweet, but that song puts me in a sad mood," I told Cadoc.

"The same for me. It makes me kind of lonely."

He gave me a crooked smile, and before I could stop myself, I said, "Summer rains make me lonely sometimes. I don't know why. Maybe because my mother died in the summer." Embarrassed at sharing so much, I busied myself with adjusting my grip on the reins. "Sorry," I muttered.

"It's well enough. You can speak about her if you wish."

I'd only talked with Matthew about my parents' deaths. He'd been with me through all of it—the shock of my dad's death in a freak accident on a paleontology dig and my mom's long illness a few years later. I shook my head. "Thanks, but not now. Someday I may tell you about her."

"I'd like that."

Tears prickled my eyes. I turned my head away and studied the trees lining the other side of the road.

The clouds grew thicker throughout the day. By early afternoon, we reached Phelip's Pond. The guards and Prince Brenden searched for traces of Prince Aiden to confirm my viewing of him in this place.

While Prince Brenden and his guards carried out their search, Cadoc became agitated and paced the perimeter of the clearing. After three rounds, he walked to the massive oak that dominated the middle of the space and spoke to no one in particular. "Something disturbing happened here."

Prince Brenden stopped his search. "What's that? How do you know?"

Cadoc shook his head and resumed pacing. The prince raised an eyebrow at Carys. She said, "With his magical skill, Your Highness, he can sense emotions that linger in a place, though he has to sort through it before he can answer your questions."

Cadoc completed one more circuit and came to a stop near the prince, who stood under the oak. "Your Highness, something happened in the last day or two—a quick event that caused a flood of emotions—anger, fear, and others I cannot sort out. Some in the party may have left the area ahead of the others."

A faint rumble of thunder accented Cadoc's words. Silvery sheets of rain hung from leaden clouds in the distance. Prince Brenden scanned the horizon and called us together. "Get a shelter ready. Let's eat quickly before the storm arrives. We'll discuss the meaning of this later."

Everyone scrambled. Carys and I cut bread and cheese into chunks. Kain, Conroy, and Prince Brenden secured the horses at the western end of the area, where the trees would block the wind a little. Matthew, Cadoc, and Alec rushed to cut a pile of pine branches from a thick stand of pines at the eastern end of the clearing. They lashed them together to make two brushy lean-tos that faced each other. A reluctant Dolph helped them while keeping an eye on the sky. When the work was finished, we gathered in the shelters. The rain arrived as we took our first bites of the cold meal. Water dripped off the ends of the roof boughs, but inside we were dry and comfortable.

By the time Dolph asked if there was any tidbit for dessert, the wind had picked up, thunder rolled, and lightning lit the sky beyond the trees to the west. Rain poured in a deluge, running in rivulets past the shelters and dripping through gaps in the pine needles. After one bright flash, Matthew counted the time until we heard the crash of thunder. "The lightning's about a mile away," he said.

"And coming closer fast," Cadoc said. "I've never seen a storm this intense."

"Nor I," said Prince Brenden with a frown. "Rumblestorms of any strength are rare events."

He wasn't the only one worried. I usually didn't mind

thunderstorms, but normally I could get indoors when they hit.

"I'm uneasy, Your Highness," Kain said. "The weather shouldn't have changed this quickly. Makes me think there's magic in it."

Cadoc said, "Prince Aiden couldn't do this, could he?"

Prince Brenden answered. "He has no magical talent. It would take a powerful magician to whip up a storm this fierce. Sorceress Mairsil had skill with weather. I thought she was long dead. Perhaps she is not. This storm is reminiscent of her magic. Look." He pointed outside the shelter. "Icestones."

Hail the size of cherry pits pelted the grass, turning it white. The wind lashed at the trees. Flashes of lightning streaked across the black sky. The ground shook with a great peal of thunder. A gust of wind tore at the shelters, carrying off a few boughs. Across the clearing, the horses reared and pulled at their tethers.

Prince Brenden jumped to his feet and barked orders. "Kain, Conroy, come with me. We'll secure the horses. Alec, take the others into the woods. Shelter under that dense clump of pines we passed on our way here." Arms thrust over their heads to block the hail, he and the guards sprinted across the open space.

When they reached the shelter of the ancient oak, they paused to wipe the water off their faces, leaning, or resting a hand against the trunk. In that same moment, a crack of thunder split the air and a bolt of lightning hit the giant tree. All three of them dropped in an instant.

Carys let out a terrible, high-pitched scream. All of us, except Dolph, ran out to the fallen men, oblivious to the storm. While we checked out the horrific scene, Dolph joined us, his cape stretched over his head as a hail-shield. Kain was pinned under a massive branch that had split off the oak. Conroy and Prince Brenden lay motionless beside the tree.

Adrenaline pumped through me. Our first aid instructor's voice rang in my mind. "Get that branch off Kain," I shouted. "Matthew, check Conroy for a pulse." Matthew rushed to Conroy's side, while Alec, Dolph, and the twins rushed to heave the branch off Kain. I knelt by the prince's still form, pressing on his chest, silently urging him to live.

The hail stopped as abruptly as it began, leaving behind a soft rain. Alec and the others managed to lift the great branch off of Kain and tossed it to one side. Carys took a step back, her fist to her mouth. I could barely understand her words through her sobs. "His chest is crushed—he's dead. Kain's dead."

Kain's eyes were open wide, staring but unseeing. A moan escaped me. It was clear we could do nothing for him. I shook my head and returned my attention to Prince Brenden. Cold rainwater trickled under the neck of my tunic and ran down my back as I pushed on his chest over and over again, stopping occasionally to listen to his heart. Nearby, Matthew did the same for Conroy.

After several minutes, Matthew sat back on his heels. "Conroy's breathing on his own. He's still out cold. With luck, he'll make it."

I put my ear to the prince's chest. His heart beat steadily. Salty tears mingled with the rain running down my face. I looked up to find Cadoc and Alec standing by my side.

"He's alive," I said.

Dolph squatted in silence, his gaze fixed on the forest. I don't think he really saw it. Carys knelt by Kain's body, one hand on his arm. The oak crackled with dancing yellow flames. I stared at the scene through a misty curtain. It was like watching a play with the action halted at the end of an act. Any moment now, the actors would take a bow, and life would return to normal.

One of the horses whinnied, breaking through my

shock. Matthew glanced from Conroy to the horses and back again.

"Alec," I called. "Can you secure the horses? They're scared, and we need them to get to Ardara."

The guard shook himself. "Aye. Cadoc, Dolph, with me."

I turned back to the prince. He and Conroy still needed attention.

To ease an invalid's recovery,
be patient and understanding.
~Elementary Guide for Healers

15

AFTERMATH

*W*hile Alec, Cadoc, and Dolph tended to the horses, Carys and I stayed with Prince Brenden, trying to revive him. Matthew cradled Conroy's head in his arms. The guard stirred and uttered soft moans. Matthew put a hand on his chest to keep him from rising and called out. "Alec, come quickly. Conroy's coming around."

Alec trotted over. "I'll stay with him. Help Cadoc with the horses."

The rain tapered off and the wind stopped blowing. The fire at the top of the oak tree had died out, leaving behind a bitter, smoky scent. Alec kept up a steady stream of talk, comforting his friend. The horses strained at their tethers and their ears flicked back and forth as though on swivels.

Matthew stroked the neck of his gelding, Colby, and murmured in his ear. The horse stopped pawing the ground. Not for the first time, I wished I had his way with creatures. As Matthew passed from one horse to another, they calmed at his touch. Each one gave a toss of a head or swish of a tail before settling into stillness. I overheard the boys' conversation when I retrieved dry blankets from a saddle pack.

"I tried to quiet them. It's no good," Cadoc said. "You come along and all's right in their world. I ought to be jealous. For true, I'm grateful." He gave Matthew's shoulder a quick squeeze. "You do well."

"Thanks. I find animals . . . easier to relate to than people. They're more straightforward. No hidden agendas." He pushed the hair out of his eyes. "Okay. Let's move them into the woods where it's drier."

Cadoc took hold of Willow's bridle. "Aye. After that, we'll build a shelter near them on this side of the clearing."

Beyond the oak tree lay the messy pile of branches that remained from our first set of lean-tos. The extent of destruction from the storm made me jittery. I caught a whiff of air perfumed with the scent of horse. Comforted by the familiar smell, I turned my back on the wreckage and rejoined Carys and our patients.

Once they'd moved the horses, Alec and the boys set to work on the shelter, assisted by Dolph. An hour and a half later, we were all gathered inside a large, sturdy structure of pine branches. Carys treated stress with a meal, the same as my mother. She spread food out on a cloth, and we ate our fill of dried meat, biscuits, raw carrots, and peaches.

Conroy sat a little apart from the rest of us. His body sagged, and he was quiet. "How do you feel?" I asked.

He swallowed the carrot he was munching while he considered my question. "My right arm is like deadwood. I can move my fingers,"—he wiggled them—"yet they're prickly, like someone stuck them with pins." He pushed up his shirtsleeve. "See this feathery mark that goes from my elbow to shoulder? What happened?" He swiveled his head around as though searching for something. "Where's Kain?"

I winced, wondering how he could have forgotten. The lightning strike didn't hurt him physically as much as Kain or the prince, but it must have affected his memory.

"You were struck by lightning, mate," Alec said. "That feathery mark's a scar."

Conroy screwed his face up in confusion.

Alec continued. "When you and Kain ran to help the

horses, you stopped by the oak and put your hands on it. Lightning hit the tree . . . a great branch killed Kain." With no response from Conroy, Alec tried again. "Do you not remember? I told you the story when you woke up."

Conroy shook his head. "What about Prince Brenden? Why's he asleep?"

Alec sighed. I answered, keeping my voice calm. "It's all right, Conroy, your memory will come back. Prince Brenden touched the tree too. He's in a coma." I glanced over to where the prince lay sleeping. "It'll take some time for him to wake up."

"What's a coma?" Conroy asked, flexing the fingers on his right hand with his left. "What happened to my hand? I can't move my arm."

Like Alec, I gave up explaining.

"Prince Brenden's in the dark sleep," Carys said. "Try not to think about it. When we get to Ardara, the royal healers will help both of you. Why don't you rest?" Conroy lay down obediently and pulled a blanket over himself with his left arm.

Matthew went outside and I followed. The air was cool and refreshing. We checked on the horses' pickets and water supply. Halfway back to the shelter, Matthew bent over and vomited.

A water flask lay on top of a pile of supplies. I handed it to him. He took a long swallow and wiped his mouth with his sleeve. "My head throbs." His gaze swept the dark countryside. "Every day in this world pulls us deeper into a nightmare. I wonder what Grandpa's going through."

"At least he's with Beli and Lord Humphrey. He's probably healed from his injury and feasting every night with the king. I hope his heart stays strong until we get back home. Living in a medieval world is a lot harder than teaching about it."

Matthew laughed a bitter sound. "I was wrong. We don't belong here."

Three pterodactyls soared overhead. Their black silhouettes passed in front of red Kuklos, which shone brightly through ragged clouds. Instinctively, I drew closer to Matthew. The breeze kicked up, and he covered one eye with his hand. Holding onto his arm, I led him back to the others.

Cary's brows drew together when she saw Matthew. "Injury?"

"Sick. Headache," he replied.

Carys rose and smoothed her tunic. Her tail hung down, limp as rope. In spite of her fatigue, she was all business. "I've got something to help that. I'll make a fire."

"Don't bother. I'll be fine," Matthew said, putting out a hand to stop her.

She clasped his hand with both of hers. "It's not only for you. We need to keep the prince warm." Even though Matthew's cheeks turned pink, he didn't pull his hand away.

"The lass is right," Alec said. "Clear skies will bring a cold night. Dolph, be a good fellow and help the twins collect firewood." Dolph mumbled a reply, then followed Carys and Cadoc into the woods. Alec seated himself next to Conroy, who had fallen asleep again.

I tucked Prince Brenden's blanket under him and felt his forehead. "One good sign. No fever."

Matthew balled his hands into fists. "How will we get to Ardara? We have no way to transport the prince, Conroy's paralyzed and can't remember anything for more than a few minutes, we're low on food, and . . . and there's Kain." He dropped down in a corner of the shelter.

Matthew's negativity rattled me; it was so unlike him. Having lost Kain, I was determined to get Prince Brenden and Conroy to the royal healers before they grew worse. "We're not helpless. Alec will get us there." I smiled at the guard. "Right?"

He nodded. "For certain, lass. We'll need a wagon." He

combed a hand through his curly hair.

Before the storm, we'd ridden through a tiny settlement with about a dozen cabins clustered on either side of the trail, their fenced yards holding back the forest. "What about that last group of houses we passed by?" I asked. "Can they help?"

"They'll have no choice. I'll command a wagon in the name of the king. Seeing as Conroy's not fit, Dolph can go with me in the morning. It will do him good to be useful. We'd best get an early start." Alec stood, his head brushing the branches at the top of the shelter. His tail switched back and forth. "Before we sleep, we need to bury Kain."

Cadoc helped Alec prepare for Kain's burial while Carys and I made a fire. Before we could light it, we magically dried the wood. Carys pointed her wand toward a thick branch and said, "*Desicaré.*" Steam rose from the branch at once. I pointed Kain's cherry wand at a pile of twigs and repeated the spell. Something must have been off in my pronunciation. Rather than dry the wood, my sleeves grew wet and heavy.

"What happened?" I said, shaking droplets off the drenched cloth.

Carys laughed. "You reversed the direction of the moisture. Instead of pushing it away, you drew it to yourself. Give it another go." After several tries, I managed to dry out a puny pile of twigs and make my sleeves merely damp rather than soaked through.

Once the fire blazed, Carys boiled herbs to make a tea for Matthew's headache. He took the mug she offered with a shy smile, and then he sipped the steamy brew in silence while he stared into the fire.

The disaster of the thunderstorm played out in my mind as I rubbed my thumb along the polished surface of Kain's wand. *He would still be alive if they hadn't paused under the tree.* I grimaced. *There is no going back. Although, it will be better for all of us if the prince is conscious when we reach Ardara.* "Carys," I said, "can you bring Prince Brenden out of his coma?"

"I've never dealt with anyone in the dark sleep. This is beyond my training." She spread her hands in apology. "As you know, the side effects of magic can be unpredictable. I don't dare attempt a healing. Besides, given a little time, he may wake on his own. As Matthew says, sometimes it's best to let the body heal naturally."

I hugged myself. I was cold despite the fire's heat. "After seeing Conroy's condition, I wonder if the prince will ever recover from the lightning strike."

Carys said, "Our best hope is to get him to the royal healers as quick as can be."

When Kain's grave was ready, everyone except Prince Brenden gathered around it. Alec and Cadoc slowly lowered the guard's body into the earth. We bowed our heads as Alec said a prayer. "Blessed Ancestors, may you welcome this champion and guard of the royal family with open arms. Keep him close and treat him well. He was a friend to many and a brave defender of good Prince Brenden." I swallowed back tears at the tenderness in Alec's voice.

We each tossed a handful of wet soil into the open pit. Without warning, Conroy let out a wail of grief. "Kain was my best friend. Someone's attacking Kylemore. Who wants to wage war on us?"

He remembered the attacks; maybe his memory was returning.

"Mate, it could be that Sorceress Mairsil isn't dead after all," Alec said. "An age ago, Kylemore suffered through a civil war. Maybe she wants to start another one. Or, it might be Kelby or Shea. Those kingdoms have been itching to fight ever since the last war ended in a stalemate."

Conroy spun around in a circle, searching the clearing. "Where's Prince Brenden? What happened to Kain? I don't see them."

Dolph spoke up. "Alec, sir. I'll take Conroy back to the

shelter and get him settled and all."

The minstrel wasn't disturbed by Conroy's forget-fulness. Earlier, Dolph had told me that when his parents were sick with mountain fever, he'd nursed them for weeks on his own. He said, "They spoke nonsense all the while until they died from the sickness. I'd go along with it and follow their thoughts wherever they led. It soothed them, my being patient with them."

Alec thanked Dolph. "Off you go, minstrel. Have a good sleep, Conroy." The two shuffled off to the shelter together, Dolph's striped cloak swishing softly as he went.

Alec turned back to Kain's grave, ready to fill it in. Cadoc cleared his throat. "Um, Alec, besides Sorceress Mairsil and our neighboring kingdoms, couldn't Prince Aiden be behind the attacks?"

Alec gave him a sharp look. "Mind who you share that thought with, lad. Prince Aiden's a rough man, yet a loyal prince." Cadoc tilted his head to one side.

The guard must have seen Cadoc's doubt mirrored on the rest of our faces. "All four of you need to understand. Prince Aiden's not had it as easy as the others. He's not a king like Darren or a future mage like Brenden. His sisters even have more power and freedom than he does. Two of them married princes in Kelby and Shea."

"Nuala told me about Princess Eolande and Princess Kiara's weddings," Carys said, a dreamy expression in her eyes. "She said they were lovely ceremonies." Cadoc poked her with his elbow, and she grew quiet again.

"Right," said Alec. "Those two have a lot of influence in their adopted kingdoms. Then there's Princess Skyla, the eldest of all the royal siblings. She hasn't married, and she gets to do what she wants. She refused the crown so she could travel all over as head of the Diplomatic Corps."

"D'you mean you could've had a Queen Skyla for your ruler instead of King Darren?" I asked.

"Aye, lass. By tradition the eldest child is considered

first when the old ruler dies. When the crown was offered to Skyla, she turned it down. She enjoys roaming the countryside and didn't want to be tied to the castle."

A movement overhead caught my eye. I grabbed Cadoc's hand. After a second glance, I released my breath and Cadoc. Instead of the sinister pterodactyl I expected, a creature similar to the twins' pet lizard Solo glided a foot above our heads. It landed in a nearby tree. I pictured Solo sleeping in front of the fireplace at the Dunstan's farm, and my racing heart slowed down.

Cadoc put his arm around my shoulder and pulled me close. Embarrassed to be startled by another harmless creature and grateful for the warmth of Cadoc's body, I slipped my arm around his waist. He smiled down at me, then spoke to Alec. "I recall when King Darren's father, King Raghnall, joined the spirits of the ancestors. Da said there was a delay before King Darren was crowned. I never knew why."

The guard gave a small nod. "Now you do. Prince Aiden hasn't gotten to do what he wants. He's served under the Captain of the King's Army for years, yet King Darren won't let him take charge. It would make anyone bitter." I almost felt sorry for the redheaded bully.

Alec looked long at each of us, checking that we understood. "Prince Aiden may be spiteful, yet he's as loyal to Kylemore as Prince Brenden. I wouldn't have told you all this if it wasn't important you understand. Say no more about it, if you value your freedom. The king doesn't take kindly to charges against his siblings."

I twisted my silver ring around my finger, thinking about everything Alec had said. Prince Aiden had a lot to be jealous about. *Maybe he is loyal to the kingdom. Then again, maybe not.*

After we buried Kain, we took turns keeping guard in pairs through what remained of the night.

There was no change in the prince's condition by

morning. After breakfast, Alec and Dolph rode to the tiny settlement and returned with food and a wagon. The wagon was half filled with hay. We placed blankets over the hay and lay Prince Brenden on top. Carys watched over him and Dolph kept Conroy company during the long day of travel. Conroy regained some feeling in his forearm, but there wasn't much improvement in his memory.

Matthew and I led the extra horses while Cadoc and Alec took turns driving the wagon. Mud sucked at the wagon's wheels, making progress slow. Thick clouds grew in the west, dampening our spirits. Fortunately, no rain fell all that day. In fact, the ride was uneventful. I wondered how long our luck would hold.

As difficult as it may be, treat your
enemies with compassion—for
your sake as much as theirs.
~Handbook of the Eyes and Ears of the King

16

PRISONER

A couple of days after the lightning disaster, Alec hunted for food, Dolph watched over the prince and Conroy, and the rest of us held a brainstorming session. Although Prince Brenden's breathing and heart rate were normal, he remained in a coma and we couldn't feed him. He couldn't even swallow when we put a cup of water to his lips. His skin became drier to the touch every day and turned wrinkly. It was a race between getting him to the royal healers and death from starvation or dehydration.

"How do they treat people in the dark sleep on Earth?" Carys asked. As a healer, she seemed totally discouraged about not knowing how to help him.

Matthew said, "One way is to put a needle, a tiny hollow metal tube, in their vein and pass water and nutrients through that."

Carys frowned. "I don't know how we could do that."

Cadoc said, "Is there any other way?"

"When my mom was in the hospital, I remember seeing a man hooked up to a feeding tube," I said.

"Such an odd expression. What is a 'feeding tube'?" Carys said.

"They stick a tube into your stomach and send liquids through it. Maybe we can put one down his throat."

Cadoc said, "What are they made of, these tubes?"

"Rubber or plastic, I guess."

Cadoc squinted at me.

"Of course. You've never heard of rubber or plastic."

"Can we make them?" he asked.

Matthew brushed the hair out of his eyes. "Sorry, no."

Carys tugged on the tip of her tail. "The tube would need to be strong and the right size to fit in your throat. Flexible, too."

"What are you thinking, sis?" Cadoc asked.

She looked up with an excited expression. "There's a plant that grows in the stream. It's called bladderbulb." She giggled. "It has hollow stems and pouches on the bottom shaped like a goat's bladder."

Cadoc laughed. "The stems are long enough, for sure. As long as my arm."

Matthew said, "Have you seen any around here?"

Carys nodded. "Aye, downstream. It's not far."

"Let's try it," I said. "We can mix honey with the water, so he'll get some nourishment."

"And a pinch of salt," Matthew suggested.

Cadoc raised an eyebrow. "Salt?"

"We all have salt in our bodies. There's salt in our blood, sweat, tears. We should add a little to keep him balanced."

Carys shrugged. "As you wish. Beyond doubt, you speak true about salty tears and sweat. I do not know the nature of blood."

Carys and Matthew went off to collect the plants, and I boiled water to sterilize them. When Carys and Matthew returned, they soaked the plants in the boiled water, cooled them, then cut them into sections long enough to reach the prince's stomach. There were enough pieces to last for the rest of the journey, assuming we didn't get lost. Cadoc stirred a large spoonful of honey and a tiny bit of salt into a cup of the sterilized water and we took the supplies to the prince.

My doubts about the project had grown during the preparations. I put a hand on Carys' arm. "I don't see how you're going to get the tube inside him."

"I'll strengthen the stem with a spell, so it won't break off. I'll coat the outside of the stem with chamomile oil to relax his throat. There are more spells I can use if need be."

With some difficulty, we managed to get the tube down the prince's throat. Carys poured a fair amount of fortified water into him through the tube. His skin was a little smoother by the time she finished. If she could get as much into him every day, he might make it to the royal healers in time.

The next night, I lay awake on my bedroll listening to the soft noises of the forest. It had rained in the morning, and the ground was still moist. The dampness muffled sounds, but once in a while I could hear a small animal skitter through the underbrush. A lump formed in my throat as I remembered Kain's calm response when I freaked out over the eomaia on our night watch shift. The scrabbling of the little creatures didn't bother me anymore. Flying creatures, especially pterodactyls, were a different matter. I wished Kain was still with us. He could have helped me get over my fear of them.

A shout pierced the quiet night. One word, loud and clear. "Alec!"

Matthew and Alec were keeping watch. I jumped up and crept to the edge of camp toward Matthew's voice, then peered into the woods from the shelter of a large pine tree. Alec crashed through the bushes toward Matthew. The guard was a few feet away from him when an arrow sang through the air, followed by a sickening grunt on impact. I choked back a shriek as Alec thudded to the ground.

A little man rushed at Matthew. I ran from the shelter of the pine. Matthew and the stranger struggled, rolling over on the wet ground, but I couldn't get close enough to intervene. There was a blur of movement as a second man ran through the trees toward us. He stopped short, let out a squeal, and fell in a heap. The assailant ignored the distraction. He grabbed Matthew's throat with one hand while jabbing a knife at his arm with the other. I danced around them and snatched at his wrist. The man swung his knife at me. I jumped back out of reach. He stabbed Matthew's arm. Matthew howled and lashed out with his dagger. It stuck in his attacker's side. The man grunted in pain and his hand fell away from Matthew's throat.

Matthew rolled away, out of danger. Cadoc arrived just then and pried the injured man's knife out of his hand. Then he tossed it aside and held the man down with a knee on his chest. Breathing hard, Matthew pulled his dagger free. Cadoc remained on top of the man while he peeled off his own tunic and cut it into strips with his belt knife. I helped him hoist the stranger to his feet and wrap some of the strips around his middle to staunch the bleeding. Then Cadoc tied him to a tree with knotted lengths of cloth.

Matthew's clothes were covered in leaves and mud. The gash in his arm bled freely. I pulled a large sycamore leaf out of his hair, then wrapped my tunic around his arm. I shivered, partly from the cool night air and partly from the shock of the attack. Giving my arms a quick rub, I told the boys I'd check on Alec.

On the way to the guard, I passed the second attacker. A bow lay on the ground next to him. One side of his head was covered in blood. Cadoc must have used his sling to take the man down. A quick check told me he wasn't breathing and had no pulse. I continued on to Alec. I hated that I was becoming used to the violent side of this world.

An arrow stuck out of the right side of Alec's chest. His eyes were closed, and he didn't move. An ashy tone overlay his deep brown skin. I put my ear on his chest and was relieved to hear his heart beating with a steady rhythm.

"Is he dead?" Cadoc's words startled me. I hadn't heard him approach.

"No, unconscious. We'll have to be careful when we move him. I don't know how deep the arrow's gone. Do you think there are more of them coming for us?"

"These two were probably scouts and won't be missed for a while. I think we're safe for now." He rubbed the back of his neck. "I won't rest easy until we reach Ardara."

"What brought you out of camp? You and I weren't set to take over the watch for another half an hour."

"Couldn't sleep. I sensed dark emotions on the air. I was tracking down the source when Matthew yelled. I regret I was too late for Alec."

"He's stable. I hope Carys can help him."

"She'll do what she can. We'll need a board to carry him to camp."

A rumpled and bewildered Dolph arrived then. "What's happened?"

"Is my sister all right?" Cadoc asked.

"Aye, she's well. She's guarding the prince and keeping Conroy quiet."

Cadoc set Dolph to keeping watch over Alec while he and I returned to Matthew and the wounded stranger. Although blood soaked through the tunic I'd wrapped around Matthew's arm, he was steady on his feet, pointing his dagger at the man's heart. Cadoc untied the assailant from the tree. He was a small man, and Cadoc tied his arms behind his back with ease before marching him to our camp. Matthew and I trailed after them. The man tilted to one side, trying to protect his wound.

Carys met us at camp and rewrapped the man's middle. Cadoc tied the prisoner to a tree once more. This time he let the man sit on the ground for comfort. "As soon as we bring Alec back, I'll have Dolph guard him." Cadoc checked the strength of his knots. "We could use one of your air walls, sis."

"My pleasure." Carys drew out her wand. The prisoner watched her warily as she performed the spell to enclose him and the tree in a solid wall of air.

The next hour was a busy one. Carys put a clean bandage around Matthew's arm, then the boys and Dolph used one of the boards from the side of the wagon to carry Alec to the shelter. Conroy wept and pulled at his hair when he saw how badly Alec was hurt. Carys gave Conroy tea spiked with sleeping herbs so she could concentrate on the wounded ones. Leaving the arrow in place, she cleaned Alec's wound and rubbed painkilling ointment on his skin. While she tended to him, Matthew and Cadoc buried the dead attacker.

Leaving Alec with the sleeping Conroy and comatose Prince Brenden, Carys and I met up with the boys when their task was finished. We returned to the prisoner and Dolph, who'd taken over guarding him once the air wall melted away. Cadoc looked at the stranger with disgust. "Carys, will you aid him or leave him to suffer? It matters naught to me."

"A healer must always do what she can, enemy or no. For true, I haven't the energy to heal everyone. He'll get what remains of my strength when I've tended to the others."

She sighed and pulled on the end of her tail. "There's not much I can do for Alec, other than keep the wound clean and reduce his pain. I dare not remove the arrow. It could cause more damage. We must get him to the royal healers."

"We'll leave at first light," Cadoc said. "Take care of Matthew's wound now."

Carys and Matthew trudged back to the shelter. I was uneasy, watching them go. Her arm was wrapped protectively around his shoulders. He leaned toward her, his thick chestnut hair brushing her cheek. Maybe it was his injury that caused them to walk so close together, except I thought it was more than that. I glanced at Cadoc and blushed. Matthew and I had both ignored my advice about not getting emotionally attached.

I stayed with Cadoc while he questioned our prisoner. When a direct approach didn't work, he slipped in trick questions. Still, the man revealed nothing of importance.

After a while, Carys and Matthew joined us where we sat by a small fire. Matthew eased himself down next to me.

"All patched up?" I asked.

He nodded and flexed his arm, showing me how well he could move it.

"Oh, no, did the healing make you lose your voice again?"

He gave me a rueful smile.

"Is it gone completely?"

Another nod.

"That's too bad. Your wrestling partner isn't talking either. Carys, can you do anything with him?"

She faced the man, clasped her hands in front of her, and spoke in a quiet tone. "I'm a healer. I can relieve your pain. May I examine your wound?"

The slightly built man looked up at her, suspicion in his black eyes. His entire being radiated hatred. When she took a step closer, he kicked out with a swift jab to her shin.

"Dragon spit!" She hopped back a step and rubbed her shin. "Listen, man," she said, all softness gone from her voice. "I'll examine your wound, even if we need to pin your legs to the ground!" She glared at him, her tail vibrating. Dolph rushed at the man and slapped him hard across the face, then sat on his thin, flailing legs.

"Thank you kindly," Carys said, and knelt next to the glowering, motionless prisoner. "Cadoc, please bring a torch. Kallan, fetch my medicine bag and some of that tea I brewed for Conroy."

Dolph moved aside, and Carys held the man's chin firmly while she looked him in the eye. "You've lost a lot of blood from that wound. You're in pain and weak. We won't harm you. I'll lessen the pain, and we'll take you to the king. He can decide what's to be done with you. That's not our task."

The wiry man sagged against the tree. Some of the fight seemed to have gone out of him. He allowed Carys to examine his side without a fuss. I brought clean strips of cloth. Carys cleaned the gaping wound and put a thick layer of ointment over it before wrapping fresh bandages around his middle. While she worked, she sang a chant to ease the pain. She didn't have enough strength to heal the gash.

Once she tied the last cloth in place, Dolph spooned a bowlful of stew into the man. When it was gone, Carys made him drink some of the same tea she had given Conroy. Within minutes he was sound asleep, his pointed chin resting on his thin chest.

"I'll guard the prisoner for the next few hours," Dolph said.

Cadoc squeezed the minstrel's shoulder in appreciation. "Many thanks. I'll take the next watch."

The twins, Matthew, and I returned to the shelter. Alec slept restlessly, moaning when he stirred. Carys rubbed more painkilling ointment on the skin around the arrow shaft. "What did you learn from the prisoner?" she asked Cadoc.

"He's called Pons. He spewed a lot of foul insults, though not a word about the one who sent him. His accent marks him as one from the Terrapin Archipelago. I discovered a map of Kylemore in a pocket of his tunic."

"How did they find us?" I asked.

"It may be that they're following Prince Brenden," Carys said. "Who sent them? Prince Aiden or someone else?"

Cadoc said, "I've no idea. One thing I know for true. As long as we're with the prince, we're all in danger."

I shifted my gaze from one twin to the other. "Do either of you know the way to Ardara?"

When the situation appears
bleak, do not panic.
~Handbook of the Eyes and Ears of the King

17

JOURNEY'S END

I glimpsed the royal city of Ardara through leafy chokecherry trees that edged the forest. A castle of red stone stood on a distant hill surrounded by a large, walled city. Although the sun was past its peak, it would be many hours before it sank below the jagged cliffs on the horizon. The obstacles that stood between our little group and the king appeared harder to overcome than the thick stone walls surrounding the city.

Since the attack by Pons and his pal, we'd been lucky. Although Conroy didn't recall the directions all the way from Phelips pond to Ardara, at each turning his memory came back for the next step. Since we didn't know who was behind the attacks on the kingdom, we needed to reach King Darren himself. He was the only one we could trust.

During breakfast, we discussed our plan for entering the city. "Why don't you want to seek help from the guards at the city gate?" Dolph asked Cadoc. "Ardara's a large city. It's a fair distance from the gates to the castle. The guards can take the prince, Alec, and the prisoner off our hands."

"What if Prince Aiden *is* a traitor, and he's behind the troubles in the kingdom?" Cadoc replied. "We don't know who's in his pay. We might not make it to King Darren if we run into any of his henchmen. They'd be happy to finish off Prince Brenden."

I asked, "Couldn't you mind brush them? Find out who we can trust?"

Cadoc shook his head. "Nay. They'd notice it. Mind you, they might not know what it was. Even so, they'd feel it, and there's no telling how they'd react."

"What if the guards at the castle won't let us see the king?" the minstrel asked.

"We'll make a racket and they'll bring the king to us. For true, I don't think the castle will be a problem. We have only to pass through the city gate."

Since no one had any better ideas, we decided to go with Cadoc's plan to try to enter the city unnoticed. The dry wood of the wagon creaked as we started our descent into the valley that ran along the eastern side of Ardara. I breathed in the scent of wild roses that hung in the warm, still air.

When we reached the valley floor, our rutted path joined the King's Road and we found ourselves in a stream of people headed toward the royal city. My spirits rose. With such a crowd, we might be able to slip by the city sentries without attracting attention.

The guards waved some people through and stopped others to ask their business in Ardara. Our group stuck to the middle of the road, letting the crowd flow around us. Cadoc drove the wagon while I sat beside him on the high plank bench. Carys made sure Prince Brenden and Alec remained hidden under hay in the wagon's body. Cadoc had cut the arrow shaft that pierced Alec, leaving a short stub sticking out of his skin. Conroy and Pons came behind the wagon. Pons walked with his head down, connected to Conroy's horse by a rope tied around his waist. Dolph and Matthew brought up the rear with the extra horses.

Cadoc had warned Pons to stay quiet. He promised we would plead for mercy for the little man in exchange for his cooperation. If Pons caused trouble with the sentinels,

Cadoc said he would ask for the harshest sentence possible. Pons grumbled, but in the end he agreed to Cadoc's request.

The wagon passed through the city gates without incident. I turned in my seat and watched Conroy and Pons draw even with the gate. They were hidden from the guards' view by a wave of travelers. I held my breath. Assuming they stayed hidden, and Matthew and Dolph were as lucky, our whole party would be in the clear.

Pons and Conroy were a few steps past the sentries, under the arch of the city gate, when Pons shouted, "Help! I'm being held captive. I'm a citizen of the Terrapin Archipelago. Help me!" He struggled against the rope that linked him to Conroy's horse. The horse took a few sideways steps, making Pons stumble. The wiry little man regained his footing and remained upright.

"Here, now, what's this?" one guard asked as he went to investigate. Another guard halted all traffic. Cadoc kept driving the wagon.

Matthew and Dolph still hadn't made it through the gate. I pulled on Cadoc's sleeve. "Stop. We mustn't get separated." He ignored me and kept the horses walking, although at a slower pace.

We heard Pons' light voice rise above the rumblings of the crowd. "They took me." The wretched man pointed at Cadoc, Carys, and me. My mind raced, thinking up an explanation the guards would believe.

One of the sentries shouted, "Stop that wagon!" Cadoc urged the horses to a faster pace.

"Can't stop. Must reach the castle," he said under his breath. Intent on his goal, he saw only the road ahead.

The guards ran after us, lances held aloft. One called, "Stop, in the name of the king!"

We bounced over the uneven cobblestones. A lance pierced the wagon's side, right behind my seat.

Carys yelled at Cadoc. "Hold the horses. You'll get us all killed!"

I grabbed the reins and pulled the horses to a halt. Cadoc turned and saw the thick shaft of the lance stuck in the wood inches from Carys. "Beg pardon," he said, his voice rough. "Don't know what I was thinking." Beads of perspiration stood out on his brow. His hands shook.

Guards, each bearing a sword or lance, surrounded our group. One addressed Conroy. "You're wearing the royal colors. Who are you?"

"My name is Conroy Sommer. I am a personal bodyguard to Prince Brenden of Kylemore."

"Who's this man tied to your horse? Where's the prince?" The man asking the questions was larger than the rest. He was black-haired and bearded, with broad shoulders and bulging biceps. His dark eyes flashed when Conroy hesitated to answer his questions.

When he continued, Conroy spoke haltingly as though he were working the facts out in his mind. He pointed to Pons and said, "He's a prisoner." Next, he pointed to Cadoc. "That fellow tied him up this morning. My memory isn't so good since Kain, he was another guard, got killed. Prince Brenden was injured then. Alec, another guard, was shot with an arrow. These younglings are hiding the prince and Alec under the hay in the wagon." He seemed pleased with himself for remembering all the details. Matthew and Dolph had caught up to us. Matthew stared wide-eyed at Pons. Dolph's mouth was wide open.

A chill settled in my bones. What Conroy said was a string of facts with no explanation about why those things happened. No matter what we kids said, we were doomed. Who would take the word of a bunch of teenagers over that of a royal guard? I was dizzy and moved my feet further apart to keep my balance. I wondered if Kylemore used poison or hanging for the death sentence.

The guards swarmed over the wagon and threw handfuls of hay onto the street. I felt faint. Gray spots danced in front of my eyes. People shouted, but their voices were muffled, as if they came from a great distance. I caught a few words; "treason" and "hangman's noose," then the world went black and silent.

When I came to, I was swaying gently. I heard someone pull shutters closed. The sound was amplified, as if I wore headphones turned to max volume. My head hung upside down. I saw dangling fingers pointing toward the heels of a pair of black boots striding along a dirty cobblestoned street. I was slung over the shoulder of a muscular man who smelled of sweat and ale. My chin itched where it rubbed against his rough tunic. I reached up a hand to scratch.

The man came to a halt. "Awake, are you? You can walk on your own."

He put me down. I recognized him. He was the guard who had questioned Conroy. He grabbed my arm and forced me to walk up the steep, narrow street lined with shops and houses. A pale face stared out of one window, and a curtain twitched in another. A skinny white dog trotted past us. It was eerily quiet. The two of us were the only people outdoors. My legs felt like noodles. Limp, cooked noodles. They wouldn't support me much longer. My steps slowed. He stopped, then tied my hands behind my back with a prickly piece of rope.

Does he really think I'm a threat? "You don't need to do that. I won't cause trouble."

"You've already caused trouble. If I had my way, you'd be hanged at sundown. Lucky for you, it's not my call. We'll see what King Darren has to say about you and your companions. You nearly killed the prince. *Actually* killed one of his guards and injured more."

"It wasn't like that. If I wanted to kill the prince, why would I smuggle him into the castle before finishing the job?"

"Treasonous brat, you'll hang for your crimes, you hear?" He struck the side of my face with the back of his hand. With my hands tied, I had no chance of breaking my fall. My head smacked against the cobblestones and darkness overtook me once more.

18

AUDIENCE WITH THE KING

I became conscious as I was about to sneeze. The place where I was had the scent of a musty cellar—the cool, stale air was tinged with the acid-sweet odor of mouse droppings. I imagined the sun never reached here and people didn't come here often, wherever 'here' was. Someone had untied my hands. I moved my head a little, and my cheek scraped over rough stone. I was lying on the floor. My face hurt where the guard had struck me, and my head hurt where I'd hit the cobblestones. I forced myself to open my eyes.

I was in a small rectangular cell, with three stone walls and one made of thick vertical metal bars. The cell had two narrow metal cots with thin mattresses and a pot against the far wall that I supposed served as a toilet. The only source of light was a tiny window set high in the wall. Carys sat on one of the cots, tugging the tip of her tail. She regarded me with a level look. "You were out for quite a while."

I viewed her from a cockeyed angle. That made me dizzy, so I hauled myself into a sitting position and drew my knees up. "Why didn't you wake me?"

She let go of her tail and sat on the floor next to me. "It seemed kinder to let you be. I did check you over. Nothing

153

was broken, and you weren't bleeding. I let you rest so you wouldn't worry."

"Thanks. I guess. Where are we anyway?"

"In the royal dungeons."

My head snapped up. "What! We have to get out of here. People in dungeons always come to bad ends. At least in the books I've read. Where are the boys?"

"In another cell. As are Dolph and Pons. We're stuck until they take us to someone in charge."

Swallowing my fear, I asked, "What if they don't?"

"You think they'll ignore people who harbor a prince in the dark sleep? The guards claim we hurt Prince Brenden. The king will want to hang us by morning. Our best hope is to reach Poppa or your grandpa. If they're even here."

This little speech made me sick to my stomach. Not wanting to retch in the small space, I lay down again on the cool stone floor and closed my eyes. Time crawled, but it was probably only half an hour later that we heard heavy footfalls in the passage outside our chamber. I roused myself and Carys and I huddled together, arms wrapped around each other.

I felt helpless and weak as a newborn kitten. Not the image I wanted to portray to our captors. "Hang on," I said and inched away from Carys. "Let's be strong. We're innocent."

"You be strong. I'll pretend," she whispered as a pair of shiny black boots appeared in front of the bars of our cell door.

My gaze followed the boots to trousers that were stuffed inside them, up a tunic with the royal staff insignia, to the black beard and hard eyes of the guard who had questioned Cadoc and knocked me to the ground.

I mouthed "Iron Beard?" and Carys nodded, eyes wide. The notorious guard Rolant mentioned on our first day in Kylemore. My limbs grew weak, remembering his reputation. Then I noticed the breadcrumbs in his beard. I imagined a flock of sparrows hiding in the black tangled mass, darting in and out to feast on the dry crumbles. Much better. He was still dangerous, but not so scary.

He looked us over where we sat on the dirty floor, his eyes gleaming with malice. "Come. You're wanted upstairs."

A second man in the passage rattled a ring of keys until he found the one he wanted and opened our cell door. We scrambled to our feet. As we slipped into the passageway, Iron Beard blocked our way.

"Not so fast." He spun me around, and a wave of dizziness passed over me. He bound my hands behind my back with a length of rope. The other guard did the same to Carys. As he knotted the rope around my wrists, Iron Beard said, "You don't have a tail. Why don't you and that other brat have tails?" My mind went blank. I couldn't think of any reasonable answer.

Carys said, "It was a troodon attack."

Iron Beard raised his hand and slapped her across the cheek, leaving a bright red mark. Carys bit her lip, but not even a tiny yelp escaped her.

"She can speak for herself," the guard growled.

"It was a troodon attack," I repeated, recovering my wits. "We were young and tried to snatch some eggs from a nest. The parents came after us and clawed our tails. They turned red and nasty and had to be cut off. I don't like to talk about it."

"Hmpf," Iron Beard grunted. I couldn't tell if he believed me. The guards shoved us in the small of our backs and we started walking.

At the end of the passage, stone stairs spiraled upward between two curving walls. The guards pushed us up the blocky steps. I shook off Iron Beard's hand and received a harder shove in return. When we reached the top, we found ourselves in a circular hall jammed with people. Matthew, Cadoc, Dolph, and Pons were there, along with a collection of guards.

I was relieved to see Matthew and Cadoc showed no sign of injury. I didn't care what Iron Beard might do to me. I pushed my way through the crowd to them. Matthew was closest. When I reached him, I leaned my head against his chest. His hands were tied behind his back too. He rested his chin on the top of my head. Iron Beard grabbed my arm and snatched me away. Matthew tried to yell at the guard. Since his voice was still weak from Carys' magical healing of his arm, what came out was a froggy croak. He settled for glaring at the burly man.

The glare had no effect on the guard. He led us down one wide passageway after another. Other guards flanked our group. All at once, Iron Beard stopped. I plowed into him and stepped on his heel.

"Sorry," I muttered. The look he gave me was dark and unforgiving.

We were in a wide corridor that ended at a pair of tall oak doors. Iron Beard stepped in front of the doors and spoke to our little band of prisoners. "You'll be meeting with King Darren. One false move and I'll run you through myself." He patted his sword in its scabbard, then nodded to the guards who stood at either side of the doors. They pulled on the thick iron handles, exposing the room within.

I expected to see King Darren sitting on a throne in an elegant chamber with Queen Meara at his side. Instead, I saw richly colored tapestries hung on the walls, comfortable chairs strewn about, and a couple of long tables made of heavy dark wood lined up in the center of the room. One was covered with rolls of parchment. The other held refreshments. My mouth watered at the sight of food; we hadn't eaten for many hours.

The king sat on a raised platform behind a writing table along one long wall. He was slightly built with delicate features and black hair that fell to his shoulders. Another man stood near the parchment-covered table. Prince Aiden. My stomach clenched at the sight of him.

King Darren spoke. "You and your men may leave us, Glendon."

Iron Beard, or rather, Glendon, gaped at the king. "You wish us to go, sire? Beg pardon, these are dangerous criminals, Your Majesty."

"I am grateful for your concern. Tie them together in pairs before you leave. My safety is assured with Prince Aiden and the guards outside the doors." It was a clear dismissal.

Glendon and his men tied me to Carys, Matthew to Cadoc, and a trembling Dolph to Pons before taking their leave. As he tied the rope binding me to Carys, Glendon leaned in close and said in a low voice, "I'll see you back in the dungeons, brat." Bile rose in my throat. I turned away from him as much as the ropes allowed.

When Glendon's party left, King Darren stepped down from his platform and stood in front of us, his hands clasped behind his back. "Younglings, I've been told a little about you and I know your names. However, you two," he nodded toward Pons and Dolph, "are completely unknown to me, and you have all arrived under distressing circumstances. I wonder, can I trust any of you?"

Several of us tried to speak at the same time, and the king raised his hand to silence us. Turning to Prince Aiden, he said, "Brother, what can you tell me of the younglings?"

Prince Aiden walked around our untidy group, making eye contact with each of us. When he finished, he returned to King Darren. "Your Highness, I met them when Brenden and I searched for ruffians in the Great Forest. Unfortunately, the criminals eluded us."

What was he playing at? I started to protest, then bit my lip in frustration at a stern look from the king.

Prince Aiden continued, "When we parted, they promised our gullible young brother they had valuable information for you and begged him to bring them here. I should have trusted my instincts and insisted he return home with me. Sadly, the evidence shows they schemed with these others," he nodded toward Pons and Dolph, "to harm Brenden and his guards."

I could stand it no longer. "That's not true, Your Majesty. We *did* capture the criminals. Prince Brenden is our friend. We'd never harm him."

The king pressed his lips together and considered Prince Aiden and me in turn, as if weighing the truth of our statements.

Prince Aiden appeared ready to contradict me when the doors opened wide. Two people entered. One was a woman I'd never seen before. The other was the baron, Colum Humphrey. Relief flowed through me. If the baron was here, Grandpa must be at the castle too.

Lord Humphrey took three steps into the room and stopped as though he had walked into a wall. "Sire, what's the meaning of this? I know these younglings. I've questioned them and found them trustworthy. Why are they restrained?" He stared at Dolph and Pons. "Who are these men?" The minstrel lowered his eyes. In contrast, the fierce warrior stared back, unblinking.

King Darren passed a hand over his brow and returned to his padded chair behind the writing table. "Colum, much has happened in recent days. I'm trying to sort things out. Skyla," he said to the woman, "it's good to see you." He shifted to face us captives. "Let's start over. Until I've heard your version of events, you will remain bound. My sister, Princess Skyla, has not met any of you before. She will help me judge the truth of your statements. Clear enough?" Our heads bobbed in understanding. She had a kind appearance, but I'd need to hear her speak before making any judgments.

The king said, "Let's begin." He waved a hand at me. "You seem eager to talk. Kallan, is it?"

I nodded, too nervous to speak.

"Begin with the morning you set out for Ardara."

I gathered my thoughts. "The others can verify what I say, Your Majesty. Pons here, is a spy. He attacked us, and Cadoc discovered a map of Kylemore in his tunic. You may not want him to listen to this. Also, he's injured and needs a healer."

King Darren rested his chin on his hand. A thoughtful man. I had hope he would believe me. *Can I avoid telling him where Matthew and I came from?* I didn't want to complicate matters more than I had to. The king was all that stood between us and the gallows.

Making his decision, he called to one of the guards who stood at the oak doors and directed him to take Pons to the healing ward for medical attention. He gave orders to keep him there for later questioning. The little man glowered at me as he was led out.

It took a long time to relate the events of the past few days. Despite my pounding head and dry throat, I didn't stop until I'd told the king all about our travels from the farm to the city gates. I stumbled over my words when I got to the part about the thunderstorm and Kain's death. Willing myself not to cry, I hurried on to describe the rest of our journey.

The king was especially interested in my Far Seeing of Prince Aiden at Phelips Pond and Cadoc's reading of the emotional turmoil that lingered there. A surprised expression and a flash of something else—maybe fear—crossed Prince Aiden's face during that part of my report.

"When Matthew's voice returns, he can give you more details about the attack by Pons and his partner. Our only thought was to get Prince Brenden and Alec to the royal healers and take Pons to you for questioning, Your Majesty," I ran out of words and stopped. I couldn't read the king's reaction. At least he'd listened to everything I said.

He propped his elbows on the desk and interlaced his fingers. "An incredible tale. If it's true, you're a courageous lot. Before I ask more questions about this journey, I have one about the trip to Avonflow when you met my brother, Brenden. You say he caught the criminals. Prince Aiden says they escaped. Explain."

"I'll tell you what truly happened, Your Majesty. May I have something to drink before I start?"

Princess Skyla gave me a sympathetic smile. "Darren, I believe we can trust them enough to untie them. They must be hungry, thirsty, and exhausted. Can we make them comfortable before we continue?"

The princess had compassion. My spirits rose a little. The king agreed with her suggestion, and the princess and Lord Humphrey untied our ropes. I rubbed my wrists, relishing the freedom to move again. We were allowed to sit in the cushioned chairs that lined the map table and have a drink of cider before I returned to my narrative.

I told the king how we'd discovered I was a Far Seer, then described our encounter with Prince Brenden and his message for Prince Aiden to meet us in Avonflow. I described the capture of Morcant and the other criminals, the way Warehouse Man died, and how our two groups had split up at Prince Aiden's request. The whole time, the rusty-haired prince watched me like a hungry bird peering at a bug.

King Darren addressed his brother. "Aiden, I haven't heard these details before. Is the lass lying?"

Prince Aiden's lip curled in disgust at the king's question. "Your Majesty, did I bring any men back to Ardara? If Brenden were able to speak, he could vouch for me. As it stands, you must decide whether to trust the word of the brother you've known since his birth or that of a foreign-born youngling."

So, the king does know we came from another world. The baron must have told him about Earth. I was happy I didn't have to explain our origins along with everything else. King Darren stroked his beard while he regarded the prince. Our lives depended on whom he believed. I twisted my silver ring around my finger, waiting for the king to speak.

The tall oak doors burst open. A thin young man clothed in cobalt blue robes entered. His soft leather shoes made a shushing sound as they passed over the stone floor. He stopped directly in front of the king and bowed low.

When he straightened, he spoke loudly enough for everyone to hear. "Your Majesty, Prince Brenden is awake."

Beware the raptor in the family tree.
~Royal Guidebook of Diplomacy

19

EXPLANATIONS

Our future and our lives depended on what Prince Brenden said. If he backed up his brother's version of events, we were doomed. If only I'd been able to capture Ethel before she escaped through the tunnel. I would never forgive myself if we rotted in prison here or worse because I'd let a chicken outrun me.

The twins and I clamored to see the recovering prince. Matthew gazed at the king with pleading, puppy dog eyes. King Darren shook his head and we fell silent. He spoke to the young man who had brought the news of the prince's awakening. "Thank you, Apprentice Blyth. Tell Prince Brenden I'm on my way."

The apprentice turned and raced back to the healing wing, his robes swirling behind him. King Darren wasted no time. "Aiden, Colum, with me. Skyla, please stay with our visitors. If Brenden is well enough, I will send for you and the younglings." He ordered one of the guards stationed outside the door to watch over us until he returned. With that, the three men left.

I stared after them. *Is Prince Brenden well enough to remember what happened in Avonflow? Why didn't Prince Aiden bring the criminals to the castle? Why did he lie?* My sketchbook had been taken away, and anyway, the drawings of the criminals were so faded now I could barely see them. I wasn't sure I remembered their faces well enough to make a new drawing that could work. I sank into a soft chair and rested my aching head against the thickly padded back.

When I looked up a while later, Princess Skyla was speaking to a messenger. Wrapped in my own thoughts, I hadn't noticed him enter. He was a slender, curly-haired boy, probably around ten or eleven years old. He stood with his head inclined toward the princess and listened intently to what she said. They weren't close enough for the rest of us to overhear. Soon the boy straightened, and Princess Skyla said in a louder voice, "Many thanks, Thane. Off you go." He bowed and then walked to the oaken doors with his back straight and chin held high.

When Thane left, the princess turned to Dolph and the rest of us. "It will be a while before we have news of Prince Brenden. Please, take some refreshment."

Dolph poured a goblet of blackberry wine and put two fruit tarts on a small silver plate. Appearing as comfortable as he might in his own home, he strolled to an armchair near a window overlooking a straw-colored lawn and settled in. The rest of us followed his lead and grabbed silver plates, heaping them high with food.

A furry head peeked out of the princess' dusky pink overtunic, pointed nose sniffing the air. Princess Skyla stroked the speckled mammal that emerged and set him on the floor. "It'll soon be dinnertime, Breckin," she murmured. He was small enough to fit in her hand. Russet dots were sprinkled across his tan fur like confetti tossed in the air that stuck wherever it landed. The bright-eyed creature tilted his head left, then right, and limped over to Matthew, holding one back leg off the floor.

"Why's he limping?" Matthew croaked. The creature wound himself around Matthew's legs and climbed awkwardly onto his lap. Matthew ran his hand over the furry body, feeling gently around the injured leg.

"He sprained his leg in a fight last night," Princess Skyla said. "He shies away from most people. He must trust you." She didn't take her eyes off of Matthew. *She doesn't trust him as much as Breckin does.*

Breckin laid on his back, purring softly, his eyes locked onto Matthew's. Grinning, Matthew gave his hairy chin a thorough scratching. A grin spread across my face too. "Matthew has a way with animals. Always has," I said.

"I can see that," the princess said. "I am fond of animals myself, so we have something in common."

Carys sat next to Matthew and examined Breckin's leg. "I concocted an ointment," she told the princess. "It could heal his leg in a few days." She gently probed the sore muscle. "If the guards didn't throw my belongings away, you can have it. It's in my medicine bag."

Cadoc said, "She speaks true. She's used it on me. It heals muscles faster than any salve from our village healer."

"Thank you," Princess Skyla said. "Your possessions are safely locked away. I'll direct someone to find the ointment."

I took a closer look at Breckin. "That's an eomaia," I said. "Kain and I saw one in the woods. He told me you have one for a pet." I sighed, remembering the fallen guard. "Kain was a kind man. It was awful when we lost him in the lightning storm."

"It must have been a terrible experience. I'm grateful you and Matthew knew enough magic to save my brother and Conroy."

"It wasn't magic, it was CPR . . . uh, something we learned in a class."

She gave me a soft smile. "Whatever you did, it worked."

Strangely, the princess reminded me of my mother right then. I traced the knot pattern on my ring and then poured a goblet of cider from a silver pitcher on the refreshment table.

Carys asked, "Princess Skyla, while we're waiting for the king, could we see our poppa, that is, Beli Whelan, and David Webbe? David is Matthew's grandfather."

The princess frowned. "I know of Beli Whelan. I sent Thane, the messenger, for him. David Webbe . . ." She shook her head. "I don't know anyone with that name."

My sip of cider went down the wrong way. My eyes watered and I coughed. Cadoc slapped me on the back.

In the middle of my coughing spell, Beli came into the room. His silver hair was tied back in a ponytail with a strip of leather. He was as lean and hard-muscled as I remembered him. When he spotted the twins, he opened his arms wide in greeting. Carys' eyes were bright, and she grinned as she hugged him. Cadoc gave Beli an extra-long handshake, holding on with a firm grip.

Beli bowed to the princess and looked Dolph up and down, taking in his colorful clothing. Cadoc introduced him to the minstrel and we all sat around the map table. The baron and Beli were both at the castle. Even if he was wounded, Grandpa should be here too. I couldn't wait any longer to find out what had happened to him. "Excuse me, where's Grandpa? Is he all right?"

Beli put a hand to his head. "Has no one told you? We took an eastern route and were ambushed. Your grandfather was seriously wounded. Not to worry, he'll recover. The closest healers were in the Pannmordian Valley, so we took him there for treatment."

Matthew sucked in his breath.

Beli must have sensed our panic because he said, "David will be all right. I left a guard with him, and the Pannmordian chief is an excellent healer. When he's strong enough to travel, my guard will bring him here. Let your mind be at ease."

My mind wouldn't be at ease until we were home again. We talked for a long while. Beli filled us in on their interrupted journey to Ardara and answered all our questions. Next, it was our turn.

As we finished describing our journey to the royal city once more, we heard King Darren's voice outside the oak doors. I was instantly on edge and wondered if Prince Brenden had convinced the king of our innocence or if he believed Aiden's lies. The doors swung open, revealing the king and Lord Humphrey. Prince Aiden was not with them. The baron strode to the refreshment table and filled two goblets with blackberry wine. He gave one to the king and took a long sip from his own cup.

Princess Skyla said, "Darren, what did you learn about Brenden?"

"The healers say he'll recover fully. He supports Kallan's version of events in Avonflow." The king seemed to suppress a smile. "Aiden claims what he meant to say was that the vandals eluded him alone, not Brenden as well. On their journey here, Aiden's party stopped overnight at Phelips' pond. The criminals escaped, taking one of Aiden's bodyguards with them. I understand why he chose to keep the embarrassing incident quiet."

King Darren became serious. "If you harbor any suspicions of my brother, you may let them go. He is a man with more pride than is good for him, that is all. Countless generations ago, our family came to rule after a civil war. My brother has no desire to destroy all we've built." I squirmed under his intense gaze.

He continued, "We interrogated Prince Aiden's other guards. We're left with one conclusion. The bodyguard helped the vandals escape and fled with them." The king eyed us while he sipped his wine.

"Where is Aiden now?" Princess Skyla asked.

"He and I questioned the prisoner Pons in the healing ward after we spoke with Brenden and the guards. Pons is from the Terrapin Archipelago. The land where our dear Aunt Mairsil fled to long ago." His voice dripped with sarcasm when he referred to Mairsil as their "dear" aunt.

"I'm convinced she lives and is behind all our troubles. Mairsil's the real traitor in the realm. She's turning vulnerable subjects, including Aiden's guard, against me. What's more, she's sneaking troops into Kylemore, and I believe she plans to take the throne by force." He set his half-empty goblet on the table. "Therefore, Aiden is preparing for battle. I have named him Captain of the King's Army and am sending him with troops to meet the challenge before it grows too large. Let's hope we're in time."

King Darren ran a hand through his wavy black hair. "I'm hungry enough to eat a whole agrio. Let us go to the great hall."

For once, I had no interest in food.

*Use magic sparingly. It drains one's
energy, and the result may
not be what is desired.*
~Master Ailfrid
The Art and Discipline of Magic

20

CASTLE DAYS

Once King Darren decided we hadn't caused Prince Brenden's injuries or Kain's death, Queen Meara insisted the four of us be moved from the dungeons to spacious rooms on the third floor. She even invited us for a private midday meal in her sitting room. To prepare, Carys and I used her routine for shiny hair, brushing it one hundred strokes. We all wore our best clothes, but we were shabbily dressed compared to the queen, who wore an emerald green gown trimmed with ivory lace. She was a friendly woman in her mid-twenties. Servants brought us bowls of pea soup and plates of moa steaks, baked potatoes, and thick slices of dark bread. We finished the meal with fruit tarts and cups of honey-sweetened tea.

The queen entertained us the whole time with stories about the king and his siblings. When we finished eating, she laid a hand on her stomach, and I gaped at the small mound in her middle.

A dimple brightened her smile. "Aye, it's true, Kallan. I am with child."

"I'm sorry. I didn't mean to stare. When are you due?"

"Due?"

"I mean, when is the baby expected to be born?"

"Ah, I understand." She gave her stomach a pat. "We expect the birthing day to be in the new year, in the middle of Meteri's first cycle."

"We'll be back home by then. I hope it goes well. Do you have any names picked out?"

"Some evenings, I present possibilities to the king as a distraction from the attacks. We have had some lively discussions on the matter."

I laughed, imagining the serious king arguing over baby names with the cheerful queen.

Beli stayed in Eyes and Ears quarters in the bailey, the large courtyard within the castle wall. He and the twins agreed to remain in Ardara until Grandpa had his audience with the king. After that they would escort us "Earthers" back to the gateway on the Dunstan's farm, assuming the king was convinced we were no danger to Kylemore. A fine plan that unraveled like a fraying rope.

We'd been in the castle for five days, waiting for Grandpa to arrive. It had rained continuously for the past three days. The drought seemed to be over, whether by natural or magical causes. The twins, Matthew, and I stayed indoors as much as possible. Within a few days, Matthew recovered from the side effects of Carys' magical healing of his arm and his voice returned to normal. More bright spots: Alec had been healed from his arrow wound, Conroy's mind was improving, and Prince Brenden was nearly well.

This morning, rain colored the world pewter gray. Inside the castle it was always cool, no matter how warm the temperature outdoors. During the day, bright fires burned in deep-set fireplaces. Servants banked them at night, and within a few hours the rooms grew cold. It was barely past dawn. The fire in the room I shared with Carys had not been built up, so I lay in my thick feather bed, cozy under the plump coverlet, and reviewed the events of recent days.

The day after our arrival in Ardara, the boys joined Carys and me in our room and I did a Far Seeing of Grandpa. He was lying on a pallet in a room with a domed ceiling. Fabric or animal skins were stretched over a skeleton frame made of slender poles crossed with thin strips of wood. Cadoc pointed to the wall of the dome. "That's a Pannmordian dwelling, for true. Poppa told me about them once after he traveled through their valley." It was reassuring that Grandpa was where Beli said he'd be, but he didn't seem to be in good shape.

"He's thin," Matthew said. He ran a hand through his hair. "What's that on his leg?"

Carys squinted at the picture. "It may be a splint. I think his leg is broken." Seeing Matthew's expression, she added, "He may not be as bad off as he looks."

Matthew put his face close to the drawing, his nose inches above the page. "He looks pretty bad."

Using magic and seeing Grandpa's condition made me cold and nauseous. I let go of the sketch, pulled up a stool in front of the fire, and stretched out my hands to the warmth. "Wish we could go to him. Sorry, I can't do any more viewings of him for a while." I hugged myself. "Carys, will I ever get the hang of this? Seeing visions still makes me sick."

Her tail switched back and forth. "With most magic, the greater the distance the magic's used, the more energy it takes. If you wanted to see Poppa in the bailey it wouldn't make you so ill. Most of your Far Seeings have been over many miles. No wonder it takes a toll."

Before we left the farm with Prince Brenden, the twins' parents had loaded us up with supplies, including weapons. Marilea gave us each a belt knife, and Rolant made us carry daggers and slings. We spent time during the sunny days at the castle being tutored by Cameron, one of Princess Skyla's guards. He had a crooked nose and a patient manner. We learned to defend ourselves with the knives and daggers and did target practice with the slings.

Later in the week, when the rain kept us indoors, I gave Carys drawing lessons and she taught me about healing plants. We also hung out in the royal library and leafed through books such as *The Art and Discipline of Magic, Elementary Guide for Healers, Chronicles of Kylemore,* and *Natural History of the Western Kingdoms.* Quite a different selection of titles from the libraries I'd visited in New York.

Matthew and Cadoc played countless games of Nine Men's Morris. They moved stones around a board that Cadoc drew with charcoal on a page from my sketchbook. Back home, Matthew played the game on the Internet. He'd told me it dated back to the Roman Empire. It had an equally long history in Kylemore, where they called it Merelles. The boys were evenly matched. As soon as one game was over, the loser would insist on a rematch.

Sometimes Carys and I watched them play, keeping quiet so they could concentrate. At those times, my thoughts drifted to the summer cabin we'd left so abruptly a few weeks ago. As strong as the lure of magic was, and as much as my stomach still flip-flopped when Cadoc grinned at me, I longed for home. Since coming through the gateway in the cliff, I'd felt like an outsider. It was the same lonely feeling I'd had whenever I went to a new foster home.

We learned our way around the castle and grounds with the help of the young messenger, Thane. Although he was always polite, the light of mischief lit his eyes, and I soon discovered he was a first-rate snoop. He let slip the word "Earth" and a few other bits of information that were supposed to be private. One day when he and I met in an empty hallway, I confronted him.

"How do you know so much about us, Thane? Our origins are to remain secret."

"I know, Miss Kallan. They are secret. I haven't told so much as a kitchen mouse about you."

"Keep it that way. You haven't answered my question.

How'd you find out so much?"

He squirmed under my glare. "I might have overheard Mister Beli and the king talking one day. After I delivered some refreshments to them in the king's study. I . . . I had trouble shutting the door, see, so some of their words floated out to me."

"I do see. From the amount you know, you had a lot of trouble shutting that door. Is there any reason I shouldn't go straight to King Darren about this?"

He paled. His blue eyes were wide. "Please don't, Miss Kallan! He'll send me to an orphan house."

"You're an orphan?" My mood softened.

"Nay, miss. My da's dead. My ma . . . She can't take care of my sister and me. Mary, she's my sister, works in the kitchens. She's ten, a puny little thing. I'm eleven. Being older, it's my job to take care of her. King Darren lets us stay here 'cause he and our da were mates in university."

"I'm sorry about your parents. You're lucky to live here with King Darren."

"Aye, miss, we are." His chin trembled. "Honest, I haven't told anyone 'bout you. I . . . I like collectin' things. Feathers, interesting stones, bits of wind-worn wood. And information," he added reluctantly. "I keep it to myself, most times. In this case, I thought you'd tell me about where you come from if I let on that I knew a little." He stopped and studied my face. His lower lip quivered.

I let him fret for another minute. When tears brightened his eyes, I said, "All right. I won't go to the king. At least not yet. In return, you must promise to keep quiet about us." I crossed my arms. "And, you can give us information about Kylemore and the people here. I'm not asking you to tell secrets, only help us learn our way around. Can you do that?"

His head bobbed up and down, and a grin split his face. "Sure, I can, Miss Kallan. Be happy to."

"Better make it official." I spit in my hand and held it

out to him. He spit in his and we shook on the deal. I sent him on his way with another warning not to discuss our pact with anyone else except the twins and Matthew.

After the evening meal, anyone who was free gathered in the great hall to hear Dolph sing and tell tales. We went every night. Visiting noblemen and their wives, as colorful as a flower garden in their fine clothes, sat on benches. Liveried servants, finished with their work for the day, stood along the edges of the room. A few times Thane and his shy sister, Mary, sat with us. Dolph played his lute while he sang. When his voice tired, he played the flute. Sometimes the instrumentals made me as happy or sad as his stories and songs.

A gust of wind rattled our bedroom windows and disrupted my reverie. Carys stirred in her sleep. I burrowed deeper under my covers, turning my thoughts to yesterday.

At breakfast, Cadoc had abruptly stopped buttering his bread, his knife held in midair above the slice. He blinked a couple of times. "I've got it," he said, then returned to buttering his bread.

"Got what?" Carys asked.

"An idea. I think I know a way we can go to see your grandpa. We'll ask Poppa to take us. If he's willing, King Darren ought to agree to the plan. Since Poppa's in the bailey, we'll have to send him a note with a messenger. The Eyes don't allow anyone who's not one of them or an official of the castle near their quarters."

"Do you think Beli will agree?" I asked, already packing my bags in my mind as a bubble of hope filled me. Matthew stirred his tea, listening.

"Why not? He'd rather be in the thick of things than passing the time playing chess and Merelles."

Carys put a hand on her brother's arm. "Are you sure that's all he's doing—passing the time? He hasn't been to see us in days. Maybe he's too busy with Eyes and Ears business to take us." A needle of doubt stabbed me, and I stopped my mental packing.

Cadoc brushed off her concern. "It would have to be serious business for him to turn us down. I'll send a message." He rose and flashed his bright smile at me as he passed. His brown eyes sparkled. The bubble of hope slid past the needle of doubt and grew once more.

We spent the day preparing for the journey. We mended clothes, inspected our weapons, and made a list of supplies to take. I was lighthearted for the first time in days. By the evening meal we had not received a reply from Beli, so we went to the great hall to hear Dolph's entertainment as usual.

He played an especially catchy tune near the end of the evening. Carys and I sang it, to the boys' annoyance, all the way to our room, across the hall from theirs. We climbed two flights of stairs and trooped to the end of a long corridor leading back from the main part of the castle. Carys and I laughed as we sang, walking arm in arm. As we finished the fourth or fifth rendition, we entered our room. Our laughter cut off as soon as we crossed the threshold. At the sudden quiet, the boys followed us into the room to see what silenced us.

Beli sat on a low stool at the side of Carys' bed. His face was expressionless. "Take a seat, all of you." He gestured to the bed. We sat in a row like a flock of birds on the castle turret.

"I received your message, young'uns. Bad news, I'm afraid. I've been called away. I leave at dawn."

Carys spread her arms in appeal. "Poppa, why now? Can't you take us to the Pannmordian Valley first?"

"Nay, lass. Two cities on the western coast are under attack. I can't say where I'm headed. I'll travel through Ardara on my return journey. If you're still here, we'll return to the farm together. If the Earthers are cleared to go while I'm away, I trust you and your brother can get them safely home."

He considered us for a minute. "You four have been tested these past weeks. Cadoc, you're more like your da every day, thinking things through before you act. Carys, you're taller than your ma and as capable as she is. Next month, you'll both turn sixteen. Fully grown and ready to take your place in the world."

He narrowed his eyes at Matthew and me. "If memory serves, David told me you two turn sixteen the following month. As different as Betherion may be from Earth, I expect sixteen-year-olds in your world can shoulder every bit as much responsibility as they do here."

Matthew made a sound that could pass for agreement. He tended to withdraw into himself and say little when he was disappointed or sad. Not knowing how to answer, I nodded. I was pretty independent at home. Here I felt like a child.

"I am sorry to disappoint you," Beli said. "But the war is heating up, and we know David is in good hands. The Pannmordians are a caring people. Lord Humphrey's guard will bring your grandfather here safely. Now, I must go." After a flurry of hugs, handshakes, and bits of advice to "stay alert" and "keep out of trouble," he left.

"Cadoc, where do you think he's truly going?" Carys asked. "One of the coastal cities? Or the Terrapin Archipelago?" Worry creased her brow.

"The Archipelago is where Pons hails from, so it's possible." Cadoc studied her. "What's wrong? You're not usually so concerned when Poppa goes away."

"The Archipelago is where Ma and Da were ambushed when they were Eyes and Ears.

Cadoc put a hand under his sister's chin and lifted her face so their eyes met. "That was a long time ago. Poppa's tough. He can take care of himself."

She gave him a shaky smile. "You're right."

Cadoc nodded and released her chin.

Carys sighed. "I only wish we could have gone to see

David. I wish the war was over."

"When that day comes, we'll celebrate," Cadoc said. "For now, we'd best get some sleep."

The boys left, and Carys and I got into bed.

I'd woken this morning to another day of rain, my head heavy from a restless night. All my bright hope had fled with Beli's departure. Once again, the four of us were on our own. My thoughts were cut off by a knock at the door. Carys woke and stretched while I went to see who disturbed us so early in the day. The boys tended to give a hard, quick rap. This was a polite, "sorry to wake you" kind of knocking. I wrapped a blanket around my nightclothes and cracked open the door. Thane stood there, dressed in his crimson and gold uniform.

"Good morning. I have a message from King Darren."

"Give us a minute." I closed the door and we hurried into our clothes. When we let Thane in, he stood at attention to deliver his message.

"King Darren wishes to speak with both of you. He said you should eat breakfast first. Best make it a quick one." Thane blushed. "The quick eating is my idea, not his. I have given the same message to Cadoc and Matthew. I shall lead you all to the stables as soon as you are ready. The king waits for you there."

"Do you know what the king wants?"

"No, Miss Kallan. But—"

"But, what?"

"I, um, heard him talking with Princess Skyla. They . . . they want to send you far away."

The wisest rulers give care and
protection to all their subjects,
in every corner of the realm.
~Calder Fionn
Chronicles of Kylemore

21

CALL FOR AID

*A*fter a hurried breakfast, we followed Thane through the castle grounds, wrapped in cloaks to keep out the rain. It had lightened to a fine drizzle, and the air smelled clean.

"Thane," I said, "Do you know where the king wants to send us?"

"No, Miss Kallan. I didn't overhear that part."

"Crap. Say, have you ever heard who's behind the attacks on the kingdom? Could it be Prince Aiden?"

Thane stumbled. "Prince Aiden! Nay, miss."

"Are you sure?"

"Aye. He's full of anger, Prince Aiden is. My da told me the reason. Prince Aiden's da, King Raghnall, never cared for him much. Think how that would make a person feel."

"Why didn't Raghnall like him?"

"Prince Aiden reminded King Raghnall of *his* da, King Delaino. See, King Delaino was a warmonger who loved to show his power. Raghnall was a peaceable man. Then Prince Aiden was born, and it's like the Living Spirit put King Delaino's essence into Prince Aiden's body. You know what a person's essence is?"

"I have an idea. Could be what we call a soul. Or maybe a personality."

He shrugged. "Maybe so. What I'm sayin' is, some folk get their anger out in words, some by fightin'. Prince Aiden's the fightin' kind. For true, he's loyal to the kingdom. My da said so, and he never lied, may the ancestors hold him close." He put a hand on his heart.

After a minute, Matthew said, "What about this Sorceress Mairsil? Who's she?"

A shudder ran through Thane's thin body. "She was a nasty one. My da told me 'bout her. Mairsil was Raghnall's elder sister. Power mad, she was, and there was no reasoning with her when she got a notion in her head. She was a powerful sorceress, too. Could control the weather and all." He took a quick peek at the sky. "Being the oldest, Mairsil should've been queen when King Delaino died. Her da didn't trust her though, so before he died, he made her brother, Raghnall, king instead."

The family history was confusing. It also sounded important. "Do I have this straight? King Delaino had two children, Mairsil and Raghnall. When Delaino died, Mairsil wasn't allowed to be queen. Prince Aiden's a war lover like his grandfather Delaino, and he's a loyal subject."

"Aye, Miss Kallan. You Earthers are quick learners." He gave me a sweet smile, a reward for being a bright pupil.

I still had my doubts about Prince Aiden. There was no point in discussing them with Thane. Instead I asked, "What happened to Mairsil?"

"No one knows for sure. Word is, she died in the Terrapin Archipelago. 'Though I overheard some nobles talking the other day. They think she's still alive."

"And she wants to take the throne by force from her nephew, King Darren?"

"So they say. That's all I know, Miss Kallan. For true." He blew out a big breath.

Cadoc said, "Enough of politics and history. I've heard

Princess Skyla has a menagerie attached to the stables. She has some rare animals. Even a dragon, if the rumors are true." He looked at Thane for confirmation.

Rainwater slid off Thane's blond curls and ran down his cheeks as he nodded. "Aye, she keeps all manner of beasts. Even a dragon."

"How did you hear about it?" Matthew asked Cadoc.

"From Fergus of all people. He delivers cloth to the castle for his da on occasion and has a habit of sneaking around where he doesn't belong. He claims he saw a dragonet, a baby dragon, last time he was here."

We crossed a wide expanse of sodden grass. By the time we reached the building, our cloaks were damp, and our trousers were soaked halfway to our knees. We entered a stable made of wood and stone and proceeded down an aisle lined with stalls. Torches blazed in sconces fastened to posts. A handful of people clustered in a stall at the far end. Princess Skyla's honey blonde hair shone gold in reflected torchlight.

We walked quickly to join them. As we passed the enclosures, I stole glances at the animals within. Some were bulky shapes covered in fur or feathers; most were horses. We walked too quickly for me to identify the others. None remotely resembled a dragon.

Princess Skyla bent over a dinosaur lying on a bed of straw. Two strangers stood along the back wall. Focused on the dinosaur, they ignored us. King Darren knelt by the creature's side, stroking its long neck. The slender-bodied dinosaur was as long as the king was tall—about six feet— with short front legs and muscular thighs. It looked to be the same species we saw in the woods where we picked queen's button mushrooms with Cadoc on our way to Avonflow. That one glowed with health. This dusky green and brown animal didn't seem strong enough to live through the day. Its whispery breaths mingled with the sound of rain dripping off the slate roof.

What's wrong with him?" Matthew asked, dropping to his knees next to the king.

"Her," corrected Princess Skyla. "We don't know. Her name's Merc. She was a gift from a baron in the southern part of the kingdom. I've never taken care of her kind before. She was healthy when she came a few weeks ago. She's weakened with the passing days."

"What've you been feeding her?" Matthew ran a hand over the body, pausing when he reached her side where it rose and fell with her breath.

"Dead rats," said a harsh voice. I took a closer look at the strangers at the back of the stall. The speaker had a light brown ponytail and a heavy brow. His hazel eyes were spaced farther apart than normal, and his nose was broad and flat. All the other people we'd met in Kylemore wore clothes made of cloth. This man was dressed in animal skins. He reminded me of pictures I'd seen of Neanderthals. His silent companion was at most three feet tall and wore leather pants and a matching vest over a soft shirt. He had pointy ears, like a movie elf. I whispered to Thane, who stood next to me. "Who are those two?"

He raised himself up on his toes and whispered back, "The tall one, Hackett, is a Pannmordian. The quiet one, Nairne, is a wood elf. All intelligent races must send representatives to work in Ardara to show their loyalty to the king."

"Has she been eating much?" Matthew asked Hackett.

"No. She drinks, yet she eats little."

"The shape of her teeth and her muscular legs say she's a hunter," Matthew said. "I think she needs live food." Hackett scoffed and Matthew repeated his point. "She wants to catch her dinner."

"Do you have any ideas to help her?" Princess Skyla asked Matthew.

Matthew thought for a bit. "Can you make a broth with animal bones? Caino, or mice, or whatever's available?

She's so weak, she'll need to be hand-fed for now. Once she's stronger you can try her on small live animals."

"Fetch a bowl of the rat broth we feed Yaeno, if you please, Hackett," Princess Skyla said. The Pannmordian left the stall. "Yaeno's one of our furred creatures, and rat broth is one of his favorite meals," she explained.

Cadoc stood outside the stall, directly behind me. "Merc has a strong will to live," he said.

"How do you know this?" King Darren asked.

Cadoc shrugged. "I cannot say, Your Majesty. I can sense her life force and . . . her emotions. It is also true," he added, "that she's not afraid. She trusts those here to make her well." He shifted his feet. "Especially Matthew."

The king appraised Cadoc with a steady eye. We waited in silence, listening to Merc's soft breathing until Hackett returned with the broth.

Princess Skyla motioned to the wood elf. "Nairne, please hold the bowl." She spooned the mixture down the dinosaur's throat. When it was half gone, Merc opened her red eyes and fixed them on the princess.

"Let's leave Hackett and Nairne to the feeding," said King Darren. "We have business to conduct."

The princess spoke to the men with quiet authority. "Feed her broth every two hours. Tomorrow give her live mice. If she's not ready, continue with the broth until she is strong enough to hunt."

"Aye, m'lady," said Hackett.

King Darren noticed Thane whose gaze was still on Merc. "Thane, thank you for bringing the lads and lasses here. You may return to your station."

Thane's chin dropped toward his chest, then he squared his shoulders and bowed. "As you command, sire." He turned on his heel and walked back the way we'd come.

We followed the king and princess to a well-ordered tack room. King Darren took the only chair. The rest of us settled on tack boxes and blankets on the floor.

King Darren said, "Matthew, thank you for your assistance. Kallan, I'd appreciate it if you'd do a Far Seeing of Prince Aiden." The king wouldn't have asked if it wasn't important. Still, I didn't want the chilliness and nausea that followed a Far Seeing. Stifling a groan, I pulled my sketchbook from an inner pocket of my cloak and set it on top of a tack box.

"Do you need help recalling Prince Aiden's features?"

"No, Your Majesty. I already made a drawing of him for Prince Brenden." I opened to the sketch.

King Darren picked up my right hand and held it in his. "This ring, it's an unusual design."

I forced myself to keep my fingers relaxed in his grip. "My mother gave it to me. It's been in her family for generations." His comment made my scalp prickle. Nuala had been interested in the ring too. *Why does it attract their attention?*

He smiled. "It's a beautiful heirloom." He let go of my hand, then set my sketchbook on his lap. "You've captured Prince Aiden's intensity and, I must say, a certain . . . attitude I recognize." He cleared his throat. "Well done."

Princess Skyla smiled at her brother. "It's true. It's a good likeness. Aiden's toughness makes him a good choice for Captain of the King's Army."

"Aye." The king turned to me. "Let's see how it goes with him."

I took the sketchbook and held it loosely. I blotted out the stable sounds and let my mind fill with the prince. The drawing slowly changed. Details filled in the background, and Prince Aiden's pose shifted. He was inside a tent. He leaned over a map and pointed to a spot in the middle of the parchment. Four knights with serious expressions were gathered around him. A patch covered one knight's eye, and his face was swollen. Another had a bandaged hand. From the shape of the wrappings, it looked like he was missing a couple of fingers. After a minute or two, Prince Aiden dismissed the knights. Once they'd left, he scratched his bushy red beard and studied the map again.

King Darren touched my wrist and I let the sketchbook drop onto the tack box. The picture quickly reverted to a somewhat faded version of my original drawing. The king stared at the portrait. "Thank you, Kallan." Although his next words were spoken in an undertone, we all heard him. "The situation grows more serious every day."

"It is fortunate that you put Aiden in charge of the army when you did," said Princess Skyla.

"Aye, it is." He turned to us kids. "I've received a request for aid from a distant community. There is much sickness among the people and animals. I will send Princess Skyla and Prince Brenden, along with Healer Oran, to assist them. Oran is the best healer I have available. I can't spare more because of the battles up north and in the coastal cities. I intend to send you four as well."

How do you tell a king that you don't want to do his bidding? This was no quick task like the Far Seeing. I'd never agree to leave the castle when Grandpa lay injured in the Pannmordian Valley. We needed to go there, not some remote village overrun with sickness.

"Carys," King Darren said, "you're a healer-in-training, and I've heard tell you've discovered new ways to use plants for injuries and illness. Cadoc, your unique talents would be valuable. This is a diplomatic mission as much as a medical one. As your king, I request you two accompany Princess Skyla and the others."

He addressed Matthew and me. "Even without magical talent Matthew, you know animals and how to help them. Kallan, your ability as a Far Seer may be useful on the journey. In addition, your quick thinking after the lightning strike saved lives. I know in my bones you two should go with the party."

We remained silent.

The king continued. "I am wary of coincidences. There

must be a reason you turned up here at this time. Perhaps the Living Spirit has sent you in aid of Kylemore. You have exhibited rare talents and shown loyalty to my family. The kingdom needs you." He rested his hands on his knees as though in no hurry for our answer.

I broke the silence. "Your Majesty, where is this community that requests help? Who are they?"

There was a distinct twinkle in his eye. "Ah, didn't I say? The people of the Pannmordian Valley."

A squeak escaped me. Cadoc and Carys stared at each other, then she spoke for them both. "We are honored to serve, sire. I ask only that a message be sent to our ma and da, so they know our whereabouts."

"Consider it done," answered the king. "Earthers, since you have not yet pledged fealty to me, I will not order you to go. You may remain here if you choose. However, with Healer Oran's help, it's likely your grandfather will be strong enough to return with you when the mission is over."

Matthew half rose from his seat in his eagerness to respond. However, I spoke first.

Rubbing my ring for courage, I said, "We too, are honored to serve, Your Majesty. In exchange for our assistance, I ask for an escort of knights or mages to the gateway on the Dunstan's farm when this is all over and Grandpa is well."

King Darren closed his eyes and rubbed his forehead.

"It's been weeks since we came through the cliff," I said. "Conditions may have changed. We might need help getting home."

The king opened his eyes. When he spoke, his words twisted my insides. "Lass, I will send an escort with you. Know that it may not do any good. The gateways are unpredictable and once closed, they cannot be reopened by even the most powerful mages. I ask you to leave yourself open to the possibility of remaining in our world."

Magic springs forth naturally
from the essence of the mage.
Its strength cannot be predicted.
~Master Ailfrid
The Art and Discipline of Magic

22

OF FLOWER AND FLAME

*K*ing Darren left the stable, and an uncomfortable silence settled on the group. My heart raced when I thought of the gateway to Earth closing before we could reach it. I recalled ordinary activities I'd taken for granted. *Riding my bike to school on paved roads. Going to the movies. Surfing the Internet. Watching television with Grandpa and Matthew. Texting on my cell phone.* A flood of homesickness overcame me. The sooner we could get to the Pannmordian Valley, the greater our chances of going home. I rose to return to the castle and pack.

Princess Skyla stood and brushed bits of hay off her skirt. "Before we prepare for the journey, I wish to show you my menagerie and conservatory." Her face glowed with enthusiasm. I frowned, wondering if she hadn't heard King Darren's words. We didn't have time for a tour.

Cadoc stood between the princess and me, shuffling his feet with indecision. Matthew wore a pained expression. I knew he wanted to travel to Grandpa. All the same, he could never pass up a chance to see new animals. Carys' ebony tail quivered with excitement. She grinned at the princess. "Wonderful. We've heard you have some rare animals here,

Your Highness . . . and plants too. We'd be pleased to learn about them."

"I've collected plants from all over Kylemore and a few specimens from neighboring kingdoms. As for the animals, many have been injured or abandoned. When they're ready, I return them to the places they naturally belong. I keep only the ones that cannot survive on their own in the wild lands. This is a refuge for them."

I had no choice but to follow the others.

As I'd noticed earlier, horses filled most of the stalls. An assortment of wildlife occupied the rest. One creature looked like a rabbit-eared horse with spreading toes. It was droopy and listless. Princess Skyla discovered an infected sore on its leg. There was a rough bit of board on one wall that could be responsible for the injury. Carys suggested using her herbal cream. Princess Skyla called for the stable hands overseeing Merc to come. She instructed Nairne to collect the cream from the castle and Hackett to fix the rough board.

We moved on to other stalls. Most of them had features of Earth mammals, although I didn't recognize many. Yaeno, the rat-broth-loving animal the princess mentioned, was about three feet long, and judging by his tooth-studded snout, carnivorous. An animal that resembled an opossum sat on a thick branch in another stall. It had a long tail, bony shoulder blades, and huge eyes for hunting at night. One creature, a cross between a dog and a crocodile, had a shallow stone basin for bathing. Matthew took time to study each one. He asked me to sketch them. I glared at him and he backed down, saying, "Another time, then." Even though they were a fascinating collection, I was eager to pack.

When we'd seen all the animals, the princess opened a door at the end of the aisle, and we entered a lush, emerald world. We stood in a long, rectangular greenhouse with a translucent peaked roof that appeared to be made of flattened animal horns fastened into wooden frames. Large sections of the walls were filled with panes of pale green, slightly wavy glass separated by lead bands. The room was bright, and beyond the grassy area outside, I could see a leafy woodland. It must have cost a fortune to build a room with so much glass. I forgot my hurry to prepare for our journey. Somehow this humid, green room made me feel at home.

"Welcome to the conservatory," Princess Skyla announced with pride. "Look around while I care for the plants."

Carys turned in a circle, oohing and aahing at the variety of plants. Ferns in a dizzying range of green shades filled one corner. Some stood a foot or two tall while others had lacy umbrella fronds that loomed over our heads.

Bushes in clay pots lined a long table. One bush was covered in bright pink flowers that had a bitter medicinal odor. Crimson flowers as large as dinner plates grew on another. Carys walked over to a bush with yellow buds. One flower was fully open. "Kallan, have you ever seen such a pattern on a rose?"

I joined her by the plant. "No. The swirls are cool. It's like someone drew waves with a cinnamon stick on butter."

Carys ran her fingertips gently over the buds and glossy, dark leaves. "I wish we were staying here a week or two longer. I'd love to see it when all the flowers bloom." She laughed and let her hand drop to her side. "Poppa always tells me, 'Buds open in their own time, they'll not be forced by the will of a lass.'"

"Beli's a smart man," I said. A movement caught my eye and I pointed. "The dragonflies are as big as my hand! Their wings remind me of stained glass."

Carys grinned. "For true. Like the glass panels in the royal library."

Princess Skyla wandered up and down the rows, watering, pinching off dead leaves, and loosening soil with a tiny rake. The boys were at the end of the room, staring through a door that led outside. They were deep in conversation, talking in low, excited voices. Cadoc's tail thrashed back and forth and his hands waved around as he spoke.

Carys and I went to see what was so interesting. A black metal cage sat in the middle of a large circle of dirt, which the morning's rain had turned to slick mud. Here and there large rocks poked up through the ground. I pressed my palms to my cheeks when I saw the animal inside. "What's in the cage?"

The princess regarded the turquoise reptile that clung to the iron bars, its head reaching two-thirds of the way to the top. "That beauty is our dragon. When Prince Brenden last visited our sister, Princess Eolande in the north, he discovered him. The dragonet was weak, near death. He'd been abandoned. My brother named the little fellow Simon and brought him here to recover until he's old enough to be on his own." She dusted her hands off. "Prince Brenden has a way with dragons. In fact, he's the only one who can get close enough to touch him."

Matthew stared at the scaly animal. "How long before Simon can be set free?"

"Not until he's fully grown. For a dragon, that's about ten years. We believe Simon is roughly eight months old. We'll move him to bigger enclosures as he grows."

"Can we see him up close?" Cadoc asked.

"Aye, as long as you are careful. He is too young to control his fire. That's why we've removed the grass around the cage." Princess Skyla opened the conservatory door and led the way to the dragon's enclosure.

"Fergus spoke true," Cadoc whispered to me as we walked outside.

Simon's length from head to tail was about the same as Willow, but that's where the similarity ended. The dragon's scales shone iridescent in the sun. His tongue flicked out to sense the air, and he warbled a melody of notes as he studied us with large, midnight blue eyes. I hung back. I don't trust young creatures, human or otherwise—they're too unpredictable. Besides being young, this one had an expression of arrogance that made me as timid as Thane's little sister, Mary.

Cadoc circled the cage about two feet away from it. As he walked, he kept his gaze on Simon. He must have been reading the dragonet's emotions. Simon paced inside the cage and watched Cadoc in return. If he continued on the same path, I saw that Cadoc would soon trip over one of the exposed rocks.

I shouted, "Watch your step!"

Too late.

Cadoc's boot came up hard against the rock and sent him sprawling on the ground. The dragonet shot a brilliant orange jet of flame through the bars. Cadoc yelped and rolled to a seated position. He held his left hand against his chest. "Living Spirit, he burned me!"

Carys, Princess Skyla, and I ran to him. The princess helped him up, and Carys took his hand in hers to see the damage. A red streak the width of a finger ran up the back of his hand and arm, halfway to his elbow.

"It's not too bad," Cadoc said. "I think we can let it heal naturally." He snatched his hand out of her grasp and waved his arm back and forth, letting air flow around it.

Carys scanned the plants at the edge of the forest. She hurried to a fat-leaved succulent similar to aloe, without the thorns. She tore off a few leaves, then squeezed their juice over the burn. Cadoc's tight face muscles relaxed.

I scooped up some soft mud and layered it on top of the plant juice. Carys gave a satisfied nod at our first aid treatment. "That should do until we get back to the castle. Then you can soak it in cool water. If the cook lets me in the kitchen, I'll make an infusion of oak bark to prevent infection." Cadoc muttered thanks to both of us, and we turned to leave.

We all stopped short at the sight of Matthew and the dragon. I bit my tongue to keep from shouting as I'd done with Cadoc. Simon's head and neck were through the bars of his cage, and he crooned while Matthew stroked the scales on top of his head. Matthew appeared equally happy. Princess Skyla stood a few feet away, watching with a wary expression.

"Prince Brenden isn't the only one who has a way with dragons," Carys said. Matthew patted Simon on the head, then we returned to the conservatory.

Princess Skyla said, "Matthew, will you revisit Simon before we leave for the Pannmordian Valley? I think he's been lonely without Prince Brenden. No one else can get close to him besides the two of you, and I want my brother to rest until we leave."

"No problem, Your Highness. I'll come back tonight and before breakfast."

Halfway through the conservatory, I stopped in front of the butter and cinnamon rose bush and gasped. All the buds were fully open. A spicy scent hung in the air. I called out to the others. "Amazing."

Matthew frowned. "Why so excited?"

"You and Cadoc were watching Simon, so you didn't see. Only one flower was open when we were in here earlier. The bush was shorter, too. It came up to my shoulder, and now it's level with my chin."

Carys stepped back from the plant and thrust both hands behind her back.

I remembered how she'd run her fingers over the buds. "Carys, you said you can't force the buds open, but you must have." Judging by her pale cheeks, she was as surprised as I was.

"No one has that power," she said. "I—all I did was run my fingers over it and imagine it in full bloom." She stretched out her hands and turned them over as though she'd never seen them before. "I did grow chilly when I touched it. Princess Skyla, is it possible to speed up plant growth?"

"Some mages can increase a plant's natural healing qualities. I don't know of any who can hurry the growth of a plant."

Carys crossed her arms and stood with her chin jutting. "Then I couldn't have made it grow. If I had this skill, I'd have seen it before." I was amused by Carys' reluctance to accept her new talent. She reminded me of myself after my first Far Seeing. Neither of us wanted powers we didn't understand.

"That's not for certain," Princess Skyla said. "Magical talent often reaches its full strength as the mage becomes fully grown. Training can help one learn to control the raw power once it reveals itself. That's what mentors and the professors at university do."

She cut a flower from the bush with her belt knife and considered the blossom from all sides. "Only magic could make this plant grow and bloom with such unnatural speed. Carys, this must be your doing. We need to inform the king and Prince Brenden. It's not clear how we can use your skill to our advantage. All the same, it's another rock for our sling."

Suddenly, I was impatient to get on our way. Every time I started to get comfortable in Kylemore, my understanding tumbled like pieces in a kaleidoscope and the pattern was completely new. I'd been at peace when we entered the conservatory. After the rose bush sprouted unnaturally, I couldn't get that comfortable feeling back again.

Princess Skyla glanced at Cadoc cradling his burned hand, his tail drooping. "Come," she said. "It's time for tea."

Not all spells can be undone.
~Master Ailfrid
The Art and Discipline of Magic

23

BY TRAIL TO THE VALLEY

*T*he king met with his advisors in the conference room the next morning, so Queen Meara saw us off. She wore a thin woolen cape with the hood drawn up to shield her from a light mist. After Carys and I checked our saddlebags, she gave each of us a parcel wrapped in cloth.

"I had the cook prepare honey cakes," she said. "There are enough for all of you." The heat of the honey cakes soaked through the cloth. I sighed with pleasure and breathed in the fragrant scent of toasted oats.

"Many thanks, Your Majesty," Carys said, taking her parcel. "We'll hand them around before we leave. They'll keep the chill off until the sun breaks through this mist."

The queen smiled briefly then smoothed her skirts. "My husband has been distracted in recent weeks," she said. "It is vital that Kylemore remain united in the face of these attacks. Some subjects who have suffered from the drought, ruined fields, or poisoned water are siding with the rebels. They demand the impossible of the king." She clasped her hands together. "Pockets of rebellion have appeared from the southern coast to beyond the Kintare Woods in the north. Know that King Darren—that we both—are grateful for your willingness to go on this mission. It is one less worry on his mind."

Carys said, "As our local healer, Nuala, says, we are

happy to use our gifts in service to the kingdom."

"I don't know how much help we'll be, but we'll try," I said. "Matthew and I are eager to see Grandpa, too. Please thank the king for sending us."

Queen Meara nodded and went back inside. We distributed the honey cakes, then mounted our horses, and the journey to the Pannmordian Valley began.

We could see the effects of the kingdom's troubles in the villages we passed through. The lack of rain had stunted the growth of vegetables and herbs in kitchen gardens and the oat and wheat crops in the fields. When the drought ended, the frequent, heavy storms took out a lot of the plants that had managed to hang on. The villagers were quiet, hollow cheeked, and unfriendly. Princess Skyla and Prince Brenden thought it better that we keep to ourselves and camp out in the woods outside of the settlements.

"I thought the water was poisoned," I said one day when the twins, Matthew, and I sat around the fire after the evening meal. "We've been drinking from the streams all along the way."

"The streams here are clear," Cadoc said. "It's the Lowri River and Lake Carlow that are tainted, as well as the River Catriona that flows south out of the lake all the way to Avonflow. Folk for hundreds of miles depend on the rivers and lake for water and fish. It's been hard on them. I heard Prince Brenden's guards talking about it. The king doesn't know how or where the poison is getting into the water."

In the afternoons we had free time. When it wasn't raining, the four of us would play checkers, chess, or Nine Men's Morris, or we'd tell stories and compare Kylemore with upstate New York. Except for the unfamiliar birdsong and the routine tasks that Carys and Prince Brenden carried out with magic, such as lighting campfires, it could have been a camping trip back home. Sometimes I even forgot about the threat of the gateway closing up before we could reach it.

As relaxing as the journey was, three days into it I found myself scowling at Healer Oran's back as he swayed in rhythm with his broad, black horse. The healer had been rude to us kids ever since we'd left the castle, and he'd chewed us out that morning for being too noisy at breakfast. I hadn't resented anyone so much since Billy Hamlet teased me incessantly after my mother died. Billy's taunts had mirrored my own thoughts at losing both of my parents: "You're a nobody. No one cares about orphans."

One day, I'd had enough. When he called me a nobody at lunch, I punched him in the stomach. While he caught his breath, I hooked a foot behind his ankle and brought him down. With tears streaming down my face, I straddled him and pummeled his chest. "That's not true," I shouted over and over again. I hoped if I said it enough times, I'd believe it myself.

Billy had a rough home life and had always been jealous of my close-knit family, but there didn't seem to be a reason for Healer Oran to treat us like nobodies. Maybe all kids annoyed him.

We stopped riding for the day, and I dropped my thoughts of Billy and the healer to help make camp. The guards cooked stew over the campfire, using vegetables from Ardara and small game they killed earlier in the day. There were biscuits to soak up the juice and wild berries for dessert. Everyone was in a good mood, even Healer Oran.

After supper Alec asked Prince Brenden, "Isn't the headwater of the Lowri River somewhere around here?"

"Aye. There's a spring that flows from an outcropping up that hillside. I planned to go there after the evening meal. We don't know where the poison's getting into the water. I want to see if it's fresh at the source. The location of the spring isn't well known or easy to access. Still, it bears checking out."

I asked, "Can we come with you, Your Highness?" Ever since I saved his life, I was extra-protective of the prince.

Healer Oran replied to my question before the prince could speak. "That's not necessary. There's nothing you could do there."

"In truth, Oran, I think it's good for them to come," Prince Brenden said. "They've proved their worth more than once. You may be surprised at what they can do."

"As you say, my lord," the healer said with a stiff nod in the prince's direction. When Prince Brenden turned away, Oran scowled at me. Once he turned around, I stuck my tongue out at him. Childish, I know, yet satisfying.

Leaving a couple of guards at camp, the rest of us hiked to the spring while the light still held. Long shadows stretched across the leaf-littered forest floor. In a quarter of an hour we came to a place where water bubbled out from the space between a set of massive granite boulders.

"This is the start of the Lowri River? The one that runs into Lake Carlow?" Carys asked, looking from the spring to the thin stream that burbled down the mountain and out of sight.

"It's hard to believe the lake and the wide river have such a humble beginning," Princess Skyla said.

Cadoc stood on one of the boulders, massaging his temples. The burn he got from Simon was healing, although it was still bandaged. I walked to the base of the massive rock. "Are you all right? Is your burn hurting more?"

He dropped his hands to his sides and peered at me through narrowed eyes. "It's not the burn. I smell something unnatural." He scanned the forest floor. "The ground has a dark cast to it. Can you see it?" All I saw was the brown of soil and decaying leaves in every direction.

Prince Brenden addressed the group. "Does anyone else smell anything unusual? See anything strange?" The casualness of his voice was contradicted by his completely still body. No one spoke up except Matthew, who said he smelled only the woods, and that their scent and appearance were normal.

"Describe what you smell and see, Cadoc," Prince Brenden said.

Cadoc surveyed the area from his perch atop the rock. "The air tastes bitter. The ground's darker near the rocks, blackish. It's gray further out. A few feet out from the spring the color is its usual brightness." He shook his head. "No, that's not right. The forest floor appears as it should everywhere, the darkness is layered on top of it like jam over bread."

"This must be the source of the poison for the lake and the river," Prince Brenden said. "It appears you can detect magic through your senses as well as emotions and intentions. Your talent may be growing." His hands were on his hips, his usual pose when he was deep in thought. "Oran, do you know what spell's been cast? Is there a counterspell to block it?"

Healer Oran placed a hand on one of the massive rocks and bent his tall frame low to sniff the water. He straightened and tugged on his pointy gray beard. "I believe I know the cause, my lord. As to a counterspell, there is none." Then he gave a sad smile. "That is, a spell exists, yet we can't make the potion it requires. If we had the ingredients, we could simply stuff a bagful down the spring and recite the incantation to counteract the poison."

"What's needed for the potion?" Carys asked.

"No one has the ingredients, Your Highness," he said, addressing the prince.

The prince crossed his arms. His voice was tight. "Healer Oran, what does the potion require?"

The healer pulled a small, green, leather-bound book from a pocket of his cobalt robe, the color worn by all healers. He leafed through the book until he found the page he wanted, then he slid his finger partway down the page. "Here it is, 'Hudor Claen.'" He named half a dozen plants, then closed the book. "The plants can be found in every healer's herb bag. What we don't have is the last ingredient.

Chicken feathers. This is an old spell, written before those birds died out."

"We have feathers!" I jumped up from the fallen branch on which I'd settled. "We brought chickens with us from Earth. Matthew made quills. They're at camp. I'll get them and Carys' medicine bag." I started running down the mountain.

Healer Oran shouted after me, "Halt! It still won't work."

I grabbed onto a slender tree trunk to stop my descent and swung around, glaring up the hillside at the healer. The man was infuriating.

Prince Brenden turned his dark eyes on Oran. "Healer, please explain."

"My lord, the lass may be mistaken about the birds. She assumes they're the same as our chickens. They might be different creatures altogether. Further, the evil that lingers here is the work of a powerful wizard or sorceress. It would take an equally powerful mage to counteract it. I regret neither your skill nor mine are enough to stop the flow of poison. The final reason, my lord, concerns the danger of succeeding."

"Which is?" the prince asked with a hint of impatience.

"If we could manage the counterspell, the effect of the magic would be so large it could attract the attention of whoever poisoned the water."

I was tired of his negativity. "Could? It's not definite they would know of it?"

Oran sneered at me. "One shouldn't take chances with magic, lass. We don't know how far the magic would reach. It's best to be cautious if the consequences are unknown." He shoved the book into the pocket of his robe. "Bah. This is a meaningless discussion. No one here has the strength to cast the spell."

Dusk had fallen while we spoke. The foliage had lost its color, dimming to shades of gray. The prince spoke with decisiveness. "Then we shall push on to the Pannmordian

Valley. I'll send a messenger bird to the king. Perhaps he knows of a mage with strength enough to make the attempt. We'd best get back to camp. I want an early start in the morning."

Although Princess Skyla was older and the diplomat in charge of communication with the Pannmordians, Prince Brenden was clearly in charge of the journey to the valley. He picked up a fallen branch and lit one end by uttering "*Ignis*" while touching the wood with the tip of his wand. He held the torch aloft and led the way.

Cadoc and I brought up the rear. "It'll be weeks before they send anyone here, if they ever do," I said, keeping my voice low. "Think of all the fish dying and the people who need water but can't get it from the rivers and lake. What about the animals that will drink the water and die? Oran should at least attempt the spell."

Cadoc gave my hand a squeeze. "We'll not budge him."

We walked in silence, his warm hand holding mine. I hated to admit defeat. After a few minutes, an idea came to me. "What if *we* gave it a try?"

He stopped walking and dropped my hand. "Blisters! We're not trained mages. We don't know how either of our magic works, not really. I was scared sick by the evil I saw back there. Put the thought out of your mind."

I sighed. "I suppose you're right. That magic must be strong to affect you so much. How do you feel?"

"As if a giant pummeled my head." He massaged the top of his head. "I dare say I'll recover."

∞

We lay in a ring around the ashes of the campfire that night. My mind was in turmoil. Countless villagers and animals suffered every day from the lack of pure water. One of the guards said people were dying in greater numbers each week. We'd seen plenty of desperate villagers on our travels.

The struggles of the past months were etched into their faces as worry lines and downturned mouths. Children were also affected. Many were sallow-skinned and played unnaturally quiet games. Scrawny dogs wandered into our camp at mealtimes, nosing around for scraps. We'd come across carcasses of wild animals who'd died from thirst or poisoned water. Carys said using too much magic could burn a person out so they'd never do magic again. It might even kill them. It felt as though a rock lay on my chest, pressing me into the ground. I couldn't save my mom from cancer, but I might be able to help these strangers. Was I brave enough to take the risk?

I waited until I heard the regular breathing that signaled sleep from my companions. A red crescent Kuklos was the only moon that night, and thin clouds dimmed its brightness, spreading a pale ruby veil over the ground. Alec and Conroy stood guard, their backs to the sleeping circle.

I turned on my side and adjusted my saddlebag pillow. Healer Oran lay a couple of feet away from me. A corner of the "pocketbook of spells" as I thought of it, poked out of his cloak, which he used as a blanket. The book's golden-edged pages glowed softly in the moonlight. It tugged at me like a magnetic pole, north attracting south. I stared at it until my eyes watered, then I gave in and pulled four chicken feather quills from my saddlebag. Next, I slipped out from under my blanket, crawled to Oran's side, and edged the book slowly out of his pocket. It was nearly free when he mumbled in his sleep and shifted his position, pinning my other hand under his elbow. Swallowing a yelp, I slowly eased my hand out and rubbed it until the pain was gone.

Once I'd stored the spellbook safely in my tunic, I crept to where Carys slept, checking that the guards continued to face away from the sleepers. Carys' medicine bag lay next to her head. I picked it up with the softest of sounds and slipped her wand inside my tunic. Next, I moved on to

Cadoc. Crouching low, I covered his mouth with my hand and whispered in his ear. "I'm going to use Oran's spell. Want to come?"

He opened his eyes and blinked a few times. I removed my hand. He licked his lips then whispered, "Are you daft?"

"Possibly. If you want to help, meet me by that thick pine at the edge of the woods. I can't wait for long." I patted his cheek in farewell, then walked as quietly as I could, darting glances at Alec, Conroy, and the sleeping figures. The guards were in conversation on the other side of the camp. It wasn't usual for them to be so relaxed while on guard duty. They must not expect any danger in this part of the woods.

The tattered clouds cleared, exposing Kuklos' curved face, and brightening the wine-colored light to a pale rose. The odors of decaying leaves and fresh pine needles mingled on the soft breeze.

When I reached the first line of trees, Cadoc began to walk toward me. Watching from the shelter of the pine, I saw Alec break off his conversation with Conroy and intercept Cadoc. Not waiting to see what happened next, I turned and plunged deeper into the forest.

Attempt new spells under the
watchful eye of an experienced mage.
~Master Ailfrid
The Art and Discipline of Magic

24

PLAYING WITH MATCHES

$\mathcal{J}$ stowed the feathers and Oran's spellbook in Carys' medicine bag. Then I went a little deeper into the woods to wait for Cadoc. For once it wasn't raining. The moonlight was dim, and needles blanketed the floor, muffling Cadoc's footsteps. I didn't hear him until he was nearly upon me.

"How'd you get away from Alec?" I asked.

"Told him I was still shaken up by the poisoned headwater, so I'd walk a bit." He shifted his weight and studied the ground.

"What'd he say?"

"He warned me to stay close to camp. Sure you want to do this?"

I considered everything Healer Oran had told us. With my limited knowledge, experimenting with magic was as dangerous as a four-year-old playing with matches. Shivering with nervous energy, I hugged myself. "I don't understand why Oran wouldn't try it—maybe he's afraid to fail in front of the prince. Or maybe he's not as good as everyone thinks he is." I shrugged. "If a trained healer can't do it, what chance do I have? Even if it does work, I don't see how the sorceress, or Prince Aiden, or whoever's behind this evil, can possibly know about it."

"How the enemy learns of it doesn't matter. It's still a possibility."

I groaned. "Listen, I have to try. Oran's spellbook—it stuck out of his robe and . . ."

"And what?"

"This sounds stupid. It . . . it pulled at my mind and wouldn't let go."

His tail switched back and forth. "I'm not sure that's a good sign."

"Hey, if we're lucky, we'll save some lives. What's the worst that can happen?"

"I shudder to think. Another thing Alec said. He and Conroy will search for me if I don't return by the time their watch is over. We've got half an hour, three-quarters at the most—less if they discover we're missing."

"Rats. We'd better be quick about it."

The only sound in the forest was the wind sighing through the branches. Soughing, my mom used to call it. Sometimes she and I would lie on a blanket in the backyard on breezy evenings, listening. The memory comforted me, and I rubbed my ring for luck. Cadoc and I searched for a stick to act as a torch. He uncovered a dry, stout one, and I touched Carys' wand to the end of it, saying, *"Ignis."*

This was one spell I was comfortable with. A thrill of excitement ran through me, and I smiled at the flame that sprang up. It was like drawing or painting—I was proud I could do something that others found difficult or impossible. With luck, the water-cleansing spell would work as well as this simple one.

We were about to start up the slope again when I heard a slow flapping of wings overhead. I nearly dropped the torch. "What was that?"

Cadoc put a hand on my arm to calm me. "I couldn't see it well. Relax. It's gone."

Before I lost the little courage I had, I picked up the

pace and kept it up until we reached the boulders where the stream of water started. It was incredible that this was the beginning of the long flow of water that ran through the Lowri River, Lake Carlow, and the River Catriona, reaching all the way to the sea. I sank to the ground at the base of one of the big rocks, as much to let my heart stop pounding as to prepare for casting the spell.

"Let's see the book," Cadoc said. The torchlight flickered on the pages as he leafed through it until he found the one with the heading, *"Hudor Claen."* When he'd finished reading the list of ingredients aloud, he pulled a clean handkerchief out of his pocket and spread the cloth on one of the large rocks.

"Put the herbs in the center."

I handed him the torch and fished around in Carys' medicine bag, holding each packet of herbs in the torchlight to make certain to choose the right ones. When I had everything on the list, I consulted the book. "Hmm, we have to grind them." I tied the cloth into a bundle, then pounded it with a stone until the herbs were reduced to tiny pieces. A pungent odor wafted up, mixing with the scent of decaying leaves.

When I finished, Cadoc consulted the book. "Now the feathers. Stick three of them through the bundle, at right angles to each other." I did so and tucked the fourth one behind my ear. I was conscious of the minutes ticking by. *How much longer do we have before the guards discover us?*

I held the bundle out to Cadoc. "Your arms are longer than mine. Shove it deep between the rocks, so it won't come loose."

He handed me the torch and took the bag, then plunged the length of his unbandaged arm into the burbling flow of water. When the bag was safely lodged in the space beneath the rocks, I squeezed the water from his sleeve.

"Now," he said. "you say the spell."

I studied the words in the dancing torchlight. "Maybe

you should call on the ancestors or Living Spirit. We could use their help."

"To be sure." Cadoc closed his eyes to think up a petition. The breeze had died away and the woods were silent. In the quiet we heard rustling down the hillside, and a jolt of adrenaline flowed through me.

Cadoc's eyes flew open. "No time. They're coming. Say the spell!"

I held the torch above the open pages with a shaking hand. Cadoc wrapped his hand around mine to steady it, and he held the book still. Taking a deep breath, I focused on the spidery writing and read the lines, my voice slipping into a chant:

> *"Purest water, flow from the ground,*
> *Mix with herbs that heal.*
> *Chicken feathers, purge the poison,*
> *Channel away the evil."*

We could hear voices now, although the conversation was too faint to be understood.

"Say it again," Cadoc urged.

I repeated it two more times. Without thinking, I pulled the feather from behind my ear and held it over the water spilling out of the ground. Each time I repeated the spell, my voice grew louder until at the end I was shouting. After the third chant, I opened my hand and let the feather fall into the water.

"What have you done?" Healer Oran wailed. I raised my head, startled to see the group frozen in place behind the healer.

Churning water gushed out of the ground, flowing over the debris of the forest floor. Cadoc grabbed my arm, and we climbed atop one of the massive rocks, away from the torrent. Leaves, branches, and stones tumbled in an ever-widening river of muddy water that cascaded down the mountain. Anything loose was swept away.

As distressed as I was at the flood, part of my mind noted that the flow was headed well west of the campsite, toward a part of the forest we'd already traveled through. I was relieved our horses and belongings were safe. My knees weakened, and I lowered myself to the flat top of the rock. I was cold and nauseous. Cadoc sat and wrapped his arms around me.

All of the others, except two of the guards, had come to the headwater. They gawked at Cadoc and me as though we had unleashed a great evil on the world.

Healer Oran found his voice first. "How is this possible? Mere younglings. It's not possible." His gaze moved from the river of mud to the two of us clinging to each other.

Finally, Prince Brenden spoke. "It appears Earth chickens do match the ones that used to exist here. Younglings, I am grateful for your service to the kingdom; however, you should never have attempted this alone. Do you have any idea what might have happened if the spell went wrong? Besides that, you took Carys and Healer Oran's possessions without permission."

He considered the tumultuous stream flowing downhill. "Oran, why is there so much water?"

"The purity of the chicken feathers draws deep ground water from all around to purge the poison, my lord. The spell will channel it to the sea. Some trees here may soon wither from lack of water. Their roots grow deep, and between the rains, they depend on the water that is stored in the ground."

I hadn't thought of the consequences beyond cleaning the water. *How many plants and animals have I hurt with my action?* Even though I hated to give the healer any credit, he was right about some things.

The prince addressed Cadoc. "Can you sense a difference in the air? Is there enough torchlight to see if a black film still covers the ground?"

The others had brought half a dozen torches with them,

which made a large pool of light around us. Cadoc stood and surveyed the area. He pointed his nose high and sniffed the air like a wild animal. "The black film is gone, and the air smells clean, Your Highness. I believe the ground is clear of the taint."

Healer Oran said, "My lord, if the spell has worked as well as it appears, the river and lake will be pure."

"The kingdom is in your debt," Princess Skyla said. "It is clear that your intentions were honorable. Regardless, you should not have taken the book and herbs without asking."

"Yes, Your Highness." I was grateful for her support, mixed as it was with a scolding. "I'm sorry. The book stuck out of Oran's cloak and called to me in a way I can't explain. Carys, I . . . I'll replace the herbs."

"We'll gather them together," Carys said, her voice sad. "I only wish you'd told me."

I hung my head. She knew the dangers of magic far better than I. If she'd argued against it, I didn't think I'd have had the courage to go through with the spell, so I'd kept her out of the plan.

"Healer Oran," I said. "Punish me. I took the book, not Cadoc."

He glowered at me from under his thick brows. "I fear the enemy will detect the counterspell. As I warned you, the spell is so intense that if the sorceress or her messengers are within ten miles of this place, she will be aware of it. There's nothing to be done about that."

He tugged on his beard. "My greatest concern is that we have in our midst mages who are more powerful than Prince Brenden and myself. Untutored mages. Unpredictable mages. Testing and training, not punishment, is what I recommend. For all four of you."

Goosebumps rose on my arms.

Matthew sputtered. "Me too? I can't even do magic."

"That may be true. Nevertheless, you have an unnatural

210

ability to understand animals. We need to know how deep that understanding goes. I repeat, all four of you."

Prince Brenden agreed. "Testing and training it is. We begin in the morning."

We returned to camp, a silent, thoughtful party. When I stepped out of the fringe of trees marking the edge of the woods, a pterodactyl took off from the thick pine where I'd waited for Cadoc earlier and flew westward toward Ardara and the Terrapin Archipelago. I had a feeling if the sorceress didn't know about the spell already, she would soon find out.

Tread lightly in the dragon realm.
Few are safe in their territory.
~Weylyn Blevins
Natural History of the Western Kingdoms

25

UNEXPECTED ENCOUNTER

True to his word, Prince Brenden began our testing the following morning before breakfast. The camp was in a flat, grassy clearing. The guards prepared the meal by the fire pit in the center while we met with our teachers at the edges. Carys was to be trained by Healer Oran; Cadoc and I were paired with Prince Brenden. Matthew's trainer was Bolin, Prince Brenden's new guard who had replaced Kain.

I was relieved to be taught by the prince instead of the haughty healer or Bolin, who was Kain's younger brother. He and Kain were both serious, and their build and mannerisms were similar. For me, Bolin was a daily reminder of Kain and his tragic death. He also had a habit of bobbing his head like a sparrow eating seeds when he spoke with the princess, Carys, or me. I didn't know how to talk with someone so shy.

Prince Brenden handed me a smooth, slender wand about a foot long from the supply of spare weapons. "Take this. When we return to Ardara, the wandmaker can craft one especially for you. Before we practice spells though, I want to learn more about your visions as a Far Seer."

I tucked the wand away in my tunic and waited for instructions.

"Calm your mind and picture Alec," he said to me. "What is he doing?" Automatically, I swiveled around, searching for the guard.

The prince chuckled. "You can't see him. I've sent him out of the camp. Concentrate as you do with a Far Seeing. Try to reach him with your mind."

This is going to be harder than I thought.

He told Cadoc, "Take a walk. Use your magical sense as well as your normal ones. Make a mental map of the emotions you find."

Cadoc said, "A mental map? I don't follow."

"Do you detect anything that appears different in the ground, or smells different in the air when you sense a mood? You've done this by accident. I want you to do it intentionally."

Cadoc shuffled off like a lumbering bear. His head swung from side to side as he sniffed, nose pointed toward the ground.

I wanted to calm my mind as Prince Brenden suggested. Problem was, I didn't know how. Eyes closed, I pictured Alec as I remembered him from the night before, when we all gathered around the fire pit after Cadoc and I had purified the spring water. Alec and Conroy stood on the other side of the circle, their faces lit by the flickering torch flames. They'd thrown wary glances our way, as though we were dangerous enemies, not friends who'd once saved their lives. The image unsettled me and left me clueless about Alec's location this morning.

I scuffed my boot in the dirt. "I can't do it."

Prince Brenden pursed his lips in thought. After a minute he said, "We'll try another way."

I didn't want to try another way. I wanted to go home where life was dull and predictable. The river formed by the water-cleansing spell rattled me. Performing a spell that big was frightening; it went way beyond lighting a torch or making an air wall. I'd puked twice and spent half the night trying to warm up. When I woke, I was exhausted and weak. *What are the limits of my magical talent? I used it for a good cause last night. Could I harm someone with it again one day, as I had with Warehouse Man?* I no longer knew myself.

Prince Brenden rummaged in Alec's saddlebag and pulled out a pewter mug. He put the mug in my hand and wrapped my other hand around the cup. "Think of Alec holding his mug, drinking from it. Think only of Alec." He stepped aside and fell silent.

Eyes shut, I thought of the friendly, brown-haired guard. The sounds of birds and other conversations in the camp faded away. I was in a quiet space that held only the mug and myself. In my mind's eye I saw Alec.

"He's standing knee deep in a river. Scooping up water and pouring it over his head. Now he's shaking himself like a dog coming in out of the rain." I opened my eyes. "Where is he?"

"I sent him downstream to explore the waterway you and Cadoc enlarged last night." Prince Brenden turned toward the south and whistled a loud bird call.

I stared at the mug grasped tightly in my hands. "Freaky. I only need something belonging to a person to see them in my mind. I don't need a drawing to find them."

Alec came into view on the other side of camp. He shouted, "Did I do well, Your Highness?"

"You did fine."

The guard joined us. He stared at his mug, which I still held.

"I . . . I was warming it up for your tea." I handed it to him.

He turned it over as if checking for leaks. "I see. Thank you." He walked off, holding the cup gingerly.

Cadoc returned. He wasn't a lumbering bear anymore. Smiling as though he were eager to share a secret, he said, "I sense a mixture of emotions, Your Highness. There's excitement, and also fear on the route we took to the headwater last night. For years I've been able to sense emotions that linger in a place. I never saw them before now. I let my mind go loose and drifted into a hazy world of color. The regular colors are there, and others sort of float above the surface like fog."

He rubbed the back of his neck. "Where I sense excitement, the air is orange. Fear is a deep, dark violet. I know it sounds daft." He studied his boots.

"I believe you," Prince Brenden said. "I suspect you and Kallan, and perhaps Carys, have talents we haven't seen in the kingdom for an age. Matthew's acceptance by the dragon, Simon, is also a rare occurrence. We need to discover how your skills work, what their limits are."

Cadoc's tail stiffened, and I rubbed my ring.

"Don't fret," the prince said. "We'll figure it out. Presently, it's time for breakfast."

∞

Two days later, the morning sky was overcast. I rode next to Matthew, listening to the murmur of conversation and twittering of birds. The trees were widely spaced, allowing us to see far into the woods on either side of the path. It was midmorning when I caught a movement in the woods and brought Willow to a halt.

"Matthew," I said when he'd reined his horse in next to mine. "Don't make any sudden moves." I pointed toward the trees. "Dragon."

Matthew sucked in his breath and froze in place.

Alec saw it about the same time I did. "Halt. Dragon to the left," he called.

The others stopped. We were mesmerized by the scaly creature. It was fawn colored and about twice the size of Simon. I got the impression it was a young animal. It spread its leathery wings and stared back at us. Slowly, it walked toward us, flicking its tongue in and out.

I said, "Simon did the same thing with his tongue. I think it's tasting the air. It reminds me of a Komodo dragon from home."

Carys said, "I thought you didn't have dragons on Earth"

"We don't. Not real ones. Komodo dragons are big lizards. No wings or fire. Still, they're dangerous. Their bite is so nasty that even if they don't kill their prey right away, the victim will die in a few days from blood poisoning."

Cadoc nodded toward the dragonet. "Being burned to death might be worse. It's good we stopped, or we might have been attacked from behind."

"How would that creature catch us? It's small and slow," I said.

"I'm thinking of its mother," Cadoc replied. "She must be nearby."

"I forgot about her."

"They don't generally eat people," Carys said. "If the mother shows up and she's hungry, she might go after the horses."

The dragonet was about fifteen feet from the trail. The horses stamped and tossed their heads as the reptile drew closer. Prince Brenden, near the front of the line, turned in his saddle. "Dismount. Hold your horses," he ordered.

"Carys, can you use magic against a dragon?" I asked.

"No. Dragons have powerful magic of their own, besides the fire I mean, and they're highly intelligent. Magic can't save us." Despite the warmth of the day, her arms were covered in goose bumps.

Healer Oran made comical shooing motions, flapping his hands toward the dragonet. A guard flung a stone into the woods, where it thunked against a tree trunk. The dragonet paused, then continued ambling toward us.

A rumbling noise deep in the forest caught everyone's attention. Now my arms were covered in goose bumps too.

"There's Mom," Matthew said in a hushed voice. "She's beautiful."

"I'd say terrifying," I whispered back, unable to look away.

The huge beast tramped through the sparse woods, sunlight glinting off her amber scales. She was far away from us. Apparently, she had good eyesight or a terrific sense of smell because she shifted her gaze between our group and the dragonet. Her wings were folded alongside her body and her tail swished back and forth, sweeping debris to the side, leaving a dirt path behind her. She moved with a determined stride, advancing toward her baby.

"Walk slowly. Stay on the trail," Prince Brenden said in a firm, quiet voice. The line started moving again. The dragonet made trilling sounds like Simon had done. Its mother answered with deep rolling tones. Puffs of smoke escaped from Mom's nostrils.

As she came even with the baby dragon, Matthew handed his reins to me. He took one slow step after another toward the woods. He held a fistful of dried meat strips wrapped in paper which he'd taken from his saddlebag.

"Matthew, no!" I said in a fierce whisper, reaching for him. I caught only air. My heart thumped in my chest. Cadoc took one step toward Matthew then stopped, fists clenched at his sides. The others watched in silence.

Matthew flapped a hand at us to keep us from following. He walked in a low crouch, pulling the wrapping from the meat. When he'd freed it from the paper, he tossed the dried strips to the dragonet. They scattered, landing in a wide area near the creature.

Both dragons halted their advance, their tongues flicking in the air. An instant later, the baby pounced on the pile of meat. After staring at Matthew for a few moments, Mom turned her attention to the food as well.

Still crouching, Matthew backed away until he rejoined us. I handed him his reins, and the prince signaled the group to start moving. One guard took up the rear, to make sure the dragons didn't come after us. An unnecessary precaution. Their sole interest was the meat Matthew had given them. I tore my gaze away from the dragon pair, hoping Matthew's offering would last long enough for Mom to forget she'd seen us.

*Be sensitive to the needs
and customs of others.
~Royal Guidebook of Diplomacy*

26

PANNMORDIAN VALLEY

*T*here were no signs of the dragons for the rest of the journey. Healer Oran, the guard Bolin, and Prince Brenden coached us on our individual talents during breaks. In the evenings, Princess Skyla educated us about the Pannmordian people, their history, culture, and politics. It was pretty dull stuff until she told us how they came to be in Kylemore.

"Legend says, in an earlier age, a band of Pannmordian hunters, men and women, came here through a tunnel of stone in pursuit of an animal. When they tried to return home, the tunnel was gone. They searched for many weeks. It was not to be found. They settled in a valley filled with caves and have remained there ever since." I stared at her, struck by the similarity to our own entrance to the kingdom.

The princess held my gaze for a bit before continuing. "They still have the domed skull of the beast their ancestors hunted. It's a revered relic with large, curving tusks. They call it 'Great Beast.' There is no similar creature in Kylemore or the neighboring kingdoms."

"Wooly mammoths used to live on Earth," Matthew said. "They had domed heads and curving tusks. Could be the same animal. Maybe the Pannmordian ancestors were

221

some of our Neanderthals. There aren't any more Neanderthals on Earth, but Hackett resembles drawings I've seen of them."

"It's possible," Princess Skyla agreed, as she poked the fire, sending a spray of glowing sparks into the inky sky. "It would explain why the Pannmordians have no tails."

What if our gateway closes up too? As always, I pushed that thought to the farthest reaches of my mind and then turned my attention back to the history lesson, which continued late into the night. My head buzzed with fatigue when we curled up in our blankets around the fire pit.

On the tenth day of our journey, we entered a steep-sided valley. A wide river flowed through a lush pasture. Pine trees and willows lined its banks, and wildflowers littered the grassland in a dazzling array of bright colors.

I scanned the valley to get a feel for the place. The north slope was covered in dense forest. On the south side, lots of dark caves broke up the gray rock face. Tent-like domes were scattered around the valley floor, spewing smoke from cook fires through openings in the top. The domes were made of animal skins stretched over some sort of frame that held them up.

"Where is everyone? We need to find Grandpa," Matthew said.

"Indoors, out of the heat?" Carys suggested.

She and Matthew had sat together by the fire the night before, talking quietly long after the rest of us had gone to bed. I'd fallen asleep to the rise and fall of their voices. Ever since Cadoc and I had purified the water on the mountain, Matthew spent more time with Carys than us. It made me sad; I wanted us all to be friends again.

"We'd best announce ourselves," said Princess Skyla. She whistled a trio of notes, waited the span of two breaths, then repeated the sounds. An answering call pierced the air, coming from the closest dome. A stocky man and two muscular young women came out, all three dressed in animal skins. The man held a tall spear upright by his side. I saw no weapons on the women, but I was sure they were armed too. They stood still, watching us closely as we rode up to them.

"Greetings, Princess Skyla, Prince Brenden," said the stocky man when we dismounted. He bowed, and the females curtsied. As sturdy as the females were, their movements were graceful.

"Good morning," replied Princess Skyla. "This is Bearach," she said, indicating the man. "And Isla and Senga." They were all tailless and similar to Hackett, with thick bodies, brow ridges, receding chins, and long arms.

Matthew said to Bearach, "Please take me to the hut where my grandfather is staying. His name is David Webbe. He was hurt and brought here to recover."

Bearach shook his head. "I am sorry, child. David is not here. He left days ago with the baron's guard."

"How can that be? He had a broken leg," I said, my voice rising.

"His leg was healing. The guard of the baron made a frame to protect it. In that way, David rode upon a small horse. He wanted to reach King Darren quickly, the sooner to take you home to your world."

Princess Skyla's brows rose at his final words. So, the Pannmordians knew we weren't from around here. Conversations were easier when we didn't need to hide who we were. I wondered if some of the Pannmordians would want to come to Earth with us. Probably not. They'd been here so long that Earth, if it was their home world, was ancient history to them.

"How did we miss him?" Matthew asked Prince Brenden.

"There are several trails that lead from this valley to Ardara. They must have taken a different route." He reached out a hand to touch Matthew's shoulder. When he noticed Matthew's grim expression, he let his hand drop.

"Matthew, I am sorry he's gone. It is good he has recovered enough to travel. Do not be concerned. He will wait for us at the castle."

It would take us two Betherion weeks to travel back to Ardara. I hoped Grandpa stayed at the castle. He might decide to return to the Dunstan's farm after talking with the king. We could spend months chasing each other around the kingdom.

Matthew stuffed his hands in his pockets. I tugged his sleeve to get his attention, then spoke quietly so the others wouldn't hear. "Want to go straight back to Ardara? Maybe they'd let us go with a guard."

"No. It's safer to stay with the prince and princess. When there's time, maybe you can do a Far Seeing, make sure he's okay."

I was relieved Matthew wanted to stay. I wasn't eager to come across the dragons again with only one guard to protect us.

When the princess finished exchanging greetings with the Pannmordian trio, Prince Brenden, Cadoc, and Matthew went with Bearach to tend to the sick moas. Isla and Senga led Princess Skyla, Healer Oran, Carys, and me to the domed hut they'd emerged from. The guards split up; two went with each group and two remained with the horses.

Senga pulled back an animal skin flap on the large hut and we filed in. Close up, I could see the frame was made of saplings and bone. Around the edge of the dim enclosure, a dozen or more people lay on mats on the floor. A rock fire ring took up the center of the room. Smoke rose through a hole in the dome's peak. A large woman, decorated with feathers, sat on a low stool near the fire stirring a fragrant stew in a large pot.

Princess Skyla knelt in front of the woman on the stool and lowered her forehead to the ground, stretching her arms out in front. Carys and I followed her example.

"Greetings and good health to you, Leader Doileag," the princess said. When Carys stayed silent, I did too. I peeked under my elbow at Doileag. A shell pendant dangled from a leather thong around her neck, and streaks of auburn paint slashed her forehead and cheeks.

"Greetings, Princess Skyla," Doileag said, her voice strong and deep.

The princess rose, and Carys and I did the same. I was confused. This valley was in Kylemore, so Princess Skyla's family ruled over the Pannmordians, yet she treated Doileag the same as she would the ruler of another kingdom. Then again, with their legend of coming from another world, I figured the Pannmordians might not be as loyal as the rest of King Darren's subjects.

After Princess Skyla made the introductions, she got straight to the reason we had come. "Your message said there is much sickness in the valley. What can you tell me?"

The old woman put the stirring spoon on a rock near the pot and rose. She held herself like a queen. "Many have fallen ill with fever, chills, coughs. They have aching bodies, headaches, tiredness the likes of which I have never seen. First the birds were sick, now the people. Many moas have died. Eight of our people are dead."

She touched the shell pendant with her fingertips then spoke to Oran. "You are a healer. Can you stop this evil?"

He crossed his arms. "We will need to see the ones who are ill. There are some in our company who know much about animals. Together we will search for a cure." A diplomatic answer, I thought. Encouraging, without promising anything.

I wanted to take precautions so we wouldn't catch whatever disease had sickened the Pannmordians. "May I speak, Leader Doileag?"

"What would you say, child?" She regarded me with open curiosity.

I explained that at home, we tried to avoid sneezes and

coughs, and we washed our hands often to prevent caretakers from getting ill.

"Are you a healer in your world?"

"No, I am not. Still, I have learned much from our doctors, that is, our healers." Better not to mention they couldn't save my mom.

After some discussion, Doileag agreed to my methods. I asked for hot water and soap to wash our hands between patients. The fire had too much heat, so Healer Oran magically warmed a bowl of water to a comfortably hot temperature. Doileag provided us with chunks of soap, and we scrubbed up. As a precaution, I tied my handkerchief around my face, covering my mouth and nose, and made the others do the same. We went from patient to patient in pairs, Carys with Oran, and I with the princess.

We checked for fevers, problems with breathing, and poor skin color. One little girl on a woven mat, covered with a thin blanket, coughed several times and moved her legs and arms restlessly. I felt her forehead. Her skin was hot and dry, her eyes glassy with fever. She moaned and grabbed my hand, holding tight. Doileag came over to soothe her.

"Be calm, child Mela. All will be well."

Isla spoke to Doileag. "Shelter Rock, she needs water and a cool bath."

Shelter Rock? I wondered where that name came from.

The old woman laid her hand on the girl's cheek and nodded. "Aye, the fever burns strong in her."

Mela's condition reminded me of the hours I'd spent by my mother's bedside in the months before she died. Then I remembered the twins' little sister, Annilea, who got sick and never recovered. I wondered where Mela's parents were. They must be worried about their daughter. It's hard enough to lose a parent. It couldn't be any easier to lose a child. Mela squeezed my fingers, and I promised her I'd do what I could to make her well.

Isla filled a clay bowl with water and together we ran cool cloths over Mela's feverish body, doing our best to keep her sleeping gown dry. All the while, she held my hand and kept her gaze on my face. Isla held a gourd of water to her lips, but Mela wouldn't drink.

"I have an idea." I snatched up a clean cloth from a nearby pile, dipped it in the gourd, then squeezed drops into her mouth. It was like feeding a sick bird. Doileag brought a bowl of soup and a small carved wooden spoon to me.

"Come on, Mela, you need your strength." I put my arm under her back to prop her up. Spoonful by spoonful, I got the broth into her, along with a couple of pieces of meat. Isla and I cooled her with wet cloths again and patted her dry. When we were finished, she fell into a deep sleep. I soaked my hands and arms in Healer Oran's bowl of hot water longer than usual before going on to the next patient.

After all the sick people in the dome had been cared for, we cleaned our handkerchief masks in the hot water and went outside to talk. Carys asked Healer Oran, "Do you know what the illness is? They're much sicker than they should be if it's only a cold."

"You speak true, on both accounts." He stroked his pointy beard.

I said, "I think it's the flu."

The healer frowned. "Pardon?"

"Influenza. Matthew and I had the flu last winter. Same symptoms—fever, headache, cough, everything. It was awful. It took a couple of weeks to get back to normal."

"Some of these people are dying," Healer Oran pointed out.

"People die from the flu too," I said.

"How are the birds connected?" Carys asked.

My eyes stung from the smoke of the cook fire. I rubbed them, which made it worse. "That, I don't know. Matthew might have an idea."

"Let's ask him," Princess Skyla said.

We found him and the others by the fence that enclosed the moas' pasture. I explained what was wrong with the people. Matthew agreed it sounded like the flu.

"What about the birds?" I asked. "What's wrong with them?"

He shrugged. "I don't know. It's pretty bad. You can see for yourself, they're zombies, staring into space."

I felt a stab of pity for the creatures. Their feathers were ruffled instead of laying smoothly along their bodies. Some of them stumbled and staggered around. Others stood still with their heads drooping. Tears welled up, and I wiped them away with the back of my hand.

"Cadoc, do you sense any dark magic here?" Prince Brenden asked.

Cadoc sniffed the air. Then he cocked his head to one side and eyed the pasture. "Nay, sire. I cannot detect any magic. Their illness must come from natural causes."

Matthew said, "Bearach says they won't eat or lay eggs."

"Do you think this," I swept my arm, taking in the collection of ill birds, "could be connected to the sick people?"

Matthew studied the mountains that bordered the valley, considering. "Pipit, I think you're onto something. Remember when we studied diseases in biology? Some can be passed on to humans from animals. With avian flu the birds often get sicker than people."

My heart swelled with gratitude for his quick agreement. "That could be it. The moas got it, then passed it on to the Pannmordians. Flu must be new here. No one seems to know about it. At home, bird flu passes from birds to people, rarely from person to person. I guess that's another difference between our worlds."

The others had listened to our discussion with frowns, ear pulling, chin rubbing, and blank expressions. Now Healer Oran raised his hands in protest. "Illness spreads from birds to people? Impossible!"

"It was 'impossible' to cleanse the mountain water," said Prince Brenden. "Perhaps we should hear them out."

Matthew gave me an encouraging smile as I twisted my silver ring around my finger, thinking how to explain diseases so it would make sense.

I cleared my throat. "We learned in school that a lot of sickness is caused by tiny living things we call germs. They're so small you can only see them with powerful tools. Usually, they affect one kind of animal, or only people. Some germs can make animals sick, then the animals can give the germs to people and make them sick too."

Matthew said, "On Earth, lots of different animals can make people sick. Pigs, for example, and insects like mosquitos and fleas."

"We don't have those creatures here," Princess Skyla said. "What can you tell us about this illness?"

I said, "Flu's spread by liquid that comes out of your body in sneezes and coughs. If you touch sick birds, you can get germs on your hands. When you rub your nose, mouth, or eyes, the germs can get inside your body."

"Colds get passed around the same way," Matthew said. "They stay with people, though."

"Can you truly see these 'germs' with powerful tools?" Carys asked.

"Yes," Matthew said. "Yes, you can."

"Enough with the school lessons," Healer Oran said. "How do you treat this 'flu'?"

Matthew and I exchanged glances. I said, "You tell them."

"All right. With the birds, I hate to say it, you have to . . . end their suffering. Birds that look healthy now will be sick before long. You'll need to kill all of them."

"With no birds, where will we get eggs?" Bearach asked, his face dark with anger. "We eat moas when they grow old. We need the food." All the Pannmordians around us grew angry.

Cadoc said, "We raise moas on our farm. Ours are healthy. I'm sure my father will give you some to start a new flock."

Prince Brenden said, "A generous offer and a good start. We'll find more from other farms in the kingdom. You won't go hungry, Bearach."

"How do we care for the people?" Carys asked, fingering her medicine bag.

"We can tell you what Grandpa did for us," I said. "If it's the flu, most of them should recover with good care."

Bearach studied Matthew and me. "Shelter Rock will call the council together. You tell them about the moas, what we must do. Convince them of the truth of your words. A warning. If the council decides you mean to harm us by killing our animals, it will not go well for you." He looked at the others in our party. "For any of you."

Prince Brenden crossed his arms. Princess Skyla murmured soothing words, and Bearach's posture became more relaxed.

I bit my lip. The princess laid a hand lightly on my arm. "Be at ease. You have explained it once. I have faith that Healer Oran can convince the council. The words of a royal healer carry some weight, even this far from Ardara."

The healer paled, then straightened his shoulders and set his jaw. In spite of myself, I felt sympathy for the grouchy man.

Magic can be useful in battle
as well as in healing.
~Master Ailfrid
The Art and Discipline of Magic

27

TURMOIL

The council meeting was held in a copse of pines near the river. The small grove of trees was not their usual meeting space. Ordinarily, they gathered in an oversized dome that housed the mammoth skull. Since it was a revered historical object, outsiders were not allowed in that space. On the way to the pine grove, we stopped by the dome for Doileag to collect supplies for the meeting. The twins, Matthew, and I managed to peek inside when Bearach held the flap aside to let Doileag enter. The huge skull sat on a heavy wooden platform in the center of the dome. Large, curving tusks stuck out from the skull's front.

Leaving that hut, we walked with the twins behind the others in a tight little clump. Matthew said, "There's no doubt that skull is from a mammoth."

"Yeah," I agreed. "It matches the one we saw at the Museum of Natural History in New York City."

Cadoc's jaw dropped. "You have seen others?"

"We have," I said. "Mammoths are extinct now. Scientists have found quite a few fossil skulls similar to that one, and bones from the rest of the body. They're kept in special buildings, museums they're called, along with other rare and old things."

"I think the Pannmordians really were Neanderthals from Earth," Matthew said.

Carys said, "Maybe that's why they keep to themselves in this valley. They're closer to their ancestors here."

I expected there would be a lot of arguing at the meeting and asked Doileag if I could skip it. I'd lived in two homes where my foster parents bickered all day and shouted at us kids. Now, quarrels and yelling gave me terrible headaches. However, the Pannmordian leader insisted Matthew and I be there in case Healer Oran couldn't answer all the council's questions. She ordered Cadoc and Carys to stay behind, but they protested and insisted they wouldn't leave us. Before the drama got out of hand, Princess Skyla intervened and reminded Doileag that we were in the princess' care, and she wanted all of us to attend the session. The Pannmordian leader made a sour face, but in the end, she agreed.

As we followed the path to the copse of pines, I studied the sky. Cadoc nudged me. "There's a violet haze around you. What are you afraid of?"

"The pterodactyls circling overhead. Do you see them?"

He followed my gaze. "Aye. Why do they cause you fear?"

"I saw pterodactyls when we first came to Kylemore. They headed west. I saw some in Avonflow and more in recent days. They were flying west too. That's where the Terrapin Archipelago is. Where Sorceress Mairsil may be. I'm afraid she's keeping an eye on me." I laughed. "I know it sounds silly."

Cadoc took my hand in his. I wished we were on our own for the afternoon, getting to know each other better, rather than facing the council. We held hands until we arrived at the shady copse of trees. The air was filled with the scent of pine needles, damp earth from the muddy riverbank, and grass warmed by the sun. The Pannmordians arranged themselves on one side of the circle, across from the rest of us. We kids sat together, our knees touching in a small gesture of support.

Doileag opened the meeting by placing the objects from the mammoth dome in the center of the circle. There were a spearhead and a large flat rock with a painting of hunters chasing an animal that resembled a wooly mammoth. The elders chanted some formal words, and when they were done, Healer Oran described the way Matthew and I believed the bird flu was spread. The council gave him their full attention, asking a question now and then.

When Healer Oran finished, Princess Skyla spoke. "We cannot risk the disease spreading beyond this valley. I regret we must destroy your birds. King Darren, your ruler, will see that you receive moas to begin a new flock." After her announcement there was much discussion among the council members.

The day was warm, in spite of dark clouds that hid the sun. The heat made me drowsy. I leaned against Cadoc's arm and let the hum of the Pannmordians' conversation hover around me like bees in a field of clover. At times, their voices rose in anger. Then the princess would speak, and they'd settle down again. I must have dozed off. I woke with a start when Cadoc shifted position and my head slipped off his arm. The group rose, stretched, then brushed grass off their clothes. I had no idea what they'd decided to do about the moas. An elder returned the official spearhead and rock painting to the mammoth dome. The rest of us started back to Doileag's hut. A meadow separated the river and copse of trees from the dwellings. The air had been calm when the meeting began. Now the grass swayed in a breeze. The dark clouds were thicker, and the air was cooler. I heard a distant rumble of thunder. Since the drought ended, it had rained nearly every day, often with thunderstorms. It wasn't natural.

When we entered the meadow, an immense black shadow swooped across the grass. Heart pounding, I ran back to the cover of the trees.

Everyone else ran the other way.

An eagle-shaped bird, as large as a horse and carriage, dove into the treetops. This must be a roc. It clawed at the foliage, trying to reach me. I cowered deep in the center of the trees. Thick slate feathers covered its sturdy body. Its talons were as thick as my wrist. The curved beak was dagger sharp. From its throat came grating, screeching sounds. I wrapped my arms around a tree trunk. Rough bark scraped my forearms. The bird cocked its head to one side. A fierce golden eye the size of a dinner plate examined me. I screamed.

The Pannmordians threw spears at the giant bird. The beast ignored them. It tore at the branches with its talons and beak, intent on reaching me. The trees shook with the fierceness of the attack. My breath came in shallow gasps. Pine needles showered the ground, branches cracked and splintered. The roc made headway into the protective layer over my head. I spared a glance at the crowd in the meadow. The roc had no interest in them; I was its target. *Why me? Maybe Sorceress Mairsil does know about the water-cleansing spell.* I clenched my jaw, irritated that Healer Oran was probably right.

Prince Brenden and Healer Oran stood side by side, their wands pointed toward the grove. Carys' arms were stretched wide. She had an air of intense concentration. I watched in awe as a wide path of thick grass and wildflowers grew as tall as my head, stretching from the others to where I clung to the tree, frozen with fear. I had no time to marvel at the strength of Carys' talent. The air around me grew warmer, then I heard Cadoc and Matthew charge toward me through the swath of tall grass.

Cadoc yelled, "Run!" at the same time Matthew shouted, "Come!"

Fear held me in its grip. I hugged the tree harder, my nails digging into the rough bark.

"Come on!" Matthew called. "Oran and Prince Brenden

will burn the roc out."

The treetop burst into flame, and the bark grew hot. Glowing embers showered the ground. With a great effort, I wrenched my hands from the trunk and ran to the boys. Crouching low, I stumbled toward the sound of their voices as they continued to call to me.

They caught me, one on each side, and we squatted down in the tall cover of grass Carys had created. An explosion rocked the air, and we watched the tree splinter, sending chunks of wood and tongues of flame high in the air. The giant bird caught fire and struggled to stay aloft. A length of branch stuck in its body like the shaft of an arrow. The stench of burning feathers overpowered the sweet smell of the meadow.

We huddled in the grass, hands over our ears, trying to shut out the roc's agonized screeches. A heavy thud shook the ground. We peered back at the fire. Beyond the trees, its great, gray body heaved a few times, then grew still. Prince Brenden pointed his wand at a towering charcoal cloud, directing it to hover over the grove. Rain pelted down, dousing the fire.

The boys and I made our way to the others. Carys smiled weakly. "I feel ill." She put a hand to her head and collapsed in a heap. Matthew snatched up her wrist, checking for a pulse. Cadoc put a hand on her forehead.

Healer Oran didn't need to examine her. He said, "She did too much magic. It drained her energy. We must act quickly, or she could die."

"She's going into shock," Matthew said. "We need to warm her up."

Doileag said, "Carry the child to my hut. We will follow."

Rain still fell from the hovering storm cloud. Cadoc hoisted his sister over his shoulder then splashed through puddles to the hut. Matthew, Prince Brenden, and Healer Oran followed close behind. I started after them. Doileag grabbed my arm and whirled me around to face her.

Bearach reached a hand toward her. She growled at him and he dropped his arm to his side. The Pannmordian leader was shaken, her voice gruff. "Why did the roc bird pursue you, child Kallan?"

Princess Skyla intervened. "She's an innocent, Doileag. War is looming. The enemy sent the roc. We need your help to defeat the intruders."

Leader Doileag shook her head, sending out a spray of raindrops. "No. Our valley is not part of this war."

We were interrupted by the sound of pounding feet. A boy ran on the path, thick drops of mud flying in the air with each step. He stopped short when he reached us and bent over with his hands on his knees, sucking in air with ragged gasps of breath.

Doileag let go of me and regarded the boy. "What is wrong, child Brackel?"

He choked out his answer in short bursts. "The far forest. Shalby hunted with me. A fierce animal dropped from a tree. Sharp teeth. Strong and quick. Shalby's dead." Brackel dropped to his knees, rain mixing with his tears.

Princess Skyla said, "That sounds like the animal our minstrel warned us about. The enemy has released this horror, Doileag. The war has come to your valley."

Brackel raised his head at the word 'war.' He clenched and unclenched his fists. "Leader Doileag, I tried to fight. My spear struck its leg and the killer limped with the pain. It was not enough. The beast fled to the mountains." He hung his head. Rain dripped from his dark hair onto the muddy ground.

Bearach hoisted Brackel to his feet. He cupped the boy's chin in his hand. "You were brave to face the evil one. Let pride dwell with the sadness in your heart."

We took shelter in Doileag's hut. Carys and the boys sat near the fire. Carys leaned against Matthew, while Cadoc gave her sips of water from a gourd. She was as pale as cream.

Healer Oran told Doileag, "We'll know by morning. She

must stay near the fire tonight." The old woman nodded.

The hides that covered the hut's slender frame softened the steady drumming of rain. The air grew sour with the smell of wet fur as the Pannmordian's clothing steamed in the warmth of the fire. I was nauseous from the odor and from worry over Carys' condition and Doileag's suspicion of me.

In between bouts of sobbing, Brackel described the animal's appearance and the attack on Shalby in more detail. "As big as this." He stretched his arms wide. "The front legs, short and strong. Short fur, brown with spots the color of night. Yellow knife fangs." He held out his hand and traced a line from the tip of his middle finger to below his wrist. "As long as this."

"What kind of ears?" I asked.

He thought about it. "Small, pointed spear tips. And black hairs on its face, as long as the fangs." He swept his fingers in front of his cheeks, as though stroking invisible whiskers. We hadn't seen any cats in Kylemore, but this sure sounded like a feline. A large one. I wondered if it could be a saber-tooth.

Doileag directed the boy to take Bearach to Shalby's body. "Return him to his mawmaw and pawpaw. He will be buried with dignity." Prince Brenden and the council members went with them.

The stocky leader then addressed me. "Two attacks in one day, and child Carys struck by magic sickness. Three bad omens. There were no animals like Shalby's killer here until you came. You bring evil, child Kallan. You must leave the valley." She turned away and stirred the stew pot with jerky movements of the ladle.

My cheeks grew cold as the blood drained from my face. I stammered, "What? I didn't cause Shalby's attack." Matthew and Cadoc started to defend me; their words rang sharp, a blacksmith's hammer striking iron. Isla and Senga, who strung shells on leather thongs near the back of the dome, picked up their spears and crossed the hut to stand at Doileag's side.

Princess Skyla motioned for the boys and me to go outside. We left the flap open when we filed out. Through the gap, I saw Princess Skyla sit down next to Doileag. The princess' soothing voice floated through the gap, although I couldn't understand the words. Isla and Senga went back to their work, which encouraged me. A misty drizzle fell, soaking the boys and me to the skin. The princess spoke for a long time while Doileag remained stiff and unresponsive. Finally, Princess Skyla came out and closed the flap behind her.

"I'm sorry. I must send you three away for a while. Stay with Alec and Conroy near the edge of the woods where we entered the valley until I can convince Doileag it's safe for you to return. I will come for you when I can."

"What about my sister?" Cadoc's hands were balled into fists. He took a step toward the hut.

Princess Skyla put a hand out to stop him. "I checked on Carys a few minutes ago. Her breathing and heartbeat are steady. Healer Oran and I will watch over her through the night."

The princess wiped my wet face with a clean handkerchief and tucked it securely under my belt. She hugged me, tight and quick. Putting a hand on each of the boys' shoulders, she gave them a little squeeze. "Hold peace in your hearts. All will be well." Lifting the flap, she went back inside.

"Sorry, guys." I led the group toward the valley entrance. My feet slapped the mud with each step.

"It's not your fault," Cadoc said. "You're in a cloud of red. Don't be so angry." He tried to hold my hand, but I pulled it free.

"Would you stop doing that?" I stamped my foot in a puddle, splashing us both.

"Doing what?"

"Reading my emotions. It's creepy."

"Creepy? I'm concerned about you."

Matthew drew up on my other side and spoke over my head. "Some advice, bro. Women like to hide their feelings. Then they can dance around an issue, give off false signals, and get huffy when guys can't figure out what they want."

How does he know all that? Maybe he learned more than I thought dating Sarah.

"Reminds me of the troodon mating ritual," Cadoc said, grinning. I straightened my spine and sniffed.

"You're inside her skin, and it freaks her out. Throws her off balance."

Matthew laid an arm across my shoulders, and I let it rest there. "I'm okay with being tossed out of the valley, Pipit. I'd rather sleep under pine boughs than in a hut filled with wet animal hides any day."

I had to smile. It was like old times. My foster brother may spend a lot of time with Carys, yet he and I were still friends.

By the time we found Alec and Conroy near the entrance to the valley, the rain had stopped. Cadoc explained the situation, and we all worked to set up camp. Together we erected two sturdy shelters, making a triangle with the one Alec and Conroy had already made for themselves. The work took my mind off Carys and off Doileag's accusations. The boys took one of the new shelters, leaving the other for me. It was too wet to start a fire, so we ate the last of the cheese and smoked meat we had brought from Ardara. Cadoc borrowed my wand and waved it over our clothes, uttering a spell to draw the water out of the cloth.

"Wish we knew what's happening in Doileag's hut," Matthew said when our meager meal was finished and we were dry.

"I can check," I said.

"How?"

"Princess Skyla gave us a link." I pulled out her handkerchief and concentrated on the princess. "She's giving Carys something to drink. Carys seems more alert." I couldn't bear it if she died after saving my life. Letting my mind roam around the hut, I found Mela. She slept. Her fingers were curled around the edge of her mat. I couldn't bear it if she died, either.

I broke off the vision. "Sorry. I'm cold and tired." Tucking the handkerchief into my belt, I burrowed into my bed of pine boughs and shut out the world.

I sometimes find it difficult to make
my thoughts clear to others.
~Kallan MacKinnon, tenth-grade essay

28

SHOW AND TELL

*J*n the morning, Princess Skyla and Prince Brenden found the boys and me rested and hungry. The princess brought us fried flatbread and plums, which we ate while she told us her news. "Carys is recovering, though she's still weak. Doileag is satisfied Kallan had nothing to do with Shalby's death, and you are all welcome to return to the village."

Prince Brenden poured spicy tea from a hollow gourd into our mugs. The fragrant, warm liquid woke me up.

"Thanks," I said. "Your Highness, how did you convince Doileag I'm innocent?"

Princess Skyla said, "It appears some hunters spotted an animal in the mountains last week similar to the one that killed Shalby. With all the sickness, they didn't want to cause more worry, so they didn't report it to Doileag until last night. Her argument fell apart then, and she understood you weren't to blame for yesterday's appearance."

She added, "After some coaxing, Doileag agreed to let you visit the sick with us, Kallan. I think you can help, and I want her memories of our visit to be good ones. She's waiting, let us go."

A short while later we set out to visit the sick with the Pannmordian leader. A rainbow stretched from one side of the valley to the other. Doileag said, "It is a good omen, child Kallan. The Blessed One wills you to stay with us."

I took it as a peace offering. "I'm grateful for the Blessed One's message."

We went from hut to hut and cave to cave. Healer Oran had no magic spell to kill the virus; he made people comfortable and gave them herbal tea to help them sleep. Matthew and I told them to drink plenty of water too. We insisted the people caring for them keep their mouths and noses covered and wash their hands often.

Afterward, Princess Skyla's party and the village council gathered together. I urged the council to put all the sick together in a few caves to stop the illness from spreading. Doileag resisted. I struggled to keep my voice patient. "Germs go in the air and make people ill. Keep the sick ones together, and the germs reach fewer healthy people. You shouldn't have lots of caretakers. Let a small group take turns caring for them."

Doileag didn't think it worth the effort to move the sick when they were suffering so much. After we talked more, it was obvious she didn't really believe germs could travel from person to person. "Please," I said, "Let me show you how the sickness spreads."

"Is there danger?"

"No danger. Some mess."

I asked her for a big gourd, then told everyone to choose a clamshell from a large pile in the leader's hut and take it to the river. At the riverbank, I filled the gourd with water and said, "Scoop water into your shells." Next, I dug a handful of red mud from the riverbank and put it in the gourd. I stirred it with my fingers. "Now stand in a semi-circle facing me." I motioned to show them what I meant. They hesitated, then did as I asked.

I drew my hand out of the gourd and flicked my fingers

242

as I coughed. Muddy drops splashed on the others' arms and into their shells. I dipped my fingers in the dirty water again and pretended to sneeze while spraying the drops. I repeated this process several times, until Doileag grumbled, and Cadoc backed away from the muddy water that splattered his tunic.

I set the gourd on the ground. "Did the mud splatter your arms and clothes? Is the water in your shell dirty?"

Doileag scowled. "Aye. You have soiled us with your mud. Why?" Her black eyes glittered, and muscles bulged in her arms. She was smart and tough. I understood why the Pannmordians had chosen her as their leader. I wouldn't want her for an enemy. Thinking hard, I tried to make my explanation clear.

"The germs are too small. I can't show them to you. I have seen some at home with a special tool. When people sneeze or cough, they spray germs on you, like I did with the mud. If you don't wash them off, the germs can go in your mouth, or nose, or eyes. Then they get inside your body and make you sick. Do you understand?"

Doileag studied her shell and arms. She said, "These germs are there? For true?"

"Yes, I mean aye," said Matthew, coming to stand next to me. "Germs make fevers, coughs, and sneezes, even though you can't see them. Imagine walking into an empty hut and finding a pot of stew ready to eat. You don't see the person who cooked it, you see what they made."

Doileag stirred the dirty water in her shell with a finger. When the water was completely mixed, she said, "I will do as you say, strange one."

On impulse, I knelt in front of the sturdy woman and spoke to her feet. "Thank you. It will take time, but your people will get well sooner if you use my plan."

Doileag touched my shoulder. "Princess Skyla says you cleaned the poisoned water of the River of the Forest. Also, you persuaded Cadoc to help you. Pannmordians have two names. My mawmaw and pawpaw named me Doileag when I was newly born. 'Shelter Rock' is the name I have earned. My people know I stand solid against all that would harm our valley. They seek safety from me, and I shelter them."

She filled her shell with clean water and poured it over my head. "I name you 'Healing River' because you cleaned the forest water and used the river to show me how to care for my people."

My face warmed in a blush while the cool water dripped down my neck. "I am honored, Shelter Rock." I wondered if she would take my new name away if more people died.

Cadoc sent a message to his father with one of Prince Brenden's messenger birds, the same kind of toothed bird as the twins' pet Aeron. He told his dad that royal guards would collect several moas and deliver them to the Pannmordians. Princess Skyla added that the Royal Treasury would pay Rolant for the birds. The prince sent his remaining messenger bird to the castle, requesting help in moving the moas and asking that Grandpa wait at the castle for us.

Over the next five days, some of us helped the villagers tend to the sick while others put down the moas. I spent time with Carys and Mela every day, doing what I could to help them regain their strength. For the first couple of days, Carys was so weak that I spooned broth into her like I had for Mela. Once they were stronger, we had fun together. Mela begged for stories, and I told her fairy tales that my parents had read to me when I was small. When I ran out of story ideas for the day, Carys and I played checkers or Nine Mens Morris until she got too tired.

It wasn't all hard work and drudgery. The air was fresh and clean, and the meadows were filled with wildflowers. One day I made flower chains for Mela, Carys, and myself. In the afternoons the boys and I cooled off with the Pannmordian kids in a quiet pool that jutted out from the river in the shade of a willow tree. Isla, one of the first

Pannmordians we met, showed the boys and me paintings of animals in several damp, musty caves. The art was colorful, and the lines well drawn. Isla was a good artist and taught me their technique of mixing paints. When I learned that Mela's parents had died a few days before we arrived, I made a collection of paintings on clamshells for her, showing scenes of the Pannmordian Valley. Isla gave her a leather pouch to store them in. Mela clutched the pouch tight in her fist as she fell asleep.

Only one more Pannmordian died during the week we remained in the valley. There were three new cases of flu the first day, one each on the second and third days, and none after that. Matthew and I trained more Pannmordians in proper ways to care for the sick. Gradually, the tension in the community eased.

When we were saddled up, ready to return to Ardara, Princess Skyla asked Doileag, "Will you join us in the fight against the enemy?"

"Healing River and the rest of you have done much to help us. The council will consider your request." Which, I noticed, was an answer that held no promises.

Consider the consequences
before engaging with dragons.
~Weylyn Blevins
Natural History of the Western Kingdoms

29

CHOSEN

We were a few days out on our return trip to Ardara when Prince Brenden asked me to do a Far Seeing of Prince Aiden.

"Sure thing." I retrieved my sketchbook. The information we might get was more important than any sickness I would feel afterward. Curious, the others gathered around me. Having an audience made me nervous. Once I focused on Prince Aiden, I forgot about them. In the drawing, Aiden struggled with a man who looked like Pons. A battle raged behind him. Armored knights fought clusters of men who were clothed as Pons had been in knee-length trousers and vests buttoned over shirts made of coarse fabric.

Cadoc's tail swished back and forth. "They have no armor. Why haven't our troops defeated them?" Then we saw a silver flash in some of the warriors' shirt openings.

Matthew sucked in his breath "They're wearing armor under their clothes. They're so light on their feet, it must weigh less than the knights' gear."

"Some of them may wear magical protection besides," Prince Brenden said. "Magic is rare on the Terrapin Archipelago, but their magic is of a different nature from ours. It's difficult to break through."

"What are those?" Matthew pointed to several large creatures that had entered the scene. One lifted a big rock and sent it crashing into an advancing line of knights.

Princess Skyla said, "Giants from the Wyvam Mountains." She grimaced. "They're not the most loyal of subjects."

Prince Brenden scratched his beard. "Mairsil's got more allies than we thought. It'll take a combined force to defeat them. Additional troops from Ardara. The Pannmordians too, and it wouldn't hurt to recruit the wood elves."

Princess Skyla said, "I wouldn't count on the wood elves, Brenden. You know how they keep to themselves. If the battle's outside their own burrows, they'll stay underground and pretend it has nothing to do with them."

Prince Brenden turned away. "I've seen enough." He called one of the guards over. "Duff, I'll write a message to Doileag. We need healthy Pannmordians to join the battle. I'm sending you and Nevin back to the valley. If my message isn't sufficient, you must convince them to join us. Tell them the battle's in the Kintare Woods. Pannmordian warriors should head there immediately. After you deliver the message, return to Ardara. The rest of us will continue toward the castle. With so many younglings present, I'm not prepared to join the fight." The guards gathered supplies while Prince Brenden composed his message.

I shivered as I shut my sketchbook. "Dang it," I said to Carys. "I wish I knew how to keep magic from making me so cold."

"Nuala says to calm yourself and let the warmth in, though I don't know how to go about it."

Healer Oran sniffed. "Typical village healer. Can't explain things clearly. You must still yourself and draw in energy from your surroundings. It's best to take it from the air. Since it's warmed by the sun, there's plenty of heat for the taking, even on a winter's day. Empty your mind, breathe deeply and slowly." He spread his arms wide.

"Merely open yourself to the vital forces that swirl 'round you."

"That's clear enough," Cadoc muttered under his breath. Carys stepped on his foot. She and I thanked the healer for his advice. It was the first time Oran had shown any kindness toward us. It was only decent to show some gratitude.

The clouds had darkened during my Far Seeing. Thunder rumbled in the sticky afternoon air.

"I've never seen so many thunderstorms in all my life," I said.

Cadoc peered at the thickening clouds. "Rumblestorms are quite common in Kylemore in the summer. And yet, not this common. Sorceress Mairsil was a good weather witch. I wonder if she is alive after all and has a hand in this. First the drought, now unending storms. Though I still don't trust Prince Aiden, the signs point to the sorceress as the true enemy."

Shafts of sunlight broke through the clouds and the air took on an eerie golden tint. It reminded me of a solar eclipse I'd observed with my mother years ago. The shadow of a tree lay across the side of our garage. The image danced with hundreds of crescent-shaped suns projected through gaps between the leaves. Comforted by the memory, I rubbed my ring and could almost feel my mother hugging me. Peace settled over me in spite of the coming storm, and I returned my thoughts to the present. The prince was ready to move out. I patted Willow's neck, then hoisted myself into the saddle.

The wind picked up as we rode, rattling branches. Rain lashed at us, and my hair flattened into a streaming cap. Brilliant streaks of lightning were followed by loud cracks of thunder and hailstones the size of lima beans. The icy spheres stung as they bounced off my face. I lowered my head, covering it as best I could with an arm, and scanned the area from under my sleeve, searching for shelter.

"Cave!" Princess Skyla pointed to a dark opening halfway up the hillside. We hobbled the horses in a dense growth of trees and then scrambled up the slope on foot. I slipped on a mixture of mud and wet leaves and slid downhill on my belly until I struck a bush that held fast. Cursing, I grabbed at the bush, pulled myself up, and rejoined the others.

An apron of flat rock extended several yards in front of the cave. The rock was split into sections by deep cracks. We hurried across the slick surface, and when we were inside, Carys and Prince Brenden used magic to dry our clothes.

The hailstorm was over by the time we were settled. The rain continued. Fortunately, the cave was large and dry. The roof slanted down toward the back wall, which was solid with no tunnels leading away from the chamber. The floor was sandy and littered with the bones of small animals. I wondered what larger animal had fed on them. Aside from us, there were no living creatures in the cave. As we sat in silence, a faint whimpering noise came to us from outside.

In an instant, Matthew crept toward the cave entrance. Prince Brenden spoke sharply. "Matthew, have a care."

Matthew nodded and then slipped outside onto the rain-soaked apron of rock. Alec, Conroy, Prince Brenden, and Cadoc moved to the entrance for a clear view of him. The rest of us crowded behind them, peeking through the spaces around their bodies.

Matthew called over his shoulder. "It's the dragonet we saw on our way to the valley. Its leg is stuck in a crack in the rock." He kept walking until he reached the boundary where the rock surface met the leaf-covered forest floor.

From my cramped position behind Cadoc, I watched Matthew bend over a dark mound near the end of the rock, his body shifting back and forth as he worked the creature's leg loose. My heart skipped a beat when I noticed the bulky shape of the mother dragon in the distance. She moved toward the cave. Her scales shone with a soft golden color. She walked with surprising grace, not hurrying her steps. Her gaze was fixed on Matthew and her baby.

Prince Brenden headed toward Matthew and the dragonet, walking with care on the slippery rock. Matthew continued to work on freeing the baby's foot. As soon as he pulled it out of the crevice, a creature dropped from a tree to the wet ground several yards away, landing with a soft plop. It had fangs and a muscular, feline body. A saber-tooth cat. It slunk toward the dragonet and Matthew. Both he and the prince seemed unaware of the danger.

I shrieked a warning. The dragonet limped toward its mother, the saber-tooth in close pursuit. Matthew hurled his dagger. Prince Brenden drew his sword and chased after it. Matthew's dagger stuck in the cat's shoulder. It yowled and broke stride. The dragonet gained distance from the cat. Prince Brenden formed a glowing ball of fire that quivered in his hand. Before he had a chance to hurl it, the mother dragon shot out a tongue of flame. I felt suspended out of time. The dragon fire glided across the forest until it collided with the saber-tooth's chest. The big cat reared up and screeched. The sounds of its struggle came as if from a great distance as I watched it writhe in slow motion against a blurry background of greenery. The dragon kept up its fiery assault until the saber-tooth was still.

Time snapped back to its usual pace. Prince Brenden's fireball winked out, and he strode toward the cave. He called for Matthew to hurry. Matthew pulled his dagger from the saber-tooth's carcass. The dragonet joined its mother and Mom nuzzled it. Then the large creature lumbered toward Matthew with her young one trailing after her.

"Matthew, to the cave," Princess Skyla shouted.

But he didn't come back. Instead, he took a few steps in the dragon's direction. I dug my nails into my clenched fists. Matthew stopped right in front of the mother dragon.

It was incredible. They appeared to be having a conversation.

We couldn't hear anything. Using his hands, Matthew demonstrated how he'd pulled the dragonet's leg free from the crack in the rock. The mother dragon bowed her head. Then Matthew stood still, his hands stretched out as though ready to catch something. The dragon scraped a claw against her chest, flicking out a large amber scale that landed in Matthew's open palm. He bowed to the dragon and they parted. The dragon returned to her waiting baby, and Matthew returned to the cave with a dreamy, unfocused expression on his face.

Inside, he held the scale up for us to see. It was nearly as large as his palm, triangular in shape, with a bumpy surface and smooth edges. Conroy pulled a length of leather cord from a trouser pocket, poked a hole near the base of the scale with the tip of his belt knife, then threaded the leather through the hole. He tied the ends together, forming a loop that he hung around Matthew's neck.

"That was risky, lad," Prince Brenden said.

Matthew shook his head. "No risk. Her name's Heulwen. She said she wanted to give me a token—for what I'd done for Cai. That's her son. She called me 'Cyneweard.'" He ran a fingertip over the bumpy scale.

My breath came fast. "You talked with her?"

"Yes. In my head."

I asked Prince Brenden, "What's it mean, 'Cyneweard?'"

"It means 'royal guard.'" He blushed. "It is a rare honor to receive a name from a dragon. It's been nearly a hundred years since someone's been dragon-named." I wouldn't have thought it possible, but the prince seemed to be jealous of Matthew.

Princess Skyla said, "It means you have been chosen. The golden dragon must hold a high place in their company. Otherwise, she couldn't name you a royal guard. Being chosen means dragons will help whenever you're in need. It also means . . ." She hesitated, her tail slowly sweeping out an arc. "They expect you to protect and defend their kind."

Matthew swallowed hard and gripped the scale.

Prince Brenden's voice was barely above a whisper. "It also means you are linked with the dragons for life."

No one had anything to say after that. The adults drifted to various parts of the cave to wait out the storm. The twins joined Matthew and me near the opening. We sat in a tight group. Cadoc squinted at Matthew, checking his emotional aura.

Carys said, "May we see the scale?"

"Sure, pass it around." Matthew took the leather loop off his neck and handed the scale to her.

It was heavier than I expected. "What do you know about dragons?" I asked the twins.

Cadoc said, "Most of what we've learned comes from the Keane tribe. Dragons are as smart as people, probably smarter. It's hard to build their trust. Once you do, they'll remain loyal for life. Unless you betray them. If you do that, it's best to leave the kingdom and never return."

I handed the dragon scale back to Matthew. "What's the Keane tribe?"

"A small band of people who live in the mountains near Dragon's Nest," Cadoc said.

Matthew asked, "Why don't they send representatives to Ardara, like the Pannmordians and wood elves do?"

Carys answered. "They do. You probably didn't see them at the castle. They spend most of their time in the royal library. They're an ancient tribe and know a lot about dragon lore. All the official books about dragons were written by Keane men and women. They pore over old books and check them for accuracy. When they learn more facts, they write new chapters. It's dull work, if you ask me."

"Important work, though," Cadoc said. "Most people don't understand dragons nearly as well as the Keanes. One of the best is Wulfric. The Keanes are neighbors to the dragons and keep mostly to the far mountains of Kylemore.

Not much bothers them. The mere presence of the dragons keeps the giants and other threats away. The dragons protect the Keanes and they teach the dragons about people, so the benefits go both ways."

Matthew asked, "Why aren't any of the Keanes dragon riders if they're so close?"

"A few have been, in the past. I don't know why there aren't any now. Maybe they fear heights." Cadoc winked at me, and I stuck my tongue out at him.

He turned to Matthew again. "They say, if the dragons take any new riders from the Keanes, it's likely to be Wulfric. Most of the old dragon knights came from Ardara and other regions of Kylemore. Dragons have long been allies of Kylemore's people, yet it's rare for them to take a strong enough liking to anyone to give them a name." His gaze lingered a while on the amber scale which hung once again from Matthew's neck, securely fastened to the leather cord. He squeezed Matthew's shoulder. "Well done."

"It's a big honor," Carys said, slipping her hand in Matthew's. I gave my foster brother a bright smile. Yet, I couldn't shake off the anxious roiling in my gut.

Battles are not won by
magic and weapons alone.
~Master Ailfrid
The Art and Discipline of Magic

30

A VIOLENT DISTURBANCE

*W*hen the storm passed, we took to the trail again. A cold north wind showered us with droplets from the branches overhead. After we'd ridden for an hour, Cadoc stiffened in his saddle. He halted and shouted to Prince Brenden. "Your Highness, I smell smoke. There's a fire in our path."

The prince reined in his horse. "Lad, are you certain? I don't smell anything."

"I'm sure. It's a faint scent, blowing in from the west."

"Your senses are sharper than the rest of ours. We'll go as far as we can and then turn south. We're on the edge of the Kintare Woods. Going north would bring us closer to the battlefield."

I brought Willow up next to Cadoc's gelding. "Do you think the fire is from a lightning strike? Could the sorceress really have caused the storm?"

"Lightning's probably to blame for the fire. Whether or not the sorceress is responsible, I cannot say. Be calm. Heading south, we'll ride away from her troops. I don't think a roc could find us in these thick woods, either." He smiled, and the churning in my stomach lessened.

Plumes of vapor rose off the rain-drenched ferns, and

birds twittered. A fire in such wet conditions seemed impossible until we crested the next hill. Flames and billowing smoke filled the forested valley below us. We halted. There was fire and smoke as far south as we could see.

"We'll have to leave the trail and head north," Prince Brenden said.

"That . . . that will bring us near the battle," Carys said.

"You're right, it's a problem. We'll try to stay south of the action. There's no trail to follow, so stick close together." The prince and his stallion started up the muddy mountain and the rest of us followed.

The afternoon wore on and the sight of distant flames kept us on edge. The woods were abnormally silent; there was no birdsong or insect buzzing, no breeze. The air had an orange twilight hue, but it was still hours before the day's end. My breath caught at the sight of a pterodactyl perched in a gnarled tree. I stopped Willow, flapped my arms, and hissed to make it take flight. It didn't budge. Then the clouds shifted, and sunlight lit up the trunk. I ground my teeth; the black shape was only the stub of a broken branch.

We were forced to go further and further north to skirt the blaze. When the sun sank below the treetops, we took a break near a small stream, letting the horses drink. My eyes stung and I had a headache. Bits of ash floated in the air, irritating my throat. I took long swallows of water from my flask.

Matthew tipped his flask and poured a stream of water over his face. He wiped off a layer of wet grit with his sleeve. "At least we're keeping ahead of the fire," he said.

"For how long?" Cadoc responded as we remounted. "The wind might shift in the night. We won't be safe until we're far west of this inferno. It's another four days until we reach Adara." He raised his head, sniffing the air, then shouted, "Your Highness, there's trouble."

"What is it?" Princess Skyla asked.

"Thick emotions. An attack from the north. Coming fast."

The guards reined in, spacing themselves around the rest of us. I unsheathed my dagger and searched my mind for the facts I'd learned about using it. Healer Oran shaded his eyes with his hand as he scanned the forest. Princess Skyla fitted an arrow to her bow while Matthew bent over his gelding's neck and spoke to him in a low voice. Muscles flexing, Cadoc eased his sword out of its scabbard. Carys and Prince Brenden drew their wands.

The forest exploded in a whirl of activity.

Dozens of men, slightly built like Pons, poured down the hillside with swords drawn. Our party was greatly outnumbered, and the closeness of the trees and bushes made escape difficult. Soon, the horses' shrill whinnies blended with the grunts and shouts of the people. My ears rang with the sound of clashing metal.

Oran and Prince Brenden uttered lyrical spells that twined together like braided rope and sent streams of air pushing at the small army, knocking many of them to the ground. Once the enemy soldiers were knocked down, the spells cut off and the prince and healer joined the guards in attacking the invaders with swords.

I looked away, unable to bear the sight of them hacking away at each other. Carys threw bursts of flame from her wand at the attackers. My dagger was no use in this battle. I did know enough magic now to make a difference, though. If I could get around behind the invaders, I might be able to trap them in place with an air wall. I turned Willow around and headed downhill. I planned to make a wide circle around the fight, then work my way above the skirmish.

It grew dark and the mare and I made slow progress. An area of dense undergrowth blocked our way and forced us to go farther downhill than I wanted to. The sounds of fighting dimmed. I became disoriented and panicky. There was no clear path back to the battle.

A blur of motion off to the side and a wiry man shouting something I didn't understand as he rushed toward me. I thrust my dagger at him. He was out of reach and jabbed Willow's front leg with his blade. She let loose a terrifying squeal and reared up. She struck the man's shoulder with a hoof when she came down. He sprawled on the ground. Her next step landed squarely on his middle. He screamed but managed another slash at the horse's leg.

Willow reared again. I tumbled to the ground, rolling out of the way of the fleeing mare. The wounded man lay nearby, groaning. He was short, with black hair and dark skin. His tail lay limp at his side. His good arm gripped his middle, and his mouth was twisted in a grimace. Keeping my distance, I drew my wand, ready to encase him in a wall of air. After watching him for a minute or two, I tucked the wand in my belt. He had made no attempt to rise or speak. Willow's trampling must have caused serious internal injuries.

I approached him with caution. He followed my steps with pain-filled eyes. I lowered myself to the ground and sat out of arm's reach. He ran the tip of his tongue across his lips. Although he looked nothing like my tall, fair-haired mother, he wore an expression of suffering eerily similar to hers when the cancer pain took hold of her. It struck me then how much people have in common with each other, no matter where we come from.

I remembered the simple gestures that helped my mom when she was sick and offered him my water flask. He reached for it, then winced and quickly returned his hand to his stomach. I moved closer and held the flask to his lips. After a few swallows he pulled his head back. He showed his gratitude with another expression that reminded me of my mother. I set the flask down and wrapped my fingers around his hand. We sat together in silence while his breathing slowed and finally stopped.

I drew my knees to my chest, wrapped my arms around myself, and took deep, steadying breaths. I don't know how long I stayed there, huddled in thought. I was nearly asleep when I heard Matthew calling me.

"Here I am." I waved a hand in the air. I didn't have the energy to get up.

Guided by thin moonlight, he picked his way through the brush and sat by my side. "Pipit, are you all right?"

"No, not really." I told him about the attack, sparing no details. He wrapped his arms around me, and I buried my face in his chest and wept.

When I had cried myself out, we made a shallow grave for the warrior, digging with flat stones and broken branches. Once we'd covered him with soil, we marked the place with a small stack of rocks and wished him on his way to the ancestors, or wherever people's souls went in this world when they died.

"I feel guilty about his death," I said.

"Don't. Willow killed him, not you. Your actions eased his passing. That's the best anyone can do for another at the end. Let it go."

The memory would be with me for a long time. Matthew was right, though. I'd done all I could for the man. "I'll try. What happened to you? How'd you get separated from the others?"

"I saw you head downhill. The fighting was fierce, and someone stunned my horse with a spell—don't know who cast it. I fought on foot for a while, expecting you'd come back any minute. When you didn't, I called to Cadoc and Alec to help me search for you. I couldn't get their attention over the noise of the fighting. It was pretty dark by then. If I waited too long, I wouldn't remember what direction you'd gone, so I left on my own. What was your plan anyhow?"

My plan sounded stupid to me now. "I wanted to help without hurting anyone. Figured an air wall was my best hope." I shrugged. "When I circled around the fighting to get in place for the spell, I got lost."

He smiled. "Lost, but not forgotten. It's too dark to search for the others tonight. With any luck, Prince Brenden's party will find us before breakfast." He retrieved my dagger and the stranger's sword and wiped them clean. Then he strapped the dead man's sword belt around his waist and slid the sword into the leather scabbard. Worn out, we searched the area for a safe place to sleep.

When accidents happen,
serious injury may result.
~Elementary Guide for Healers

31

LOFTY RESCUE

s soon as it was light, Matthew and I followed a narrow game trail up the mountain in search of our companions. An ashy breeze irritated my eyes. We'd slept in a hollow oak trunk that was dry and somewhat protected from the chilly night air. I curled up tight against the curve of the trunk and breathed in the sweet, woody scent. When I was younger, my family pitched a tent every summer in a campground bordering a lake in the Adirondacks. In the evenings, we'd catch snatches of conversation and laughter from nearby campsites. This was not that. I rubbed my silver ring for luck against wild animal attacks. Crazily enough, it seemed to work; nothing disturbed our sleep.

After we'd hiked a couple of hours, we stopped to survey the valley to the south. Matthew said, "Judging by the smoke, we need to keep heading north."

"I don't like being forced closer to the battlefield, although I suppose the others went that way too." My voice was raspy. The sharp angles of the narrow switchback trail zigzagged above and below us. I shuddered. "This is steeper than the trail to the waterfall on Grandpa's land. If we slip, it's a long way to the bottom." I've always been afraid of heights. My dad said it's a fear babies are born with, and

261

most people get over it. Apparently, I'm different from most people.

Matthew gave me an encouraging smile. "Keep looking ahead." He started up the trail again.

Around noon we reached a large clearing and stopped to rest. The slope wasn't as steep further up the mountain as it was below. Here the trail was wider, and the air was warm, if hazy. We called out for Prince Brenden, Princess Skyla, and the others, cupping our hands to magnify the sound. We didn't hear a reply.

I did a Far Seeing to locate Carys, using a medicine bag she'd given me. I could only make out that she was in a forest and Cadoc was with her. "There's no way to tell what part of the forest they're in." My shoulders slumped.

"At least they're alive. 'Course, they could be as lost as we are."

"That's a cheery thought." I tied the medicine bag back onto my belt. We'd had nothing to eat since lunch the day before. I searched the clearing and found some flowering plants I knew had edible roots. When I straightened from collecting the plants, I heard a faint rhythmic sound. I whirled around, expecting to find a roc or pterodactyl. Nothing. I called out to Matthew, "Do you hear wings?"

He trotted over and put his hand on my arm. "Don't move." He pointed to a large animal flying toward us. "Dragon."

I held my breath as the scaly creature flapped steadily in our direction then landed in the clearing. From head to tail it must have been twenty feet in length and its wingspan was at least twice as long as its body. It folded its amber wings and studied us. Shaking off Matthew's hand, I took small steps backward until my hands touched the smooth bark of a tree, then hid behind a leafy branch.

"It's Heulwen, the dragon that gave me her scale," Matthew said. "She knows me." His voice was thick with emotion. He listened intently. "She wants us to go with her."

"Did she call you that name again?" I peeked around the branch and found the dragon had bent her knee and lowered her head.

"She did. It's Cyneweard. Come. It's all right." He stretched out his hand toward me.

Sunlight glinted off the scale dangling from the leather strap around his neck. The color of the scale exactly matched the shimmering beast that loomed above us. My head swiveled toward the dragon, to Matthew, and back to the huge, scaly beast. "Are you out of your mind?"

"She can fly high enough to see the battlefield. We should be able to spot the others." He turned back toward the dragon and continued speaking to me. "Do you think you can ride her?"

"No way! I don't want you to, either. We should stay together." Fear crept into my voice. The woods were unfamiliar, and an attack could come at any time as it did the night before. "Matthew, it's too risky. If you fall off, you'll be killed." I wrapped my arms around myself to stop shivering.

He ignored my concerns. "I'll be fine, Pipit. Stay here. We'll fly back to this clearing as soon as we can."

"Do you really think you can control a dragon?" My voice rose to a high pitch.

Matthew spoke as though he were explaining an obvious fact to a young child. "You don't control wild animals. It's a matter of understanding them. They're individuals, same as people. I saved her baby. She wants to return the favor."

I cursed and kicked at the ground, sending up a spray of dirt and debris. "You'll never make it. Please don't leave me."

"Trust me. I'll be back before dark. Stay here."

He walked alongside her, stepped past her neck, then pulled himself up, settling in to let his legs dangle in front of her wings. He laid his torso along her neck and wrapped his arms around it. Then he nodded and took a deep breath.

I groaned as the dragon lifted into the air and flew northward, toward the mountaintop. I watched until they were out of sight, then sat in the cool shade of a maple tree to eat the roots I'd collected. They were pithy, and my mouth was dry when I finished. I downed most of the contents of my flask in big, noisy gulps. I returned to the maple and waited with my hand wrapped tight around the hilt of my dagger.

The forest was quiet in the afternoon heat. I grew drowsy, and despite my best efforts, fell asleep. It was midafternoon when I woke, and I was still thirsty. I drained the rest of the water from my flask and checked the sun's position. There was time to return to the stream where we'd filled our flasks that morning.

I traveled through cool, shady woods, following the faint game trail. It was narrow and there was a sharp drop-off on one side. The leaf litter hid slick patches of mud, like on the path to Grandpa's waterfall. I let memories of the day we entered this strange world distract me.

I rounded a bend in one of the switchbacks and lost my footing on a particularly large strip of mud. The world turned topsy-turvy, with the sky in view one moment and brown soil the next. Brambles caught at my clothes. They couldn't stop my tumble down the steep slope. Crap! A stump. My head smacked the rotting wood with a dull thud. Another somersault threw me against a huge oak. I came to rest with my leg twisted under me.

For several minutes I lay still, propped against the oak, taking deep steadying breaths. My head throbbed. My leg was worse. I'd never felt such intense pain. I could almost hear my first aid instructor reminding me to do a thorough examination. I checked each arm and leg and probed my sides for broken ribs and bleeding gashes. The damage seemed limited to a swollen lump on my forehead and the twisted leg.

When I tried to sit up straight, the effort made me dizzy and I vomited my meal of pithy roots. Tearing off a large piece of fern, I wiped my mouth and sank back in a cleft of the great oak's trunk. *How will Matthew ever find me?*

I closed my eyes to shut out the pain. A bird chirped and a small creature, probably a mammal or lizard, scrabbled up a nearby tree. Muffled footfalls approached me. Closer and closer they came. Whatever it was sounded larger than a dog, smaller than a horse. I held my breath, waiting. When I could bear the suspense no longer, I opened my eyes. The bushes in front of me parted, and a small, hairy man strode toward me.

Some people like surprises.
I'm not one of them.
~Kallan MacKinnon, tenth-grade essay

32

ENTANGLEMENTS

The approaching stranger was short, but that was the only feature he had in common with Pons and his countrymen. Nestled atop his curly auburn hair sat a pointed hat trimmed by a striped feather on one side. A thick tangle of beard reached halfway down his chest. His shirtsleeves ended an inch or two above his wrists, exposing thick hair on his arms. Even though I knew I'd never seen him before, he looked familiar. Before I could search my memory, he drew back his foot and kicked my injured leg. A fiery pain exploded inside my shin.

"Ow!" I howled. "Why'd you do that?"

"You're blocking my way. My dwelling lies under your tail." His voice had a light, gravelly tone, like pebbles tumbling over each other when waves retreat from the shore.

Through clenched teeth I managed to say, "I haven't got a tail."

"What happened to it?"

I stared at my lap. "I don't want to talk about it."

"Fine. Don't. Simply remove yourself."

"I can't."

"I'll help you." He pulled on my arm.

"Stop! You're hurting me. My leg is broken."

The little man took a couple of steps back, then rested his chin in his hand while he stared at me with icy eyes that matched the silver streaks in his beard. A tingle flowed through my thighbones, shins, and feet, as though an invisible force vibrated them, testing for cracks. When the tingling stopped, the peculiar man took off his hat and bowed. "So it is. I offer my deepest apology."

"Apology accepted. In case you have any ideas of thumping me on the head, it hurts too. What are you, anyway?" His lips pursed, and I remembered my manners. "Sorry, that's rude. I mean, who lives under trees?" That didn't sound much more polite, but I was in too much pain to care about niceties.

"Wood elves, of course. I am known as Lord Elwood Trow, also named Master of the Taggla Forest, the portion you see, and what lies beyond. Who wanders the Taggla Forest alone?"

Now I remembered. Nairne, the stable hand at the castle in Ardara was a wood elf too. However, the man in front of me carried himself like a royal, not a servant. Imitating Lord Trow's manner I said, "I am known as Kallan MacKinnon, also named Healing River. My brother Matthew and I are part of a diplomatic mission to the Pannmordians. We were returning to the royal city and got separated from our companions." I couldn't quite keep my irritation with Matthew out of my voice when I added, "Then my brother flew off on a dragon, and I fell down the mountain, ending up in front of your . . . dwelling."

Lord Trow didn't bother to hide his doubts about the truth of what I said. He narrowed his eyes and held my gaze. I refused to blink or turn away. In time, my eyes watered from the strain. My limbs grew cold when I suspected the elf was rummaging around in my thoughts.

Finally, he shook his head, breaking eye contact. "So you say. So you say. If you'll excuse me, I must think." He turned his back to me and began to hum.

The air was much clearer than it had been that morning. Licking my forefinger and holding it out, I discovered the wind had shifted, taking the fire ash and, I hoped, the fire, in another direction. If Matthew could communicate with the dragon as well as he thought he could, they should return to the clearing soon. I wondered how strong the dragon's sense of smell was. Maybe it could sniff out my location.

I shifted my leg. Jolts of pain sliced through me and beads of perspiration broke out on my forehead, then dripped into my lap. My ears rang, and the world turned gray. I was near to fainting.

I lowered my head as far as I could. "Hey, Lord Trow. Need some help here." My words came out in a whisper. He whirled around and was at my side in an instant.

"Great mushroom caps! Don't pass out, lass. We need to get you inside." He waved his hands over my leg in an intricate pattern that he repeated half a dozen times while mumbling an incantation: *"Unicom, Skrinium, Capsium."* The pain in my leg shrank to a tiny core near the break. Somehow, he convinced me to roll over on my hands and good knee. He supported my broken leg, and I dragged myself through a rough opening at the base of the trunk.

We entered a large dirt room which, judging by the pots and pans hanging from hooks in the overhead roots, was a kitchen. I couldn't tell how tall the room was. From the look of it, I'd have to bend my knees to keep my head from brushing the ceiling. I rested my head on the cool, hard-packed earth. Lord Trow lowered my bad leg to the floor, careful not to bump it, and pulled a pile of blankets out of a chest that sat along a side wall. He spread two of them out on the floor near me. "Lady Trow, we have a visitor," he said, directing his words toward a passageway in the rear of the room.

"Clamber over here, now. Then you can rest." He raised

269

his head and called out toward the passageway again. "Lady Trow, your assistance is required." With the elf's help, I inched my way over to the blankets and collapsed, shutting my eyes against the world. I didn't care if a dragon breathed fire into the room, I was staying put.

Someone covered me with more blankets and tucked a pillow under my head. The pillow was soft and spongy, like moss. I was too worn out to open my eyes. Whoever it was smelled different from Lord Trow. It must be the lady he'd called for. The brim of a cup touched my lip and I took a small sip. The liquid was thick and sweet, tasting of honey mixed with nuts and orange blossoms. I drank it all, and with my energy used up, let myself drift into a deep sleep.

∞

The mingled scents of carrot soup and fried mushrooms woke me. I was lying under a thin, surprisingly warm blanket that appeared to be made of the same emerald green moss as my pillow covering. I ran my hand along its soft surface, trying to figure out where I was. Nothing in the dimly lit room was familiar. My breath came in shallow, rapid spurts.

A short, slender woman with bony elbows was singing. She slid several orange biscuit-shaped discs from a griddle onto a wooden tray.

"Excuse me," I said, raising my voice above the singing. "Where am I?"

"Under the place we met," said a voice I recognized. It belonged to the strange little man I'd spoken with earlier. I searched my memory for his name and came up empty. Then I spotted a pointy hat on a shelf and remembered. Lord Trow. I couldn't see him from where I lay, nor could I remember how we met, but I did find some comfort in his gravelly voice.

"You picked a good time to wake, dearie. I am Lady

Trow," said the woman as she set the tray of orange discs on a sturdy wooden table in the center of the room. "Can you manage some food, Miss—?"

"Kallan. Kallan MacKinnon. Thanks for the offer. However, I can't stay. I'm in a hurry." I had an urge to get to a special place before nightfall. What that place was, I didn't remember. I only knew it was up the mountain rather than downhill. I forced myself to look at my hostess rather than the tempting meal set out on the scrubbed table. Lady Trow's hair was walnut brown and framed her face in soft curls. Her eyes were a warm hazel. My stomach grumbled, and I put a hand over my belly. In a flash I remembered leaning against a tree trunk on the edge of a grassy clearing, eating pithy roots. "There's a clearing I have to reach while it's still light outside."

A frown flitted across the little woman's face, then she beamed a smile at me. "Certainly. But food first, for strength. Lord Trow will help you up. After the healing, your leg will be stiff. I haven't seen such a bad break since our son Sylvan tumbled out of the tallest tree in the glen so many years ago."

I had forgotten about my leg. It all came back to me now—the dragon carrying Matthew away, the slippery mud, the jolting trip down the mountainside, the rotted stump and final somersault flinging me against the oak tree. I rubbed my fingertips across my head. The tender lump was still there, coated with a sticky substance.

"I put ointment on your bump. Mind you, your head will be sore for a few days," the woman said in a bright, cheerful tone. "Your leg and tail are all fixed up. Two out of three is—"

"My tail?" I said, twisting on my blankets. Sure enough, the end of a hairy, black tail stuck out from under the edge of the blanket. I grabbed the tip of it. "Oh, no! Is it a side effect of the healing magic? How long . . . how long will it last?"

Lord Trow snorted. "The High Magic of wood elves has no side effects like the Common Magic humans use. Such gratitude. You were so distressed about losing your tail, you couldn't even speak about the loss. Lady Trow thought it a kindness to grow it back. You see, Urmed, I tell you it's better not to have dealings with humans."

"It was kind of you. Very kind," I babbled. "I'm grateful. Really. I was surprised, that's all." I softened my voice, hoping to pacify the grumpy man. "I'm impressed you'd go to so much trouble to help a stranger."

"Humpf," was his only response.

I couldn't imagine how I would manage with a tail. *Can I control how it moves? Will it hurt if I sit on it? How hard will it be to stick it through the tail slit in my borrowed trousers? And the privy?* I shuttered.

It occurred to me that Lord Trow might be important in the wood elf community. I remembered Princess Skyla speaking about the wood elves' powerful magic during one of her lessons on Kylemore's history. Their magic was probably one of the reasons Prince Brenden wanted them to fight the Sorceress' troops. *How can I convince them to join the battle when they prefer to keep to themselves?*

I sat up, careful to hold my tail to the side so I didn't trap it. Lord Trow helped me to a standing position. Surprisingly, the ceiling was just high enough for me to stand up straight, except for where the largest roots dipped below the rest. Little by little, I shifted my stance until I put my full weight on my right leg, then I sighed with relief. "There's no pain. That's terrific. Thank you again, Lady Trow." My leg felt like it was enclosed in an invisible brace. I thought it best not to mention that fact.

"Of course, there's no pain. When Urmed heals, she does a thorough job."

"Now, Elwood, leave off. The lass is our guest, and our skills are unknown to her."

"Please tell me more about wood elves," I said as I took

a seat on a long bench next to the table. The bench was low, and my knees poked up higher than my seat. As soon as I sat, I jumped back up, wondering what I'd squashed. My tail. How quickly I'd forgotten. I tried again, holding the furry thing aside until I was settled. Eating with the odd couple seemed to be the quickest way to get back up the mountain to meet Matthew. Besides, after all the work Lady Trow had put into cooking the meal, it would be rude not to eat. The last meal I'd eaten was the handful of roots, and I'd puked those all over the ground. My mouth watered at the mounded platters of food.

"May I ask what those are?" I pointed to the circular orange discs.

"Walnut yam cakes, sweetened with honey," Lord Trow said. "My lady bakes the best cakes in the forest." They were delicious—nutty, slightly sweet, and dense as a veggie burger. I asked for a second helping.

While we ate, Lady Trow gave me a brief summary of the wood elves' history. Her family came from the woods north of here, while Lord Trow's had lived in the Taggla Forest for generations. Their marriage cemented relations between two powerful clans.

Once, when I shifted position, I trapped my tail under my leg. I tugged it free without attracting the attention of my hosts. I didn't want to make a habit of sitting on it. I finally solved the problem by draping it behind me to hang over the back of the bench.

I considered how to approach the subject of the war. I knew of nothing that would entice the wood elves to leave their safe homes and risk their lives in battle. Princess Skyla was good at bringing people around to her way of thinking, but I was no diplomat. I wondered if the princess and the others were all right, then forced myself to concentrate on my own troubles. Reaching the clearing as soon as possible was my top priority.

When we'd finished the meal, I stood and stretched my

leg, testing it. No pain and the tightness was easing up. "That food was amazing. I have to go now. Thanks for—"

"Not until you have Urmed's apple tarts and a cup of bee balm tea," Lord Trow said, arching a bushy eyebrow for emphasis. "The tarts are still warm."

"Bee balm tea will help your head heal, dearie," Lady Trow said as she cleared the dishes from the table.

I resigned myself to staying a little longer. This time I took care to drape my tail over the bench before sitting down. I cast about for a topic of conversation while I sipped my tea. "Does your son Sylvan live with you? Do you have other kids? I mean, children?"

Lord Trow sat back in his chair and brushed a few crumbs from his beard. "That we do, lass. We have four young'uns, scattered all over the woods. Sylvan and our daughter Keitha live with their families in the Kintare Woods."

With a start, I sat up straight, sloshing hot tea onto my hand. I wiped it off on my tunic and stared at Lady Trow. "The Kintare Woods? Haven't you heard? There's a battle going on there right now."

She gasped. Lord Trow stood up so quickly his bench fell over. "What do you mean, battle? Explain yourself."

He acts like I have something to do with it. Deciding to keep my lingering doubts about Prince Aiden to myself, I said, "Sorceress Mairsil, King Darren's aunt, has started a war against Kylemore. She's brought troops from the Terrapin Archipelago, and giants from the Wyvam Mountains are fighting with her. There are others on her side, too."

"How do you come by this information?" Lady Trow demanded. "You claimed to be on a diplomatic mission."

I explained in as few words as possible what had been happening in Kylemore since spring—the drought, ruined fields, and poisoned water as well as the attacks on villages around the kingdom. Then I told them about the new predators the Pannmordians had found in their valley. "Prince Brenden said the threat's so great that they'll need all the warriors they can get and he's hoping you'll join the fight. I'm sure he'll send an official request soon. Since you haven't received it yet, I'll ask for him. Can you help?" I held my breath, waiting for Lord Trow to speak.

He stirred another spoonful of honey in his tea. After a minute he laid his spoon on the table. "In recent weeks, I've had similar reports. I didn't believe them to be true. Nairne, one of our representatives currently in the royal city, mentioned problems around the kingdom in his latest message." He made a gesture of apology with his hands. "You have to understand, Nairne has been known to exaggerate now and then. I thought he was trying to sound important."

Lady Trow tugged a lock of her hair. "Elwood, if she speaks true, perhaps we should reconsider our position of isolation."

"Would it help if I did a Far Seeing of your daughter to make sure she's safe?" I asked. "Do you have an item that she used a lot? We could check on your son, too."

After a short consultation, they agreed to the Far Seeing. Lady Trow took down a mug from the shelf that held dishes, and I wrapped my hands around it. Within a minute an image came to me of a short, curly-haired woman standing next to a tree with a toddler hanging onto her skirt. She was arguing with a soldier, who appeared to urge them to leave the area. I relayed everything I saw to the Trows.

"How do we know you're not making it up?" Lord Trow asked when I'd handed the mug back to his wife.

"I'll draw a picture of the woman and child I saw, and you can decide if they are your daughter and grandchild." I still had my belt pouch with some pieces of charcoal and a scrap of paper inside. I drew the curly-haired woman and barely finished the sketch of the toddler's face when Lord

Trow snatched the paper out of my hands. He stared at it, then waved it in the air.

"If our young 'uns are in danger, no giants or islanders will keep us away. Urmed, fetch me Farrac." He turned to me. "We're joining the battle, lass, and you're going with us."

Before the elves retreated into isolation,
there was a time when they were
close allies of humans.
~Calder Fionn
Chronicles of Kylemore

33

JOINING FORCES

*L*ady Trow hurried down a tunnel to fetch Lord Trow's mysterious "Ferrac." She returned carrying a large curved animal horn. Lord Trow looped the leather cord that was fastened to the horn around his neck and waved a hand at the opening that led outdoors. "Out you go, lass. It's time for a gathering of the clan."

I wanted to make my intentions clear while the three of us were alone. "Listen. I'm not going to the battlefield, only as far as the clearing. My brother will wait for me there, remember? We're going to Ardara."

"By yourselves? Do you know the way?"

"No, but I'm sure Matthew's found Prince Brenden and the others by now. They'll take us."

"Does life always work out as you plan, lass?"

Even though I refused to speak, my tail drooped in answer to his question. The traitorous furry rope made it hard to keep my thoughts to myself.

I led the way out of the burrow and was surprised to find it was nighttime. The air was chilly, and brilliant stars littered the velvet black sky. Metiri was full and bright while Kuklos was a berry red gibbous.

I followed Lord and Lady Trow down a dirt path. My tail

quivered, either from the cold air or because I was anxious to find Matthew and the others. We'd been walking for ten minutes or so when I heard the sound of rushing water. My heart sank when we got closer. A long tree trunk served as a bridge across a ravine. Cautiously, I approached the ravine's edge. It was deep, and a stream flowed far below the bridge.

"I can't cross that," I said, stepping back onto firmer ground.

Lord Trow snorted. "Afraid to cross a stout bridge? How have you survived this long, lass?"

Lady Trow touched my elbow and spoke in a soft voice. "Ignore the man, dearie. You may have forgotten since you lost it long ago. Your tail will help you balance. You'll be across in the blink of a firefly."

My feet wobbled on the first few steps. I tilted to the left, then overbalanced to the right. Instinctively, I flung my arms out to the sides. They windmilled in small circles while my tail jerked from side to side in reaction to my shifting weight. Once I righted myself, I took several steady steps to the middle of the bridge. Lowering my arms, I kept my gaze on the back of Lady Trow's curly head for the rest of the crossing. Without conscious effort, my tail adjusted itself to keep me balanced. When I reached the end of the long trunk, I jumped down to land firmly on solid ground. I laughed in delight and gave the end of my tail a little pat.

In another ten minutes, we reached a circular clearing with a large, flat rock in the center. Lord Trow stepped up on the rock and held Ferrac to his lips. It had been hollowed out and the tip cut off. He blew three short blasts followed by two long ones. Every few minutes he repeated the call, and soon wood elves poured into the clearing from every direction. It took a while for them all to arrive. There must have been more than three hundred by the end. Women and men mingled together, all curly-haired and wearing vests and trousers that blended in with the forest colors.

Some used walking sticks. A few carried slender wands. None of them had tails.

Some elves rode into the clearing on corgis. These were taller, shaggier, and wilder versions of the twin's farm dog, Howell. They were dark brown with ginger accents. Large patches of white fur stood out bright along their shoulders, and that's where the elves sat. I remembered my mother calling corgi's white patches "fairy saddles." This wasn't Earth, so if elves wanted to ride them instead of fairies, who was I to question them. The elves were around three to three-and-a-half feet tall. Many rode with their feet only inches above the ground.

I tried to make myself invisible, leaning against a tree trunk at the edge of the clearing, but Lady Trow planted herself next to me. All the wood elves paused in front of her, sweeping off their hats and bowing. They'd give me a quick glance before joining the others near Lord Trow's rock. Although they weren't exactly hostile, none of them were friendly. I ran my thumb along the raised pattern on my ring and greeted each elf with my brightest smile.

After a time, the clan quieted down to listen to Lord Trow. As he spoke, he surveyed the elves, stopping now and then to let his gaze linger on an individual.

"Taggla clansmen. I call you here to prepare for battle. As you know, we elves do not normally trouble ourselves over human squabbles."

Scattered shouts of "Hear, hear" broke out in the crowd.

"Today, we must break that tradition. There is a battle raging to the north. It threatens our kin who have moved to the Kintare Woods." There were pockets of muttering in the crowd, and some of the elves shuffled their feet or exchanged uneasy glances with each other.

Lord Trow went on, "This battle concerns us. The enemy has fierce animals that drop from trees to tear their victims apart. To the east, they've broken through to the Pannmordian Valley. Our corgi pack is not safe. In addition, the enemy has enlisted the giants and brought them out of their northern haven in the Wyvam Mountains."

Several elves spat on the ground and more than a few shook their fists and cursed. After giving them time to work up their anger, Lord Trow finished. "If you are not convinced this fight is ours, know that the enemy is using bolts of fire from rumblestorms to burn down the forest to the south and has enlisted warriors from the Terrapin Archipelago to the west. The battle is making its way to our glen from every direction of the compass."

The mention of fire added fear to the elves' anger. Their whole community could be wiped out in a blaze. Lord Trow talked a little longer, whipping up their emotions. There was much shouting, fist waving, and foot stomping. At some point he must have decided they were agitated enough. He blew Ferrac again and sent them off to prepare to leave at dawn. When we returned to the lord and lady's underground home, I was exhausted. It was warm inside the burrow, and Lady Trow insisted I have another cup of bee balm tea before lying on my mossy bed in the kitchen to catch a few hours' sleep. I was angry with myself for missing my meeting with Matthew and had troubled dreams.

We ate a hurried breakfast at first light, then met up with the other elves in the place the clan had gathered the night before. They organized themselves into six divisions, and we marched up the mountain in formation with Lord Trow in the lead. When we reached the clearing where Matthew and Heulwen had left me, it was empty. I hadn't really expected to find them waiting. All the same, I was disappointed. We marched north for hours, finding no sign of the battleground.

In the afternoon, I offered to do a Far Seeing of Princess Skyla. I drew a sketch of her on a slab of bark, using the burnt tip of a stick Lady Trow prepared for me. Lord Trow recognized the part of the forest where she was, and in the early evening we encountered guards posted at the perimeter of an army camp. At the sight of Lord Trow and the elves, the guards snapped to attention. One ran off to report on our arrival to whoever was in charge.

Before long, we arrived at the camp where Princess Skyla and our other companions were staying. The princess was huddled with a few soldiers, studying an item one of them held in his hand. Carys tended to a campfire. I broke rank and dashed into the camp. Carys spotted me and ran to meet me. We clung to each other in a warm embrace. I'd never been so glad to see a friend.

Over the ages, the outcome of many a battle
depended upon the skill of a Far Seer.
~Calder Fionn
Chronicles of Kylemore

34

ONE STEP BEHIND

I stepped back from Carys' embrace. It had been two days since we'd seen each other. Even in the dusk, I could see dark circles under her eyes by the flickering light of the campfire. My tail switched back and forth in agitation. It was weird how it sometimes moved on its own. Questions tumbled out of me. "How are you? Where are Matthew and Cadoc? Prince Brenden? Can we start back to Adara in the morning?"

Carys looked past me at the hundreds of elves arranged in tidy columns at the edge of the camp. Then she examined me as I had studied her. Her gaze caught on my furry black tail. She smirked. "And you don't think you fit into this world. Want to tell me about it?"

I grabbed the end of my tail to stop its swishing. "Later. It's a long story."

Princess Skyla spoke with Lord Trow, then the princess sent a messenger to inform Prince Aiden of the wood elves' arrival. As he trotted through the camp, I noticed something familiar about the way the messenger carried himself. "Is that Fergus?"

"Aye. He's joined up with the king's army. Prince Aiden thought he'd serve best as a messenger for now. He's had no training as a page or squire, and he's good at moving through the woods without being noticed."

"I bet his da isn't happy he's left the shop."

"Not a bit."

I'd had enough small talk. "Where are Matthew and Cadoc?"

"Out searching for you. The dragon brought Matthew here, then she left to take her baby to Dragon's Nest. It's in a valley up north, between those mountain peaks." She waved her hand up the slope. "Matthew says when the dragonet's old enough, mother and baby go off by themselves. They bond and the dragonet learns to hunt. The Fledging, they call it. That's why we saw them in the woods all on their own."

"Enough about dragons. We have to find the boys."

"Nay, we'll stay here for now. They're safe enough with Alec," Princess Skyla answered. I hadn't noticed she'd joined us until she spoke. "Wandering off will waste time. They have orders to return here by noon tomorrow at the latest."

I didn't ask what the plan was if I didn't turn up before they got back. Something must have shown in my face though, because Princess Skyla said, "If you hadn't found us and they returned empty-handed, we would send a whole regiment out to search for you."

I nodded, grateful for the reassurance. "Princess Skyla, I don't know how much food the elves brought with them. If they're half as hungry as I am, they could eat everything you have on hand and still not fill their bellies."

She looked behind me toward the elves. "I think they can take care of themselves."

The wood elves had spread out in small groups under the trees and were busy preparing for a meal. Some collected wood for cooking fires, others unwrapped packets of meat and vegetables, and a few carried pots filled with water they must have gotten from a nearby stream. Corgis were being fed and watered, much as humans would tend to horses after a long day's ride. At a few campsites, elves were already cooking meat over low flames. The aroma wafted in our direction, and my mouth watered.

Princess Skyla beckoned me to sit near the campfire with her and Carys. "Let us eat, and you can tell us the tale of your tail." She grinned and held out a large bowl of stew and a thick slice of bread. As much as I wanted to go search for Matthew and Cadoc, I knew it was better to stay put, so I accepted the food and settled in to tell them about my adventures since we'd been separated. When I'd answered all their questions, I rolled up in a blanket near the fire and, safe among friends, fell fast asleep.

∞

Prince Brenden joined us for breakfast, and I repeated my story for him. Matthew and Cadoc hadn't returned in the night. I urged Prince Brenden to send out a search party. Despite my pleas, he decided to wait a while and left to speak with Lord Trow. Soon the elves dispersed to join Prince Aiden and the king's army.

When the midday meal was being served up, Alec led Matthew and Cadoc into camp. I ran to meet them, ready to give Matthew a hug. He held me at arm's length and stared at me.

"Is that a tail? What have you done?" He frowned and let go of me. "Turn around."

Alec had left to talk with Prince Brenden. Cadoc took a step toward Matthew, then stopped.

Anger rose inside me making my head hot. "I'll do no such thing. I worried myself sick about you, and all you can say is 'what have you done?' You make it sound like I *asked* for a tail."

"If not, why do you have one? Why weren't you at the clearing? We chased all over the woods searching for you, and here you are, rested and contented as . . . a cat." He stood with arms folded across his chest.

"I don't get it," I said. "Why are you so angry?"

He blinked rapidly, but a tear leaked out. *He was really worried about me.* He brushed the tear away with the back of his hand. My mood softened and I held out two fingers toward him, using the private peace signal we'd made up in third grade. His fingertips touched mine, and he spoke softly so only I could hear. "You're my best friend. I'd never forgive myself if anything happened to you."

Tears welled in my eyes. I tried to make my tone casual. "It's all right. I waited in the clearing for a long time, then—well, a lot of things happened. Come, have a bowl of stew."

Princess Skyla filled two wooden bowls and handed them to the boys. "When you're done," she said, "we have something to discuss."

Cadoc took the bowl from the princess and set it down on a flat rock, untouched. He beckoned for me to follow him. Matthew scowled and jabbed his spoon into his stew. When we were out of earshot of the others, Cadoc stopped. He held onto my arms and studied my face. His eyes were full of worry. "Are you all right? I fretted about you since that skirmish the other night. Matthew hardly ate, he was so concerned."

"I'm okay. Sorry for the trouble. It wasn't fun, although things were much easier when I met the wood elves."

He frowned. "Easier? Perhaps. Nevertheless, I don't believe for a minute that you asked for a tail. How did that come about?"

My mouth twisted in a grimace. "I fell down the mountain, broke my leg, and landed in front of Lord and Lady Trow's home. That was lucky. When Lady Trow healed me, she put me in a deep sleep first, so I couldn't object. Really, it was all a misunderstanding. I gave them the impression I'd lost my tail. She was simply being kind, growing it back. It would be rude to ask her to take it away again."

He held me in a tight embrace. "The wood elves generally keep to themselves. Poppa says they're helpful when they see a need." He released me and kissed the top of my head. "Your tail suits you. It's as pretty as the rest of you."

My cheeks grew hot. "Uh, thanks." I stepped back and took his hand in mine. "Let's get you fed." We walked back to the campfire and he gobbled down his bowl of stew.

As soon as the boys had finished eating, Princess Skyla sat on a tree stump and gathered the four of us around her, with Prince Brenden at her side. She pulled a small packet out of a pouch at her waist. Something was wrapped in a scrap of leather. She peeled back one flap after another, then showed us what was inside. Several strands of thick, black hair were tied together with a narrow length of ribbon.

"Where'd that come from?" Carys asked.

Cadoc was sitting on the ground next to me. At the sight of the hair he leaned back, as though there was a bad odor in the air. He pointed to the packet. "That's oozing with hatred and evil. Whose hair is it?"

Princess Skyla held the packet in a tight grip by the leather wrapping, careful to avoid the hair. "There were signs of a campground in the area. These strands were found stuck in a broken stump of a tree." She waved the packet toward us. "We believe the hairs are from Sorceress Mairsil. If so, they are extremely valuable." She turned to me, and I knew what was coming. My tail trembled in anticipation of her request.

"Kallan, would you be so kind as to do a Far Seeing of the sorceress?" She didn't make a move, and the silence stretched out between us. The hair repulsed me. I didn't want to touch it or have anything to do with the sorceress. However, the fate of the kingdom might depend on finding out where she was.

"Okay," I said and reached out for the packet. I closed my eyes and breathed deeply, running my fingers along the silken hairs. I shuddered and reminded myself how much depended on learning the sorceress' whereabouts, then blocked out everything except the silky strands.

After a minute or two, a picture formed in my mind. I saw a woman with black hair, wearing a silver-colored tunic. She rode a mount as dark as midnight through a forest, accompanied by four other riders. The forest was no different from others I'd seen, and I couldn't find anything special that would mark its location. I watched the little party make its way through the woods, waiting for something unusual to show up. No luck. The only thing that changed was the amount of sunshine. The woods thinned out a little, and the light grew brighter as they rode. Nothing distinctive ever appeared in the area. When my leg fell asleep, I lost my concentration.

I opened my eyes. Everyone was watching me. I stretched my legs and winced at the pins and needles that ran up and down my calf. I shivered with cold. Although Princess Skyla was gentle with her questions, I knew she was disappointed.

I told them what I'd seen. "It could have been anywhere. Near the end, I thought the curve of the path and the trees looked familiar." I said it to give the princess hope and found I almost believed it myself.

Princess Skyla said, "Let's try again in a little while. Maybe you'll see something you recognize for certain then. At least we know she's on the move. If we can learn enough next time, we might be able to stop her before she puts her plan into action."

Carys brought me a blanket, and I laid down near the fire. I was exhausted from the vision and wanted to sleep for a week. Healer Oran was in the camp and brought me a cup with a potion that smelled of nutmeg. I drank it down in a few swallows. The healer still didn't like us kids, but he'd gained respect for us in the Pannmordian Valley. I gave him the empty cup and was asleep within a minute of laying my head down.

It was evening when I woke. Cadoc hurried over to me. "How are you?"

"Warmer and rested. Thirsty." He brought me a cup of water, and I gulped it down.

"Could you do another Far Seeing now? I've been examining that hair and I don't believe we have much time before disaster strikes."

"Yeah, I'm okay now. Let's find Princess Skyla." Fergus and Prince Aiden had come into camp sometime while I slept, and they joined the group that gathered together for the Far Seeing. I didn't want to attempt the vision with Prince Aiden right there. I reminded myself that Cadoc didn't seem to have a problem with him now. Even if Prince Aiden was mixed up in the sorceress' plans, I figured someone in our group would know if he tried to communicate with her.

I settled into a position I hoped wouldn't make my legs fall asleep and held the hair tight in my fist. Right away, I recognized where the sorceress' party was. I opened my eyes and pushed the hair into Princess Skyla's hand, breaking contact with the magic.

"I know where they are! They're on the trail we took from Phelips Pond after the thunderstorm. I don't understand. Why did the sorceress leave this part of the forest? Isn't this where the battle's being fought?"

Prince Aiden shook his head, his shaggy red hair dancing in the firelight, his face a mask of worry. "She's left her troops here to fight and keep us distracted. With a small party, she'll be able to slip inside the castle. The king and queen are in danger. Can you tell how far they are from the royal city?"

"If their camp's where I think it is, they're a full day's ride away. They seem to be settled in for the night."

"What can we do?" Carys asked. "Can you send a messenger bird?"

"Nay," Prince Brenden said. "A pterodactyl attacked and

killed the lot of them. We'll have to count on the castle guards to intercept them."

Prince Aiden was too agitated to stay still. He paced in front of the fire. "And if they can't? Mairsil's a master of deceit and illusion. She'll cast a spell and have the guards believing she's Skyla returning in advance of the rest of you."

"There may be a way to reach the castle ahead of her," Matthew said from his perch on a fallen log.

Prince Aiden spun on his heel. "Are you planning to fly, youngling?"

Matthew's lips formed a tight smile. "Yes, that's exactly what I had in mind." He drew out the leather cord that hung around his neck and held up the amber scale. "Heulwen, the dragon who gave me this, can get there in a day."

Prince Aiden's jaw dropped. He whirled to face Prince Brenden. "What do you know of this, little brother?"

Prince Brenden walked over to stand behind Matthew as if protecting him from Prince Aiden's quick temper. "It happened in the cave region west of the Pannmordian Valley. Matthew has been chosen as a dragon guard. The golden dragon Heulwen named him Cyneweard. The dragon riders live again, big brother." He smiled at Prince Aiden as though he had scored points against him in a game. His expression said, *I may be the younger prince, but Matthew gained his special status when he was with me, not you.* I wondered if males everywhere turn each interaction into a competition.

Prince Aiden sneered, "A tailless outlander chosen as a dragon rider? A wild fantasy. Come, lad, tell me where you got the scale. It's dangerous to tangle with dragons. Didn't my brother tell you that?"

Matthew tucked the scale inside his tunic. "He did. I acted on my own. Heulwen is the ruler of the Camulus clan of dragons. I saved her son, Cai, from certain death. In return, she chose me as a dragon guard. She can get to the castle faster than any other creature around. I don't think she'd fly without me. She can probably carry a second person, though. Maybe it will be enough."

Prince Aiden said, "It will have to be, lad. Or the kingdom is lost." It was the sincerity in his voice and his sad expression that convinced me at last that he had nothing to do with the sorceress and her traitorous war. As soon as I let go of my suspicions, my shoulders, which always tensed up when I was near the red-haired prince, relaxed.

"Who will go with Matthew?" I asked, wondering which prince would win the argument that was sure to come.

"That's simple, lass," Prince Aiden said. "You."

Each person with magical abilities
is unique. Choose the best
individual for each task.
~Master Ailfrid
The Art and Discipline of Magic

35

FLIGHT

I balked at Prince Aiden's decision to send me to the castle with Matthew. My stomach heaved like a dozen butterflies hatched at the same time. I wiped sweaty palms on my trousers. "You . . . you want *me* to go? That makes no sense. You're the Captain of the King's Army. Prince Brenden knows magic and he's good with a sword. Matthew and I are kids. Younglings. Besides," I added, hating to admit any weakness to him, "I don't do heights."

Carys and Matthew turned their attention to Prince Aiden, waiting for his response. Cadoc came to stand next to me. His presence had a calming effect, although not enough to squash the jitters in my middle.

Fergus took a step toward the prince. "I could go in her place, Your Highness." The cloth merchant's son was much more respectful than when we first met. He'd been bitter about working in the shop with his father. Now, as part of the army, he seemed happier. I didn't trust his motives, though. *Is he truly reformed? Or seeking recognition and fame?* He smiled at me. It was more of a smirk than a sign of friendship. I gave a tiny nod and mouthed, "Thank you."

"Matthew is the only person who can communicate

with the dragon," Prince Aiden said. "Kallan is a Far Seer. She's the only one who can keep track of where Aunt Mairsil is. That will be critical when the evil hag enters the castle grounds." Fergus shoved his hands in his trouser pockets. A scowl replaced his smirk.

Prince Aiden turned his attention to me, and I refocused on him. "From what I've heard, you can wield *some* magic. Unless Doileag's act of naming you 'Healing River' was a mistake?"

I felt sick, knowing I could help if I had the courage to face my fear. But I didn't have it. What he was asking was totally different from crossing a ravine on a log bridge. My mouth opened and closed a couple of times before I could speak. "Not a mistake. Although, it doesn't change the fact I'm terrified of heights. I cannot fly on a dragon."

"I have a thought, Your Highness," Fergus said. "We could make a harness with two pouches, like saddlebags. Big ones that can hold a person. Matthew and Kallan can ride on either side of the dragon for balance." I studied him and didn't detect any gloating or mischief in his body language. Maybe he realized there was no quick path to glory. If he wanted Prince Aiden's respect, he was going to have to earn it.

"Excellent suggestion," Prince Aiden said, clapping a hand on Fergus' shoulder. "The army needs clever minds like yours. Your da's loss is our gain." Fergus beamed. He was getting the recognition he craved. Prince Aiden rubbed his hands together. "Let's figure out how to construct these human saddlebags."

The others brainstormed what to make the pouches out of (army tents), how to securely fasten them together (reinforce the seams with magic), and how to attach the whole apparatus to Heulwen so it would stay in place for the entire twenty-hour flight (long straps wrapped around her middle). They all ignored my protests. I sat by the fire and let the discussion swirl around me. Even if I conquered my height terror, the whole plan was off if the dragon refused to take us. I argued with myself for the better part of an hour.

Matthew withdrew to a thicket at the edge of camp to call on Heulwen. Earlier, he'd explained their communication system to me. He would hold onto the scale and call the dragon in his mind. She would reply into his mind. It was some kind of magical telepathy. If they were close, he didn't need the scale at all.

After a while, Princess Skyla and Carys came to sit with me. Carys held a drawing in her hand. "This is our plan. We'll make the pouches long enough so you can lie down. We'll also place them high enough on her sides so you can see each other over her back and talk if you want to."

I studied the sketch and had to admit they'd taken my fear of heights into account. The pouches resembled long cocoons. I could be completely encased and never have to see the ground if I didn't want to.

"What do you think?" Princess Skyla asked. Her tone was neutral, but her body, as she leaned forward, was tense as a bow.

While the others prepared the harness contraption, I had considered the issue from every angle. It was time to make a decision. "I think I can do it. I have to try, anyway."

Princess Skyla sighed in relief. "Thank you kindly. Drink some ginger and chamomile tea before you go. The ginger will settle your stomach, and the chamomile will relax you. You might even sleep."

I seriously doubted I could fall asleep on a dragon. "Has Heulwen agreed to the plan?"

"Let's ask Matthew. He's on his way over."

Matthew joined us. His eyes sparkled and he slipped restless hands in and out of his pockets. "Heulwen has agreed to fly us to the castle. I told her about Prince Brenden's dragon, Simon. Apparently, he and his mother became separated when they were on Simon's Fledging journey. Heulwen wants to bring Simon home to Dragon's Nest. She says that if he's away from the clan too long they'll reject him, no matter that he was one of their hatchlings."

"Prince Brenden named him Simon," I said. "What did the dragons call him?"

"He didn't have a name yet. Their moms name them during the Fledging."

"What happened to Simon's mom?"

"The dragons discovered the remains of her body. Looked like she'd been attacked by a band of giants. Simon was nowhere to be found. They figured the giants killed him and carried him off."

I took a deep breath. So much depended on our trip. I had to see this through.

It took a couple of hours to create the saddlebag pouches. Matthew and I gathered weapons, water flasks, warm clothes, and blankets. The air would be cold at the altitude Heulwen would fly. Prince Brenden and Prince Aiden outlined what to do when we arrived at the castle and gave us a parchment note with the royal seal to get us in to see the king. If all went well, there would be several hours for the castle guards to prepare for the sorceress' arrival. While Matthew and I made our preparations, about a dozen people fashioned the saddlebag pouches and harness under Fergus' direction. The finished contraption was large and sturdy. Carys sealed the seams with magic to reinforce the stitching.

Heulwen needed plenty of space to land. She flew to the far side of the clearing in which the camp was located. Matthew held a silent conversation with her, and then two men fitted the carrier onto her back, securing the harness straps under her belly.

My stomach twisted in knots again as I watched the men work. Cadoc came over and whispered in my ear. "Come. We need to say a proper goodbye."

I let him lead me by the hand into the trees where we

were hidden from view. He wrapped his arms around me, holding me tight. I rested my head on his chest and breathed in his spicy clove scent. His heart beat a steady rhythm in my ear. "I'm scared," I said in a husky voice.

"You're a brave lass. You will succeed." He caressed my hair, smoothing it over and over with long strokes.

"What if I can't? I wish you could go with us. I could be braver if you were there too."

He loosened his grip on me and took a step back. Moonlight lit his face and softened his features, like a marble statue worn smooth with time. He placed a hand over his heart. "Though I'll not be on the dragon, I'll hold you close in spirit."

"I'll keep you close too," I said and put a hand over my own heart. My tail swept out a slow arc.

He pulled me to him. His breath was warm on my face. We drew closer, and then his lips touched mine, soft and warm in a tender kiss. I leaned into him. My body softened, fitting into the curve of his arms. When we finally broke apart, we gazed into each other's eyes in silence for a while. My heart hammered in my chest and my knees grew weak. I wondered if this was love. Whatever it was, I could hardly bear the thought of being separated from him.

"I'd better go." I stepped away before I completely lost the strength to leave.

"Wait." He held onto my arm. "Take this." He put something small and hard in my hand, closing my fingers around it. "The acorn Ma gave me after I set the barn on fire. It made me brave, remembering her courage when she saved Da's life. Let her bravery pass into you."

I swallowed a lump in my throat and tucked the acorn in a pocket. "I'll keep it safe and return it when I see you again." He followed me back to the clearing where Heulwen waited.

On the way, we saw Matthew and Carys emerge from a nearby clump of trees. They were holding hands. I didn't think the pink glow of Carys' cheeks was entirely due to the moonlight.

When we reached the group gathered in the clearing, Matthew and I tossed our gear into the pouches. After a quick round of goodbyes, we climbed up ropes that Carys had attached to the pouches with magic and settled in next to our supplies. My pouch was a pea pod, with me and my gear the peas. If Matthew and I sat up, we could see each other over the dragon's back. When I lay down, the pouch's sides rose above my head.

Heulwen spread her wings, and with a powerful thrust from her back legs we lifted into the air, rising above the treetops after two or three wingbeats. The angle of ascent was as steep as a roller coaster. The force pushed me to the back of my narrow carrier. I stifled a scream, then reached up and held the edges of the pouch in a white-knuckled grip.

Before long, we leveled out, and I braved a look around. Overhead, stars sparkled in the inky spaces between the clouds. Kuklos was a curved, raspberry crescent, while Metiri was full and brilliantly white. I peeked over the edge of my pouch. The ground was far below us; the crowns of trees appeared as small bushes. Heulwen swerved to the left, tilting my side downward, and a swooping sensation hit my stomach. I withdrew my head and focused on my breathing until I was sure I wouldn't puke. After a while, the flight became smooth again. The pouch swayed a little as Heulwen pumped her wings, but it didn't swing wildly. I got used to the gentle rocking motion and relaxed. If I ignored the sound of the air whistling by us, I could almost pretend I was in a hammock in the backyard of our cabin.

We rode in silence for a couple of hours, then Matthew asked how I was doing. We peered at each other over Heulwen's scaly amber back.

"I'm okay," I said, surprising myself. I was beginning to enjoy the quiet flight. "How about you?"

"All right. If it weren't for the sorceress, this would be the best experience of my life."

I laughed. "I wouldn't go that far. Matthew, we can't tell anyone about this when we get back home. They'd never believe us. Or worse, they might try to find this place."

"I know. We'll need a good excuse for missing weeks of school."

I noticed we both avoided discussing our romantic experiences with the twins, as well as the possibility that the gateway to Earth would close before we could return to it. "Family Services will ask a lot of questions," I said. "Do you think they'll let me stay with you and Grandpa? I can't take another foster home."

Besides not making it home at all, this was my biggest worry. I wondered if Grandpa still wanted to adopt me. After all, if I hadn't lost my hold on the chickens when we discovered the gateway, we wouldn't be in this mess. Matthew could have rescued Ethel before the twins ever noticed him.

He frowned, and then shrugged. "After all we've been through in Kylemore, convincing Family Services to let you stay with us should be a snap."

"I suppose."

"First, we need to stop the sorceress. Want to do a Far Seeing now?"

"No. Heulwen's wings make it too breezy. I only have a few of the sorceress' hairs. If I lose them, we'll have no way to keep tabs on her when we get to the castle."

"Right."

We lay down, each occupied with our own worries. I alternated between rubbing my silver ring for comfort and Cadoc's acorn for courage.

The sky lightened with the dawn, and Heulwen descended toward a clearing. We were still in a woodsy area, with no city in sight.

"What's going on?" I asked Matthew.

"Heulwen needs a break. She says she's not used to carrying so much extra weight."

"I hope she recovers soon. We don't stand much chance of surviving if the sorceress arrives at the castle before us."

We climbed down the ropes attached to the pouches. After stretching our legs, we took advantage of the dense bushes to relieve ourselves of the tea we'd drunk before getting underway. We checked the harness to make sure it was still fastened securely and wasn't rubbing on Heulwen's scales. She told Matthew she was thirsty. Although we could hear a burbling stream, the foliage was too dense for the bulky dragon to reach it. Fretting at the lost time, Matthew and I repeatedly filled our flasks and poured the water down her throat until she'd drunk her fill. Then I did a Far Seeing of Sorceress Marisil. She was still in the woods but getting closer to the castle—it would be a race to see who got there first.

When Heulwen indicated she was ready, we climbed back into our pouches, and she took to the air once more. Matthew and I played a game, imagining what animals the passing clouds resembled. Eventually, I drifted into sleep.

I woke as we came in low toward the castle grounds, skimming the treetops. Inside the wall enclosing the lower bailey behind the castle, I saw one of the guards. He was stretched out on the grass next to the guardhouse, arms spread wide, eyes staring at the sky. I didn't think he was imagining animals in the clouds. From the vacant look in his eyes, I didn't think he would imagine anything ever again.

Though it be hard to do,
one must confront evil.
~Handbook of the Eyes and Ears of the King

36

CONFRONTATION

*H*eulwen glided to a stop next to Simon's cage. As the dragon's feet hit the ground, I bounced in my container. Once she folded her wings, I went down the rope, then sprinted toward the guardhouse. Halfway there, I realized Matthew wasn't with me. He had unfastened Heulwen's harness, allowing it to slip to the ground. He seemed to be communicating with her. "Matthew!" I yelled. He broke off the conversation, unlatched Simon's cage, patted Heulwen's side, then ran to join me.

We checked on the guard lying near the guardhouse. He wasn't breathing and had no pulse. In the stone wall surrounding the enclosure, there were wooden doors next to the guardhouses on the east and west side. The door on the east side had been blown off its hinges, and bits and pieces of wood lay scattered about. Some of them were charred and still smoldering. I shivered, realizing we must have missed the sorceress' arrival by minutes.

The walkway near the top of the wall that was usually patrolled by guards was empty. A group of bodies lay in a heap at the foot of a staircase leading up to the walkway. Some were dressed in Kylemore's royal colors. Four wore black uniforms—they must be the sorceress' companions

I'd seen in my vision back in the camp. I was impressed with the castle guards for taking them all out. *If only they had managed to get the sorceress too . . .*

"Where is everyone?" Matthew asked. "The castle's usually swarming with people. You'd better do a Far Seeing," He pulled me into the guardhouse. "We need to find the traitor quickly."

"I'm on it." I took the hair out of its leather wrapping and settled my mind as quickly as I could. "She's in that hallway that leads out of the kitchens, heading toward the front of the castle. Wait—she's got someone with her."

"A guard?"

"No. I can't see the face. Too small for an adult. She's holding a wand against a kid's back." I put the hair into the leather packet and shoved it in a pocket. My tail twitched and my heart pounded.

"Let's go," Matthew said.

We left the guardhouse, running as fast as we could. I was tired and chilly from the Far Seeing, so I couldn't go at top speed. I shuddered when we passed the dead guard. If he couldn't escape the sorceress, what chance did we have? We were near Princess Skyla's conservatory. The door was open, but it wasn't destroyed like the one in the stone wall. We hurried through the bright room. I noticed a shoe sticking out from under a bench that overflowed with exotic plants and wondered how many guards Sorceress Mairsil and her party had killed. As soon as I finished the thought, the shoe moved a little. I grabbed Matthew's sleeve and pointed.

I drew out my wand and we approached cautiously. Matthew squatted next to the bench. I held my breath, fearing it might be an enemy. In that calm tone that soothes animals and people both, Matthew called a name.

"Thane? Are you all right?" I heard a whimper, and then the messenger crawled out from behind a pile of empty baskets. When he spotted me, he put his arms around my waist and burst into tears.

"What is it?" I asked, holding him as he sobbed.

"My . . . my sister. The sorceress has Mary, and she's going to kill her!"

"We won't let her." I patted his arm as he cried. He jerked back. A hole in his sleeve exposed a large patch of blistered red skin. "You're hurt." I almost managed to keep my voice steady.

"It was the sorceress. She grabbed Mary and me. I got free and tried to pull Mary away from the witch. Then she threw a fireball. I couldn't get out of the way in time." He cradled his injured arm with the other one. "It hurts bad."

Matthew found a rag and soaked it in a bucket that was full of water for plants. I tied the wet cloth around Thane's arm. "There, that'll keep it cool until we can find a healer. Let's rescue Mary."

The three of us ran out of the conservatory and through the stable. When we came outside again, Thane scooped up a scuffed leather ball sitting on the walkway leading to the castle kitchens. It was about the size of a soccer ball and appeared to be well made. The dirty brown stitching was probably white when it was new. Thane tucked the ball under his arm, and we trotted toward the castle.

I said, "That's a quality ball."

"It was my da's—a present from King Darren when they were at university. It's all we have left from my da. Mary and I were playing with it—it's our free afternoon—when the sorceress took us."

"What's it filled with?" I asked, trying to keep his mind off his sister.

"Chopped sponge from the Terrapin Archipelago, miss."

That blasted island chain turned up everywhere. "Smart way to fill a ball. We use air at home."

He shot me a surprised look, then gave the ball a squeeze.

Before we entered the rear of the castle where the

kitchens were, I pulled out the packet of hair for another Far Seeing. The sorceress was in a corridor near the front of the castle. A thick white fog covered the floor and swirled around the hem of her black robe. Boots and swords stuck out of the whiteness, and an occasional rounded belly. No one moved, no one challenged her. The sorceress carried Mary over her shoulder, up out of the fog. The little girl pounded Mairsil's back with her fists, but the sorceress didn't seem to notice. I stuffed the hair in my pocket, and we went inside. Using so much magic wore me out. I could hardly keep up with the boys, and I didn't think I could manage another Far Seeing.

The kitchens were fog free, and the yeasty aroma of freshly baked bread filled the air. The room was silent, and nothing moved. We found the bodies of a gray-haired cook and a plump apprentice on the flagstone floor in front of an oven. A loaf of bread rested on a wooden paddle next to them. A couple of other kitchen servants lay by the sink. I couldn't see any blood or wounds.

I asked Matthew, "Dead? Or under a spell?"

He pushed the hair out of his eyes. "A spell makes sense. That way, she'll have staff to work for her when she takes the throne. Come on. We can't let that happen."

We stopped in the doorway to the great hall, not sure where to go next. The room was empty.

Matthew asked Thane, "Do you know where Sorceress Marisil took Mary?"

The boy nodded. "I didn't want to tell her . . ."

"It's okay," I said. "Where?"

"She asked me where the king was. She was going to throw another fireball at me."

"What happened?"

He tightened his grip on the ball. "My eyes turned quick-like toward the part of the castle where the queen's music room is. I couldn't help it."

It was like pulling out a deep splinter, getting one tiny

bit of information at a time.

"And then?" Matthew prodded.

Thane's tail drooped. He looked up, eyes brimming with tears. "She pointed her wand at Mary's face—I couldn't lie to her. She named a lot of rooms on that side of the castle, and I shook my head 'no' every time. When she said, 'The music room?' I didn't say yes. I didn't shake my head either. Then she knew."

"It's all right, you had to save your sister," I said. "There are plenty of guards between the sorceress and that room. Maybe some of them have escaped her magical fog."

Thane frowned at me. "Her what?"

"A thick white cloud she's using to knock people out. I saw it in a Far Seeing. What's the quickest way to the music room?"

"There's a shortcut the servants take," he said. "She might not know about it."

"Let's hope not. Take us to it."

As we started across the great hall, Thane said, "The music room is on the third floor."

I scanned the great hall for more bodies and my breath caught in my throat. I tugged on the boys' tunics and pulled them to a stop.

"What is it?" Matthew asked. "We have to hurry."

I pointed across the room, where a corridor led to the front of the castle. A narrow band of fog flowed along one side of the hallway. A servant exited a storage room where candlesticks and tablecloths were kept and headed straight for the corridor. He carried a tall pile of tablecloths that blocked his view of the low cloud. We shouted at him to stay where he was. He turned his head to ask us a question while he kept walking. I groaned when he stepped into the thick white layer. It swirled around his legs and he collapsed, dropping to the floor like a pile of rags. The tablecloths sank out of sight in the thick mist.

A figure strolled into the great room from the direction

of the kitchen. The colorful striped cape identified the man as Dolph. He called out to us, "I say, Earthers, when did you arrive? Did you know the dragon in the lower bailey is missing? Its cage is empty."

"No time to explain," Matthew said, trotting over to the minstrel. "Find some guards who aren't asleep. Tell them the king and queen are in danger. Send them to Queen Meara's music room. Whatever you do, don't put a toe in the fog."

"Fog? Indoors? Are you daft?" Dolph scratched his head.

"Guards. Music room. Go!" Matthew placed his hands on the minstrel's shoulders and gave him a gentle push toward the front of the castle. Dolph strode off, holding the edges of his cloak to keep it from flapping.

I shouted after him, "Don't touch the fog!"

We ran to the corridor leading to the servants' staircase. The servant who'd carried the tablecloths lay hidden in the foggy half of the hallway. Luckily, the staircase door was on the clear side. We tiptoed along the corridor to avoid stirring up the mist. Thane pointed to an arched wooden door and Matthew edged it open just wide enough for a person to slip through sideways. Cool air flowed down the stairs and out into the hall where it mixed with the fog, stirring the edges of the white blanket. Thin curlicues of mist drifted across the flagstones toward us. Matthew quickly disappeared into the dim staircase, followed by Thane. I hurried after them and closed the door behind me.

Safe from the treacherous fog, we raced up the spiraling stairs. The air was hot and dry in the windowless space. A warm yellow light came from thick candles in sconces on the wall. Our shadows flowed up the rough stone, making the steep, narrow steps hard to see. I hadn't recovered from the Far Seeings or the close call from the fog. By the time we reached the third floor, I was panting and a little dizzy.

Matthew opened the door, and the sweet notes of a harp

floated to us from a closed room to our right. The music room. Queen Meara was playing a melody for the king.

The opposite wall of the corridor faced outdoors and was set off with several angled alcoves that stuck out in a V shape. Each contained a stone bench under a window for resting and taking in the view of the gardens far below. Before we'd taken two steps toward the music room to warn the king and queen about the sorceress, a shrill voice rang out from the stairway at the far end of the hall to our left. "Wretched girl. Stop hitting me. If I didn't need you to play on Darren's sympathy, I'd have killed you by now."

The three of us turned toward the voice. Two guards stood at the end of the corridor. I heard the scrape of blade against scabbard as they freed their swords. Both of them rushed down the stairs and out of sight. I blew out a big breath, grateful they could finish off the sorceress, so we didn't have to face her. As soon as I finished the thought, I heard grunts and the thud of bodies tumbling down the stone steps. Then, Sorceress Mairsil's head appeared in the doorway at the end of the hall, and she and Mary started toward us. The little girl walked behind the sorceress now, punching her back and kicking her whenever she could. The sorceress ignored the blows. She gripped her wand with one hand and Mary's wrist with the other.

I considered throwing up an air wall to hold Sorceress Marisil back, but it wouldn't be smart to do that while she had Mary in her grasp—if they were trapped together, Mairsil might decide she didn't need to keep the girl alive any longer.

When they came even with the first alcove, Thane ran to them. Matthew tried to hold him back. He managed to catch the boy's sleeve, but Thane pulled free, dropping the leather ball in the process.

The sorceress sneered at the boy and readied her wand. With a flick of her wrist, she shot a series of glowing fireballs out of the tip. Thane ducked and ran in a crooked path. The fireballs narrowly missed him and smacked into the wall inches from my face, blackening the stone. One flew right past my ear, and I breathed in the stink of burning hair. I rubbed my head and yelled for the king. Behind me, rippling music flowed under the music room door as the queen plucked the harp strings.

Thane had reached the sorceress and tugged at her fingers, trying to pry them off of Mary's wrist. Matthew ran forward, bent double, and headbutted the sorceress, sending all of them crashing into the wall of an alcove. Sorceress Mairsil was strong though, and never loosened her grip on Mary or her wand. As soon as Matthew stood up, Mairsil flicked her wand at him and said, *"Rigidio."* He stiffened and fell over, a human stick of wood. I didn't know if I could reverse a spell the sorceress had cast. I pointed my own wand at him and shouted, *"Reversion."* Matthew's body relaxed and he rolled over, then rose onto his hands and knees. He shook his head like a dog after a bath, then got to his feet and backed up toward me. The sorceress would have hit him with another spell if Mary hadn't clamped her teeth onto Mairsil's hand. Thane grabbed the sorceress' wand and tugged. She held on tight to her weapon.

We were at a standstill. I wanted to run to the music room and pound on the door but didn't dare turn my back on the sorceress. If she made me into a piece of wood, there was no one to undo the spell. Carys had taught me how to send a thin thread of fire out the end of a wand. They were nowhere near as big as the sorceress' fireballs. Still, it was worth a try. I uttered the spell, aiming for her face. A promising streak of orange light soared out of my wand, only to fizzle out halfway down the hallway. I swayed with exhaustion. I couldn't do any more magic.

Mairsil laughed at my feeble attempt. As if planned for the dramatic scene playing out in the hall, the queen's music rose to a crescendo. Matthew was by my side, saying something I couldn't hear. The sorceress stomped on Mary's foot, which caused the kitchen maid to stop biting her. Then Mairsil raised her wand arm, lifting Thane off the floor. She tried to shake him off, but he held tight until the sorceress spit in his eye. He let go with one hand to wipe his face and she managed to throw him to the ground. Still gripping Mary's wrist, Mairsil pointed her wand at me. Before I could duck or swerve, I heard the words *"Ascendi y Descendi."* I rose in the air, cracked my head on the ceiling, then crashed to the floor, smashing my nose on the smooth stone. Using my sleeve, I wiped warm blood off my chin. Still, the harp music continued. *Why doesn't the king hear us? We're making a lot of noise.*

When I tried to get up, Matthew shouted, "Stay down." I obeyed, happy for him to take charge. He set the leather ball on the floor, then drew back his foot and gave the ball a sideways soccer kick. It flew in a smooth arc, dropping to smack into the sorceress' face. At the same time, Mary bit down hard on the sorceress' hand, forcing her to release the girl's wrist. Mary ran to her brother, and he pulled her toward Matthew and me.

When enough space opened up between the sorceress and the kids, I gathered my strength for one more spell. Pointing my wand at the sorceress, I said, *"Solidiom."* The air boomed into a clear, solid wall, trapping her in the alcove. A door opened behind us, and the king stepped into the hall. He held a golden statuette in one hand. It was in the shape of a bird, like Carys' pet Aeron, only twice as big as the real bird. Queen Meara stood behind the king, peering over his shoulder.

"What in blazes?" the king said.

The sorceress shook her fist and ranted at Matthew and me from behind the air wall. "I was the eldest. I should have ruled Kylemore, not my idiot brother, Raghnall. It was my right! You cursed outsiders crossed me at every turn. My villains destroyed the fields, and you exposed them. I poisoned the river, and you cleansed the water. You stopped the Pannmordian sickness and killed my roc. Even brought wood elves and dragons together to oppose me . . ." Her voice trailed off, but the hatred in her black eyes was as deep as ever.

I was shocked by how much she knew. "But how? Did Prince Aiden tell you?"

"Aiden?" she scoffed. "Never. I would have used him if he weren't such an arrogant, stubborn man who thinks too much of himself and is eternally loyal to Darren. Nay, it was the pterodactyls."

My suspicions were true. I shivered right down to my tail. "For real?"

The sorceress' mouth was a thin red slash in a pale face. "They told me everything. I would have taken the throne by now if it weren't for you younglings." Her face hardened. "The time for talk is over. I'll take my rightful place on the throne now." Waving her wand at the air wall she muttered, *"Wearm Ager, Mollis Ager."*

With a soft whoosh, my air wall shimmered and dissolved. Mairsil pointed her wand at us again. We never heard the spell she had in mind. King Darren threw the golden statuette with all of his might, catching his aunt in the forehead. She stumbled back, cracking her head on the sharp corner of the alcove wall. Her wand clattered to the floor and she sank onto the bench. She put a hand to the back of her head and brought it out red with blood. She stared at it with widened eyes. After a few heartbeats, they glazed over. Her chin sank to her chest, her bloody hand dropped to the bench, and the life went out of her.

A thunder of boots sounded on the stairs. Half a dozen guards poured into the hall, followed by Dolph. The minstrel took in the scene and said, "Are we too late?"

When life gets hard,
I hang on to what's important.
~Kallan MacKinnon, tenth-grade essay

37

CHOICES

*K*ing Darren approached his aunt, the powerful, traitorous, Sorceress Marisil. He picked up her wand and pocketed it, then checked for a pulse. Shaking his head, he laid her hand on her chest. Her attempt to take over the kingdom was finished.

The king and queen spoke with the guards and Dolph. Matthew handed me a handkerchief to wipe away the blood from my swollen nose, then wrapped his arms around me. Thane and Mary joined us, and we laughed and cried in a group hug. I was happy King Darren had dealt with the sorceress, yet still bothered by his delay in joining the fight. When we broke apart, I said, "Thane, what took the king so long to step in. Didn't he hear the commotion?"

"The music room's got a spell on it. It lets sound out and keeps outside noise from getting in and spoiling the music." I bit my tongue to hold back a curse.

"Good thing he had that bird statue," Matthew said. "Can't imagine why he had it with him."

Thane said, "He'd forgotten it in his study and had me bring it to the music room. That's how I knew where he was."

I frowned, "Why'd he want it in the first place?"

"When he was a lad, his da, King Raghnall, gave him the statuette as a gift. His da is on his mind a lot these days, so he keeps it with him."

"Why's his da on his mind so much right now?" I asked.

Thane's habit of giving out bits of information one at a time like valuable coins, saving the biggest news for last, could be frustrating. This time, Mary spoke up, beating him to the grand finale. "The anniversary of King Raghnall's death is today." The little girl clasped her hands behind her back and looked at her feet with a satisfied smile. Thane scowled and nodded in agreement.

"I see." My ring always made my mom feel close. It made sense the golden bird would do the same for King Darren.

Queen Meara came over and we bowed and curtsied. Her middle bulged out farther than the last time we'd seen her. She said in her gentle, musical voice, "Thank you for saving King Darren and me. You've done a great service to the kingdom, and your deeds will be long remembered."

The rag I had wrapped around Thane's burned arm was coming undone. The queen rewound it and tucked the end into the wrappings. "I will take you all to the healing wing."

"Matthew and I are fine," I said. My protest was spoiled by the need to wipe a trickle of blood off my lip.

She waved away my objection. "While you may not be seriously injured, I insist you see a healer."

Matthew said, "With respect, Your Majesty, my sister and I want to see my grandfather before we go to the healers. He needs to know we're all right." I felt a warm glow inside at the word "sister."

There was sadness in Queen Meara's eyes above her smile. "He does indeed. Come, I'll take you to him." She turned away from the group clustered around the sorceress' body and led us through the stony hallways. All the sorceress' spells had ended with her death. The fog was gone, and those who'd been magicked to sleep were waking up.

I carried the scuffed leather ball. Thane held his sister's hand as we walked, and he repeatedly stole glances at Matthew. For a while Matthew ignored him. When Thane kept it up, Matthew said, "What's on your mind?"

Thane ducked his head. Then a grin lit his face, and he said, "Where'd you learn to kick like that?"

Matthew laughed and ruffled the boy's hair. "It's a game we play back home."

"Can you teach me?"

"You bet."

A few minutes later, we arrived at the healing wing. The front of the room was filled with shelves and cabinets stocked with clay jars, bunches of dried herbs, and oddly shaped pieces of medical equipment. I didn't even want to think about their uses. Behind the supply areas, rows of beds lined the walls on either side of the room; many were empty, some of them were screened off for privacy, and people slept or read in others. Although the screens were cloth on wooden frames, and the beds were simple ones with feather mattresses, the space was enough like a hospital to revive bad memories of my mom's illness. I wanted to deliver Thane and Mary and leave as quickly as possible to see Grandpa.

The queen handed the young siblings over to a healer and gave her a brief summary of the events that had taken place upstairs. I gave Thane his ball, and Matthew and I turned to leave. Queen Meara put a hand out to stop us. "Not that way."

Matthew frowned. "But . . ."

"Come," she said. She led us down the wide aisle between rows of beds, stopping at a screen hiding a bed at the end of the row. Smiling, she motioned for us to go behind the screen. There, under a soft coverlet, lay Grandpa.

"I'll leave you alone," the queen said, then walked away.

There was no lump in the covers from a splint on

313

Grandpa's leg. They must have healed that much, I thought. However, his skin was pale, and he looked thin and frail. His hair was whiter than I remembered, and he'd grown a silky beard. Matthew sat on the edge of the bed and they clasped hands. I stood next to my foster brother, trying to hide my worries.

"I was wondering when you'd show up," Grandpa said. He noticed my tail, and his lips formed an O.

"It's a long story," I said, glancing at the glossy fur. "I'll tell you when we're not so tired. I'll ask the healers to remove it before we go home." I would be sad to see it go— it was a part of me now. "Grandpa, what happened to you? Are you still recovering from the attack on Lord Humphrey's party?"

"No. After the baron's guard brought me here, I had a heart attack. The healers did all they could, but . . ." He scratched his beard. "Well, it's an old ticker, and it's wearing out. They couldn't fix it completely, even with their magical touch."

Matthew drew in his breath and Grandpa said, "Not to worry, son. I expect to be around for quite a while yet. I'm getting stronger every day. It's going to take a few weeks before I'm well enough to travel back to the Dunstan's farm, though."

"What have you been doing to pass the time?"

"Learning about the history of this fascinating kingdom. A couple of historians live here full time and we've been comparing Kylemore with Europe in the Middle Ages. Another visitor, Wulfric Keane, is a representative from a tribe that lives in the mountains near Dragon's Nest. He's an expert on magical creatures, especially dragons." He clasped his hands behind his head. "One of the healers said you two flew here on a dragon. I expect you'd enjoy chatting with Wulfric."

"For sure," Matthew said. "What did he say about—"

I'd had enough of dragons for one day and interrupted

before they could get deep into dragon lore. "Grandpa, not to change the subject, but did you have any side effects from the magical healing?"

He pushed his hair back.

I laughed. "Pointy elf ears!"

"My hearing is vastly better than normal. I can tell when mice are scuttling in the corridor at night. If the effect lasts long enough, it might be a handy fox detector when we get home. No more chickens flying the coop."

We all laughed at that. It was fun to be together as a family again.

A healer interrupted us to check Matthew and me over and tend to our injuries. We visited with Grandpa a while longer, then a footman came to take us to dinner. We ate a simple meal with King Darren and Queen Meara in a small dining room. Thane and Mary were spending the night in the healing wing. Weak as he was, Grandpa insisted on eating with us.

The queen explained she'd given the kitchen staff the night off, to rest and recover from the sorceress' spells. Queen Meara herself had prepared our supper. Like Prince Brenden, she'd spent many hours as a kid in the royal kitchens in her kingdom, testing out recipes and learning to cook. The scrambled moa eggs with queen's button mushrooms and thick slices of bread covered in honey butter tasted better than the fanciest meal I'd ever eaten in a restaurant on Earth.

Around midnight, Grandpa said he was ready for bed. We thanked the queen for the meal. Before we could leave, the guard, Glendon, whom I still thought of as Iron Beard, came to the door. He approached the king, ignoring the rest of us. His expression was unreadable. "Your Majesty, a messenger wishes to speak to one of your guests. He says it is of the utmost urgency."

"Send him in."

A minute later Glendon brought in the Dunstan

farmhand Rafe and then withdrew. A feeling of dread swept over me. What news did Rafe bring that could explain the wild look of the man? He seemed to have ridden the long distance from the farm with hardly a rest. I couldn't imagine how he'd gotten the guards to open the city gate at this hour.

Queen Meara offered him water. He thanked her and drank half a goblet in a few swallows. He set the cup on the table and wiped his mouth on his sleeve. "Master Rolant sent me with an urgent message for David Webbe from Lord Humphrey's guards. These are their words:

The way grows dim. What once a body could pass through with ease, light can barely penetrate. By the fifth day of the seventh cycle of Metiri, solid rock will meet your gaze.

The strange message could only refer to the gateway to Earth.

Rafe swayed a little when he finished. Queen Meara called for a footman to take him to the kitchen for food, then to a room for sleep.

Before he left, I asked, "Rafe, when does the seventh cycle of Metiri begin?"

"In four days, miss."

Crap! We're running out of time.

King Darren was the first to speak into the silence that followed Rafe's departure. He addressed Matthew and me. "As I told you once before, when a gateway closes, it does not reopen. You are left with two choices. Travel as fast as possible, by horse or on Heulwen, if she'll take you, and you should arrive in time to pass through the opening. However, you return home alone. Your grandfather would die on such a journey, whether by horse or dragon. Or, remain in Kylemore and create a future for yourselves here."

The king held our gaze, his dark eyes reflecting his compassion for our situation. I sat rigid as a wand, grasping Matthew's hand tightly in my own.

Grandpa's cheeks reddened. "I'll not have you stay here because of me. You two have your lives ahead of you. Your future is on Earth."

"No!" Matthew and I said in unison.

Queen Meara said, "Decide in the morning. This choice is too important to make in an instant. Reflect on it."

Matthew shook his head. "I don't need time for reflection. I won't leave my grandfather." He looked at the frail old man and his voice softened. "You can't convince me to go, Grandpa."

I went to my foster father and hugged him, burying my face in his neck. When I lifted my head, my cheeks were wet with tears, yet my voice was steady. "Grandpa, you took me into your home when I had no one. You and Matthew are my family. Kylemore will be our home."

Grandpa opened his mouth to argue, then closed it again. His shoulders slumped and he said in a quiet voice, "I have no strength to protest. I want to hear your thoughts in the morning. If you choose to stay, remember there's no going back."

I rubbed the smooth metal of my ring, but my thoughts were too jumbled for my old habit to do any good.

In Kylemore, "home" means more than
where you live and the place you
belong. It's where you flourish.
~Kallan MacKinnon, Kylemore Diary

38

CONSEQUENCES

*W*e didn't change our minds about staying in Kylemore. What mattered most was that Matthew, Grandpa, and I were together. In the days that followed, my chest ached often with the thought of home and all we'd lost. Other times, I was lightheaded with a blossoming sense of freedom and adventure. Often, knots of anxiety twisted my insides. *Where will we live? How can we earn a living?*

When we weren't trading stories of our travels around the kingdom with Grandpa, Matthew and I took long walks in the castle gardens to discuss our future. Some days, Matthew spent time in the library learning about dragons from the mountain man, Wulfric Keane, while I had tea with the queen. We got to know each other pretty well. She was curious about kids on Earth: the kind of toys we had, what sorts of games we played, and what we learned in school. When it hurt too much to talk about home, I asked her questions about being a kid in Kylemore.

The healers assured us Grandpa would get better. I didn't think he believed them. Whenever we tried to make plans for after his release from the healing wing, Grandpa would change the subject. He seemed to feel he'd let us down by not getting us back home. He needed hope—something to look forward to, but that was one thing I couldn't give him.

Rafe left with our reply to Rolant the day after delivering his depressing message. I was glad to see the farmhand go; he was a reminder of the lost gateway to Earth. Within two weeks, Beli and Lord Humphrey returned to the castle from their mission in the west, and then the twins arrived with Prince Brenden and Princess Skyla.

I wanted to tell Cadoc about our encounter with the sorceress; however, their party arrived late at night, and they were exhausted from the long trip. The next morning, Queen Meara had the kitchen staff bring the four of us breakfast in the small dining room where we'd eaten after the sorceress died.

Once we were served, the queen stopped by to welcome the twins to the castle. "I expect you have a lot of catching up to do and could use some privacy," she said before closing the door to the small room and leaving us alone.

There was an awkward silence while we ladled oatmeal and fruit into bowls, spread jam onto toast, and poured juice into our mugs. So much had happened in the time since we'd seen the twins, I didn't know where to begin. Matthew and Cadoc kept quiet too. Carys studied her toast, then broke the silence. "I suppose we'll leave for the farm tomorrow. You'll be through the gateway and home in two weeks."

"About that," Matthew said. "There's been a change of plan."

Carys flinched. "For true?"

Cadoc's head snapped up. "Beg pardon?"

We took turns filling them in on Grandpa's heart attack and the message from Rafe. It took a while to convince them that we were all right with our decision. Finally, they accepted our reluctance to talk about the gateway or home. Cadoc asked in a casual voice, "Which was harder, riding

Heulwen for twenty hours or fighting Sorceress Marisil?"

That was a subject we could talk about more easily. When we were done, they told us about their return trip to Ardara. It turned out that with the death of the sorceress, the rainstorms returned to normal. They came across pockets of rebels along the way. King Darren had sent a messenger bird to Prince Brenden, so he was able to inform the villagers that the king had killed the sorceress. Further, Prince Brenden said if they didn't show loyalty to King Darren, Prince Aiden and his troops would haul them to the dungeons in Ardara.

I never thought that I'd see my mare, Willow, again. Somehow, she returned to the castle on her own from the woods where we'd been attacked. Cadoc and I visited her in the stable where she was recovering from her wounds. She seemed happy to see us and gobbled down the carrots we brought for her.

Afterward, Cadoc asked me to walk with him in one of the castle gardens. We wandered along the gravel paths, under the light of both moons. Metiri was a dim crescent, and Kuklos was a few days past its full moon phase. Cadoc sat me on a granite bench next to a pear tree full of ripening fruit.

"Stay there," he said. Then he walked toward a path that followed the castle wall.

I started to rise then plopped down on the cool stone to wait. *What is he up to?* My legs were twitchy. One jiggled up and down. I pressed my hands on my knees and then tilted my head back to count pears. Before long, Cadoc returned carrying a wreath made of small, fragrant flowers.

He cleared his throat. "I ought to do this when Kuklos is at the full again . . ." He straightened his shoulders. "I can't wait that long. Carys may have told you, Kuklos is the moon we connect with romance. It's our custom for a lad to give a lass flowers when Kuklos is full, as a way of saying . . ." He trailed off, and I gave him an encouraging smile to get him started again.

"Well, uh, as a way of saying he fancies her. That is, he thinks she's special. If she feels the same about him, she accepts the flowers as a gift. Will you, Kallan, accept this wreath from me?"

I nodded and whispered, "Yes." I reached for his hand. "You're special to me too."

He placed the wreath on my head and pulled me close for a long, soft kiss. It was wonderful to be in his arms again and breathe in his spicy scent. When we came up for air, I fumbled in my pocket for the acorn he'd lent me. "Thank you for letting me borrow this. It made me braver when I faced the sorceress."

"Keep it. The flowers will lose their bloom. The acorn will last and keep me close to you when we can't be together."

"All right." I put the acorn away. "I'll give you a drawing of myself, as a reminder of me."

We walked back through the garden in the rosy light of Kuklos, my new favorite moon.

∞

The next morning, King Darren and Queen Meara requested that all of us, except Grandpa, meet them in the king's conference room. Even Thane and Mary were released from their duties to come.

When we were settled, I blurted out the question at the top of my mind. "Does Kylemore have a special place for homeless families to go?"

"Homeless? What do you mean?" Queen Meara said. "You may stay at the castle as long as you wish."

"That's very generous, Your Majesty." It *was* generous. The castle would never be like our house in Albany or our summer cabin in the Adirondacks, though. It wasn't our own place.

"My parents will let you stay at our farm if you want," Carys said. "You'd be close to the spot where you entered our world."

"That's good of them," Matthew replied. He didn't appear any more excited about the idea than I was. Staying with the Dunstans would be worse than remaining in the castle. It would drive me mad to be reminded every day that the home we'd left behind was just out of reach. I bit my lip to hold back tears.

King Darren sat behind his desk on the raised platform, elbows on the cluttered surface, fingers steepled. He cleared his throat, and we turned like flowers toward the sun to hear what he had to say.

"Let us set aside the question of a home for now. There are other matters we must attend to first. Cadoc and Carys, please approach."

They exchanged puzzled glances, then crossed the room to stand in front of the platform. The king stood and smiled at them. "You have both given much service to your king and kingdom these past weeks. You guided and befriended the Earthers, saved my brother and his guards, took an enemy captive, and delivered him to the castle. Your actions helped Matthew and Kallan arrive in time to save Queen Meara and me from the traitor in the realm. You showed bravery and strength of character and deserve to be rewarded."

"We only did what was right, Your Majesty. We seek no reward," Cadoc said.

"We would give our lives to protect you and the queen," Carys added.

The king nodded solemnly. "I am grateful for your loyalty and humility. However, it is my privilege and pleasure to acknowledge your service. You will be given land and treasure and will join the ranks of nobility as baron and baroness."

They gaped at him. He wasn't finished. "Carys, we do

not know the full extent of your talent as a healer and plant mage. If you agree, you will enter university this autumn, and attend free of charge."

"I'm honored. It has long been my dream to study at the university." She curtsied to both rulers.

"Cadoc," the king said, "your family has long served in the Eyes and Ears of the King. If you are willing, you'll train as an agent in that vital service. The kingdom will always have enemies. We need your talent."

Cadoc said, "I agree to your request, sire. We thank you for the titles and gifts of land and treasure." He bowed to the king and then to the queen. I wanted to rush over and hug the twins. This appeared to be a formal ceremony though, so I stayed put.

Once they were seated again, King Darren said, "Matthew, please approach."

Matthew ran a hand through his hair, tugged on his sleeves, then slowly walked to the king's platform.

The king stepped down to stand in front of him. "You have shown loyalty to me as well. You fought for the kingdom from the back of a dragon. That is something we have not seen in Kylemore for over a hundred years. You have earned the right to be dubbed a dragon knight. Kneel."

Matthew knelt and bowed his head, clasping his hands in front of himself. "Matthew Webbe, do you promise to be faithful to me, your king, to never cause me harm, and to observe your homage to me completely, in good faith, and without deceit?"

"I do."

King Darren picked up a sword that lay on his desk and tapped one of Matthew's shoulders with the flat of the blade, then the other. "I dub thee Sir Matthew Webbe, the first in a new line of dragon knights. You will receive a bountiful treasure. Prince Brenden and Wulfric Keane have some ability to bond with dragons and knowledge of the history of the dragon knights of old. They will be your tutors in that area. Prince Aiden will mentor you in battle tactics. Rise, Sir Matthew, and receive this sword as a gift from me."

This time I couldn't help myself. When Matthew stood, I ran to embrace him, careful to avoid the sword's blade. "Congratulations, Sir Matthew," I whispered in his ear as he hugged me back. When we parted, the king smiled at me.

"Returning to the subject of living arrangements, Queen Meara and the Dunstan family have made honorable offers. As kindhearted as they are, I believe, Kallan, that you would prefer a home of your own. Is my thinking correct?"

"One day, Your Majesty, it would be terrific to have our own home again."

"You already have a home here in Kylemore."

"I don't understand."

The king pulled a large burgundy book from a shelf behind his desk. He cleared a place on the map table and opened the book to a page he had marked with a ribbon. "Kallan, bring your ring." He held out his hand.

I placed my ring in his palm. He held it over the open page, blocking my view of the book with his body. "Tell me again how you came by this ring." He traced a finger over the loopy pattern on the top. Many people called it a figure eight, or an infinity symbol. My mother told me it was really two "S" pieces joined together, one facing forward, the other backward.

"My mother gave it to me. It's been in her father's family, the Sheehan family, for countless years. The ring was passed down to the eldest son in each generation. My mother was an only child, so the ring came to her. I've never seen another like it. My favorite part is the rainbow of colors that swirl through the metal."

The king stepped aside so I could see the book clearly. He held my ring next to a drawing of an identical one. The name "Sheehan" was written in a flowing script under the drawing.

"What does this mean, Your Majesty?"

"I suspected what your ring was the first time I saw it. While you traveled to the Pannmordian Valley, I met with our most senior historians. This book," he tapped the open page, "is a history of Kylemore's royal and noble families. The Sheehans were more than noble. They were a *royal* family. They ruled Kylemore for an age, beginning with King Stephen. In time, they dwindled to a small group of fewer than a dozen. One day they went riding together, and the entire family and all the guards and servants with them disappeared, never to be seen again. I believe they passed through a gateway similar to the one that brought you here."

He smiled at me. "I also believe you were meant to return to Kylemore. This is your true home. When the Sheehans disappeared, there was a . . . struggle between the noble families at the time, and eventually the Pendergast family, our family, came to rule the kingdom."

My knees felt weak. Gripping the book, I compared my ring with the drawing of the Sheehan ring again. The drawing even captured the swirling colors. "Can you explain the colors?"

"They are not part of the silver. They are a sign of the magic that's been placed into the ring."

"You mean I don't have magical talent? It's the ring that makes me a Far Seer?"

"Not at all. You have your own magical ability, separate from the ring. The Sheehans were powerful mages. When the ring was made, each living Sheehan added a bit of his or her own magic to the metal. The ring protects the rightful owner from harm and enhances their natural ability. You've had some close calls since you arrived here, yet you survived. Do you think it was pure luck that you reached the castle in time to save me from my traitorous aunt? You managed the powerful water-cleansing spell with no harm to yourself or anyone else. When you fell down the mountain, you didn't land in front of a random elf's home but the one belonging to the leader of the clan."

"I had no idea." I rubbed the smooth curve of the design with a trembling finger. I would never take the ring off again.

The king's eyes twinkled. "No doubt there are other times the ring's power worked in your favor. You even managed to grow a tail."

I blushed, and the end of my tail brushed my leg. It wasn't entirely under my control.

He closed the book and pulled a map out of the pile on the table. "I said earlier that you have a home here. This," he pointed to a spot north of Ardara, "is where the Sheehan castle was located. Their royal city was called Canibri. When they disappeared, the site was abandoned, and Ardara was built as the new royal city. The old castle still exists, although the walled city around it became deserted during the struggle for a new ruling family."

The look he gave me now was all business. "You are the rightful heir to the castle and lands and the Sheehan treasure. I planned to tell you earlier, then Rafe came with the message about the gateway before I got the chance. I had already made arrangements with the guardians of the royal treasury, in case you decided to stay in Kylemore. You will be given treasure equal to the amount the family owned when they disappeared, plus interest. It will be more than enough to repair the castle and hire servants to run the household. You will also receive artifacts dating back to the time of the Sheehans."

It was all too much. As my knees threatened to give way, Matthew came and hugged me. I whispered, "What do you think? Should I take it all?"

"Of course. It's yours."

I stood tall, willing my knees to stiffen. "Okay, Your Majesty. I'll accept the Sheehan treasure and the home of my ancestors."

The king slipped my ring on my finger. "There is one other matter to attend to, Princess Kallan."

"Princess?"

"It is your correct title since your family ruled the kingdom and never abdicated the throne."

Yikes! Do I have to help rule the kingdom? "I see. What is the other matter?"

"Kylemore can have only one king and queen at a time, and the current rulers are Queen Meara and me, as my Aunt Mairsil learned with tragic results. Beyond that, there can be only one ruling family. I hope that we can come to a peaceful agreement. I would ask you to sign this document I've had prepared. It states that you give up your family's right to rule Kylemore. You will retain your title, lands, and family riches—you'll still be royalty, minus the burden of decision making that comes with overseeing the kingdom."

I had no desire to be in charge. "Where do I sign?"

Before he handed me a quill, I had to pledge fealty to him as Matthew had done. After that, I signed my full name on the document with a flourish: *Kallan Aileen Sheehan MacKinnon.* When I finished, Thane shuffled over to me.

"Princess Kallan, I have a question."

The curly-haired messenger was a shadow of the lively, curious boy he was when we first met. The only side effect he'd had from the magical healing of his burned arm was a change in eye color, to violet. Still, he'd become anxious and fidgety ever since the sorceress had forced him to choose between his kingdom and his sister. Family rightfully won out, but he wore the guilt of giving away the king and queen's location like a suit of armor. He chewed his nails, couldn't eat or sleep, and positively would not look the king in the eye.

"What is it Thane?"

"I wanted to ask," he said, glancing at Mary, who sat on a chair, swinging her legs back and forth. "I wondered if my sister and I could live with you in Canibri." He wrung his hands and faced the king. "Beg pardon, sire, we can't stay here, neither of us. The terror was too great for Mary. As for me, well, I can't live here, knowing what I done. And we can't go back to our ma, you know that."

King Darren dropped to one knee in front of the boy. "Thane, lad. What you did was brave. You protected your sister while keeping silent about the queen and me. It's a rare person who could hold their tongue in the presence of my devious aunt. Queen Meara and I have great respect for you."

Thane's eyes widened at the praise. "Thank you."

"My wish is for you to be happy," the king continued. "You will make a fine knight one day. If memories of recent events here are too dark, and Princess Kallan will allow it, perhaps it is best for you and Mary to live with her for a while. Know that you and your sister are always welcome here, and I will continue to oversee your education and training as I promised your da long ago."

Thane stood at attention, waiting for my answer. In spite of his impish ways, or maybe because of them, I'd grown fond of the boy. "I'd be happy for you and Mary to come to Canibri. Matthew and Grandpa will live there too." I hugged the little messenger, and when I stepped back, his bright smile gave me hope that one day he would regain his former light spirit.

That settled, the only thing left to do was tell Grandpa the good news. Maybe it would be the boost he needed to speed his recovery.

I looked around the room at our new friends, and peace settled over me like a blanket. After years of living with foster families and weeks of traveling around a treacherous foreign land, my wandering was at an end. I'd found my way home, at last.

Characters

Note: Kallan, Matthew, David, and the chickens are from Earth. All others are from the world of Betherion.

Aiden Pendergast: A prince of Kylemore, younger brother of King Darren

Beli Whelan ("Poppa"): (bell'eye we'lan) Carys and Cadoc's maternal grandfather

Bodyguards of Prince Brenden: Alec, Bolin, Conroy, Kain

Brenden Pendergast: A prince of Kylemore, youngest brother of King Darren

Cadoc Dunstan: (cad'oc dun'stan) A fifteen-year-old boy who lives on a Kylemore farm. Cadoc's twin sister is Carys.

Carys Dunstan: (care'iss dun'stan) A fifteen-year-old girl who lives on a Kylemore farm. Carys' twin brother is Cadoc.

Darren Pendergast: King of Kylemore

David Webbe (web) ("Grandpa"): Matthew's paternal grandfather and Kallan's foster father

Doileag: (dol'-ak) Leader of the Pannmordians

Dolph Molyngton: (dawlf mol'ing-ton) A minstrel and storyteller who travels around Kylemore

Durst: A stocky criminal working for the traitor behind the attacks on Kylemore

Fergus Brady: A schoolmate of Cadoc and Carys

Iron Beard (Glendon): A guard at the royal castle

Kallan MacKinnon: Narrator. Fifteen-year-old orphan from upstate

New York. Matthew's best friend and foster sister

Lord Colum Humphrey: (col'um hump'free) A baron of Kylemore.

Lord Elwood and Lady Urmed Trow: Wood elf clan leaders

Mairsil Pendergast: A sorceress and aunt to King Darren and his siblings: Brenden, Aiden, Skyla, Eolande, and Kiara

Marilea Dunstan: (mari-ə-lee'a dun'stan) Mother of Cadoc and Carys, daughter of Beli, and wife of Rolant

Mary: A ten-year-old kitchen servant at the royal castle in Ardara and sister of messenger Thane

Matthew Webbe: A fifteen-year-old orphan from upstate New York. Kallan's foster brother and best friend.

Meara Pendergast: Queen of Kylemore, wife of Darren

Morcant: (more'can't) A burly, bearded criminal working for the traitor behind the attacks on Kylemore

Nuala: (noo'la) A healer who serves the village of Daire and surrounding area

Pannmordians: People of Kylemore who resemble Earth's Neanderthals and live in the Pannmordian Valley

Pipit: Matthew's nickname for Kallan

Rolant Dunstan: (row'lant dun'stan) Father of Cadoc and Carys and husband of Marilea

Seisyll: (sieze'ull) A thin, curly-haired criminal working for the traitor behind the attacks on Kylemore

Skyla Pendergast: A princess of Kylemore and elder sister to King Darren

Thane: An eleven-year-old messenger at the royal castle in Ardara and brother of Mary

Wulfric Keane: A dragon expert from the Keane tribe

Creatures

Aeron: (air'on) Carys' pet toothed bird. Aeron's species, *Boluochia zhengi,* is extinct on Earth.

Agrio: *Agriochoerus* is a mammal. Extinct on Earth, they grew up to six feet long and about 185 pounds. Betherion *Agriochoerus* grow up to four feet long and 100 pounds. Herbivore.

Cai: (kye) A young dragon (dragonet), son of Heulwen

Caino: *Cainotherium* is a hoofed mammal (ungulate) the size of an Earth rabbit. Herbivore. Extinct on Earth.

Chickens Chanticleer (chant'ə-clear), Ethel, and Tess: chickens belonging to Kallan, Matthew, and David

Eomaia scansoria: A small mammal, about four inches long. Extinct on Earth.

Heulwen: (hay'l-when) A female dragon of the Camulus clan, mother of Cai

Howell: Carys and Cadoc's pet dog, a corgi

Moa: A type of large, flightless, herbivorous bird. Extinct on Earth since the late 1700s. Earth's moas grew up to twelve feet tall. Betherion's moas may reach a height of six feet.

Saber-tooth: Saber-toothed cats became extinct on Earth about 10,000 years ago. Earth saber-tooths could weigh up to 600 pounds. Betherion saber-tooths weigh up to 100 pounds.

Simon: A young, motherless dragon

Solo: A gliding, insect-eating reptile and pet of the Dunstan family. Solo's species, *Coelurosauravus jaekeli,* is extinct on Earth.

Troodon formosus: (trow'o-don for-moe'sis) A feathered, birdlike dinosaur. Betherion Troodons are about six feet long. Omnivore. Extinct on Earth.

Places

Ardara: (are-dare'ah) The royal city of Kylemore

Avonflow: A seaport in southern Kylemore

Betherion: (bə-thear'ion) A world that is "the next world over" from Earth. The world Kallan and her foster family enter when they begin their adventure.

Canibri: (kən'ih-bri) The ancient royal city of Kylemore

Daire: (dare) The nearest village to the Dunstan farm

Dragon's Nest: A mountainous region in northeastern Kylemore where the Camulus clan of dragons live

Kelby: (kell'bee) The kingdom to the north of Kylemore

Kintare Woods: A forest in central Kylemore

Kuklos: (kook'lowss) The smaller of the two moons of Betherion. Reddish in color.

Kylemore: (kyle'more) The kingdom in the world of Betherion where the story takes place

Metiri: (mə-tir'ee) The larger of the two moons of Betherion. White in color. Months on Betherion are measured in cycles of Metiri. There are ten cycles per year, (thirty-five days each), twenty-five hours in a day, and five days in a week.

Shea: The kingdom to the east of Kylemore

Taggla Forest: A forest in eastern and central Kylemore

Terrapin Archipelago: A nation west of Kylemore that is made up of twelve islands

The Great Forest: a large forest in southern Kylemore

Wyvam Mountains: A northern Kylemore mountain chain

Acknowledgments

This book came about through years of imagining, writing, and rewriting. However, it did not arrive at its final state by my hand alone. I am grateful to all who encouraged me and everyone who suggested ways to enhance the story. Many thanks to Paula Chinick of Russian Hill Press, artist Susan Marchand, copy and developmental editor Linda Todd, and cover designer and copyeditor Jordan Bernal. Any errors that remain are mine.

Special thanks go to Jim Boyle, who was a constant source of support, and Kerry Boyle Liu, who provided thoughtful feedback throughout the project. Rob Boyle, Nicki Araneta, and Eric Liu, your interest in the story gave me boosts of energy when I needed them. I appreciate the support, suggestions, and time contributed by Nikki Padilla, Jaynee Spence, and my critique partners and beta readers in the California Writers Club Tri-Valley Branch. Much gratitude goes to Nathan Wolf for his interest and insights. All of you made it a better story

About the Author

Patricia J. Boyle and her husband, Jim, live in Livermore, California. They have two adult children who are married and have children of their own.

Patricia grew up in upstate New York, spending summer vacations in the Adirondacks. Since childhood, she has been awed by the natural world and fascinated by mathematics. These interests led her to earn a degree in math and earth science education from Cornell University. Afterwards, she studied weather at the State University of New York at Albany, earning a masters' degree in atmospheric science.

In Bennington, Vermont, Patricia taught math and computer science at Southern Vermont College. Later, she worked as a research meteorologist at the Naval Post-graduate School in Monterey, California. When she and her family moved to Livermore, Patricia taught math and science for nearly two decades, working with students in elementary, middle, and high school.

In recent years, Patricia has turned to writing poems and short stories and indulging her love of fantasy tales. This is her first novel.

Find out more about Patricia and her current projects, Kylemore, and the world of Betherion at www.patriciajboyle.com.

CPSIA information can be obtained
at www.ICGtesting.com
Printed in the USA
LVHW011706180121
676809LV00001B/13